THE NEW MEXICO SCOUNDREL

A Skyler Moore Thriller

R. Scott Wallis

THE SKYLER MOORE THRILLER SERIES

THE MAINE NEMESIS
Book One – Available Now

THE NEW MEXICO SCOUNDREL
Book Two – This is It!

THE NEVADA SABOTEUR
Book Three – September 27, 2019

THE ALASKA SCALAWAG
Book Four – February 28, 2020

THE JOHNNY WAINWRIGHT THRILLER SERIES

SCOUT'S HONOR
The All-New Revised Edition – Summer 2019

SCOUT'S NAMESAKE
Book Two – Summer 2020

For Kristin

"Because it's never too late for a new chapter."

—

A WARNING, OF SORTS:
THIS IS BOOK TWO

You don't necessarily need to read the very first Skyler Moore novel, *The Maine Nemesis*, to enjoy her New Mexican adventure that follows, but it couldn't hurt. In the first book, we meet our hero in her quirky hometown of Wabanaki, Maine, along with a rather colorful cast of supporting characters. Of course, murder and mayhem ensue. It's a fun, fast-paced, 'Down East' adventure that leads Skyler and her friends to Miami Beach, New York City, and Las Vegas. Read it second, if you want—all the books stand-alone—but please keep in mind that spoilers here within will ruin twists and turns in *The Maine Nemesis*. It's the nature of a series.

That said, enjoy it any way you see fit. Who am I to tell you what to do? I'm not your father. (Or am I? Maybe I'm your long-lost evil half-brother. Or a third cousin, twice removed. We might never know the whole twisted truth about how we're really related, but I still won't try to run your life or tell you what books to read or in what order. I promise.)

—R. Scott Wallis

P.S. Please read *The Maine Nemesis* first.

PROLOGUE

Just moments before sunset, Georgia Reece, a renowned and much sought-after opera singer, who had performed with famed opera companies from Milan to Sydney, arrived home after a shopping spree downtown. She gathered the many bags of clothes and accessories, her Louis Vuitton purse, and a half-full Starbucks cup—which she'd already decided would be swapped out for a glass of wine once she was settled—and made her way into her new house.

Once behind the towering front door, she dropped her packages and purse to the floor. Georgia was faced with a horrific mess and she was having a hard time processing what she was seeing. Despite a commanding presence on the stage—her celebrated coloratura soprano voice once made a Serbian colonel, known around the world for his excessive brutality, weep openly—Georgia was an extremely reserved and restrained person when she was alone, and she painstakingly created an ultra-private oasis within her own walls.

That oasis had been violated and smashed that chilly December afternoon.

She walked warily from room to room, unable to process the senseless destruction. Drawers were ripped from every piece of furniture, the contents scattered on the floor. Most of the paintings were off their hooks. Couch pillows, papers, and clothing were strewn everywhere. Even pasta and crackers were dumped from their ripped-open boxes in the kitchen. It just made no sense. *What on Earth were they looking for in the cracker boxes?*

It dawned on her that she should be more nervous than mad as she discovered more messes around every corner. *Could the perpetrator still be in the house? Why hadn't she activated the previous owners' alarm system yet? Should she run back to the safety of her locked car?*

But the house was numbingly quiet, so she continued, cautiously, with a fireplace poker in one hand and the Starbucks cup in the other.

When she reached the Great Room, she found the entry point. Glass from a ten-foot-high window was shattered all over the stone floor and a ceramic vase that had been on the patio outside lay on the cowhide rug, broken in several large pieces.

It was the grey ashes on the floor in front of the fireplace that finally sent her into despair. She set down her weapon and coffee and fell to her knees and quietly sobbed as she used her bare hands to scoop her mother's remains into a pile. Dumping potpourri from a crystal bowl—one of just a few of her possessions still intact—she salvaged as much of the ashes as she could. And when the gruesome task was finished, she washed her hands, then dialed '911' on her cell phone. She explained to the woman who answered that her home had been ransacked and she was promised that a police cruiser would be dispatched immediately.

Georgia had closed on the house just ten days earlier. It was her first home purchase, having only lived with her parents and in dorm rooms, various rented apartments, and properties owned by her two late husbands.

Both men had been cruelly taken from her way before their time—one succumbed to cancer three years after they wed and the other dropped dead of a heart attack on their honeymoon.

Moving to New Mexico to buy the large house on the mountain-side overlooking downtown Santa Fe, was her way of starting over. It was therapeutic. A new beginning. A new chapter in which she longed for serenity, peace, and, most hopefully, an escape from the deaths that repeatedly interrupted what was otherwise a lovely life. Not only was she unlucky in the husband department, but she'd been forced to say goodbye to both of her parents prematurely. Most recently it was her beloved mother, the woman who was now partially contained in the crystal potpourri bowl and partially littered all over Georgia's brand-new floor.

It was almost too much for her to bear. But by the time the doorbell rang, she was out of tears.

Two officious, by-the-book Santa Fe Police Department officers walked through the house with Georgia, asking questions along the way. She explained that she was new to the neighborhood and knew few people in town. She had no known enemies. And, surprisingly, she couldn't identify anything in the house that was missing.

"The jewelry appears to be untouched," she said when they arrived at the large walk-in closet. "It's not ridiculously expensive stuff, but there's several thousands of dollars worth of stuff in here." She picked up the diamond necklace that had been a wedding present from her second husband. "This was insured for $10,000, for example."

3

"Oh, right. I see. *Not* ridiculously expensive," one officer said.

"Was there a handgun in the house?" the other officer asked.

"Never."

"Cash?"

"A few dollars," she said, shaking her head. "I never have cash on hand."

"Stock certificates, bonds, anything like that?"

"All in a safe deposit box back in New York." She began to sit down on the side of the bed, but an officer stopped her.

"Don't disturb anything, please."

"There's what looks like a painting by Picasso in the living room," the other officer said. "That can't be real."

"It is," she said calmly. "Is it still there? I hadn't noticed."

"If I noticed it, you can assume it's still there," he said.

"I'm sorry. I'm a little shaken up. My mother's ashes were dumped on the floor."

There were many more questions, but no one could come up with a motive. An evidence team was ordered up from Albuquerque with the hopes that the perpetrator may have left a usable fingerprint behind.

"I'd consider getting a security system, ma'am," the older of the two officers suggested. "Unfortunately, break-ins are on the rise in this neighborhood. It could be that this was just a bunch of kids who had no idea what any of this stuff was worth. They might have just done this as a thrill. Out of boredom or something or other."

"Boredom? Well, isn't that great," she said. "But, yes, I think upgrading the security is going to be the first thing on my to-do list. I have something here; I just haven't activated it yet."

"I'd get that window replaced A.S.A.P., too, ma'am. It's supposed to get down into the twenties tonight. We might even get some snow."

She was unsure who to turn to for that kind of task and it was already dark outside. She was stronger than this, and she'd certainly dealt with worse tragedies, but nevertheless, she began to cry again. Feeling sorry for the widow, one of the officers called his construction worker brother-in-law to see if he could come to her rescue.

"I appreciate that more than you can imagine," she said after the officer got off his phone.

"It's the Santa Fe way, ma'am. Just part of the job."

"It's not, I'm sure. But thank you for going above and beyond the call of duty. I really do appreciate it."

An hour later, while the forensics team dusted doorknobs and glass doors for prints, a weathered looking, middle-aged man, dressed in paint-splattered, well-worn clothing and heavy construction boots arrived in an ancient pickup truck with several large pieces of plywood. When Georgia went out to the front driveway to greet him, his mouth dropped open.

"Miss Reece," the man said, approaching with two extended arms. He took hold of her hands and his heavily tanned face beamed. "I am such a *huge* fan. I'm so sorry that this has happened to you."

"Thank you," she said. "I'm afraid I don't know your name, kind sir."

"Diego, ma'am. Diego Ferrera. I know it doesn't look like it, but I've been an opera fan since I was un pequeño chico. My mother was obsessed with the music and my brothers and I grew up listening to little else. I saw you in *Rigoletto* this past summer. Your performance was nothing less than breathtaking."

"Estoy muy halagado, mi amigo," Georgia said in a perfect Spanish accent as she led him hand in hand through the house and into the Great Room. "And I appreciate you coming to my aid this evening. As you can see, I have a large hole in the back of my house."

"We'll have this patched up in no time," Diego said. "And I'll get someone to replace that window pane tomorrow. There's a great glass company in town. We can get it done."

"My hero."

"Anything for you, Miss Reece. *Anything.*" And the man got to work.

One of the original responding officers walked up to Georgia's side. "Are you someone famous?"

She despised that question but was relatively used to it. "I guess so. In some rather small circles. I'm an opera singer."

"Ahh," the officer said. "Never been to an opera. I hear the Santa Fe Opera is a pretty cool venue though."

"It is, indeed. Very unique, with its open-air theater. Every seat has little screens so that theatergoers can read along in English. You should give it a try some time. It's breathtaking up there."

"I'm more of a metal fan."

"I understand. Opera certainly isn't for everyone."

"How famous are you? Do you have fans?"

Georgia raised an eyebrow. "Well, Diego here seems to be a fan. People do know me, sir. Some seem to even like me. What are you getting at?"

"Could this mess be the result of your fame?" the officer

asked as he gestured around the room. "A deranged fan or something of the kind?"

"I couldn't even fathom that, officer. I've heard from a few people over the years, but nothing that stood out as questionable or disturbing in any way. No one has ever harassed me in public or at one of my homes. I travel freely, and I'm only recognized in public a very tiny fraction of the time. I'm very rarely on television or in magazines. Most people don't know this face."

"*Diego* knew your face."

"Like I said, it's very rare and it surprises me every time it happens."

"Well, it might be worth exploring," he said flatly. "And I'd get that security system activated just as soon as you can."

Georgia found it very difficult to sleep that night. It might have been because she left every single light on in the house. It might have been because the house still looked like a tornado had ripped through it. Or, it could have been because there was a complete stranger sleeping on her living room couch. Diego insisted on staying when she commented that she didn't feel safe in the house but wasn't too keen on checking into a hotel. And while she was both unnerved and touched by his gesture, she didn't know how to turn down his magnanimous offer. He was a police officer's brother-in-law who loved *Rigoletto*, so he couldn't be all that bad, she decided.

CHAPTER ONE

In the English basement office of her Washington, D.C. brownstone, Skyler Moore was finishing up some paperwork after a long day of conference calls and meetings that had all but completely drained her energy. She'd been working non-stop for months, foregoing her usual late-autumn vacation to see to an ever-growing client list. She'd recently hired two new gung-ho associates, but the work continued to pile up. Her boutique public relations business was booming—mostly because she signed superstar pop singer Carissa Lamb to her roster—and the focus of the company had rapidly transformed from mom-and-pop products and small non-profits, to all-things celebrity and entertainment.

Skyler was slightly out of her element but energized by the new challenges that she was facing on a daily basis. She'd recently returned to the nation's capital after a whirlwind business trip that took her to New York City, Las Vegas, and Los Angeles where she'd met with her top clients—she insisted on regular face-to-face interactions with the people who paid her bills.

She had more work to do, but her suitcases were still packed and sitting in the bedroom upstairs; she dreaded having to deal with them, but knew she'd never get anything done until the task was done. Her boyfriend was also clomping around somewhere above her head in the creaky old house and she was having a hard time concentrating.

She headed up to the kitchen on the ground level where she poured herself a glass of pinot grigio before continuing upward to the second-floor master suite. Thankfully, the house was quiet now that the staff had gone home. She constantly second-guessed her decision not to move the company to larger digs somewhere downtown but appreciated her effortless commute; the quick elevator ride to the basement level was certainly better than braving D.C.'s congested streets on a snowy day. Washingtonians simply didn't know how to deal with the white stuff and the city had pretty much come to a screeching halt when the first flurries started to fall that morning. The government was put on liberal leave. Public schools were closed tight. The grocery stores were devoid of toilet paper and milk. It made Skyler long for her hometown back in Wabanaki, Maine, where several feet of snow didn't put a dent in anyone's day and the hordes didn't run out to buy up every single last loaf of bread.

"It's really coming down out there," he said as she entered the room. "Looks like home."

She walked over to the bay window and stood next to him. It was a bittersweet moment. He was scheduled to leave the next morning and she'd gotten used to having him around. But he was bored. He needed something to do other than playing endless video games and getting in her way when she tried to work. And Wabanaki needed him more than she did. And while she certainly earned enough money to support them both, he'd appreciate some of his own money in his pocket again.

"I wonder if my flight will get off on time," Leonard Little said absently. "They don't know how to clear the runways here."

She slipped an arm around her boyfriend's firm wide back and pulled him close. "I'm going to miss you."

"Me too," he said. He turned to face her and kissed her lightly on the lips. "But it's not forever."

He'd been a police officer back in their childhood hometown in Maine. Skyler had known him since they were kids, but it wasn't until last summer that they'd started an accidental sexual relationship that quickly turned into a love affair. When Leonard's estranged wife had been brutally murdered, the unlikely pair teamed up to help find the perpetrator. When they followed a lead to Miami, they started having sex and pretty much never stopped. It was fast, unexpected, and altogether satisfying, especially since the never-married Skyler had been relatively unlucky with maintaining healthy relationships over the years.

Then after a very unfortunate July—which involved the death of both a close mutual friend and Leonard's father, who had been the Sheriff of Wabanaki for decades—the new couple decided to flee Maine to live in Skyler's house in Washington, D.C. But now he was going back to the scene of the crimes. And it hurt them both.

"The new Sheriff needs you. Your town needs you," Skyler said. "You're doing the right thing, darn it."

"I can't believe Kristin broke *both* legs. Porter emailed me photos of the car accident. It didn't look *that* bad."

Skyler crinkled her brow. "What are you talking about? The whole front end was smashed in like an accordion."

"Yeah, that's true. I guess that *would* do it."

"Um, yeah, dummy. And I feel so badly for her," Skyler said. "Lord knows that Porter and the rest of those deputies aren't up to running that police department without her at the helm. But you're right, it's not forever. Legs heal. And you don't really have a choice now, do you?"

Skyler was going to miss the sex. She didn't know where the relationship was going—they never talked about it—but whatever it was, the sex hadn't tapered off since the start. That made her very happy.

And as usual, they had sex before falling asleep in front of the bedroom's gas fireplace that night. The snow stopped falling sometime overnight, a warm front blew in, and Washington Reagan National Airport was open for business as usual the following morning, taking Leonard 'Down East' and away from Skyler.

* * *

The chartered Cessna Citation Sovereign touched down at Las Vegas' McCarran International and taxied to Advanced Aviation, a fixed-based operator for private aircraft on the southwest corner of the airport. With a championship heavyweight bout between the evenly matched Serota and Felix scheduled to take place that evening at the Mandalay Bay Events Center, the tarmac was absolutely overflowing with aircraft of all shapes and sizes. Brenda Braxton peered out the window and wondered where the pilots would find room to park on the crowded ramp. She was pleased when they managed to squeeze in between two mid-size jets, the engines were powered down, and the cabin was depressurized.

Knowing that the desert winds do embarrassing things to women in dresses on runways, Brenda changed into a pair of pants for deplaning. With a large tote flung over her shoulder and a dog leash in each hand, she descended the stairs and climbed into a waiting minivan. Within minutes, she and her dogs were speeding toward the Golden Cactus Resort and Casino, the relatively new, four-star property on the northern section of Las Vegas Boulevard, otherwise known as The Strip. The Golden Cactus was in a part of Las Vegas presently undergoing a resurgence, with several new resort properties being constructed to the north and south. Similar to the Sin City-revitalizing building boom of the late 1980's, this one was producing innovative casino projects designed for the 21st century. Heavily themed, family-focused projects were out. Opulence, high-energy, and adults-only concepts were very much in vogue.

Brenda was in love with the Golden Cactus and what the developers had created, and she felt very at home there.

For better or worse, she was on the move a lot, overseeing her ever-growing empire of restaurants, hotel projects, cookbooks, a television cooking show, and a line of sparkling wines that sold quite briskly every time she appeared on Q.V.C. to hawk them. Her celebrity chef cred was hotter than ever, but it was taking a serious toll on her body and mind. She was simply exhausted—despite a head office staff of seven full-timers—and more than ready for an honest to goodness, sit-and-do-nothing kind of a vacation.

But that would have to wait.

After being escorted to her usual suite, along with Mulder and Scully—her sibling Lemon Treeing Walker coonhounds, named after the two main characters in her beloved *The X-Files* television show—Brenda flopped down on the bed with her

13

smartphone and tapped a few buttons to call her best friend.

"Hey there," Skyler said when she picked up. "As usual, you have amazing timing. I'm between meetings and having my seventh cup of coffee."

"Just today, I read an article on the plane about the benefits of eight cups of coffee a day," Brenda said. "So, darling, you have one more to go. Hey, listen, I just flew to Vegas from Santa Fe. I feel like I never left; I was just here yesterday, for goodness sake. I should probably just move out west, huh? Anyway, I'm having a big dinner thing at my Golden Cactus restaurant tonight. We're debuting the new menu for the casino suits. And Carissa is coming."

"Right. She mentioned that to me yesterday. She's very excited."

"Me too. You know I haven't seen her since all the craziness went down in Maine. I'm amazed she's still talking to me."

"Oh gosh, Brenda, you know nothing sticks to that girl. She probably forgot all about it on the plane ride home."

Brenda was incredulous. "How do you forget getting held captive at gunpoint by a mad man?"

"He wasn't a mad man!" Skyler said a bit more loudly than she intended. It was still a sore subject and she felt like she would always be unnerved by the memory of losing their mutual friend to mental illness. "He was our friend and he...just lost his way." She paused for a moment, realizing how silly that sounded. "You know what I mean."

"I do, honey, and I'm sorry. Let's change the subject." Brenda eased off the bed and walked over to the floor-to-ceiling plate glass window. She peered down at the street fifty-three stories below. "So, did he really leave?"

"Leonard? Yes. First thing this morning. I think he's looking at a few months as acting Sheriff. I don't even know if we'll be spending Christmas together."

"I'm surprised that didn't come up."

"It won't come as a surprise to you, Brenda, but we don't really talk about important stuff all that much," Skyler said.

"The sex still good?"

"Duh."

Brenda laughed. "Listen, I have a proposition for you. I mentioned it a while ago, but now I want you to seriously consider it."

"Here we go."

"No, it's a good thing, Skyler. I'm here in Vegas for a few nights and then I'm jetting *back* to Santa Fe for this thing called, The Winter Wine and Beer Fiesta, as a part of the Franklin-Lowery hotel project I'm doing. I'm working very closely with the guys who are developing the hotel chain and I'm not just doing the restaurants for them, I'm really involved in all aspects of the project now. I'm talking décor, the staff uniforms, marketing, even helping to pick out the perfect mattresses for the sleeping rooms. It's quite an undertaking."

"Geez, lady. I seriously don't know how you have the time. Have you cloned yourself?"

Brenda chuckled. "I wish. But this is the slow season for me. I've already done all the television I'm doing for the year, we just put the new cook book to bed, and this is fun for me."

"Alright, so, what's the proposition?" Skyler asked.

"I very much want you to come spend a few weeks with me in New Mexico. We can be there for Christmas and New Year's Eve and I promise that we'll have *all* the fun. Santa Fe has some very good restaurants, more art galleries than almost anywhere else, and loads of cute little shops. Oh, and there is this very hard-to-describe, interactive art installation called Meow Wolf that you really do need to experience; it's a trip and a half." Brenda took a second to catch her breath, then asked, "So? Are you game?"

There was a long pause.

"Skyler Moore! Why are you hesitating?"

"Alright," Skyler finally said. "I'll come, even though I have no idea what this Meow Wolf thing is. I guess I can do whatever needs doing in Santa Fe just as easily as I can here. Plus, it's one of the few states that I've never stepped foot in."

"Yes! Alright! Happy day! I'm booking us in at the Four Seasons hotel for this Friday. Then we can move to a rented house, or something, so we'll have more space."

"You mean so the *dogs* will have more space."

"That's true, yes. They always come first. But I am very excited about this, Skyler. And you'll just love Santa Fe. It's a bit nippy this time of year, but the sun is very warming, even on the coldest of days. They call it the high-desert, you know. They're at like six or seven thousand feet above sea level. You'll just love it, I promise. It's beautiful."

"Okay, geez, I'm sold. I'll book a flight. How do I get there from here?"

"Commercial to Santa Fe from D.C.? You'll have to change in Denver or Dallas depending on who you fly. Shouldn't be too bad," Brenda said.

Skyler waited a few beats, then said, "Excuse me. You're not sending a plane?"

The chef was caught off guard. "I *totally* will, honey. Do you want me to do that?"

"Of course not, silly. I was kidding. I have about a zillion frequent flyer miles. Plenty for a first-class upgrade. I'll be fine. You save your fractional jet hours and just buy me a few expensive dinners."

"Okay, that's a deal I can stomach. *Whew.* You just saved me about $20,000. I literally started sweating, but you do know that I'd do that for you, right, Skyler?" She laughed heartily, startling the snoozing dogs. "Or at least I'd *offer.* Alright, I can't wait to see you, honey. It's been, what? Months? Okay, bye, honey."

Brenda hung up without waiting for Skyler to say goodbye. She spent a few minutes loving on the dogs, jumped in the shower, and then slipped into a sparkly black pant suit with a matching jacket. She arranged for a dog walker through the hotel's concierge before taking the executive-level express elevator down to the ground floor. She enjoyed the long stroll from the lobby, through the casino—it was really hopping, with nearly every table game seat taken and thousands of people at the slot machines—finally ending up at *Brenda's Kitchen,* her sixth and most recent eponymous restaurant.

She pow-wowed with her head chef and the maître d'hôtel, then went to the cozy private dining room next to the wine cellar to check on the place cards. The president of the holding company that owned both the casino resort and the television network that produced and broadcasted her cooking show, was coming, along with his former-Olympian figure skater wife and a small army of casino executives.

Carissa Lamb, the hotel's headlining entertainer, breezed in first, sporting a long, dark brown wig and oversized Jackie-O style sunglasses. The celebrity chef and the pop singer had become fast friends the previous summer and Brenda had introduced Carissa and Skyler to each other. The women air kissed, European-style, never making actual physical contact. Brenda learned that from the stylish singer and thought it very cosmopolitan, and she had started adding the greeting into her own interactions with *cooler* people.

"You look fabulous," Carissa said.

"And you look like no one I know."

Carissa spun around. "I'm in disguise, Brenda, darling. I mean, have you *seen* it out there? I'm told that the hotel is completely sold out all week. This city is just overflowing with people like I've never seen before. Thank goodness for strong economies, huh?"

"Better than the opposite," Brenda said. "Miss Lamb, I miss your red hair."

"Well, I still have it." Carissa pulled off the wig and sunglasses and shook her head. She was stunning and somehow made it all look so effortless. "Is this better?"

"Much."

"I've missed you terribly, Brenda," Carissa said. "I watched the cooking show episode that I was on. I just wish we could have watched it *together.* It came out wonderfully, don't you think?"

"Carissa, thanks to you, it was the highest rated episode we've ever aired. I really mean it...thank you."

"It was my pleasure. And *my* idea, if you'll recall. I had so much fun doing it."

Brenda waved over a waiter and the women ordered drinks—a glass of 'ice cold' champagne for the singer and a classic Old Fashioned for the chef. When the waiter walked away, she turned back to Carissa. "I feel just horrible about what happened after the taping. I was seriously afraid when you left Wabanaki that Skyler and I would never see you again."

"Oh, please," Carissa said with a fluttering of her delicate hand. "It's been totally forgotten. I choose to remember the *fun* parts of that day: cooking with you in Skyler's cute little house and having the chance to become such good, *true* friends. Hey, we all survived, didn't we? That's the important thing." She smiled and showed off her impossibly bright white, perfect teeth. "So, what's for dinner tonight?"

"We're starting with crab and cucumber rillettes as the amuse-bouche; you'll love them. Then, we have a veal tongue with horseradish-cream as the appetizer course. We'll follow that with a brie tortellini paired with roasted figs as the pasta course; I am obsessed with that dish. It's brand new. Then, if people are still alive, we have a pistachio-crusted leg of lamb with gingered carrots. And, here's the best part, Carissa—I'm not doing any of the actual cooking tonight. Hallelujah, praise the Lord."

"Come on now. You left out the best part. Certainly you are serving dessert."

"Of course. Duh. Individual apple tarts with salted caramel ice cream. The tarts are made with croissant dough instead of puff pastry. They are decidedly *deadly*. And my pastry chef makes the ice cream right here, by hand, every day. I could open a stand and make millions. It's better than Häagen-Dazs, I swear to the Swedish Gods."

"I believe you. But, exactly how am I supposed to fit into my costumes tomorrow night, I ask you that?"

Brenda smiled. "I guess you better hit up that home gym of yours…like you have anything to worry about." She looked over the singer's shoulder and watched as the head honcho strolled through the door. "Okay, here we go. The big guy has entered the building."

CHAPTER TWO

On Thursday morning, Skyler called her troops together in the small basement conference room and announced her departure. She'd booked a flight for the next morning and left the return open-ended; she promised to be back in Washington by "…the twelfth day of Christmas."

Her confused assistant asked, "What's that? It's a song, right?"

"It's a song, yes," Skyler explained, "but it's also the fifth evening of January, on the eve of the Feast of the Epiphany which takes place on January 6th."

"Why couldn't you just say that you're going to be back on January 5th?"

"Because I'm trying not to be boring. I'll be back on or before January 5th. Okay? Happy with that?" Skyler consulted her calendar. "Except that day just so happens to be a Friday, so I might not be back until January 7th or 8th. We'll see."

That was met with blank stares.

"Listen guys, I don't expect you to work the whole time I'm gone. The office will be closed from December 22nd through January 5th. So, you'll have two whole glorious weeks off. Deal?"

They all nodded in agreement.

"But next week I'll need you here to attend to a half a dozen things that we still have in the pipeline. I'll be working remotely from Santa Fe, and you'll need to remember that I'll be two hours behind you. New Mexico is on Mountain Time."

The team was capable enough and Skyler knew that most of her clients wouldn't need hand holding during the holidays anyway. She sent the staff back to their respective desks and snuck upstairs to her bedroom to pack her luggage. Brenda had explained that Santa Fe was upscale, yet casual, so she skipped the fancy stuff and instead focused on jeans, corduroy slacks, cashmere sweaters, a puffy down jacket, hiking boots, and one long, semi-fancy dress, just in case. All the sexy and skimpy undergarments stayed in her closet drawers; without Leonard there, she decided she might as well be as comfortable as possible.

For the first time in decades, Skyler and her best friend hadn't put a Christmas plan into place months in advance—it had been a frenetic year and everything was out of whack—so she was happy Brenda had finally come to the rescue. With her parents long gone, and her brother and his wife and kids planning to spend Christmas on the beaches of Hawaii, Skyler didn't feel at all guilty about decamping to the southwestern desert for the holidays. She almost always celebrated the holidays with Brenda and it usually involved improvised decorations, a lot of wine, and some pretty spectacular meals, the benefit of having a world-class chef on hand. Brenda would whip up her buttery Christmas cookies and prepare a roast turkey dinner with all the trimmings on Christmas Day; they'd typically invite a combination of both new and old friends to join them, too. The previous year, they were in Manhattan for the festivities and when Skyler found out that Brenda didn't have a tree or ornaments stored in her large loft, Skyler went out and bought a dozen boxes of colorful glass bulbs, spending close to $1,000 at an upscale second-hand store in Chelsea in order to create the most perfect, vintage Christmas tree. And when they were in Rome a few years before that, Skyler decorated their hotel suite with construction paper snowflakes and they wandered down to St. Peter's Square to listen to the Pope address the crowds and to marvel at a full nativity scene complete with live actors, a few donkeys, and a camel. It was quite magical.

Skyler didn't know what to expect in Santa Fe, but she was up for the adventure. She made it a point to pack a half-dozen red velvet stockings to hang by the fireplace—she held out hope that there *would* be a fireplace on Christmas Eve—and she even stuffed a Santa hat into her suitcase for good measure. Her late, Christmas-loving mother would be so proud that she took the time to root around in the attic to find the decades-old inherited items. Even when the saint of a woman had given up on her battle with breast cancer, she climbed up the attic stairs that last winter to fetch and hang her most beloved decorations throughout her house; Skyler's mother let absolutely nothing stop Christmas from being the most special time of the year and her daughter intended to make it as enchanted as she could, too, even if the circumstances weren't ideal.

* * *

Georgia Reece sat by herself at a table set for three, in a back corner of The Compound restaurant, an upscale hot-spot just off of the storied Canyon Road, a few blocks from downtown Santa Fe. It was the first time she'd left her house since the place had been broken into and she was more than just a little bit nervous about being out in public. At home, she was surrounded by the newly installed, high-tech security perimeter that she'd spared no expense on, opting for every possible devise they offered: motion detectors, glass break sensors, door and window contacts, night vision security cameras inside and out, and panic buttons strategically placed throughout the large house. She had pressure sensors installed at the end of the long driveway, too, so she'd know the moment someone entered the property in a vehicle. A motorized driveway gate had been ordered, but it would be some days before it could be installed. She had a landscape lighting designer scheduled to come the next day; she planned to tastefully light every inch of the yard, with the added emergency option of blazing it up like the inside of a sports arena at a moment's notice, if necessary. She was certain that she'd royally piss off the neighbors with that, but she didn't care...and she hadn't met them yet anyway.

The opera singer wasn't taking any chances and never again wanted to be caught off guard. She considered a handgun, but ultimately decided against it; she certainly believed in the right to bear arms, but she also knew that experienced criminals could easily turn the tables and use the weapon against her. Georgia settled on placing her father's Little League baseball bat next to her bed. And as a backup plan, there was a spray tube of mace tucked into the bedside table. She was considering adopting a dog or two, for added peace of mind, but she didn't want to rush into such an important, life-changing decision. She had enough trouble keeping herself watered and fed.

Georgia felt as if all eyes were on her as she waited for her dinner companions.

Do they recognize me? Did they read about the break-in in the local paper yesterday? Could the person who ransacked my house be in this very restaurant right now!?

Deciding that she was probably overreacting, she tried to calm herself. She took a deep breath and gulped down some wine. Then she saw them approaching the table, the two most perfect specimens of twindom.

Carter and Sullivan Lowery were in the their late-thirties, each tall, dark, and wickedly handsome. They were a spitting image of each other, although Carter—who was seven minutes older than his brother—was the conservative, buttoned-up one and Sullivan (many close to him simply called him 'Sully') was more laidback and casual. It set them apart when nothing else did. She'd known the Lowery twins for about a decade—they first met at the East Hampton wedding of a mutual acquaintance, becoming fast friends—and she absolutely beamed when they arrived at the table.

"Georgia," Carter said, embracing the diva, "you are the prettiest woman in this restaurant." His brother hugged Georgia, too, echoing Carter's sentiment.

"You're both very good liars. Sit." She waved over a waiter who took drink orders. "Tell me what you're doing in Santa Fe? I couldn't believe my eyes when you texted that you were in town."

Sullivan grabbed one of Georgia's hands and gave it a squeeze. "We're here to support you, my dear. We heard about the break-in and flew out immediately."

"Hogwash," she said pulling her hand away. "I'm the one that told *you* about the break-in just this afternoon. So, what gives?"

"We're in the final stages of construction on the newest Franklin-Lowery hotel. It's a block off the historic Plaza right downtown," Carter said. "Santa Fe has got some amazing hotels, of course, but they've never seen anything like this."

"I am sure you told me about this and it obviously slipped my ever-aging mind. But this is very exciting news. I can't wait to see it. You know that I adore the one you created in New York; it's so welcoming and warm and funky. That was the first one, wasn't it?"

"It was," Carter and Sullivan said in unison. She was used to them doing that; everyone who knew them was used to it. Carter continued on his own, "And this will be the *sixth*, can you believe it? After New York, we did Boston, then Charleston, Miami, and then Palo Alto just last year."

"Palo Alto? That seems random," she said.

"Tech money, honey," Sullivan said. "That place has been oversold since we opened the doors in January. We did 208 rooms there; we could have easily done hundreds more."

Georgia smiled. "Well, you guys certainly have the Midas touch. I'm so proud of you both. And I'm sure the Santa Fe location will be just as successful as the rest. What's the theme?"

Carter spoke up, "It's decidedly Southwestern, which is required here, with a lot of curved adobe walls, reclaimed wood beams, kiva fireplaces in every room, lighted niches galore with some really amazing local Native art, but at the same time, it's got that modern flair that we're known for, if you can picture that crazy combination. It's kind of a cross between the Southwest and Greenwich Village. Wooden roadrunner statutes sitting next to 1950's record players in every room. There will be a vinyl record lending library off the lobby. We're doing radiant-heated concrete floors, guests can control everything from their smartphones, and all of the rooms have a private patio or balcony so people can get outside. I insisted on that." Carter was quite passionate and proud of their creation.

"There's still some folks comparing Franklin to other trendy boutique chains," Sullivan said, "but it's *so* not that. I think we have a hell of a lot more warmth and charm and uniqueness. We also think bathrooms shouldn't be in the middle of the damned bedroom; people like their privacy when they're taking a shit."

"Excuse that man's foul language," Carter said. "But he's right. We're warm. And private."

"Sounds lovely," Georgia said with a sweet smile. "I can't wait for opening day. I will be there with bells on, since I live *here* now and I'm not planning to travel quite as much as I used to."

"Hold on. No more operas Down Under? No more summers in Vienna?" Carter asked. "We enjoyed traveling to Austria to see you in…oh my goodness, what was that show?"

"That show was *Tosca*," she sighed. "At the Wiener Staatsoper, the best opera house in the entire world. But, guys, I'm just so tired of all of that. I know that I'm not old, and I'm certainly not retiring, but I just don't have it in me anymore to do three major productions a year. My voice can't take it. My feet can't take it. And I don't want to live out of a suitcase 90% of the time. I just want to stay closer to home."

"And home is Santa Fe, New Mexico now?" Sullivan asked. "What about New York? You're a New Yorker, for God's sake."

"I still have 1020 5th Avenue and I'll never, *ever* sell it, no matter how many Peter Thiele suck-ups make offers. I grew up there. And despite what happened to me *here* on Tuesday, I absolutely love Santa Fe, too. I can't wait to show you the view from my new backyard. It's to die for."

"Well, as someone who lives out of a suitcase 90% of the year, I feel ya," Carter said. "It would be nice to dislike my neighbors for an actual reason."

"Bite your tongue," Sullivan said, as he dug into the appetizers that Georgia had ordered before they sat down. "We have three more hotels in the pipeline after Santa Fe."

"Kill me now," his brother said.

"You'll live. This business is making us very comfortable and you love it." Sullivan turned back to the singer. "We could stop and retire young, but why? I'm having so much fun. I love building things. Creating experiences."

Georgia added some tuna tartare to her plate. "As long as you're having fun, that's all that matters. You should keep going, if you have the energy and drive. Absolutely." After she swallowed some of the appetizer, she put a hand on top of Sullivan's hand. "How's that little brother of yours?"

The twins sighed in unison.

"Do we need to talk about him?" Carter asked. "He's a mess."

Sullivan shook his head. "He's not a *mess*. He's pulling his shit together. He's been up, he's been down, and he has his demons, but he's in school right now and he's doing fairly well, by all accounts, and he leaves us alone most of the time. And the best part: he's not bunking with me anymore. He's got his own apartment in Hell's Kitchen. He seems to like it over there."

Georgia smiled politely. "Well, Darby is certainly a character. I only met him once or twice, but he left...um...an impression. I'm glad your younger brother is doing well."

The twins nodded in agreement but were eager to change the

subject.

"So, when are you performing again? Is anything on the calendar at all?" Carter asked.

"For the first time since college," Georgia said, "I have absolutely nothing planned until next summer, when I'll be playing Mimì in *La bohème* here at the Santa Fe Opera. We start rehearsals for that in late-May, so I have six months off. Six *glorious* months off, boys."

Carter held his glass of wine up for a toast. "To Georgia and her six glorious months off."

Georgia and took a sip of her wine and smiled at the gorgeous, single brothers. She was perpetually curious about why neither were ever attached to a lady and never quite believed them when they swore they were married to their work. But whatever their real story was—maybe she'd never know—she was happy to have their familiar, beautiful faces with her in Santa Fe. The combination of the brothers' presence, along with the great wine, finally allowed her to relax and enjoy the evening.

Outside in the cold night, two figures stood in the shadows between cars in the parking lot. They had a perfect view through a side window of the opera singer as she dined with the twins.

CHAPTER THREE

Skyler had flown in small planes before but never packed in so tightly. On the first leg from Reagan National, she was in a comfortably wide first-class cabin, but then on the second flight, it seemed as if she was sharing that same amount of space with 47 others. Luckily, it was a short hop from Denver. After they touched down, she peered out of the Embraer commuter jet's window as it taxied to the gate at the Santa Fe Municipal Airport. It was the *only* gate the tiny airport had. She watched as a long metal ramp was pushed up to the aircraft's front left door, complete with a built-in awning covering the sloped walkway. She felt a rush of cold air fill the cabin when the flight attendant opened the door and moments later, Skyler was outside, walking into the postage stamp-sized terminal building. It was dated, but, she thought, not without charm, and she quickly claimed her luggage. A sharply dressed young man was waiting for her, holding a piece of paper that read, "S. Moore."

"Do you know the way to San Jose?" she asked the kid.

"You can't get there from here." He smiled. "It's cool, ma'am. I'm from the Four Seasons."

She followed him to a silver Mercedes S.U.V. with the hotels' logo painted on the door.

"This is the first time anyone's asked for a password before.

Have you been picked up by nefarious dudes in the past?"

"Kind of, sort of, not really," she said as she slid into the seat. "I did get in the wrong sedan in Rome once, but no one was trying to kidnap me. I just didn't understand what the fellow was saying. But I did have a celebrity client who was picked up at L.A.X. by someone who was absolutely *not* from the intended black car service. It's a long story, and she ended up being fine, but it was terrifying for her when she realized she was being taken in the opposite direction from where she was supposed to be going."

"How'd she get away?"

"When they stopped at a red light, she bailed and ran like the dickens. She got to a small motel and called the police, but the driver, the car, and her luggage were never seen again."

"That is scary," the driver said. "Who was it?"

"Mmm, I shouldn't say," Skyler said. "Client privilege and all. It never made the news. Although, we considered leaking it for the publicity...and to help others who might not be so lucky."

"You're in P.R.?"

"Yes, for better or worse."

"I'm actually studying journalism and public relations now," the kid said, surprising Skyler, since she thought he looked no older than 16 years old. "I have one semester left. I interned at an F.M. radio station down in Albuquerque this past summer, and I really want to get into terrestrial radio after graduation, but I know it's dying a quick death. But P.R. seems cool, too."

Skyler marveled at the mountains in every direction as they pulled out of the airport and headed north on the highway. "I was a disc jockey at my school's radio station for three of the four years I was in college. I loved every second of it. But I think that, if I lived here, I'd want to do something outside. It's just so gorgeous."

"That's the Sangre de Cristo Range to the right," he said, pointing. "It's the very southern end of the Rocky Mountains. Santa Fe is beautiful. I've lived here my entire life. But, it can be kind of sleepy."

"Oh, I know all about sleepy," Skyler said. "I grew up in a tiny town in Maine called Wabanaki. It was named after an Indian tribe that lived there hundreds of years ago."

"I'm part of the Tesuque Pueblo just north of here. It dates back to the 1200's."

"Pueblo?"

"It's another name for a reservation. But it sounds nicer."

"Very cool," she said. "This country sure does have a rich history."

They drove in silence for the last few miles. They passed the bohemian-looking Tesuque Village Market—which Skyler hoped to return to; she loved unexpected, out of the way businesses—then they turned right on State Road 592 and headed up into the foothills. They soon arrived at the Four Seasons Rancho Encantado, an extremely private compound overlooking the Rio Grande Valley. Dozens of individual guest casitas made up the property, all featuring patios or terraces with endless, unobstructed views of the rolling desert landscape and mountains beyond. As Skyler made her way into the reception building, the sun was just beginning to set, cascading a rich orange-red light into the space. She was greeted warmly at the front desk and then whisked off to her casita in a large golf cart. The bellboy gave her a quick tour: the room had a king-sized bed, a fireplace, a well-stocked bar, a couple of comfortable-looking easy chairs, black and white desert photographs on the walls, and a massive concrete floored bathroom with a large walk-in shower and a deep soaking tub. After the hotel employee left her alone, she stepped out onto the patio and marveled at the last sliver of sun that was about to disappear behind the mountain top in the distance.

"Welcome to Santa Fe," Brenda's voice said from behind the stuccoed wall to her right. Skyler leaned out and stuck her head around the wall. Brenda was there with a glass of champagne in hand. She was wearing a long fur coat. "Get over here. My door is open."

Skyler pulled on her jacket and found her way through Brenda's suite—stopping for a few seconds to greet Mulder and Scully—then stepped out onto the patio. "Fur? Really?!"

Brenda did a twirl. "Like it? It's new."

"I do *not*."

"It's fake."

"I love it!" Skyler went in for a big hug. "Where's my glass?"

Brenda popped back into the room and fetched Skyler a glass of bubbly. Back outside, they talked while they watched the magnificent light display in the sky as it transformed from evening into night.

"The desert is amazing. But it's so deafeningly quiet here. How does anyone sleep?" Skyler asked.

"Isn't it something? But I'll take this over ambulances and screaming drunks any day."

"It's colder than I would have thought."

"Just wait until tomorrow. The desert sun warms you to the core."

Skyler tightened up her coat; she was shivering a bit. "How was Vegas?"

"A big hit all around, I'd say," Brenda said proudly. "The suits loved the dinner, seemed pleased with the new menus, and everyone left fat and happy. And Carissa told me to tell you, 'hello.'" She took a sip of her wine. "So, I'm curious, how are you getting on without Leonard?"

Skyler sighed. She didn't like being defined by her relationships with men, but it was Brenda, and she could get away with such questions. "I'm fine. I was so busy the last few days, I hardly noticed he wasn't there until it was time to go to bed. I hadn't slept alone in months. He's busy, too. Wabanaki has pretty much turned into a ghost town for the winter, he tells me, but I guess there's a lot going on police-wise. Leonard says there's quite a bit of new development happening this winter. Someone actually bought the Lobster Shanty lot and they're building a new Japanese restaurant on the site."

Brenda nearly choked. "A Japanese restaurant in Wabanaki? Now I've heard everything."

"I wrote down the name. Hold on," Skyler said, pulling up the Notes app on her phone. "*Omotenashi*. The woman who is developing it is someone named Jai Yu."

"Okay, yes, I know her in passing. A fine chef and restaurateur. She started in Tokyo, then branched out to Las Vegas, New York, and London, as I recall. But *Wabanaki?* I am just flabbergasted. How would that even be on her radar?"

"Are you kidding me? Our little town is coming up in the world, thanks to last summer."

"Amazing what a few corpses do for your reputation."

Skyler bristled. "Can we go inside? I'm freezing my tits off."

"What a lovely image." Brenda led the way back inside and Skyler closed the heavy sliding glass door. They settled into the easy chairs. "So, we have a lot on the schedule."

"You mean *you* do," Skyler said topping off her glass. "I'm here to decompress and relax for a change. Although, I will have to work a little bit next week. Just a little bit."

Brenda wrinkled up her face. "I have work to do, too, but it's going to be fun stuff. The Winter Wine and Beer Fiesta is tomorrow, and I'll be manning a booth there with the boys."

"The boys?"

"Carter and Sullivan Lowery. They're the developers of the Franklin-Lowery hotels. You met them in New York, I'm sure."

"Oh, yes. The twins that look like they just stepped off a fashion show runway. So very dreamy."

"Yep. *And* smart and creative. Did you see the *60 Minutes* piece on them last month? No? These two took their dad's construction firm, landed some Silicon Valley investors, and now they're rich as all get out. I'm always a little suspicious of self-made people. Or people who aren't me, at least. But if you have to get in bed with someone…"

"Wouldn't that be something?" Skyler said with a sly smile.

"Stop it. They're both so sweet. Or they both seem sweet. But I guess there must be something wrong with them; no two can be *that* perfect."

"So, what happens at this fiesta? What is the booth even for?"

"We're doing what you've taught me so well, lady, we're starting to build local support and excitement for the hotel. Public relations, I think you call it. And we're doing it all by ourselves. Since it's so close to Christmas, I have no assistants with me and neither do the boys—they sent their whole hotel development team back to New York and they're managing the project, and the fiesta booth, alone. But we'll survive, just like in the old days. I'll have my cava on hand for people to taste and I'm doing these cute bite-sized lobster rolls. And the boys will have renderings of the hotel rooms and the lobby and all of that. They usually repurposed older buildings for their hotels, but this is the first time they're building something from scratch from the ground up."

"Cool. I'll help anyway that I can," Skyler said. "I'm good with this kind of thing."

"It's why I made you come out here."

"Great." Skyler didn't know there was an ulterior motive, but she'd do anything for her best friend.

"And we'll have some super yummy meals and some downtime, too, I promise." Brenda finished her wine and got to her feet. "And tonight, we have been invited to a holiday party, so we should get going."

"I haven't been to a party in ages," Skyler said as she got to her feet. "What about the dogs?"

"We're at the Four Seasons, darling," Brenda said. "They're sending over a doggie nanny!"

CHAPTER FOUR

The caterers were busy in the kitchen as Georgia breezed through the house lighting candles and rearranging knickknacks and vases of flowers. She agonized over the tiniest of details; it was just in her nature to always strive for perfection. The house was back to normal after the break-in, thanks to an interior design student that her agent had found at the local community college. While it took some convincing that the twenty-something was up for the task—Georgia would have preferred utilizing a local, experienced design firm—she ultimately gave the young woman carte blanche to replace all the things that had been broken and Georgia was very pleased with what the girl came up with. The student—her name was Emma—even managed to procure a new urn for Georgia's mother's ashes and the matriarch was back in her place in the middle of the fireplace hearth. Georgia planned to take the new urn to New York eventually, where, the singer decided, it probably should have stayed in the first place.

Emma was standing on her tip toes, putting finishing touches on the Christmas tree in the main room of the house when Georgia entered from the back hall. The girl was dressed in impossibly worn jeans and a faded navy-blue sweatshirt, her mousy brown hair pulled back into a loose ponytail. Georgia thought the outfit didn't befit a student of design, but the girl had been working like a fiend all day for her and Georgia was thrilled with everything.

"Did you bring something to change into for the party?"

Emma didn't turn around right away. She adjusted a silver snowflake ornament and swallowed hard before facing the opera singer. "I can't attend, I'm afraid."

"Oh, darling, you must," Georgia said. "The tree is amazing. Everything is." She gestured around the space. "*You* did all of this. Please stay for the party."

The girl stuffed some empty ornament boxes into a large plastic garbage bag and folded up the stepstool she'd been using. "I have my last exam on Monday, Miss Reece. I haven't even begun to study. I must get home. But thank you for the kind invitation."

Georgia gave up. The girl wouldn't fit in with the guests she'd invited anyway; but she felt compelled to invite her nevertheless, as a 'thank you.' The lady of the house smiled. "Well, do have a glass of champagne with me before you go. We can toast your good work. The bartenders look like they're about set up."

"I couldn't," Emma said flatly. "I never, ever touch the stuff." She gathered up her belongings and headed toward the kitchen. "I hope the party is a success."

Sullivan and Carter were the first guests to arrive and they were greeted at the front door by a waiter who had been tasked to be the butler for the evening; he was to greet the guests and take their coats and gifts. When Georgia spotted the brothers, she rushed over and hugged them warmly.

"Thank you for coming," she said. "Can you believe I'm

doing this so soon? I just got the place put back together."

"Everything is absolutely beautiful," Carter said as he scanned the Great Room. "I love the tree. Is it real?"

"It is," Georgia said, leading them to the 12-foot-high Norwegian Spruce. "My Christmas decorations are in storage back in the city, so all of this was purchased yesterday by an amazing local design student. It's all from Pier One and Dillard's. Can you *believe* it?"

"I'd give the kid a large bonus, Georgia," Sullivan said. "She did a bang-up job. And I want her name. We might have to hire her to do the lobby of the hotel next December."

Georgia lowered her voice to a loud whisper, "She's obviously very capable, but seems a bit…troubled. A little off, maybe." She straightened up and smiled. "But I'm being horrible. I'm very thankful for all that Emma has done for me. Emma Wade, is her name, Sullivan."

She led them to the bar where a waiter stood ready with the signature cocktail of the evening. "Cider honey syrup, whiskey, and prosecco," the young female bartender said as she handed each brother a Collins glass topped with a sprig of fresh rosemary.

"How many are you expecting this evening?" Carter asked after tasting the drink. "This is delicious, by the way."

Georgia accepted a glass, too. "Thirty or so. Mostly music folks, since I don't know many other people here. And the Governor of New Mexico is coming, naturally," she said with a self-deprecating laugh. "She's a friend of the president of the opera house and she lives just down the hill. So, I expect we'll have a lot of security people milling about, which makes me feel better about things. An advance team and a couple State Police officers came by this afternoon to case the joint. It was quite surreal."

"We'll look forward to meeting her," Sullivan said. "Having the Governor in our corner can't hurt the hotel. But I can't believe you'd be intimidated by the lowly Governor of New Mexico. You've performed for kings, queens, and presidents."

Georgia smiled but ignored the comment. "And Brenda Braxton is coming along with a friend of hers from back east."

"Perfect," the brothers said in unison.

"Are you coming to the fiesta tomorrow? It'll be in a big heated tent up at the opera house parking lot," Sullivan said. "So, I suspect you know how to get there."

"I wouldn't miss it for the world," Georgia said. "If you two will excuse me for a moment, the Governor just arrived. I should go say hello." She glided toward the foyer leaving the twins to admire the tree.

The party was in full swing when Brenda and Skyler arrived. They'd changed before leaving the hotel, but Skyler was a little miffed that she hadn't packed something more upscale-festive than the semi-fancy dress she'd picked out. "I'm not dressed appropriately for this party," she said under her breath as they handed their coats to the man at the door. "Everyone has such sparkly things on."

"You're fine," Brenda said. "They'll be looking at me, anyway, not you. I'm the celebrity. You're just in P.R."

"What is *wrong* with you?"

"I'm kidding. You look fine, honey." Brenda placed a wrapped box of chocolates—ridiculously expensive, Skyler thought—on the front hall table among a dozen other small gifts.

"Let's find the bar, damn it."

With drinks in hand, the pair wound their way through the crowd and found Carter and Sullivan standing next to the roaring fireplace. Brenda made the introductions.

"I do believe we met when you first opened your New York location," Skyler said. "I was at the hotel's launch party, as Brenda's guest, of course. She's been filling me in on your success. Congratulations on growing so fast. And the *60 Minutes* piece—impressive."

"Thank you, Skyler," Carter said. "We're really excited about the new property here in Santa Fe. It's the most ambitious project we've ever tackled. Literally from the ground up. We've never done that before."

"We could certainly use your expertise, Skyler," Sullivan added. "Have you worked on hospitality projects?"

"Not per se, but my company is branching out. We're doing a lot more celebrity work of late, and I'll be taking on Brenda's restaurants when her current public relations contract ends, so it makes sense that we'd work together, doesn't it?"

"We'll talk details next week," Carter said. "We have an in-house marketing team but partnering with outside forces can only add creativity to the mix." He turned to Brenda. "Which reminds me, have you come up with a name yet?"

Brenda shifted her weight nervously. She turned to Skyler to explain, "As you know, all my current restaurants are named *Brenda's Kitchen*, but the boys want a fresh new concept for New Mexico. I need to come up with something *el originalé*."

"I don't think that's actual Spanish, but never mind. Do you have any ideas?" Skyler asked.

"All the good names are taken," the chef sighed.

"That's silly," Sullivan said. "There must be something left. What happened to the idea of calling it *S.F.N.M?*"

"Blah," the chef said. "I'm leaning toward, *Gingersnatch.*"

"What?!" the twins said together. They looked as if they weren't sure she was kidding or not.

Carter gave a hesitant laugh. "You can't be serious."

"I'm not," Brenda said, "But it does sound fun, doesn't it?"

"It sounds dirty," Skyler said. "And I would have no idea how to market that. *Gingersnatch* sounds like a redheaded drag queen. Surely someone has come up with that before you."

Brenda cocked her head. "Alright. I'll come up with something more palatable. Something more upscale. Something that better fits my position and your fine establishment."

"You have about 14-hours," Sullivan said. "The fiesta starts at 11 o'clock tomorrow morning. We want to unveil the name as part of the presentation at our booth."

"The *pressure* of a *name,*" Brenda said dramatically. "I just detest having to make quick decisions that are so important. Really—are you all sure that *Gingersnatch* won't do?"

"You've had several months to…" Carter stopped talking. After a beat he said, "Something is wrong."

There was a popping sound toward the front of the house. It was so loud that most of the guests stopped their conversations and turned to look.

Then it happened.

An impossibly loud explosion in the foyer sent guests running for cover. Two uniformed policemen tackled the Governor to the floor near the Christmas tree, nearly toppling it over.

People screamed. Glasses shattered on the tile floor.

An oil painting above the gift table was on fire, filling the Great Room with a thick cloud of acrid black smoke.

Waiters rushed to open the patio doors and guest scrambled out of the house and into the bitter cold night.

Skyler and Brenda raced from the house and found themselves clutching each other's hand next to a frozen birdbath. They watched through a window as a policeman used a handheld fire extinguisher to put out the flaming artwork and what was left of the pile of gifts. The Governor—who Skyler and Brenda hadn't had a chance to meet—was whisked through the backyard and taken around the side of the house, presumably to a waiting vehicle.

"What the hell?" Brenda nearly screamed.

"This is insane," Skyler said. "Did a bomb go off? Who would try to blow up an opera singer's Christmas party?"

Carter Lowery appeared and handed his sport coat to Skyler. His brother took off his own jacket and put it around Brenda's shoulders. "Georgia has had some trouble lately," Sullivan said. "The house was ransacked on Tuesday. But she added a security system. And there are cops everywhere. This is just crazy. How could something like this happen in Santa Fe?"

"With the Governor here, to boot," Brenda said. "There must have been a very tight guest list."

"How *tight* could it have been," Skyler asked. "We didn't get frisked at the door and they didn't even know that I was coming, did they? Did you tell them?"

Brenda thought about that for a moment as they all watched the chaos from a comfortable distance. "I indicated that I had a plus one. I don't remember giving them your name, no."

"Apparently security around the New Mexican Governor

isn't what it is for the President of the United States," Skyler said. "But I'll tell you this, they're not going to let anyone leave this property anytime soon. That's for sure. This is one big fat crime scene."

"Great," Carter said. "And we have a big day tomorrow."

"That's what you're worried about?" Sullivan asked his brother with disgust. "A friggin' bomb just went off in our friend's house, dude."

"Okay, calm down, *dude*," Carter said mockingly. He looked around at the excited crowd then said softly, "It's still going to screw stuff up for us."

"You're screwed up," Sullivan said sharply.

Brenda threw up a hand. "Okay guys, stop. Look, they're letting people back inside. Let's go see if we can be of some help."

The opera singer was a mess. She sat on the couch in her front drawing room answering a barrage of questions to the best of her ability. Massimo Modena, Georgia's career-long talent agent and business manager sat next to her, firmly gripping one of her delicate hands to try to keep her from shaking. She was too upset to push him away. While he'd been in her life for decades—they'd even dated for a very brief time—she had recently told him about her self-inflicted performance slow-down and he became enraged, demanding that she keep working at her usual fevered pace. And although she asked him to stay away for a while, he showed up in Santa Fe unexpectedly and weaseled his way into the party.

A New Mexico State Police captain was initiating the

investigation but told the assembled that the F.B.I. had been contacted. Agents were on their way from the Albuquerque field office, some sixty miles south of the resort city.

"Do you have any known enemies?" the captain asked.

"No, sir. I've been wracking my brain. I can't imagine why anyone would want to torment me like this."

"You don't think this was an attempt on the Governor's life?" Massimo asked in his thick Italian accent. "Maybe someone who is not fond of a tiny *woman* being in charge?"

Georgia hit Massimo on the leg. "Massimo, honestly."

"What?! She's very small."

"We're not ruling that out completely, sir, but given how Miss Reece's house was broken in to earlier this week, we're going on the assumption that this is somehow connected to that. I have a man reviewing the video feed. It was very smart of you to have those cameras installed, ma'am."

"Just a few days ago, they were installed," Georgia said weakly, easily falling back into her native New York accent. "Was it one of the gifts? Can you pinpoint which gift exploded? That should help identify who left it on the front table, no?"

"Unfortunately, all the gifts were destroyed beyond recognition," the policeman said. "We'll have the forensics team do their best. It also doesn't help that the camera in the foyer is trained on the front door. It doesn't get a good view of the sideboard, since it's set back into a nook."

"We must grill every single guest," Massimo said flatly.

"We will do that, sir. And we'll be asking everyone exactly what they brought to the house, although we don't expect that someone will offer up that they brought an explosive device wrapped up with a pretty bow—it's never that easy. As far as I know, everyone you invited, as well as all of the staff, are still here, except for the Governor and her immediate security detail. The Governor's Chief of Staff is right over there by the buffet."

"I can't believe people are still eating," Georgia said with a look of confusion.

"People eat. That's what they do." Massimo said. "Why waste a good spread because of a little bomb? No one died."

In the Great Room, guests continued to sip drinks and eat the food, but all of the talk had changed from polite cocktail party conversation to speculations about the bomb and when, if ever, folks would be allowed to leave the house. But, they ate and drank heartily, nevertheless.

Brenda and Skyler sat squeezed together on an oversized loveseat near the Christmas tree. The Lowery brothers delivered stiff drinks to the women and took seats opposite.

"It's curious that the waiters and bartenders are still at work like nothing happened," Carter said.

"I'm amazed that more people aren't freaking out and demanding to leave," Brenda said. "I have the mind to suggest to the authorities that they *should* move us out of here. What if there's another bomb, for Christ's sake? A bigger one. It's certainly a possibility."

"I think that's unlikely," Sullivan said. "I'm no expert in this kind of thing, but it seems like the device was small enough that it wasn't meant to hurt anyone. Perhaps it was just a warning. Just a scare tactic."

"What on Earth do *you* know about scare tactics or anything else?" Carter spit. "He doesn't know anything more than what he sees on *Criminal Minds* reruns on television."

Sullivan mouthed, 'fuck you' to his brother.

"It was certainly scary." Skyler rubbed her cold drink glass across her forehead for a quick moment. "That little bomb did the trick. It *was* scary."

Georgia and Massimo joined the group and the twins immediately stood up, offering their chairs. The hostess looked pale. Her face had a blank, distant look when she sat down, but she managed a weak smile when she started to speak. "This isn't how I intended this evening to go. I'm so very sorry."

"Why are you apologizing to us?" Carter asked. "We're fine. The more important question is, how are *you* doing?"

"I asked that the police allow people to leave and follow up with folks later, but because the darned Governor was here, this has become something of a major incident. I'm afraid it's going to be a very long night for everyone. That's why I apologize."

"Enough!" Massimo waved an angry, dismissive hand. "What is, *is*."

"No wiser words were ever spoken," Brenda said dryly under her breath. She turned to Skyler and spoke softly so that the others couldn't hear: "This trip was supposed to be relaxing."

"I'll be okay. Surprisingly, I'm getting used to the madness that my life has become. What a year, huh?"

"Next year will be quieter, I promise," Brenda said. "We'll make sure of it."

"Are we going to find a cave in the woods for us to live in, off the grid?" Skyler asked. "If we can't find peace in sleepy places like Wabanaki and Santa Fe, we're doomed, lady."

When Brenda chuckled, Georgia turned her attention to the women. "Thank you for having such a good attitude about all of this Miss Braxton and Miss Moore. I need to stop thinking about all of this for a moment." She looked as if she were about to cry, but quickly got herself under control and fixed a small smile on her face. "I am so terribly sorry that I didn't get a chance to formally welcome you to my home when you arrived. I guess I was caught up with my hostess duties. Despite the unfortunate explosion in the front hall, I am very happy that you could come. I'm a big fan, Brenda. Oh my goodness, I'm so sorry. Can I call you Brenda?"

"Well of course you can. That's my name, isn't it? And thank you," Brenda said sweetly. "We were thrilled to get the invitation. I've never seen you perform, Georgia, sadly, but I aim to fix that *tout de suite.*"

"That will have to wait, Brenda," Georgia said. "I'm not performing again until next summer, here in Santa Fe. I've been working non-stop since college. I'm giving these tired old vocal cords a much-needed vacation."

Massimo scowled. "*Stupido!* You are in the prime of your career. They will forget you."

Georgia playfully slapped the man's leg. "Don't listen to him. He just wants his cut."

"No one will forget the great soprano," Carter said.

"Thank you, Sullivan, darling."

"I'm Carter."

"If you say so." Forgetting for a moment the gravity of the situation, she roared with laughter, then stopped herself short. "I'm sorry for that. It must get terribly old having people make fun of the *twin thing* all the time. I am so very sorry."

"Stop apologizing, Georgia," Carter said. "*That's* what's getting old."

Georgia shrugged her shoulders. "I give up."

"Your house is beautiful," Skyler interjected, hoping to change the subject. "This tree is magnificent. I don't think I thought about it before deciding to come to New Mexico for Christmas, but I am going to miss not having my tree up and decorations out this year."

"Thank you, Skyler, darling," Georgia said. "As I told the boys, these aren't even my ornaments. Well, they're mine *now*, but every single one is brand new, bought in the last 24-hours. My vintage stuff is back in New York. This is pretty, yes, but I prefer the old stuff, I believe."

"I kept my mother's and grandmother's ornaments," Skyler said. "I know what you mean."

A tired looking man in a worn, ill-fitting black suit approached and identified himself as an F.B.I. agent. He asked to speak with the opera singer in the other room and she and her manager darted away leaving the foursome alone again.

"Is she involved with the Italian?" Brenda asked the twins. "Those two seem intimate. Very close."

"Massimo is her longtime agent and manager and I believe they dated briefly when she was between husbands," Sullivan said. "She's been widowed *twice*. Both were quite tragic and unexpected."

Brenda looked around to see if anyone was in earshot. "They are doing it." It wasn't a question. "And I don't like the look of that guy."

"Brenda, honestly," Skyler said. "Who cares?"

"The F.B.I. might care," Brenda said.

Skyler took a sip of her drink. "You've lost your mind."

Brenda's face lit up and she turned toward the twins. "I have a name for the restaurant! It just popped into my head and I love it instantly. If it can't be *Brenda's Kitchen*, then it should be, *Cornerstone*."

Carter and Sullivan squinted their eyes. Skyler nodded, "I like it. But why on Earth are you thinking about that right now?"

"What else do we have to do? *Cornerstone*. It's good, right?" Brenda asked. "It's classic, solid; to me it says, '*new beginning*.' What do you think, boys?"

"I love it," Carter said after a beat.

Sullivan's brow was wrinkled and he stared at the floor. After a moment he said, "It makes me think of the corners, bricks, cement. I'm not sure that's the imagery we want in peoples' heads when they're are deciding where to eat dinner. It sounds like a construction company."

"Did you come up with that just now? While we were talking about F.B.I. agents?" Skyler asked.

Brenda shifted in her seat. "It's a word that's used a lot in the *The X-Files* books I read. There's a lot of cornerstones in the *X-Files* mythology. The Catholic Church. The Syndicate. The Elders. Deep State."

No one said anything for a moment, then Skyler turned to the twins. "You should know that Brenda is obsessed. She's got every line, from every episode and all *The X-Files* movies, memorized and she reads the novelizations and the non-fiction books about the series. It's *The X-Files*, 24-seven."

"I don't know *every* line from *every* episode," Brenda said, "but it is my all-time favorite show. When you meet my dear dogs, you'll know how much I love that world."

"We'll go with *Cornerstone*," Carter said. "I like it, it's different, and it's certainly better than calling it, *Little Green Men*. You wouldn't suggest that, would you, Brenda?"

The chef shook her head. "No. No. Of course not. Aliens aren't green. More of a whitish-grey." She turned to Sullivan and grabbed the side of his arm. "*Cornerstone by Brenda Braxton.* I think my name should be in the official title. People have heard of me."

"I agree. It's a done deal. Now if we can ever get out of here, we might get a few hours of sleep before the fiesta tomorrow," Sullivan said. He consulted his watch. "I'm sorry, it's already *today*."

Skyler was curious, so she slipped off the loveseat, walked to the front window, peered outside, then returned quickly. "Not a single news vehicle. Maybe about a dozen police cars though."

"This is Santa Fe," Georgia said. "The closest news van is probably down in Albuquerque. And I doubt local reporters monitor the police scanners like they do back East. Maybe this won't make the news at all."

"It'll make the news," Carter said to Georgia. "The governor, you, Brenda, us. All in one bombed out Christmas party? It'll make the news."

Everyone bristled but didn't necessarily disagree.

CHAPTER FIVE

Operating on just a few hours' sleep, the Lowery twins and a team of locally hired temp workers were at the fiesta site by nine o'clock that morning, busily setting up the Franklin-Lowery booth. Brenda arrived moments later with two Four Seasons restaurant employees—a middle-aged male bartender who was the spitting image of actor George Clooney, she thought, and a cute little wisp of a twenty-something prep-cook. She'd convinced them both to moonlight for her since she was in Santa Fe without her usual team. They got to work assembling hundreds of mini lobster rolls and placed dozens of Brenda's signature cava on ice. She believed that the crisp sparkling white wine, together with her small taste of Maine seafood, would be a welcomed surprise, given the sea of New Mexican hatch chili-themed foods surrounding their booth.

Brenda wasn't a food snob, in any sense. She had no problem enjoying a box of Kraft Macaroni and Cheese alongside a nice steak, but she just wasn't a fan of food clichés. While she made allowances since it *was* a chili-themed town, it was overkill; every booth appeared to be just a slight variation on the same tired thing. She was proud that the Franklin-Lowery booth would stand out with its splash of Down East seafood. It was almost like wearing a red dress to a black and white ball—it takes balls to pull it off. And she had 'em and wasn't afraid to whip them out when necessary. Balls, and "…taking risks outside of that tire old, damned proverbial box," she always said.

While the December morning was certainly chilly, the interior of the football field-sized tent was toasty. Brenda shucked her faux fur coat—she'd seen a few women give her *that* look, but she didn't care; she knew it wasn't real—and donned an apron.

"We appreciate you doing this," Carter said. "I'm guessing you don't usually get yourself involved at a local level like this."

"Don't be silly," she said as she popped a piece of lobster claw into her mouth. "I'm successful *because* I do stuff like this. From time to time you need to let the little people see you up close."

Carter looked concerned.

After a moment, her face brightened. "I'm kidding, honey. Kidding."

"Oh." He set out a pile of cocktail napkins embossed with the Franklin-Lowery hotel logo.

"Relax, brother," Sullivan said. "He can't take a joke, Brenda."

"I'm only successful if you guys are successful," the chef said. "And I have very high hopes for the Santa Fe hotel *and* the new restaurant. Cornerstone. Heck, if it does well, maybe you'll keep me on for the forthcoming properties?"

"Yeah. That's the idea," Sullivan said. "We do have a request though."

Carter put a hand on his brother's back. "You're going to ask her *now*? They're about to open the gates and the let the little people in."

"Ask me what?" Brenda's eyes widened with intrigue.

Sullivan pulled away from his brother. "We were wondering if you might convince Carissa Lamb to attend the grand opening of the hotel. That would guarantee that we make the national news, gossip sites, and social medias, really putting the hotel on peoples' radar. We'd get tons of press having her here. I have a contact at *Travel & Leisure*. I know they'd send someone to cover it."

"Well, that's an easy one, boys," Brenda said quickly. "Do not ever be timid about asking me questions like that. I'm all about creative marketing and using the friends and connections that I have to increase the bottom line." She gave a low laugh. "And Carissa is so game for stuff like that. Honestly. And if you time it right, I'm sure we can make it happen. She's an absolute doll and very, very down to Earth. But she works constantly. We have to plan carefully."

"Having one of the world's most famous pop singers, the world's most in-demand opera diva, and one of the country's most famous celebrity chefs…well, it's just a trifecta of marketing perfection," Sullivan said proudly.

Brenda closed her eyes and smiled. "Thrilled to help. And since I make money, too, it works for me. Let's just work on keeping that diva alive, for goodness sake. I'm still shaking from last night. What the hell happened?!"

Carter sighed. "Someone bombed the damned party, is what happened. I still can't believe it."

"Where is Georgia now?" Brenda asked. "You didn't leave her alone, did you?"

"No, of course not," Sullivan said. "We offered to have her come stay at the house we're renting, but she and Massimo decamped to his suite at the La Fonda hotel down on the Plaza. She didn't want to stay in that house."

"Well, I don't blame her. I wouldn't have stayed a minute longer than I had to," Brenda said. "And I *knew* there was something going on between her and that agent of hers."

Their conversation was cut short when scores of Santa Feans started approaching the booth. The twins talked up the hotel to all who would listen and Brenda's food and sparkling wine were an instant hit. The celebrity chef took countless photos with fans and signed autographs, too. By one o'clock, the food was gone and only a few bottles of wine were left. And the boys had given away nearly all of their promotional materials. Only a handful of guests were still milling about when Skyler approached the booth.

"You pretty much missed the whole thing," Brenda said. She was exhausted and sat down on an ice chest. "I'm out of lobster. Where have you been?"

"Actually, I've been here for about an hour. I ate and drank my way through the whole place and it was simply glorious. What an amazing event. It was pure heaven in bite sized pieces. My favorite. I'm sorry, you guys. I was being very selfish. But I had a ball."

"I hear the Wine and Chili Fiesta in September is four times as big as this," Carter said. "We'll have to make sure we're available for that, too."

"I'm so stuffed, I can't imagine having more options," Skyler said as she eyed a bottle in the ice chest. "But I'll have some of that cava, please. I hear it's very drinkable."

"Damn right," Brenda said as she got to her feet.

Sullivan poured her a glass.

"Brenda sends me a case several times a year," Skyler said. "I drink more of this than water, thank you very much."

Carter pulled his smartphone out of his pocket and looked at the screen. "It's Georgia. Hello?" He listened intently for a few moments. "Okay. I'll be there. Hang tight." He turned to his brother. "Massimo just left to return to Italy for the holidays and she's a mess. I'm going to go see her at the hotel."

"I thought no one from the party was supposed to leave town," Skyler said.

"Massimo does what he wants," Carter explained. "He told Georgia that he was an Italian citizen and that they couldn't make him stay and miss spending Christmas with his family."

"He might be right," Brenda said. "But I still don't like that guy."

CHAPTER SIX

After a much-needed afternoon nap back at the hotel, Skyler dialed Leonard's cell. It rang several times and then went to voicemail. At least she got to hear his sexy voice. "Hi, it's me," she said after the beep. "Having an adventure in Santa Fe, to say the least. It's cold here, but absolutely breathtakingly beautiful. Call me when you have a free moment. Brenda says, hello. I love you." She hung up and agonized over having said the 'love' word. Leonard hadn't used it yet either and she wasn't convinced he was prepared to say it out loud so soon. She brushed it off; the deed was done. She couldn't undo it.

She took a quick shower and dressed in jeans, hiking boots, a ribbed long-sleeve thermal top, and a medium weight jacket that she'd picked up at a local outdoor provisioning store on her way back from the fiesta. People weren't kidding about the weather; at night, one had to bundle up, and during the day, the sun beat the heat right into you despite the frigid wind chill.

After retrieving Mulder and Scully from Brenda's empty room, Skyler took off for the front of the resort with a dog leash in each hand. They soon arrived at the beginning of the Camino Encantado Trail that circumnavigated the resort property. It was a relatively short trail with manageable hills and the dogs seemed to love sniffing and exploring their new surroundings. Skyler marveled at the views of the mountains and valleys around the resort when she wasn't watching her footing. She nearly slipped off a large rock at the top of a crest but used the weight of the dogs to steady herself, nearly choking the poor beasts. She took a few cell phone photos of cacti, sagebrush, and the occasional lizard, which predictably sent the dogs into a frenzy of curiosity.

Skyler reveled in the quietness. It was unsettling to her how silent it was; but a welcome break from the constant frenzy of city life. She decided that she could get used to northern New Mexico and would even consider living in the beautiful place...if it just had more shopping options. A Nordstrom addict in the Land of Enchantment might be forced to make several trips to larger metropolitan cities for clothes, or buy online, which Skyler was decidedly not a fan of. She had to touch fabrics and try tons of stuff on before she settled on outfits.

She rounded the last bend of the trail and came face to face with an elderly man holding an ornate carved walking stick. His deeply weathered face came to life when he noticed her.

"Good afternoon, young lady," he said warmly.

"Good afternoon." She smiled back but she hoped this wouldn't turn into a long conversation. She tended to attract the attention of old geezers when she was out and about and it didn't always end well.

"How did you enjoy the trail?"

"It was perfect for me," Skyler said, pulling back on the leashes to keep the excited dogs from knocking over the man. "About as much as this city girl can manage in a day."

"Which city?"

"I live in Washington, D.C."

"Never been a fan of the capital city," he said, losing his

smile. "I haven't been back since before John Kennedy was shot. That makes me quite old."

"You don't look that old, sir."

"I'm a nonagenarian! Turned 94 this past September."

"You don't look a day over 80," she said, playing along.

"You're too kind," he laughed. He looked down at the ground and then slammed his walking stick forcefully onto something. "Got him! I don't like those big black bugs."

He indeed smashed to death a large cockroach-looking insect into smithereens. "Thanks for saving me," Skyler said.

"I spend most of my time at hotels now that I gave up my houses. I'm basically a nonagenarian nomad," he said with an explosive laugh. "I'll be here through Christmas and then I'm off to Maui for New Year's."

"That sounds lovely," Skyler said. She was becoming impatient with the conversation. The temperature was falling quickly and she was getting cold.

"Hawaii is my all-time favorite, but Santa Fe is a close second. I built a very fine business and worked my fingers to the bones over the past 50 years, so I deserve this easy life, I believe. But I should get on before it gets dark…and I should stop monopolizing a pretty young lady's time."

"I enjoyed our chat, sir," Skyler said, "And I especially appreciate being called a young lady, when it's obviously *not true.*"

"That's where you are wrong, *young* lady. You're young when compared to me," he said over his shoulder as he worked his way up the hill she had just come down. "Until we meet again!" And he disappeared behind a large olive tree and was gone.

Skyler continued the last few yards to the casita where she encountered a hotel employee stacking pinon wood for guest fireplaces. The dogs sniffed at the man and tried to jump up on him to say their 'hellos.'

"I'm sorry," Skyler said, pulling back on the leashes. "They love absolutely everyone."

"No bother," the young man said as he pet Mulder and Scully quite enthusiastically. "I love dogs." He pointed up at the trail with his nose. "You do know who that guy was, right?"

"No. We just bumped into each other."

"That's Foster Martin."

"*The* Foster Martin? The billionaire?"

"The very one," the man said. "He's one of our most frequent and probably oldest guests."

Skyler was impressed, and more than a little bit excited. "Well, isn't that interesting. I didn't recognize him." She wondered if she'd been rude to the old man; she hoped not.

"I'm pretty sure he owns nearly half of the television stations and newspapers in this country."

"Oh, I'm well aware," she said. "How interesting."

* * *

When Georgia answered her hotel room door, Carter immediately detected that she'd been crying. Then he saw the shiner encompassing her left eye.

"What the hell happened?" he asked as he closed the door and led her back into the main room of her suite. He sat her down on the sofa and settled in next to her. "Georgia? Did someone hit you?"

She hesitated.

"Come on, it's me," Carter said.

"Massimo and I had a little...disagreement," she managed to whisper.

Carter became enraged. "Are you fucking kidding me?!" He took a deep breath. "Excuse my language, but are you kidding me? Massimo gave you a black eye?"

"How can I show my face in public? Or even private? It's almost Christmas." She started to cry.

"The bigger issue is that your Italian asshole agent laid a hand on you. Georgia, this will never do."

"I know," she sniffed.

"Why on *Earth* would he hit you? What was the argument about?"

"Money, of course," she said. She reached for a bottle of water and took a long drink. "I need to stay hydrated."

"Yes, indeed. *Money*? I assume he's done very well representing you."

"He didn't pull any punches at the party last night. You heard him. He wants me working. Constantly. That's his way."

"He may not have pulled any punches last night, but he obviously punched *you*! Where is he? I need to..."

She cut him off. "Carter, honey, he's long gone."

"Where did he go?"

"I told you on the phone; he's probably half way to Milan by now. He caught a commuter to Denver and I think he was getting on a plane with direct service to Europe. Did you know that one could fly from Denver to Europe? I didn't know that you could..."

"I don't give a crap about that, Georgia. What I care about is *you*. And I care about Massimo not getting away with this. We'll sue him. No! Forget about suing—he should be arrested. We'll have him arrested when he steps off that plane in Italy. How do we go about getting that done?"

"He has taken care of my career from day one, Carter," she said. "He cares about me too much, is all. How do I walk away from all of that?"

"I honestly don't know who you are right now," he spit. "You're one of the most famous, sought-after opera singers in the world. Surely you can find another agent. One who won't lay his hands on his prized client. But when I get my hands on him, I tell you, Georgia, I won't be gentle."

Georgia rose from the sofa and walked to the large picture window. She watched as the last rays of sunlight sparkled above the horizon. Then something caught her eye. She looked down at the street four floors below and saw a hooded figure staring up at the hotel. It sent a chill through her body. He, or she, perhaps, was wearing sunglasses and appeared to be looking directly up at her window. Georgia stepped back a few paces. "Carter! Come here."

Carter jumped off the couch and joined the singer near the window. He looked down at the street and saw nothing. "What is it? What am I looking for?"

She tentatively stepped forward again and peered downward. "He's gone."

"Who's gone?"

"I don't know who it was," she said strongly. "But there was a hooded man—maybe it was a woman, I don't know—looking up at the hotel. Right at me."

"There's no one there now."

"Good."

"It could have been a kid or a tourist," Carter said. "The city is crawling with tourists right now, honey. It's Christmas."

"Maybe. I don't know."

Carter put an arm around Georgia's back and gently led her back to the couch and they sat down. He clutched one of her hands in his and squeezed. "You've had a hell of a week. And I am so sorry for what you've gone through. But I know you're strong. We can deal with this together." He nodded toward her suitcase sitting by the closet door. "How about we get your stuff together and you come stay with Sullivan and me at our house? We won't tell *anyone* where we are. It's private up there. The closest neighbor is a world away. The fact is, I'm not leaving you here alone, so I'm not really asking. We have tons of extra bedrooms all with their own bathrooms. You'll be very comfortable and very secure."

She considered it for a moment. "I guess I'd feel safer there."

"Done," he said as he sprung off the couch. "Let's get going. My car is in the garage. We'll stick you in the backseat and no one will even know you left the hotel. We won't even check you out. Leave the 'do not disturb' sign on the door. Good plan?" He didn't wait for an answer. "It's a good plan."

"It's a plan, at least," she said softly. "I'm sorry, Carter. I'm the last thing you should have to be worrying about right now. You have a hotel to finish."

He took both of her hands in his own. "I can do both. I cloned myself, remember? We'll get the hotel built *and* keep the beautiful opera singer safe. And we'll find out who left that crazy bomb in your house, too. I promise you that."

"I can't believe that sentence just came out of your mouth," she sighed. "A bomb at my house."

"It's unbelievable."

"It sure is."

* * *

Brenda and Sullivan walked into the Secreto Lounge at the Hotel St. Francis and found a vacant table along the wall. Brenda took the banquette seat and Sullivan pulled a heavy wooden chair across the stone floor. They each drank in the atmosphere before speaking; they were always critiquing, evaluating, judging, and borrowing ideas from competitors. They had that in common.

"It's warm and inviting in here," Brenda finally said. "Love the chandelier with the candles. They look real, but they're electric."

"Agreed. Rustic, yet upscale."

They perused the cocktail menu, Brenda selecting the Agave Way—featuring New Mexican green chili (*of course*, she thought), tequila, lime juice, and agave nectar—and Sullivan chose the Collins' Death, a doctored Tom Collins with cucumber, lemon, cane syrup, gin, acai spirits, and soda water. The waitress zipped away to place the order with the head bartender.

"I think she recognized you," Sullivan said quietly.

"Perhaps. I'm still surprised when people do."

"You're on television constantly. I'd think you'd be used to it by now."

Brenda scanned the room then lowered her voice a bit. "You'd think, but I never, ever expect it. I swear, every single time it happens I am taken aback. I just can't wrap my head around it. I suspect that people know who you are, too, yes?"

"Most people think I'm my brother," he chuckled. "But, no, it doesn't happen very often. People don't tend to know hotel developers as much as they do celebrity chefs who are on T.V. all the time. Although, we did have a woman on a plane freak out when she spotted us in first class. She said she was the very first Franklin-Lowery V.I.P. card holder. A real devotee. We looked it up later and indeed she had card number 000001. We immediately added a million points to her account when we got back to the office."

"Like frequent flyer points?" Brenda asked.

"Yeah. It takes a while to accrue them, but 1,000 points will get you a free week night stay. 2,000 points for a weekend night. Slightly more on holidays, naturally. It seems to be a popular loyalty program. You live and die by repeat customers, as you well know. She deserved that million for being number one."

"Mmm hmm," she said. The drinks were delivered and then they ordered appetizers. "It's all for research," Brenda said when the waitress disappeared. "So, I won't allow myself to feel guilty for adding another pound to all of the others I already have."

"We're going to spoil our dinner, but I don't care," Sullivan said. "What are we doing for dinner, anyway?"

"Skyler is going to meet us at your house. Carter just texted and invited us."

"I'm the last to know."

Brenda's eyebrows raised. "We certainly don't *need* to come, dear."

"Oh, I didn't mean to imply that," Sullivan said, his face reddening. "It'll be fun to have a group dinner away from the masses."

"He said Georgia would be there, too."

"I suspected as much. My brother has a soft spot for that lady."

"She seems nice."

"She is," he said after he swallowed a gulp of his drink. "I just hope she doesn't become his new project."

"Oh gosh. What does that mean?"

"Well, obviously she is quite needy right now, given the break-in at her house and the exploding presents. And, of course, we *should* help a friend, but we also should be putting 110% into the hotel. That's our main objective here."

Brenda chuckled. "I thought you were the liberal one. I would have thought that you'd be more caring and concerned."

"I'm not *uncaring*, Brenda," he said. "I love Georgia. I just don't love this distraction. Not now. This is the most important project we've ever taken on. And the most expensive."

"I get it," she said, "but friends come first. If I've learned anything in the world of business, it's that business should not come in the way of friendships. Ever. And at the end of the day, you're still a multi-millionaire with an incredibly successful business. It's all about balance."

"I'm balanced," Sullivan spit. "And I'm not a multi-millionaire. Not yet. At least not *multi* in the way I want it to mean."

"But you own controlling interest in six hotels."

"We haven't exactly made a fortune yet," he said under his breath. "It takes time. We've put nearly every dime of profit back into the business so that we don't have to continue to go out and find new investors. We already gave away a small percentage of the company. We're not willing to part with any more."

Brenda had obviously hit a nerve. "I'm happy to be a part of this adventure and I know that it's going to eventually pay off for you two...*and* me." She smiled. "Shall we put business on the back burner for the evening?"

"We shall. And we should. And I am very sorry for snapping, Brenda. Really, I am."

"It's all good," she said. "Ohhh, goodie! The guacamole is here."

They dug into the appetizer and spent the rest of their time dreaming up ideas for Cornerstone's menu. They wholeheartedly agreed that classic Southwestern items had to be featured, but they aimed to bring in unexpected dishes, too. "Santa Fe is going to get a kick in the culinary ass," Brenda said proudly.

CHAPTER SEVEN

The Lowery brothers' rented house was nestled into a narrow valley in the hills above the city. From the backyard, there were views of the rolling hills through the tall trees that surrounded the property. The house didn't sit high enough to have the commanding mountain and city views that Georgia enjoyed much closer to town. But the twins appreciated the remoteness of the property, and certainly dug the amenities. An in-ground infinity pool was covered with a tarp for the winter, but an enormous round hot tub sat nearby in a wooden gazebo. The tub was covered and kept at 103°, at the ready around the clock.

Inside the house, a 20-foot high wood-beamed ceiling towered over the Great Room, a space that included a large well-equipped kitchen, a dining area, a sunken conversation pit, and an office nook. Four ensuite bedrooms lined the back of the house and there was a tiny fifth bedroom area upstairs with its own small balcony. Georgia toured the house on her own while Carter started a fire in the massive stone hearth.

"I know how to make one thing really well," Carter said when she reappeared in the kitchen, "so, I'm making that for dinner."

"Let me guess," Georgia said. "Spaghetti."

His face fell. "How'd you know?"

She pointed at a pile of groceries on the counter. "I'm not a detective, Carter, but I spy a few boxes of pasta, several cans of crushed tomatoes, and a block of parmesan cheese."

"You got me."

"How could I not be thrilled that we're having Italian tonight?" she deadpanned.

"Oh, gosh, I'm sorry, Georgia. We can make you something else." He started rooting around in the refrigerator. "I think."

"Don't be silly. I was kidding. I refuse to even allow myself to think about that man tonight."

"Or ever again, Georgia," Carter said. "Massimo is a disgrace and he doesn't deserve his 10%. Or any percent!"

"Ten?!" she nearly choked. "Try 40."

Carter's mouth fell open. "Georgia! Why would you give him 40% of *your* money? That's insanity. I've never heard of such a thing."

"I was stupid and young and I signed a long-term contract."

Carter slammed a hand on to the counter top. "And now that contract is null and void, my dear. We'll see to that. Actually…" he pulled out his smartphone "…we should take a picture of that black eye of yours."

Georgia took a step away from him. "Why on Earth would I allow you to do that?"

"For evidence! You should also seriously consider filing a report with the local police department."

"Against an Italian citizen? In Santa Fe, New Mexico? What good would that do?"

"All the good," Carter said. "This has got to be documented for it to be official. If you want to keep him away from you, and if you want to get out of that damned contract, then this is what needs to happen. Even if he never comes back to the United States ever again, I'm pretty sure those are the hoops you're going to have to go through. And if and when he comes back, he'd be arrested on sight."

The singer sighed deeply. "Massimo has obviously had a large impact on my life and career, but I have been dreaming of jettisoning him for a while now. He's grown increasingly demanding, unreasonable, and downright scary in the last few years. And he's put his hands on me more than a few times, Carter." She paused, looked up at the ceiling, and tried very hard not to cry again. "I've made nothing but bad decisions my entire life."

"That's just not true," Carter said. "You married two amazing men and you're the toast of the opera world. I'd say *those* were good decisions."

"I married two men who both dropped dead on me and the third guy I got involved with..." Her voice trailed off. "Okay. I'm done feeling sorry for myself." She straightened up, pushing her shoulders back. She clasped her hands together and took a deep breath. "I'm done!" she sang loudly.

"Well done, Diva," Carter said with a smile. He pulled out an enormous stock pot and began filling it with water. "I'm going to start cooking. Brenda, Skyler, and my brother should be here any minute now." When the pot was on the stove and the gas jet lit, he turned back to the singer who was struggling to open a bottle of wine. "I just realized something, Georgia. I'm cooking spaghetti for one of the most famous chefs in the world. What am I thinking?"

"She'll love it," Georgia said. "She's very down to Earth and you know it." She handed the bottle and corkscrew to Carter who quickly extracted the cork.

"I guess so."

Georgia took back the bottle and filled two glasses. She proposed a toast. "To a quiet evening at home. With *no* surprises."

"I'll drink to that," he said. "And absolutely no exploding presents."

"That goes without saying." She took a long sip. "Mmm, this is very good wine. So smooth." She took another sip. "I'll tell you, I am a little miffed that I didn't get to open any of those gifts. Tell me. What did you bring?"

Carter laughed. "I have no idea. Sullivan picked up something downtown and had it wrapped at the store. I'm sure it was *very* expensive and over-the-top extravagant, and you would have loved it and cherished it forever."

They both laughed heartily and didn't notice when the front door opened. Sullivan and Brenda breezed into the house and got out of their coats. They were feeling good from their happy hour cocktails and they told Carter and Georgia in detail what they drank and ate at the St. Francis.

"How'd you get home?" Carter asked his brother.

Sullivan cocked his head. "An Uber. We're not stupid."

"I didn't call you stupid, stupid!"

"You're the stupid one!"

Brenda and Georgia exchanged looks.

"Shut the fuck up!" Carter yelled.

"Will you guys please stop it," Brenda said. "Honestly, are you eight years old?"

"They do this sometimes," Georgia said. She climbed onto a

stool at the kitchen island. "Boys will *always* be boys. Especially twin brothers."

"Georgia! Your face," Brenda exclaimed. "What happened, honey?"

Georgia turned slightly away. "We decided we wouldn't talk about it anymore tonight. I'm fine."

Brenda turned to Carter. "Did you do this?"

"Of course not," Carter exploded. "What is wrong with you? That Italian asshole Massimo did that to her."

"I knew it!" Brenda yelled. "I knew I didn't like him."

Georgia closed her eyes. "We're *not* talking about this anymore tonight," she repeated. "At all. Can we please just have a nice time?"

"We can, dear," Brenda said. She turned back to the cook who was standing over his pots in the kitchen. "Spaghetti? My favorite. I love when other people cook for me."

"Good. I was worried it might be too pedestrian for you."

"Hogwash," she said. "I'm just a simple girl."

There was a knock at the front door and Sullivan went to answer it. A rush of cold air filled the Great Room again as Skyler entered with Mulder and Scully. "I didn't ask, but I hope it's okay that I brought the dogs. I felt sorry for them being all alone in that hotel room."

The coonhounds bound over to Brenda and nearly knocked her over with exuberant, wet greetings. "Hi, hi, hi, hi, babies," Brenda cooed. She turned to Sullivan. "Is this okay, Sully?"

"What do we care?" Sullivan said. "It's not our house. And even if it were, they'd be most welcome. You know we allow dogs at the Franklin hotels, right? We wouldn't have it any other way."

"Well, that's good, because these babies go everywhere I go. And I mean everywhere." Brenda searched through the kitchen cabinets until she found some Tupperware bowls. She filled them with tap water and set them on the floor for the dogs.

"What do you do with guests who are allergic to animal dander?" Georgia asked.

"We send them to the Holiday Inn," Carter said flatly.

Sullivan crinkled his face. "What? No we don't. We set aside animal-free rooms. The reservation system keeps pretty good track of that sort of thing. We don't want anyone having an attack." He turned back to his brother. "What is wrong with you, Carter?"

"Eh. I think most supposed allergies are made up. Who could be allergic to a beautiful dog? It's all in their heads, I tell ya," Carter said.

"Tell that to my brother who is deathly allergic to peanuts," Skyler said. "Just a few and he goes into anaphylactic shock. It's *not* pretty. Believe me."

"If you say so." Carter busied himself with dinner preparations.

"Don't listen to him," Sullivan said to the women. "He just says shit like that to get a reaction out of people. If you don't react, he stops."

"Shut up, Sully," Carter said. "Why do you hate dogs?"

The group enjoyed the hearty spaghetti dinner, complete with a Caesar salad and French bread. Carter presented decadent chocolate caramel cupcakes from a downtown spot called The Great Divide Bakery and they all agreed that the twins should consider a partnership to feature the treats at the new hotel.

Stuffed and happy, Sullivan suggested a dip in the hot tub.

Brenda went pale. "No one wants to see me in a bathing suit."

"Who has a bathing suit with them? It's December," Georgia said.

Skyler had a sense where this was going and she knew everyone had just enough wine and cocktails inside them to ease their inhibitions. If she'd been alone with the twins, she would have never entertained the idea. But it was three against two, and she liked the odds. Plus, she had a very sweet spot for hot tubs on cold winter evenings. She was game and she agreed first.

Brenda was the last holdout, but it didn't take the group too long to break her down; the brothers promised to close their eyes until she was submerged and that did the trick. Sullivan scooted from bathroom to bathroom rounding up the heavy terrycloth bathrobes provided by the owner of the house, and minutes later five pale naked bodies sunk into the glorious bubbling water. They were each furnished with a plastic tumbler of bourbon on ice to sip in the tub.

"I never dreamed that I'd be sitting a few feet from my business partners, naked as the day I was born," Brenda said. "I'm not sure I'm comfortable with this."

"We don't have to let it change our working relationship," Sullivan said with a sly smile. "Just relax and enjoy it."

"The water feels so wonderful," Skyler purred.

"Heaven," Georgia said. "I definitely need to buy one of these for my house."

There was a pause in the conversation when an animal howled in the near distance. Despite the warm temperature of the water, it sent a chill down Skyler's back. "What on Earth was that?"

"Just a coyote," Georgia said. "They don't hurt people. Much."

Skyler's eyes widened.

"I'm kidding. I'm told that they stick to themselves. But their calls are something else, huh? There's so much nature to get used to when you live in the high desert. And we thought we had a lot of animals in Manhattan."

"Very different breeds of animals, for sure," Sullivan said. "But I could get used to it here. Imagine—the closest neighbor is clear over there somewhere. You can't even yell that far. This privacy is awesome. We're not in the city anymore, people."

"I like it," Skyler said. "I don't think I'd get naked in my backyard in D.C. I'm pretty sure there are Senators and diplomats who have a direct view of my back patio from their windows. I have a little bit more privacy in Maine, of course, but the neighbors are pretty close there, too. I wouldn't do this."

"Tell us about some of your clients, Skyler," Georgia said. "I'm very intrigued by your business."

Skyler took a sip of her drink. "I try not to divulge the names of the people I work for, but we're all friends here, right? My biggest client right now is Carissa Lamb."

"Oh my gosh," the opera singer exclaimed. "She's a superstar."

"And she's the most down to Earth, sweetest superstar you'll ever meet," Brenda added.

"That's good to hear," Georgia said. "You have no idea how many celebrities I have come across who turn out to be total jerks when you get to know them. I understand the need for a public persona, for the fans and all, but it all comes crashing down when you realize it's all a big fat act."

"You're not fake, Georgia," Carter said. "You're the real deal."

"Thank you, Carter. You're so sweet. But I don't have time for you now. I'm talking to someone more important than you." She turned her head dramatically. "Who else, Skyler? Who else?"

"Noah Jones is a new one."

"He is so dreamy," Brenda added.

"The *actor* Noah Jones?" Georgia asked. "I love his movies. I just saw the one where he's a spy in 1980's London. Action packed, that one."

"Yup. He's a friend of Carissa's—that's how we got hooked up together. He's starting his own boutique vodka brand and a restaurant to go with it, in Tulsa, where he's from, and he wants to eventually take the concept national. So, I'm working on that with him. I got Noah booked on *CBS This Morning* this coming Tuesday, in fact. One of my associates is accompanying him to the studio. I should be going myself, but, you know, I'm naked in a hot tub in Santa Fe."

"Priorities," Brenda said.

"I'm doing a lot with celebrity product development. Everyone has something to sell these days. That's where the real money is. Folks are absolutely cleaning up on Q.V.C. and those other shopping channels."

Carter and Sullivan exchanged looks. "What can we sell?" Sullivan asked after he read his brother's mind.

"Franklin-Lowery bed sheets and towels, maybe?" Carter asked.

"A great idea!" Brenda said. "Are they your own line or someone else's?"

"Someone else's, for the time being," Sullivan said. "But we've started talking to a manufacturing company in Turkey that creates private brands for companies. I think we could make a real killing with our own line."

"As long as they're well-made quality goods, comfortable, and reasonably priced, then absolutely," Skyler said. "And I can absolutely build a buzz for it. That's what I do, damn it."

They all laughed.

"Then that's what we'll do," Carter said. "Fuck you, Martha Stewart. It's very exciting. Franklin sheets on every bed!"

"That should be the goal—why not?" Brenda said. "I do my own olive oils and a sparkling wine, as you all know, and I've made more dough from those things than I'll ever make from the restaurants, cookbooks, and television shows. By leaps and bounds. It's insanity, but in a very good way."

A loud cracking noise came from the woods a few yards away and it got everyone's attention. They saw a dark figure sprint away from the house and out of view.

"What the heck is *that*?" Sullivan asked.

Skyler started climbing out of the hot tub. "Let's get in the house."

The quintet scrambled into their robes and darted into the house dripping wet. When the door was closed and locked, Carter found his cellphone and dialed 911.

"You're calling the police?" Sullivan asked.

"Well, I'm not calling for a pizza, dumb ass."

"Will I get *any* rest?" Georgia exclaimed, clearly shaken. "Who was that out there?"

"It may not have been because of you, honey," Brenda said trying to calm the singer. "Let's go get dried off and dressed and let the boys deal with this."

"That's kind of sexist," Skyler said. "I'm going to go out there and have a look around."

Brenda grabbed her friend by the collar of her robe. "You most certainly are not going back out there! It's pitch black, freezing cold, and you're soaking wet, Skyler. Let's wait for the police to arrive."

And they did just that.

It took the local police over a half an hour to arrive, and by that time, the group was well into their next cocktail…and the intruder, whoever he or she was, was most certainly very long gone.

CHAPTER EIGHT

After Skyler, Brenda, and the dogs were chauffeured back to the Four Seasons—and when Sullivan retired to his suite for the night—Carter and Georgia slipped into Carter's room and closed the door. They'd consumed many more drinks than was normal for both of them, and their judgement was compromised. Georgia was vulnerable and scared. And Carter was anxious and over-worked—he had been devoting all of his time to the hotel project, promising himself that he must sideline a social life—particularly a love life—until after the grand openings of the Santa Fe and Palm Springs properties.

But at this rate, there will always be hotel opening, he told himself. He worried about falling into a life of loneliness and celibacy. *What kind of life would that be?* He decided he'd refocus on work the next day.

"You know it's already tomorrow," Georgia said in a slurred whisper. She lay down on his bed and propped her head up with a palm. "It's the Sabbath, too."

Carter struggled out of his shoes, nearly toppling over a few times. He steadied himself by grabbing on to the dresser. "What are you saying?" He wrestled out of his sweater and slacks. "Should I go?"

"No. No, I want you to stay. I do. It's just…it's definitely been awhile for me."

"Same. What's up with that? We're in the prime of our lives." He sat down at the foot of the bed. He pulled off his socks with one hand and stroked her hair with the other. "You have a pretty head."

"Thank you. It was a present from my parents." She snorted at her own joke. "My goodness. Did you hear that sound I just made?"

"I did," Carter laughed. "It was super attractive."

"I guess I don't have to seduce you, Carter. It's not like this is the first time we've had sex."

"I'm not sure it's the *next* time either."

She had been staring at the lump in his black Ralph Lauren briefs, but now her eyelids were closing. "What do you mean?"

"Georgia, I've had like 183 shots of bourbon tonight, on top of all that wine."

"Whiskey dick?" she asked, not opening her eyes.

"Probably. That's not exactly what I was thinking, though. I'm just so damned exhausted. And very full of spaghetti and bread."

"That's okay, honey. I'm better in the morning, anyway. Let's just cuddle and get warm."

He lay down next to her and put an arm across her back. "I like that idea."

He was lightly snoring within 30 seconds.

What seemed like just a few moments—although it might have been much longer, she wasn't sure—Georgia turned over and sat straight up. "Carter!"

His arm flipped upward rolling his body off the mattress and he landed with a thud on the floor. He opened his eyes and found that he was staring at dust bunnies under the bed. "What the hell happened?"

"Did you hear that?" she asked in a loud whisper. She peered over the side of the bed. "Are you okay?"

"What did you hear? How long was I asleep?"

"I don't know. And I don't know what it was, but it was loud. Go look around." She pulled her legs up to her body and hugged them close to her chest. "What could it have been?"

Carter found a dry robe and wrapped it around his body. He managed to get his shoes back on and headed into the main room. He looked ridiculous in the white terry robe, bare legs, and brown leather loafers without socks.

Sullivan was standing in the hall in the exact same getup. "Did you hear that, too?"

"No, I just thought it would be fun to come out here and say hello to you," Carter said.

"Hello."

Carter hit his brother in the arm. "Shut up and find a flashlight."

"Why don't we just turn on all the lights instead?" Sullivan started walking through the kitchen and Great Room, flipping every switch and raising every dimmer that he passed. Soon the house was bathed in light. He went to the patio doors and turned on the outside spotlights. That's when he saw red brake lights at the end of the driveway. He flipped off the spotlights and watched as a vehicle continued down the dirt road and banked around a corner and was gone. "Well, someone was here. Again."

Carter was right next to him. "Who the heck was it and what did he do while he was here? It was loud."

"I'm not going out there to find out."

"Should we call the police again?" Carter asked.

"They *just* left, man, and anyway, by the time they get their butts back up here, that person in that car will be long gone." He turned the spotlights back on. "Let's leave all the lights on and go to bed. I don't see any broken windows and all the doors are still locked. We'll figure out this craziness tomorrow."

"Okay. I'm too tired to fight with you."

"Good," Sullivan said. "You're smartening up, buddy boy."

Carter would have rolled his eyes, but they were too heavy. "Goodnight." He returned to his room, lost the robe and shoes, and climbed under the covers. He didn't even notice that the opera singer wasn't there anymore. And if he had, he probably wouldn't have cared. He was unconscious within seconds.

After he relieved himself in the half bathroom off the Great Room, Sullivan found Georgia standing in the kitchen.

"What was it?" she asked him.

"Nothing that I could find. Let's get some sleep. The house is still all buttoned up."

She grabbed his arm and they walked together to his suite. He didn't give it a moment's thought when she disrobed and got between his covers. He turned off the light, dropped his robe, and got into bed with her. After a few minutes of making out, he was hard and inside of her.

"I thought you were too tired," she moaned as she received him.

"Never." He kissed her hungrily up and down her slender neck. He kept a steady pace and she seemed to be receptive to his speed and style. They both started breathing heavy and reaching a state of near-climax at the same time.

"Oh, Carter."

He froze for a moment but didn't pull out. "Sullivan. Sullivan," he said softly into her ear. "Call me by my name, please."

That's when it was her time to freeze. *Oh shit.*

In the morning light, the twins managed to take showers and get dressed, despite near-debilitating hangovers, then they went outside and scoured the grounds for evidence of the trespasser. Or trespassers, as the case may have been. They found nothing out of the ordinary.

Over toasted bagels and bananas, they discussed the immediate future with Georgia, who was still unnerved.

"Well, I'm going back to my house, for one thing," she explained. "There's no security system here and my house is much closer to town and the police station."

"I really don't feel good about leaving you alone," Carter said, "but we have so much work to do. Even though it's a Sunday."

She smiled sweetly. "I completely understand. And, like I said before, it's not your job to babysit me. I'm a big girl. I'll be fine."

"But we do need to get to the bottom of this," Sullivan said. "Someone is obviously still out there screwing with you and we need to figure out what he wants." He peeled and devoured a second banana in seconds. "I love these things. We need to get Brenda to do a banana pancake thing for the hotel. People like banana pancakes, right?"

"You are so strange," Carter said. "Focus, man." He turned to Georgia and placed a hand on top of one of hers. "I feel very good about Brenda and Skyler being at the house with you for the next week or so. Skyler is a tough cookie. Plus, having Brenda's dogs around can't hurt either."

"It'll be nice to have a full house," Georgia said. She felt him squeeze her hand and it sent a very strange feeling of electricity through her body—she knew he thought it was time for them to get busy. And when Sullivan got up and returned to his room to work on his laptop, Carter moved in for a kiss.

"You mentioned last night that you're best in the mornings," Carter said as he nibbled on an earlobe.

"Did I say that?"

"You did."

"I still need to take shower."

"Go on. I'll meet you in my room."

"But what about Sully?"

"He's going to take our rental car down to the hotel," Carter said. "And I'll take you to your house in your car. After a bit."

Georgia managed a smile then padded off to her suite's bathroom, unsure that *this* was a good idea. She wasn't exactly sure how *not* to go through with it…but she'd always thought she liked Carter best. *What a mess*, she thought. *This will end badly.*

She and Carter had slept together once after a similar night of heavy drinking with a group of friends, some seven or eight months ago back in Manhattan. But Sullivan hadn't been there, so it wasn't weird. It was sweet and energetic and over fairly quickly. They'd decided to remain friends, both claiming that they were married to their work and too busy for relationships. But she carried a thing for him and felt a little spark whenever their paths crossed.

And now she was about to do it again, a mere eight hours

after bedding his brother for the first time.

She was not pleased with herself...but she had every intention on following through. Just this once more.

CHAPTER NINE

Skyler woke up quite late. There was a text from Brenda waiting.

```
I've already walked the dogs and I'm about
to head to the hotel restaurant for a
ridiculously ridiculous Sunday brunch.
Wake up and join me, sleepyhead.
```

Skyler dashed off a reply begging for a half hour, then she jumped out of bed and into a hot shower. She felt the familiar pangs of a slight hangover once she was on her feet but knew that as soon as she put some black coffee, greasy bacon, and a few mimosas inside of herself, she'd be as good as new. A good brunch menu almost always worked its magic that way.

"You've never gotten ready that fast in your life," Brenda said as they walked from their casitas to the main building in the chilly, late-morning air.

"I didn't wash my hair. And it still smells like the chemicals from the hot tub, damn it."

"No one is going to get close enough to you to notice."

They were greeted at the front door and immediately escorted to a table near the fireplace. They had a commanding floor-to-ceiling view of the distant mountains and the crystal blue skies above, with only a few airplane contrails where clouds should have been. The ladies ordered nearly everything on the menu—as Brenda was apt to do when dining out—then sat back and enjoyed the perfectly strong, hot coffee.

"I wonder if they think you're a crazy person for ordering seven entrees?" Skyler asked when the waitress left the table.

Brenda shrugged her shoulders. "You ask me that every single time we go out. They'll probably think I'm just a big fat heifer. But, if the waitress recognized me, she'll go tell the chef, and then we'll certainly get some extra attention. I'm totally okeydokey with using my celebrity to get better service and spectacular food."

"Oh yeah. I guess that's why I hang out with you then."

"I didn't sleep well last night," Brenda said, "I've been up since 5 o'clock. I've already heard from Sullivan—he's a morning person. Anyway, apparently someone was back at the house again after we left last night. The boys couldn't find a thing in the woods when they searched this morning."

"It's so frightening," Skyler said. "Someone was definitely there. I saw him."

"And you wanted to go out in the dark and investigate. What is wrong with you?"

"I've always been like that. I need to know what's going on at all times, you know that. I hate to admit it, but I'd feel a million times better if Leonard was around right about now. A man packing heat comes in handy sometimes."

"This from the independent woman who told me that she was done with men forever a few months ago," Brenda said. She accepted a mimosa from the waitress and continued, "You used to despise guns. What has happened to you?"

Skyler sipped her drink. "Pineapple mimosas are good! Brenda, I still hate guns, but when you date a cop, it just comes with the territory. And when your new friend is being terrorized by some crazy person from the woods, maybe packing a piece isn't such a bad idea."

Brenda shook her head. "I have no idea who you are right now."

"You'll get used to me with time," Skyler said. "I just wish we could do more to help Georgia. This situation is absolutely chilling. And at Christmastime, for Christ's sake."

Brenda chuckled. "Oh, that's cute, Skyler. For Christ's sake, indeed. Anyway, I'm just glad Georgia has the twins watching out for her."

"They're quite dreamy, aren't they?"

Brenda scanned the room to see if anyone was in listening range. "Did you see what *they* were packing last night?"

"How could I miss 'em? Showers, not growers, for sure."

Brenda's face reddened. "It's been *way* too long for me. I'm acting like a horny school girl." She started fanning her face with an imaginary fan.

"School girls would be so lucky to have two twins like that vying for their attention."

"We need to change the subject. It's Sunday, for Christ's sake."

The friends broke up laughing until a man in a white jacket appeared next to the table.

"Ladies," the man said, "I'm so sorry to interrupt what appears to be a very good time. My name is Jason Day. I'm the head chef here at the resort." He turned to Brenda. "Miss

Braxton, I'm a huge fan."

Brenda stared up into the young man's face and tried not to drool. "And I need to thank *you*, Chef, for allowing me to steal a few of your people away from the kitchen yesterday for the fiesta. They came in very handy. I couldn't have done it without them."

"We were most happy to assist," he said. "That is, until I found out that you're going to be opening a restaurant at that new hotel on the Plaza," he said with a little laugh. "You'll be serious competition for us."

"Oh please, Jason. Competition is a good thing," Brenda said, "I've always believed that. I actually encourage it. More restaurants and more hotels make everyone better, don't you agree?"

The man smiled. "I guess I do. And I do wish you the best of luck with your new place. I can't wait to come try it."

"Well, Chef Jason Day, my friend Skyler Moore and I look forward to many great meals here at the Four Seasons, too. Especially this morning's breakfast."

"It's on its way, ladies," he said with a smile. "Every dish in the house."

"Yummy," Skyler said.

"It's how I roll," Brenda said.

When the chef left the table, Skyler sighed deeply.

"What's the matter?"

"Nothing. I'm fine. Just thinking about all the work I should be doing."

"It's Sunday, a week before Christmas," Brenda said. "Let's do try to relax, alright? I have to get some work done tomorrow, too, but *today* we're going to enjoy this breakfast, maybe do a little shopping downtown, and move into our new house."

Skyler crinkled her face. "New house?"

"The Four Seasons is lovely, naturally, but I thought we could use a bit more room. Especially with the dogs being here and Christmas approaching. And I really do need a kitchen."

"Alright. Where are we going?"

"Georgia's house."

Skyler's mouth fell open. "You must be kidding."

"I'm not. It was Georgia's idea. She's won't stay on at the twin's house after what happened last night. She wants to hole up at her house and she wants company. She likes the idea of the dogs being there, too."

"It is a beautiful house when bombs aren't exploding in the front hall," Skyler said calmly. "I guess I'm game. I mean, it sounds insane, though."

"There won't be any more bombs. Plus, it was just a teeny tiny bomb."

The food started arriving in waves, and they dug in.

"I'm going to have to go on Weight Watchers in January," Skyler said as she shoved some bacon into her mouth.

Brenda's face dropped. "Bite your tongue." She slowly sliced into an eggs benedict and started cutting it into tiny pieces as if that was somehow going to help control her own growing waistline. "I shouldn't have ordered this much."

Skyler realized what she'd said. "I wasn't trying to be mean. I just wasn't thinking."

"No. It's good. I'm good," the chef said. "It's research, right?" And she smiled a genuine smile before popping the decadent egg, ham, English Muffin, and hollandaise into her mouth. "Oh. Jason's hollandaise is too good."

* * *

Georgia was quite hesitant, but Carter eventually won the battle and escorted the opera singer downtown for a mid-morning visit to the Santa Fe Police Department to file an assault and battery report against Massimo. They took the photos of Georgia's black eye into evidence, promising to include them in the file they were preparing. The officer on duty wasn't too encouraging, however, explaining that since Massimo was an Italian citizen living and working in Italy, there wasn't much of anything they could do unless he returned to the city.

"We can't do much more," the officer said without apology.

"Lovely," Carter said. "Welcome to Santa Fe."

"It's not just Santa Fe, sir," the officer said, clearly annoyed.

"I told you this was a waste of time," Georgia said as they left the station.

"At least it's been officially recorded," Carter said. "That will help, perhaps, down the line."

When Sullivan and Carter left to meet their contractor at the hotel construction site downtown, Georgia closed her heavy front door and set the alarm system. The boys had repeatedly offered a room at their house, but she put her foot firmly down; she was determined to live her life…in the house that she just spent a small fortune to buy and decorate.

The authorities had finished their on-site investigation and had officially turned the house back over to her—they had come up with nothing, although results from forensics tests were forthcoming. Despite the scorched wall and ceiling in the foyer, the rest of the place was pretty much intact; there was no structural damage. And the catering crew had done a fine job cleaning up after the party, too.

She spent the next several minutes checking each and every door and window to make sure they were secure. Georgia then pulled up the live video surveillance feed on her iPad—everything looked clear outside. Appeased for the time being, she retreated to her home studio and went through her vocal exercises at an upright piano. Although she had several months before rehearsals would begin for the summer performances at the opera house, she intended to keep her voice relatively tuned.

She was halfway through neutral vowel scales—ʑ ʑ ʑ ʑ ʑ ʑ ʑ—when the phone rang. She cursed it, meaning to leave it in the other room so as not to be interrupted. She didn't recognize the number but answered it nonetheless.

"Pronto."

"Georgia Reece, please," a male voice said.

"Speaking."

"Miss Reece, this is Archibald Grey from Mallard Protection in New York City. I got your message and called just soon as I could."

"Oh, yes, Mr. Grey," she said, "Your service was recommended to me by one of my friends back East—the soap opera actress Olivia Downs. I'm so very sorry to disturb you on a Sunday."

"Our business operates 24-7, ma'am. What can I do for you?"

Georgia gave the security expert a quick rundown of the events of the previous few days. "Sadly, neither the local police nor the F.B.I. have been much help yet. It's all quite frustrating and more than just a little unsettling."

"That is very troubling, yes," he said. "But we can help. Did you have something specific in mind or shall I outline some possible..."

"I want someone here as soon as possible, Mr. Grey," she said, cutting him off. "I have a few friends who will be staying with me at my house, along with two rather large, friendly dogs, but I'd feel much better with professionals on the case. I've never felt the need for personal security in the past. This is all so new to me."

There was a short pause before he began to speak again. "I have a two-person team in Los Angeles who are just finishing up an assignment. Both are recently retired New York City police detectives. They are two of my very best. I can have them there tomorrow. Do you have room to put them up?"

"I will make room, sir. And I am most grateful."

"Their names are John Sparks and Anna Jannis. A married couple. I have your email address, Miss Reece, so I will have my assistant send our standard contract and the cost estimate. If you could look it over and sign the document, we will put everything in motion."

And she did just that. It was an expensive proposition, but the terms allowed for her to call off the team at any point, so she didn't feel locked in. She emailed back the document and within an hour received an itinerary—John and Anna would arrive in Santa Fe early the next afternoon.

Georgia busied herself with preparing the guestrooms for Brenda, Skyler, and the security team. She was thankful that she purchased the largest house she was shown; there would be plenty of room for everyone.

Both washing machines and both of the clothes dryers whirled away in the laundry room while Georgia scrubbed toilets and stocked bathroom cabinets with all the essentials. She did the work herself instead of calling in strangers, as she was normally apt to do. She was just happy to have the distraction and to be kept busy.

* * *

Over the crest of the hill to the south, Massimo Modena pulled to the side of the dirt road and put his rental car into park. He fished a pair of binoculars out of his leather briefcase and pointed them toward the back of Georgia's house. He was patient. He could wait all night if he had to.

CHAPTER TEN

With Christmas Eve just a week away, downtown Santa Fe was buzzing with tourists and locals alike, on a quest for the perfect souvenirs and gifts. It was a typical cloudless, albeit chilly December Sunday, and most of the art galleries and shops were enjoying brisk holiday business. The historic plaza and surrounding narrow streets were artfully decorated for the season and scores of artisans had set up impromptu shops on the sidewalks, their wares laid out on large colorful blankets. Indian jewelry—all things turquoise, spiny oyster shell, coral, and sterling silver dominated—and original crafts and artwork were the mainstay outside, just as they were inside the shops.

Carter watched as a plump, middle-aged woman with a thick New Jersey accent haggled with a Native woman over the price of a small dreamcatcher. She was relentless in her pursuit of a deal and wasn't backing down. Carter wanted to intervene and tell the woman in the purple velour tracksuit that she was being rude, but he thought better of getting himself involved, and certain he'd be smacked across the face if he scolded her. He pulled his sunglasses down off the top of his head and continued up the sidewalk with a cardboard tray of Starbucks coffees. He nearly tripped over a homeless man and a Black Labrador who had taken up residence in the main entranceway to the hotel.

"Watch it, bucko!" the deeply tanned fellow yelled.

Carter was no stranger to street people; he dealt with them constantly in Manhattan. "Dude, you and the dog need to find another place to perch. We've got people coming and going all the time."

"It's a free country, man. I have the right to be here if I want."

"It's a free country, you're right," Carter said, fumbling in his pocket for his keys. "But this is technically private property, so move your shit or I'll move it for you." He got the door open and squeezed inside, locking it behind him.

"I feel sorry for that poor dog." Sullivan said from across the lobby. "Is he going to move?"

"I don't know. We'll see." He set the coffees down on the makeshift table they'd created between two sawhorses and took off his coat. "When is the contractor getting here?"

"He just texted. He's looking for parking. It's not easy on the weekend, Carter. I'm just glad he's agreed to work on Sundays."

Carter sighed. "He better work every damned day for what we're paying him. We've got to stay on schedule. I want this place open by March 1st. It's a firm date, brother."

"I keep thinking we're not going to pull this off. I realized neither of us called to see about getting the fucking gas running. All those inspections. All the permits we still haven't bribed people for. The mattress delivery is delayed again. Oh, and that custom deer antler chandelier won't be here until January 15th."

"Great. That's all great. But, we will do it, man. We have to." Carter took a sip of his coffee, instantly burning his tongue. "God damnit to hell!"

"Georgia called while you were at Starbucks. She went ahead

and hired a New York City-based security team. They arrive tomorrow."

"That's gotta be expensive. But I guess that's a good thing since we can't be with her constantly. I wish the police had something to go on. Anything!"

"They'll get to the bottom of it. If the F.B.I. can't figure out who left the bomb in the house, who the heck can?"

"Geez, I don't know. This is out of my realm of expertise." Carter pulled up a folding chair and sank down onto it. "What I do know, is that I'm not letting Massimo get away with the shit storm he's created for her."

"You think he's behind all of this?" Sullivan asked.

"Not necessarily, no. I don't think the things are related. But he *did* sock her in the face this weekend and he's stealing her blind. His taking a 40 percent commission—that's highway robbery! Why did she ever agree to that? She's successful, comfortable. But imagine how much more money she'd have if she had hired legitimate representation who took a more reasonable cut? I think the police report against him was a good idea. I'm glad that she agreed to it."

"What good will that do now that he's back in Italy? I don't think countries extradite citizens for giving one chick a black eye. And little ol' Santa Fe, New Mexico certainly isn't going to ask Italy to return him over that."

"Maybe not, but Georgia could sue him. A civil suit, maybe. Officially have a judge break the contract. Go after him for damages. Maybe get back millions of dollars that he had no right to in the first place. Filing the police report was just the first step. It was necessary to get the ball rolling."

"I guess. Or maybe she should just cut ties and let Massimo

be," Sullivan said. "That might just be the easiest way out and she could save all the headaches and attorneys' fees. The attorneys are the only winners, you know."

"A coward's way out," Carter spit. "I'd fight. But we'll see."

"I think she's sweet on you."

Carter didn't see that coming. "What? No."

"Dude, totally. I see the way she looks at you," Sullivan said.

"She looks at you the *same way*, man. Half the time she doesn't even know which one of us she's looking at." The twins erupted in laughter and didn't hear when the front door opened. Their local contractor—an impossibly tall, lean guy named Matteo—startled them as he approached the table.

"Do you know that there's a guy and a dog living in the front doorway?" Matteo asked as he set down his rolled construction plans and began pulling off his jacket. "They both smell really bad."

"We're going to have to deal with that eventually," Carter said, "but it's the least of our problems today. How are we doing with the H.V.A.C. ductwork? Did you find an alternate route for the main venting?"

The trio got to work examining the plans and discussed myriad projects and timelines. After a few hours, the twins felt better about the progress and planned to start marketing efforts for the proposed March opening.

"The full crew will be here at dawn tomorrow and we'll be working around the clock," Matteo promised. "I just can't work them on Sundays. You understand."

"We're not slave drivers," Carter said. "But it is a hell of a lot easier here than in New York City, I'll tell you that. Union towns don't make things easy."

The contractor started rolling up his plans. "I'll be back for the meeting with Chef Brenda. Tomorrow at 10 o'clock?"

"That's when she'll be here, yes," Sullivan said. "And she's got some grand ideas. We might need your help reeling her in a bit."

"I'm good at that," Matteo said. "Okay, I'm leaving out the back. I don't want to deal with that hobo again."

The twins turned their attention to the front door. The homeless man was now standing up, facing the floor-to-ceiling glass doors. His pants and underwear were pushed down to his knees and he was relieving himself into the corner. The dog jumped up and scampered away.

"Good God," Carter said.

* * *

Brenda had retreated to her suite to make a business call, so Skyler lazily poked around the resort gift shop hoping she might come across something to give to Brenda for Christmas; she was also trying to avoid having to pack up her things for the move to Georgia's house. As she caressed a colorful alpaca blanket, Skyler felt a hand on her back. She turned and found herself face-to-face with Foster Martin.

"So, we meet again," the billionaire said sweetly. "I was actually just thinking about you on my walk around the property."

"Oh?"

"I understand you own a public relations consultancy."

How could he possibly know that? she thought. *This had to be Brenda's doing.* "Well, yes sir, I do. I used to be with one of the big international firms, but now I run my own boutique operation with a small team out of an office in Washington, D.C."

"I got your name from Carissa Lamb," he said as he shifted his weight and reached out to prop himself up against the wall of the shop. "She's a firecracker."

Skyler was stunned. "You know Carissa?"

"We don't run in the same circles, but our paths have crossed a few times. She performed at my eightieth birthday party in the Hamptons and I sat next to her at a state dinner for the Prime Minister of Great Britain at the White House."

"How perfectly lovely."

"There are scores of public relations people working for my company, as you can imagine, Skyler," Foster said. "What I need help with is my new educational foundation. It's in its infancy and I haven't talked about it publicly yet. But when I do, I want to make sure the initial message is well thought out. You'll help with that."

"I will?"

"Yes, ma'am." He smiled and Skyler was taken by his perfectly straight white teeth; they didn't look like they belonged in the mouth of a man of his advanced age. "My name is Foster Martin."

She took his hand. "I know who you are, sir. And I'm Skyler Moore. And I'm pleased to meet you. Officially, that is."

"It's all *my* pleasure, my dear," he said, squeezing her hand gently. "Although, I should know better than to call you 'my dear,' I suppose. It's not politically correct these days, sadly, even if it is delivered with the utmost level of respect."

"Mr. Martin, you can call me 'dear,' or 'babe,' or whatever you like," she said with a chuckle.

His smile faded a bit.

"Well, not *anything* that comes to your mind," Skyler said. "I do have my limitations. I am a lady, after all.

He laughed. "That's good to know. When can we sit down and talk? I'm leaving Santa Fe to fly to Hawaii on the 27th. Will you pencil me in for some day this week? Before Christmas?"

"It would be my pleasure. How about Tuesday? We could have lunch."

"Perfect." He handed her a business card. "This is my private number and the name and number of my personal assistant. Feel free to use either one. I'll wait to hear from you." He started walking away, out of the store. Without turning back, he said, "You decide when and where, but I very much enjoy La Fonda on the Plaza." And he was gone.

The older woman minding the shop glided up next to Skyler and both women watched as the old man walked across the small parking lot. "He seems to change his demeanor fairly quickly, but I wouldn't take it as a slight. I think he just really needed to go to the bathroom."

Skyler turned to the woman. "Are you serious?"

"He's very old."

"He's still very sharp."

"He's also very, very rich."

Skyler shook her head slowly. "That doesn't sound like something a hotel employee should say out loud about a guest to another guest."

The woman reddened. "My apologies, ma'am. I didn't mean to speak out of turn."

"It's okay. I certainly won't tell. And the truth is, he *is* rich. He's the fourth richest man on the entire planet."

"And he's *single*," the woman said with a mischievous smile.

"Now you've gone too far."

The clerk's face dropped again.

"I'm kidding," Skyler said. "I need to go pack. Have a good afternoon." She left the shop to return to her casita. She walked with an extra oomph in her step; she was more than a little intrigued about possibly working for the fourth richest *single* man in the world.

Back in her room, Skyler's iPhone rang. When she saw that it was Leonard calling, she felt a pang of excitement—the day kept getting better.

"Hello, you. What's up?" she asked.

"I am tired as shit but happy that we're finally connecting," Leonard said. "What time is it there again?"

"Two-something."

"So, four here. I haven't even had lunch yet."

"Tired and hungry. Not a pleasant combination. I thought things were supposed to be slow for you there." Skyler sank down into one of the easy chairs in her room and kicked off her shoes. She closed her eyes and pictured her boyfriend on the other end of the line. "I miss you."

"And I miss you. Maybe with you here, I wouldn't be working 18-hour days."

"You most certainly would not be doing that. Why *are* you doing that?"

"Because I have nothing to go home to. And I hate being in my grandmother's house with all those ghosts."

"Oh my goodness, Leonard, what a horrible thing to say. How's Wabanaki? How are Kristin's legs?"

"Wabanaki is fine—like I said, lots of development going on in anticipation of a busy summer season. And Kristin is in good spirits. I think she'll be back to work in three or four weeks."

"That's great news. And Christmas?" There was a pause. Skyler could hear him exhaling smoke. "Are you smoking? You quit, Mister!"

"I'm not smoking," he lied.

"I can hear you doing it. Come on. You did so well in D.C."

"It's too easy to slip back into old habits when you come home," the lawman said. "But I can stop again. I will."

"Good." Skyler updated her boyfriend on the events of the last few days, in detail.

"Geez, Sky, no rest for the weary, huh? Brenda and you need to be careful and take care of yourselves. I wouldn't go stay at that woman's house if I were you. Please don't do that."

"Brenda thinks it's a good idea."

"Who cares! What does she know about good ideas? Skyler, if the police and F.B.I. haven't been able to come up with anything, that means that the perps are still out there. I don't like this at all and I'm too far way to do anything about it."

She was happy that he cared so much—and Leonard was so damned cute when he was being protective—but the defiant, independent side of her was confident enough to help a friend without her policeman boyfriend glued to her side. "I'll be fine, Leonard." She heard him light another cigarette.

"I'm not going to pretend to like this."

"Okay, no one is asking you to pretend, just to stop smoking," Skyler said. "So, what are you going to do for Christmas? Can you come out here?"

"We've already talked about this," he said. "I'm not flying

2,500 miles for one day. And that's probably more than I can spare, anyway. These people need me, Sky. We can celebrate the next holiday together. What is it? Valentine's Day? I'll be totally done with this place by then."

"Valentine's Day is just *not* as important as Christmas, Leonard, but I understand."

"Well then, why don't you come here?"

"I'm not flying 2,500 miles for one day either," she said with a laugh.

"Why do *you* only have one day? What's keeping you in Mexico?"

"*New* Mexico, silly. And Foster Martin is keeping me here."

"The billionaire? *That* Foster Martin?"

"That's the one. I met him here on the hotel grounds. It turns out he knows Carissa and she suggested that he hire me to do the public relations for the launch of his new foundation."

"That would be a good get, Miss Moore. Damn. Good for you."

"Don't I know it. I'm going to need a bigger office. I'll probably most definitely need more people, too."

There was more silence.

"Leonard? Are you still there?"

"You're going to have less and less time for me."

"Don't be silly," she said. "I will always make and have time for you. And after the holidays, let's make sure we're not so far apart from each other for so long, ever again. Deal?"

"Deal. Oh, and I heard what you said, Skyler."

"What did I say? When?"

"On the voice mail. The other day."

She knew what he was talking about, of course. "And?"

"I love you, too."

She started tingling and she smiled widely; she hadn't felt that way in a very long time. "Cool."

He laughed. "It *is* cool. Listen, I've got to go find some food and then get down to the wharf. Some kids spray painted bad words on old man Maddox's lobster boat."

"You have fun with that. Dress warm."

"Yes, Mom."

"And there ya go," she said, "you just ruined it."

"Sorry. I love ya, bye." And he hung up.

Skyler smiled with much satisfaction. And then she kicked herself for not asking what bad words the kids spray painted on old man Maddox's lobster boat; not knowing would bother her for the rest of the day.

CHAPTER ELEVEN

It was a clear, but brutally windy Monday morning. A winter storm had blown through overnight, leaving a dusting of snow, but soon after the sun peeked over the mountain top, it quickly melted, save for a smattering of white stuff in shaded bits of Georgia's vast backyard. She stood at the kitchen sink with an enormous mug of coffee and watched as three cardinals jockeyed for position at the birdfeeder. She didn't notice when one of her guests had joined her.

"Good morning," Brenda said.

Startled, Georgia spilt half of her drink onto the window glass and into the sink.

"I'm so sorry, dear," the chef said. "I should have made my presence known from out in the hall." She put a hand on the singer's back and patted gently. "I'll make you another cup. And I will totally clean that window. Where do you keep the Windex?"

"It's fine, don't you bother with that. And I've already had three cups anyway."

"How long have you been up?" Brenda busied herself with the coffee maker. "It's only half past seven."

The opera singer sighed dramatically. "I haven't slept, Brenda. Not a wink."

"My goodness, honey. I'm so sorry. I had hoped that you would have felt more secure with Skyler, the dogs, and me here in the house."

Georgia climbed onto a kitchen stool and rested her chin in one of her palms. "I do. I really do. And I thank you so much for coming. It does mean the world to me. I'm going to be okay. Eventually." She scanned the room. "Where *are* the dogs?"

Brenda chuckled. "Mulder and Scully are definitely divas. They're still *very* much asleep. It's actually quite lovely to have lazy dogs who don't demand to go outside at the break of dawn every day. It's *especially* wonderful at home in Manhattan or when I'm up in a 50th floor hotel suite in Las Vegas."

"I can only imagine. I've never owned a dog myself. My mother was very against animals of any kind in the house. No, I take that back. We had a bird once. A yellow canary. His name was Fred."

"I couldn't imagine a life without dogs," Brenda said as she warmed her hands with the mug. "I even took my childhood dog to college with me."

"That sounds dreadful," Georgia said with a laugh.

"On the contrary. It was divine. I loved the company." Brenda leaned in closer to her hostess. "Hey, your eye is looking much better."

Georgia instinctively touched it. "It still hurts. He got me good."

"What a complete and utter asshole he is. I assume you haven't heard from him? Massimo?"

Georgia had received a lengthy, sappy-sweet email apology from her manager, but she kept that to herself. "No," she lied. She'd opened up to these people fairly quickly, and she was fine with that, but she was super sensitive to the situation with Massimo, mostly because she was embarrassed that she'd allowed him so much control over her life. And her face.

"It's for the best." Brenda pulled up another stool and settled down next to the counter. "Carter is confident that you'll do just as well, if not *better*, with fresh new representation. I believe that, too. I switched agents a few years back and I can't tell you how beneficial that was for my career. Things really took off with new folks on my side. You'll see."

Georgia slowly nodded her head and managed a small, tight-lipped smile.

"What can I make you for breakfast?" Brenda asked. "I checked out the fridge and pantry last night and you are very well stocked for someone who doesn't cook. I was impressed. I could make pancakes or omelets or whatever you like. I saw fresh strawberries and…"

"I never eat until lunchtime or later. And I'm just too…I'm just too worked up to even think about food."

"As you wish. When do the security people arrive?"

Georgia checked her watch. "Hours yet. I believe their plane lands at the Santa Fe airport at three o'clock. I'm told that they'll take a cab to the house. I'm not sure there *are* cabs to be had in Santa Fe though. But they'll figure it out."

Skyler breezed into the kitchen and pulled a wool beanie off her head and started shucking her puffy jacket. Her cheeks were red and she was breathing heavy. "It is windy out there."

"You were outside?" Georgia asked, looking alarmed.

"Yes, why? I took a short walk to wake myself up."

The lady of the house stood up and headed to a panel on the wall. "I didn't turn off the security system." She pressed a few buttons. "It's still armed, Skyler. How did you get out of the house?"

"I forgot all about that, actually," Skyler said. "I just went out into the side yard from the sliding glass door in my room, walked around to the front driveway, and down to the street. I never heard anything beeping or anything like that. I'm so sorry."

"Well, damn it all. The cameras aren't working either." Georgia slammed her palm against the countertop and turned to face her guests. "We were vulnerable all night!"

"We're fine, honey," Brenda said. "There's no one in the house except us."

"I'm calling the security company. This is just unbelievable." Georgia stormed out of the kitchen. They waited until she was some distance away before they spoke.

"She's becoming unhinged," Brenda said.

"Understandably. I'd be a mess, too. But I wouldn't rest until I got to the bottom of it."

"That's what we need to help her do." Brenda pulled out a loaf of sourdough and some butter. "I guess I'm making toast. It's the least I can do. Plus, I'm starving."

"Do you think we really need to be involved with this?" Skyler asked in a whisper. "Do we need this monumental headache? Bombs, stalkers, abusive Italians, and God knows what else?"

Brenda's eyes widened. "We can't abandon her. She's our friend now."

"She's *your* friend. I'm supposed to be on vacation, remember?"

"You are horrible. Honestly."

"You promised me some down time. It's Christmas, damn

it." Skyler was only half kidding.

"I guess I did promise you down time, and I'm sorry, but who has time for that right now? I have a restaurant to build and you have a new billionaire client on your hands." Brenda turned and put her hands on her ample hips. "By the way, I am so very excited about that, aren't *you?* Foster Martin is major big time, Skyler. Major. Big. Time."

Skyler poured herself a cup of coffee. "I'm intrigued, yes. But should I really be taking on someone so...so major big time? Someone so important? I mean, I'm going to lose control of this little business very soon if I'm not careful. What with Carissa, and Noah, and you, and all of my other clients, I'm seriously close to being tapped out. I'm supposed to be enjoying the fruits of my labor right about now, not killing myself."

"You talked about hiring more people. You can certainly justify that. Do that and do it quickly. And, my dear, you need to learn how to delegate."

"I left the firm to start my own company so that I could be lean and manageable, Brenda. So much for that."

"I think it's exciting. Up, up, up! Grow, grow, grow!"

Skyler sighed. "Right now, I just want to be cuddled up under a blanket with Leonard, with no cares in the world and no one else depending on me for anything. I can actually afford to do that for the rest of my life so why wouldn't I do that?"

"Because it's not in your nature. You're never going to be happy being a retired housewife. At least not this early in your life. And Leonard is not going to be happy sitting around doing nothing either. You both need to stay busy. It's in your collective blood. And I don't need to tell you any of this. I have confidence in you and your little public relations company."

"You know what Leonard wants to do after he gets back from Maine, right? I told you about his new master plan?"

"If you did, I don't remember. Please tell me that he's not going to run for Congress."

Skyler made a horrified face. "Honestly. Can you imagine that? No, thank goodness. He's been toying around with this idea of starting a protection agency for celebrities. Super protection for super V.I.P.s." When he first mentioned that, they'd been lounging in bed watching a documentary about the Secret Service on television. He knew he was too old to apply for such a position, so he opted to start his own protection service instead. At the time, she'd blown it off as idle talk, but he kept bringing it up and she thought he might actually be serious about the idea.

Brenda set down her knife. "Well, that's *exactly* what we need right this very minute. Let's get Leonard here."

"He'd be here right this very minute if he wasn't stuck in Wabanaki. Anyway, there's a special tactical training course out in Nevada that he wants to take. It's a very intensive program. Weapons training, defensive driving, surveillance stuff, the works. It's supposedly the second-best thing to actually going through training at the C.I.A.'s farm just outside of Williamsburg, Virginia."

"Very interesting. I applaud Leonard for his entrepreneurship. That boy has come a long way in a very short time." Brenda set a small plate of buttered toast in front of her friend. "And if he does all of that, Leonard will be very busy, so you'll have no excuses. You'll have plenty of time to build Skyler Moore Public Relations into the next Edelman or Fleishman-Hillard."

"Bite your tongue! Yuck."

"Grow it, then sell it. That's the logical progression. Then you can fly private the rest of your life."

Skyler took a bite of toast. "And will you be taking your own advice, Bren, huh? Will you continue to grow your business empire and then sell it off to someone else?"

"Maybe eventually. Why wouldn't I? I can't work forever. And I certainly can't continue to live out of my steamer trunks and cart the dogs back and forth across the country forever. Martha Stewart sold her companies with her name on everything; why can't I do that?"

"You can. But will you?"

"Someday, maybe. And then I can open a super exclusive inn in Wabanaki and settle down in *one* place."

"Maine? All year? Wabanaki in winter?" Skyler was skeptical of that. "No thanks."

"Well, I'll need a winter retreat, too, I guess. Maybe a bungalow in Palm Springs? And a private jet to get me back and forth, naturally."

"Naturally. Isn't it nice that we only need the little things to make us happy?"

Georgia appeared in the doorway. "Ladies, the security system has been tampered with. I was on the phone with the security monitoring company and they had me describe to them stuff inside the main panel in the master bedroom closet. Half of the wires have been cut. I just can't get my head around this."

"Shouldn't the security company be automatically notified if someone sabotages the inner workings of their system?" Skyler asked.

"Apparently whoever did this knew exactly what they were doing," Georgia said. "They made it look like everything was fine on the outside, when it was anything but. Every door and window could be blown wide open and no one would know it."

"What do you want to do right now, honey?" Skyler asked.

"I want to get out of here until the security people arrive and not come back until it's all fixed."

Brenda stood up and pushed back her stool. "I'll go jump in the shower, grab the dogs, and then we can all go down the hill to the hotel. I have a meeting. You can hang out there, or walk the dogs, or go shopping, or do whatever you want to do. We'll all be safer with hundreds of people around us."

"That sounds like a good plan," Georgia said. "I'll go get ready, too. This is good, because I need a few Christmas gifts. I want to get the twins something. I have no idea what to buy them, though. What do you get two thirty-something guys who already own the whole world?"

"Pussy!" Brenda yelled as she was well on her way down the back hall.

"Oh my God," Skyler said, nearly chocking on her coffee. Georgia started laughing, too, and together, they laughed quite uncontrollably for half a minute.

"I needed that," Georgia said when she regained her composure. "Brenda is a stitch and a half, isn't she?"

"The funny thing is, she means it," Skyler said.

"I had a feeling." Georgia started toward the hall, then turned around and whispered, "I've already had them both. But not at the same time." And then she was gone.

* * *

Carter and Sullivan stood in the raw space that was to become Brenda's restaurant. It was about half complete, but there was still much to be done before furniture and fixtures could be moved in. There were bundles of wires everywhere and the floor was still just bare concrete—it was basically a messy shell at that point, but it would come together quickly. It always did.

Matteo had climbed an impossibly high ladder and was tinkering with some wiring that was attached to the reclaimed wood beams that spanned the room. The twins were watching from below, most uncomfortably; they didn't have time built into the schedule should the contractor fall to his death.

"Better him than me," Carter said under his breath.

"You've never been a fan of heights."

At precisely 10 o'clock, Brenda breezed in. She had a dog leash in each hand and a large tote bag flung over her shoulder. She released Mulder and Scully and they immediately got to work sniffing every square inch of the room. When they noticed Matteo high above the room, the dogs started howling, startling the contractor. The ladder shuddered and leaned to one side and both twins threw themselves toward it to keep it from toppling over.

"What have I done?" Brenda exclaimed. "Mulder! Scully! Be quiet."

Matteo was holding onto a beam. When he got his breathing back under control, he descended the ladder.

"Sorry, buddy," Sullivan said when the man was back on solid ground.

"If I wasn't awake from all the coffee I've had today," Matteo said, "I am now." He turned to the chef. "I'm fine. Welcome to

Cornerstone."

Brenda turned slowly in place, taking in the surroundings. "I'm lucky," she said. "I can see it in my head. Many people can't visualize such things."

"Can't visualize what?" Carter asked.

"What it's going to look like when it's done. I see it all very clearly. The deep purple crushed velvet banquettes, the old oak bar, the conversation pit that we'll use for folks who are waiting for tables, everything. I see it clear as day, and it's going to be gorgeous." She walked up to the contractor and extended her hand. "Hi. I'm Brenda Braxton."

"Matteo Ferrera," he said. "It's an honor to be building this out for you."

"You flatter me, sir," she said. "*You* are the talented one. The designs your firm came up with were spot on. It's exactly what I had in mind from the very beginning. I just know that it's going to be very complimentary to the Lowerys' vision for the hotel."

"I'm delighted that you're so pleased. I hope we can get it all done on time."

"That's not really an option," Carter said flatly. "It *can* be done on time. And it must."

Sullivan placed a hand on his brother's back. "What my brother means is that we're sure that you'll do your very best to get things done for us on time."

Carter pulled away. "Your very best is all we want. I'm going to go check on the crew working in the lobby." And he was gone.

"We've got a lot of pressure being applied on us by our partners," Sullivan explained. "But we'll be fine."

Brenda had moved over to a drafting table and was pursuing the blueprints. "I'm not sure I like the placement of the reception desk. It's built-in, yes?"

"Yes. But changes will push things back," Matteo said.

"No changes, Brenda," Sullivan said. "It's all going to work."

Brenda let out a little sigh. "If you say so. So, what am I doing here?"

Sullivan and Matteo exchanged looks. Sullivan managed a smile. "As a partner, we wanted you to see where we are on everything. And the lighting designer will be here momentarily. If it makes you feel better, we have some flexibility regarding the fixtures."

"Cool." She started toward the back of the room. "I'm going to go see the kitchen." The dogs dutifully followed her out of the room.

"She's a tough cookie," Matteo said.

"She didn't get to where she is by being a shrinking violet. You have no idea how excited we are to be in partnership with her. She's going to help put this place on the map and she'll bring some fresh blood to Santa Fe's restaurant scene."

"What? No green chili smothered on everything?"

"Hardly. Brenda is very innovative. And I'm sure she'll bring some authentic Maine to the desert."

"Green chili smothered lobster," Matteo said. "Yum!"

* * *

Less than a block away, Skyler and Georgia browsed through a catch-all shop called, Marker's, a purveyor of Santa Fe-inspired gifts, trinkets, one-of-a-kind pieces of art, books by local authors, and handmade greeting cards. It was busy, but so quiet Skyler felt uneasy. As she examined an artificial tree covered with coyote-themed Christmas ornaments, she thought that music would liven up the joint; it was a little too much like a library inside.

When the book she had tucked under her left arm fell to the floor and she leaned over to retrieve it, she backed into a middle-aged man.

"Excuse me," she said.

"My apologies," the man said. He got to the book first and handed it back to Skyler. He smiled at her like he was looking at an old friend.

"Do I know you?"

"No, ma'am," he said sheepishly, "but I know who you are. At least, I know that you are a friend of Georgia Reece. I saw you two walk in together."

"Oh, do you know Georgia?"

"I've done work at her house."

"Well, then you're just the person we needed to run in to today." Skyler turned and spotted Georgia across the room and waved her over.

"Diego!" Georgia said as she approached. "It is so good to see you again."

"And you, madam."

Georgia closed her eyes for a moment. "No, no. Madam won't do. Please call me Georgia."

"Georgia," he repeated back to her.

"I'm glad you are here," the opera singer said. "I misplaced your business card and I find that I am in need of your services again. We had a small fire at the house the other evening."

"My goodness, that's horrible," Diego said. "And I did hear about that, of course. It was on the news. I hope no one was hurt."

"Luckily, no. But I have a front hall wall and ceiling that are quite singed. Perhaps you could come patch it up and repaint it for me sometime this week?"

"It would be my pleasure. I could take a look at it today, if you want, and do the repairs tomorrow. I don't have a lot of work this time of year, thanks to my brother."

"That would be lovely," Georgia said. "Any time after three would be great. I'll be there."

"And then so will I," Diego said in a most gallant sounding voice. He tipped an imaginary hat to both ladies and then slipped out of the shop.

"What a strange little man," Skyler said. "But capable, I'm sure." She smiled at her friend. Skyler worried sometimes about what she said when she thought aloud; it was a bad habit. She hoped she hadn't offended her.

"It turns out that he's a big fan of opera and of me. His brother-in-law is the Santa Fe police officer who responded when my house was first broken into. That was who recommended Diego in the first place. And, I have come to find out, that Diego's brother Matteo is Carter and Sullivan's contractor. They apparently had a falling out, so Diego isn't working on the hotel project."

"Santa Fe is a small town, huh?"

"Just as long as my house gets fixed and the security system is back up and running, I'll be happy."

They walked to the sales counter and placed their selections in front of a young woman with a shock of violet hair. Skyler put an arm around Georgia's back. "And the new security team from New York. Don't forget about them."

"I'm counting the minutes," Georgia said as she instinctively scanned the room.

CHAPTER TWELVE

Back at Georgia's, Skyler busied herself with email correspondence while sitting in front of the fireplace in the living room. Amongst scores of business emails, a single message stood out. It was from Leonard, and she loved it for its simplicity and direct-to-the-pointness:

```
Dec 18 @ 11:45am EST
From: leonard.little@wabanaki.gov
To: skyler.moore@skylermoorepr.com
Subject: Stuff

Sky,

Miss you. Love you.

--LL

Acting Sheriff Leonard Little
Wabanaki Police Department
12 Main Street, Suite P
Wabanaki, Maine 03999
Main: 207-555-4679
Cell: 207-555-1046
```

She felt her heart thump as she jotted off an equally short reply:

```
Dec 18 @ 2:46pm MST
From: skyler.moore@skylermoorepr.com
To: leonard.little@wabanaki.gov
Subject: RE: Stuff
```

Me, more. Counting the days.

—Skyler

```
Skyler Moore Public Relations, LLC
Washington, DC and Worldwide
www.SkylerMoorePR.com
Main: 888-555-1301
Cell/Text: 202-555-1733
```

At three o'clock, the doorbell rang and Georgia let a distinguished looking couple into the foyer. Georgia didn't introduce herself and instead immediately gestured toward the bomb-damaged wall.

"This is one *very* important reason why you are both here," she said.

John Sparks was an imposing, thick, but not in the least bit fat, man with an impossibly thick head of platinum grey hair. He placed his bags on the floor and closed the front door. "And we will make sure that this never, ever happens again, ma'am." He extended his hand. "John Sparks. And this is my wife Anna Jannis."

Anna was clearly her husband's equal. She, too, was on the stocky side, most likely from spending much time in the gym lifting weights. Her military-short hair was dark brown and looked like it'd been styled with an electric clipper.

Skyler surveyed the couple from a distance. She could tell that these folks meant business.

"I am very pleased to meet you both," Georgia said. She shook each hand firmly and managed a smile. "I've never been so scared in my life, but I do feel 100% better now that you are here in Santa Fe. I've only heard good things about your agency over the years from my friend, and when I spoke to Archibald yesterday, he had nothing but high praise for you both."

"That's very kind of him," Anna said, "He tries to make sure he hires people who are very good at what they do. John and I were detectives on the N.Y.P.D. Mr. Grey lured us into an early retirement to come work for him. It's paid off for everyone involved, I'd say."

"Well, perhaps New York City got the short end of that stick. I have to say, you both inspire confidence." Georgia led the couple into the living room. Skyler stood and introductions were made.

"Skyler and her best friend Brenda are house guests and they will be here through the holidays. Brenda is currently downtown at her new restaurant. Actually, you might know of her. Brenda Braxton? The restauranteur and celebrity chef?"

"Of course," John said. "We're big fans."

"And Mulder and Scully," Skyler added. "Don't forget about them."

"Oh, yes. They're dogs, though—not F.B.I.," Georgia chuckled. "Mulder and Scully are absolute lambs. I forget that they are even here, to tell you the truth. I never, ever see them."

Skyler added, "Lazy, but ridiculously friendly and loyal to Brenda. They're here somewhere and, as you can see, they didn't even stir when the doorbell rang. That tells you something about how good they are as guard dogs. We probably shouldn't rely on them for that."

"Having large dogs on the property is always a good idea nevertheless," John said.

Everyone took a seat near the fire. John and Anna each took out a small notebook and pen and were poised to take notes.

"What is the main objective?" John asked bluntly.

"To keep me alive," Georgia said with complete seriousness.

Skyler cringed but nodded her head in agreement.

"We've been briefed on everything that has transpired over the last week," Anna said. "It's troubling that the local authorities are coming up with nothing. Because the Governor was here when the explosive device went off, this event went pretty high up the ladder, I'd say, and still nothing. That's quite worrisome. It would seem that whoever planted the bomb, is extremely knowledgeable and very dangerous. Or, frankly, just very lucky."

Skyler had to stop herself from rolling her eyes. "It would seem so. So, where do we go from here?" She immediately worried that she was coming off as being a bitch, so she decided to shut up and listen.

John pushed back his shoulders. "We get the security company out here right away to get the system back up and running. Anna and I get access to the video feed and have it available on our phones and tablets around the clock. One or both of us will accompany you everywhere you go, Miss Reece, and everyone who comes to the house will be checked by one of us before they gain entry. Basically, it'll be like you're a member of the immediate family of the President of the United States. This will be close to Secret Service-level protection. And while all that is going on, we'll liaison, to the best of our ability, with the police and F.B.I. to see if we can assist with their ongoing investigations."

Anna spoke up, "It's very possible, given what's happened, that we're dealing with more than one suspect. It could be a crazed fan. A stalker. It could be a disgruntled co-worker or employee. We just don't know yet. We're going to want to dig deep into your life and try to identify possible persons of interest."

Georgia took a deep breath and placed a hand on Skyler's knee. "As I have said ad nauseam, I just can't imagine who would want to do me harm. I really can't."

"We're going to figure it out," John said. "I promise."

"Is there a money back guarantee?" Georgia asked.

Anna laughed. "No. But we've never lost a client and our track record is pretty golden. It's why Mr. Grey sent us to you. We'll figure this out, Miss Reece."

"Alright, good. But please, no 'ma'am' and no 'Miss Reece,' okay? Call me Georgia," she said, rising. "And I want you both to make yourselves at home. I'll show you to your suite."

Georgia gave the couple a tour of the sprawling house, ending at the large bedroom and ensuite bathroom over the garage that would serve as the base of operations and sleeping quarters for the married ex-detectives. John mentioned that he was pleased with the view of the driveway from the room's bay window, and Georgia left them alone as they began to unpack their clothing and equipment.

Before she left the room, both Anna and John removed their blazers, and the singer noticed that each of them had a holstered handgun strapped to their side.

* * *

"They're both packing heat," Georgia said as she rejoined Skyler in the living room. "I think that makes me feel better."

"They aren't messing around, that's for sure. A tough looking pair, those two." Skyler closed her laptop and placed it on the ottoman. She leaned close to Georgia and whispered, "I was trying to picture them having sex. I can't see it."

Georgia erupted in laughter. "You are so bad. But I was thinking the exact same thing. They seem more like brother and sister, don't they? If the brother and sister were former military and former cops who spend an extraordinary amount of time at the gym together."

"This doesn't seem very Christmassy. I'm so sorry you're going through this, honey."

"You're so very sweet, Skyler," Georgia said. "And it's ridiculously generous of both Brenda and you to spend this time of year here with me. Given these circumstances. There are certainly better places you could be spending the holidays."

"I don't know," Skyler said through a sigh. "My boyfriend is working around the clock in Maine and my only living family is my stupid brother and his young family, and, I hate saying this, I do, but we're just not very close and we haven't spent any holidays together since our parents passed away. And Brenda is feuding with her brother and aunt over financial stuff—it's all very messy, but I should let her tell you that story. So, Brenda and I throw ourselves into our work and then we go together to where ever we want to for the holidays. And this year, we're very happy to be here with you here in Santa Fe. I mean it."

"But you didn't expect all of this mess." Georgia's eyes welled up. "I'm still sorry for making it all such a downer."

"Stop apologizing. It's all going to be figured out." Skyler looked over at the Christmas tree. "Concentrate on your gorgeous tree!"

"I do love it."

John came running into the room from the back hall and sprinted toward the front door. He had a handgun in his right hand.

Georgia and Skyler jumped to their feet just as Anna ran in and commanded them to, "Hit the deck!" The female detective took up a tactical position between the women and the now-open front door. "Stay close to the floor," Anna said. She too had her weapon drawn and was aiming it at the door.

Skyler's heart began to race and she was immediately taken back to the previous summer when a similar siege took place in her house in Maine. She suddenly decided that Christmas in Santa Fe wasn't a good idea after all.

Outside on the gravel driveway, John sat on the back of a man. He holstered his weapon and wrestled the man's arms behind his back. He fished a plastic zip-tie from his pocket and bound the man's wrists together then effortlessly lifted him to his feet and pinned him to the side of the couple's rented Ford Explorer.

"What are you doing here?" John demanded.

"I've come to fix the wall," the man said. "Miss Georgia asked me to come."

John eased off the man and gently turned him around so that they were facing each other. He pressed a finger up to his right ear where an almost-invisible communication device was nestled. "Anna. Ask Georgia if she hired a man...what's your name?"

"Diego. Diego Ferrera," the man said through labored breaths.

"Diego Ferrera," John repeated.

Moments later, Anna, Georgia, and Skyler were outside on the driveway as John cut away Diego's restraints with a pocket knife.

"Diego, darling, I am so very sorry," Georgia said, trembling. "Please do come inside."

"Why were you walking up the driveway? Where is your vehicle?" John asked.

"On the street. The gate is closed. I tried calling, but no one answered."

"So, you jumped the fence?" Anna asked.

"When someone like Miss Reece asks me to get a job done, I get it done."

Skyler couldn't help but smile. "Diego, you are a very loyal man. And a very lucky one. As you can see, Georgia has called in the cavalry. Things have changed around here."

"I will be more careful next time."

"I'll open the gate," John said, "and you can drive your truck up to the house. But I hope you won't be offended if I watch you while you work."

"I'd expect nothing less," Diego said. He brushed off his pants and started walking back down the driveway.

Georgia grabbed on to Skyler's arm. "I totally forgot that he was coming. I owe that poor man a *very* sizable Christmas bonus."

"I'd say so."

* * *

Brenda and Sullivan weaved through the crowds on the Plaza, crossed Washington Avenue, and stepped into the lobby of the Inn at the Anasazi, an upscale boutique hotel in downtown Santa Fe that would certainly rival their own. It was late in the afternoon, but they were famished, and the bar was serving food. They settled into a banquette and each ordered a Spicy Paloma— a delightful serrano-infused tequila and grapefruit concoction— and a chopped tortilla salad with shrimp. Brenda also asked for an order of the crispy green beans with Cotija cheese. As usually, she was perpetually on a hunt for things she could adapt and call her own.

When the waiter disappeared, Sullivan absently commented that he was surprised that they had the handsome bar to themselves.

"Everyone must be out shopping," Brenda said, "because I know for a fact this place is sold out through New Year's Eve."

"The vibe is very pleasant," he said as he scanned the room. "Swanky, yet still casual and comfortable. I hope we can manage a feel like this."

Brenda shook her head. "No, darling. We're going to seriously show up this dump." She chuckled. "This is all very nice, of course, but our plans are nothing short of marvelous and it's all coming together, Sully. Truly. I have never felt so confident about a project. And I've built *a lot* of restaurants. Trust me."

"Carter is working my last nerve," Sullivan said out of the blue.

"Listen, I'm told that you two came out of the womb with your hands around each other's throat, but you also get along better than any two siblings I've ever met or worked with. I can't imagine it can be all that bad."

"It's not world-ending, but he's the perfectionist in the family, which is not a bad thing in the hotel industry, I guess. But, he's so hard on contractors and subs, and so damned unforgiving when things don't go as planned. He's damned demanding about everything. He's like Miranda Priestly in *The Devil Wears Prada*, without the over-priced designer originals."

Brenda's eyes widened. "Straight men aren't supposed to know who Miranda Priestly is."

"That's old-fashioned sexism, Brenda. I'm very metro," Sullivan said with a sly smile. "I can watch Mets games *and* Meryl Streep. I have a broad palate. Plus, I had an ex-girlfriend who was obsessed with that movie. I think I was forced to watch it a dozen times."

"Well, whatever you do," Brenda said, "try not to kill Carter before the hotel is done, because with him dead and you in jail, I can't get it all done on my own."

"I'm not going to kill him. But I do think that I'm going to suggest some changes."

"Like what?"

Sullivan sighed. "We're co-CEOs. We both do *everything*. Have our hands in every single cookie jar. Quite literally. *Both* of our hands. We're negotiating contracts, picking out fabrics, testing mattresses, hiring hotel managers, buying art, and even selecting the perfect shade of white for the ceilings in the suites. Brenda, we decided, together, which brand of toilet paper that we were going to stock in the bathrooms. It's just a tad short of insanity."

Brenda looked like she couldn't quite process what she was hearing. "Honey, no," she said very slowly. "You can't do all of that at this stage in your business. You're going to kill yourselves. Repeat after me: *del-e-ga-tion.* I just had this exact same conversation with Skyler. It's imperative now that you let other people help you."

"I'm not allowed to use that word because we simply don't know how to do that. I should say, fucking *Carter* doesn't know how to do that."

"Sully. Carter and you need to split up this job. Specialize. And, for goodness sake, don't be afraid to hire competent people and let them make some decisions for you. As the company continues to grow, you won't be able to keep up this momentum. Trust me, please. I learned this the hard way early on. Do you think I write every recipe and every article? Do you think I'm in the trenches developing my olive oils? I get people to do that stuff for the brand. It's a *brand*, it's not all Carter and Sullivan Lowery."

Sullivan had a pained, almost stunned look on his face. "I'll try to have a conversation with him."

"Good. It's important. And if you don't, I will. I have a stake in this now, remember?"

"Mmm hmm. I won't let you down. You're way too important to the Franklin-Lowery family."

"You're sweet," Brenda said. She took a long sip from her drink. "And accurate."

When the beans arrived to the table, Sullivan dug in. "My goodness, Brenda. What is this cheese? Parmesan?"

"Cotija. But it's in the same family. It's a Mexican cow's milk. I use a similar aged version called Anejo in a few restaurant recipes. It's salty and savory and I love it so much." She grabbed an appetizer fork and helped herself. "This is amazing. The chili powder gives it an extra kick. I have to take some notes or I'll forget." Brenda pulled out her phone and jotted down a few words. "Perfection."

"Well, don't copy this and put it on the menu here in Santa Fe," Sullivan said. "They won't like that. And it'll get out."

Brenda wrinkled her brow. "I don't *copy* stuff. I acclimatize," she said with a wicked smile. "That means, adapt."

"I'm familiar, thank you."

"And if I do develop something similar, I'll use it somewhere far away, I promise. Las Vegas, maybe. Vegas needs green beans with Cotija."

"If you say so."

Brenda's phone vibrated in her hand, and she glanced at the screen. It was a text from Skyler:

```
When are you coming back to Georgia's?
The NYC security people are here now and
they've already almost killed Diego.
```

"I have no idea what this means," Brenda said out loud.

"Don't know what *what* means?" Sullivan asked.

Brenda tapped back a response:

```
    IDK who this Diego guy is, but coming soon.
        Groceries first. Cooking tonight for
    everyone, twins, security and all. Except
        Diego. Because I don't know him. Do I?
```

CHAPTER THIRTEEN

Skyler woke up with another hangover. It was wearisome at this point in the trip and she quickly decided that she was getting too old to make herself feel this way on a semi-regular basis, especially when she was supposed to be enjoying a relaxing holiday. She struggled to her suite's bathroom and started the shower. She had a little over an hour to make herself presentable enough so that she wouldn't look like a complete freak show in front of a certain billionaire businessman.

The previous evening was a blur. As she soaped herself up, she remembered Brenda coming home with Sullivan and a slew of paper grocery bags. She recalled Georgia opening the first of what she guessed must have been several bottles of expensive wine. The security people were there, too, of course, but they drank club sodas with lime. The dogs were extra energetic because Diego was making a racket in the front hall, but he left before the rest of them sat down to eat.

Then it all fades to black.

Skyler couldn't recall what was on the menu—which in itself was a crime when you have a superstar chef making your dinner—or what else might have been consumed that was causing the suppression of memory. A nagging hangover was one thing; a total blackout was something completely different.

And it was unsettling.

When she was standing at the bathroom counter wrapped in a couple of towels, Brenda magically appeared behind her. Skyler was too tired to be startled.

"Good morning, sunshine," Brenda sang.

"How on God's green Earth are you so chipper?"

"I didn't drink gallons of tequila."

"Ahhh," Skyler said as she tried to steady her hand enough to apply eyeliner. "Shots, I presume?"

"Many."

"Super."

"It was Sully's idea; he's a bad influence. But to give him credit, or a plausible excuse, I think he was trying to erase the difficult day he had with his brother down at the construction site."

"None of this is familiar to me."

"They aren't getting along as well as they always have. Or at least Sullivan doesn't think so. In any event, Georgia, the twins, and you got pretty smashed."

"Evidently." Skyler turned around and crossed her arms. "Did I do anything that I need to be embarrassed about? Do I need to apologize to Georgia—or Leonard, for that matter—for something stupid?"

"I don't think so, no." Brenda leaned against the door frame and smiled at her friend. "You were all just silly. And *loud.* Oh so loud. But no one ended up in any compromising positions that I was witness to. Well, except for our hostess."

"Spill it."

"She disappeared with Sullivan sometime around midnight. Carter wasn't too happy about that."

"Interesting. She did tell us that she's been with both of them. Seems like it might be a potentially messy love triangle, huh?"

"Maybe so. Carter didn't really communicate that to me though."

"Wait," Skyler said. "Who's still in the house?"

"Carter requested a rideshare or a cab or something and left last night. Or early this morning, for that matter. And I'm pretty sure Sully is still in Georgia's suite. I don't know that for a *fact*, but I'll bet John and Anna know. Those two didn't look too pleased last night. I remember Georgia pleading with them to go to bed, but the cops seemed duty bound to stay awake until the last reveler was snug in a bed and the house was buttoned up tight. Actually—and you won't believe this—John is the one who walked Mulder and Scully before I turned in. He insisted on it. He said it would be good for him to patrol the perimeter. The dogs were in heaven, too; they just love men."

"How very nice for all of you."

"Yeah, because it's as cold as a witch's titty out there. And it was super windy last night, too."

"Witch's titty," Skyler repeated with a giggle. She turned around to finish her makeup. "That takes me back to eighth grade. Mrs. Reynold's class."

"I remember."

"Why are witches' titties so cold?"

"They're cold hearted bitches, those witches. Can I fetch you some coffee and a croissant or something?"

Skyler lightened. "Coffee, yes. Food, no. I'll eat something after my meeting with Foster. Maybe."

"He's going to love you." Brenda started out of the

bathroom and through Skyler's room. "Everyone does." And she was gone.

Skyler wasn't so sure that she was loved universally, but it was a nice thing to hear from her best friend. She pulled the towel off her damp hair and considered whether she had the energy to blow dry it straight or if she'd let it dry naturally, which would emphasize the curls in her long locks. She opted for the natural method and would pull it back into a ponytail before heading out of the house. Given the relative lack of humidity in the high desert, she wasn't too concerned about frizziness.

After she downed half the coffee Brenda delivered, Skyler sat down at her laptop and scanned her messages. Besides another sweet missive from Leonard, she was more than a little bit excited to see an email from her longtime contact at *Vanity Fair* magazine in New York.

```
Dec 19 @ 9:09am EST
From: isabella.bunch@vf.mag
To: skyler.moore@skylermoorepr.com
Subject: April Cover & Spread


Skyler,


I realize that I told you last week that this
wasn't going to be decided until the beginning
of the new year, but it's LOCKED IN. Ready??

Carissa will be the April cover with a seven or
eight page spread. Just her. Leibovitz is booked
to do the photos sometime in late-February, in
Las Vegas, at your request. Dates to be worked
out. We haven't assigned a writer yet; will get
```

back to you on that. Maybe Dylan or Casey—they're
both huge fans without being schmaltzy.

Would she be open to a video crew being at the
photo shoot(s)? Might be a great companion
piece for the web or social media. Could even
be a part of our new BTS doc we're working on.
Annie is always cool with crews on her set.
Well, almost always.

Let's talk the first week of January. Happy
Holidays! And, you're welcome.

Best, Isa

Isabella Bunch
Executive Editor, Vanity Fair
Main: 212-555-5151
Cell: 718-555-2368

Skyler closed her eyes and took a few silent moments to
thank the public relations gods. This was one of Carissa Lamb's
lifelong goals and the pop superstar was going to be over the
moon with excitement. The monumental 'get' might very well
come with an extra holiday bonus, too, Skyler hoped. She was
certainly doing her P.R. best, and then some.

She forwarded the email to Carissa (and copied Enzo, her
right-hand man back in D.C.) with a short note attached:

Dec 19 @ 8:59am MST
From: skyler.moore@skylermoorepr.com
To: clamb@psmail.com
CC: enzo.flores@skylermoorepr.com
Subject: FWD: April Cover & Spread

C,

OMG, see below. How much do you love me? Forward your February schedule to Enzo as soon as you can. He'll make sure everyone is on the same page.

Talk soon. So excited!

—Skyler Moore

Skyler Moore Public Relations, LLC
Washington, DC and Worldwide
www.SkylerMoorePR.com
Main: 888-555-1301
Cell/Text: 202-555-1733

Pleased with herself, Skyler jumped into an all-black outfit, tied a red silk scarf around her neck, and threw her laptop, iPad, and an old-fashioned paper notebook into her briefcase. She was out the door and behind the wheel of the rental car—after checking out of the house with Anna, the de facto hall monitor on duty.

Skyler screamed out a short exclamation of glee and pounded the steering wheel as she zipped toward the Plaza. Replaced by happiness of a job well done, the hangover was magically gone.

* * *

Georgia wasn't completely comfortable with the idea of leaving the house, but she agreed to go shopping with Brenda. Of course, that threw the security team into motion, as last-minute plans were made for a trip downtown—a whole two miles down the hill.

"We're going to go to the Mea Culpa dress shop, an animation art gallery on Water Street, and then pop into a café for lunch," Brenda said matter-of-factly. "We're not advertising it online. How will anyone even know we're there? What could possibly happen in sleepy ol' Santa Fe?"

"I bet you didn't think a bomb would go off in the living room or a stranger would stalk you from the woods or follow you to your hotel downtown," John said curtly. "So, anything *could* happen. And probably will."

Brenda placed her hands on her hips. "Great attitude."

"We're just doing the job that Miss Reece hired us to do. At any time, she can send us packing and you ladies can fend for yourselves, Miss Braxton."

"My name is Brenda. I've asked you repeatedly to please call me…" She ran out of steam. "Never mind. How soon can we leave?" She turned and looked at Anna, who seemed to be a little friendlier.

"Give us 15 minutes, okay?"

Georgia and Brenda retreated to the kitchen.

"You have to let them do their job," Georgia said in a whisper. "For me?"

"Of course." Brenda was embarrassed by her outburst but decided to brush it off. She took a seat at the bar and fiddled with a book of matches. "It's frustrating, but I understand how grave the situation is."

"I've considered leaving. I gave it a lot of thought this morning after Sully left."

"About that…"

Georgia rolled her eyes. "I'm so stupid, Brenda. I can't be

having a sexual relationship with *both* of them. I mean, how long can this possibly last? They're already at odds with each other. I'm just making things worse."

"Do you like one of them more than the other?" Brenda rested her chin in her palm. There was a twinkle in her eye; she loved this kind of stuff, which was probably why she was addicted to reality television shows like *The Bachelor*, even though she knew many people thought the medium was low-brow.

"They are so different out of bed. In bed...they're kind of exactly the same. Like, *exactly the same*."

"Down there?"

"Absolutely identical. Even how they start, what they do next, the positions they prefer. It's all so absurd. And confusing."

"I'm so intrigued. Do you think they compare notes? Maybe they've had threesomes so that they know each other's game plan?" Brenda erupted in laughter. "This is so crazy, Georgia. This should be a book. Skyler can help you get an agent. She knows everyone."

"Oh my goodness, I could never do something like that— tell tales out of school. Not me. But they *are* good. Probably the best I've ever had."

"Wow. What are you going to do?"

"Fly home to New York City to avoid getting killed by a deranged stalker and to avoid having to make a decision on what I do about my twin lovers."

"I think you should reconsider, Georgia. You have the cops here watching out for you now. Skyler and I are here. The dogs are here. And it's Christmas. If you go back to New York now, with all of us here, won't you be all alone?"

"I would be, yes."

"Then stick it out a bit longer. This is going to come to an end soon. I promise."

Georgia seemed placated for the moment. "Plus, I can't be in New York at Christmas time after what happened last year."

Brenda's eyes widened.

"I'm sure you read about it in the papers."

Brenda racked her brain. "Maybe I did, but it escapes me. What happened last Christmas?"

"I was driving on the Long Island Expressway, coming back to the city from a girlfriend's holiday party. I had three or four drinks, but I felt okay to drive."

"Oh geez. No. I don't know this story."

"I must have fallen asleep at the wheel," Georgia said softly. "I veered into the left passing lane and sideswiped another car. There was a man alone in that vehicle and he swerved to get away from me and…" Her voice trailed off.

Brenda noticed that the singer was shaking. "Was he hurt?"

"Badly. He went head first through his windshield when he hit…when his car hit a tree." She lowered her voice to a low whisper. "He died three days later from his injuries. He wasn't wearing his seatbelt…but it was still my fault. All my fault."

"Oh, Georgia, honey. I am so sorry."

Perhaps it was from all of her experience on the stage, Brenda thought, but all of a sudden Georgia composed herself and continued. "I was exonerated after my very powerful, very expensive lawyers arranged for a plea deal. I was supposed to do a month in jail, but due to overcrowding—which is common in the City—I was in and out in 18 hours. Eighteen hours, Brenda. It was just unbelievable. I got 200 community service hours, a hefty fine, and I lost my driver's license. For *life*. The saving grace was that I was never given a breathalyzer test at the scene. I claimed I only had one drink at the party and the hostess ultimately lied for me, attesting to the same. She carried a lot of weight with the judge apparently, because she is the wife of the former mayor. I was extremely lucky. The man who died...he was not."

Brenda just shook her head. "This is a book in itself."

"No!" Georgia erupted. "It can't be. If it were, then the real details would come out. As far as the outside world knows, I was exhausted and fell asleep at the wheel. Still liable, but it sounds a hell of a lot better than *passing out* at the wheel. Nevertheless, Page Six in the *New York Post* had a field day with it. I didn't lose any performance gigs, thank goodness, but I'm sure it must have damaged my once squeaky-clean reputation somewhat. Not to mention what I did to that poor, poor family."

"Did he have a wife and kids?" Brenda asked.

"A late wife who died from cancer a few years ago. But he had a daughter. I really don't know the details beyond that. I never saw the inside of a courtroom, so I never had to come face to face with anyone. My lawyers and I were scared to death that the daughter would bring a civil suit, but it's been a year and nothing has popped up. I'm still on pins and needles about it, every single day. I'm not sure what the statute of limitations are for something like that."

"I'm so very sorry, honey. And I understand why you'd want to stay away from New York at this time of year." Brenda had trouble processing the astonishing confession and immediately questioned how she felt about the woman and her apparent lack of judgement. But the opera singer did seem genuinely remorseful, *unless that too was an act*, Brenda thought. She quickly decided it wasn't her place to judge—she hadn't caused anyone's death that she was aware of, but she hadn't lived her life as a saint, either—so she pushed her shoulders back and put a big smile on her face. "So, we'll make the best of it and make sure we all have a happy and *safe* Christmas right here in Santa Fe."

"I agree," Georgia said as she took a deep, calming breath. "Now, dear, let's go shopping."

"That's my second favorite sentence, after *let's go eat*." Brenda slipped off her stool and pulled on her coat. "Let's tell the hired guns that it's time to go."

* * *

Skyler pulled her car into the La Fonda hotel garage entrance and was faced with a sign that indicated that the lot was full. A very handsome young man appeared at her open window. "Are you checking in, ma'am?"

"I am not," she said with a sweet smile. "But I'm late for a lunch date at La Plazuela. Can I please park here?"

"I'm sorry, ma'am. We can only accommodate overnight hotel guests at this time of year. We're quite booked, I'm afraid, and the garage is small."

She wasn't a regular practitioner of bribery, but she was desperate and nearly late. She fished a $100 bill out of her wallet, folded it in half, and held it out of the window. She glanced at his nametag. "Just this once, Henry?"

He didn't blink. He pocketed the Benjamin and handed Skyler a claim ticket. "You can leave the car here, ma'am. I will take care of it while you enjoy your lunch."

She grabbed her bag and climbed out of the driver's seat. She gave him a wink and strutted into the hotel, proud of herself. It was worth the money, she decided, to save the aggravation of finding parking on the street.

As she passed by the concierge desk, she noticed a middle-aged woman sitting behind a computer screen. Then she looked over at the two ladies standing behind the front desk. And a split second later, Skyler caught a glimpse of herself in a floor-to-ceiling mirror and stopped dead in her tracks. She'd managed to dress *exactly* like the hotel staff members. Her black slacks and slim-fitting jacket, white blouse, and red scarf were nearly identical to their uniform. All she needed was an embossed gold nametag pinned to her right breast pocket. Horrified, she ripped the scarf from her neck and stuffed it into her bag. But it was too late. Foster Martin was standing a few feet away, directly to her left.

"Are you moonlighting here?" he asked with a chuckle.

Skyler beamed at the old man. "I am not. It was an unfortunate accident."

"You look very city-corporate, Miss Moore," he said taking her by the arm and gently guiding her toward the restaurant. "You do realize that we're in Santa Fe, New Mexico, where blue jeans and a pair of well-worn boots is considered a dressy outfit."

"I guess I should know that by now. But I have never been here before and I wasn't sure how to dress for a…" She stopped talking.

"For a billionaire? Is that what you were going to say?"

Skyler could feel her face flush. "I guess I might have if I didn't stop myself, yes."

"This billionaire is fairly casual most of the time and he wouldn't really care if you were wearing a burlap sack to lunch as long as you brought along the public relations and marketing chops that you are so well known for."

"I'll remember that for next time," she said with a chuckle. "Burlap sacks are all the rage this season."

They were greeted warmly by the hostess and escorted to a small table beside the fountain. After getting settled, Skyler looked around the atrium and marveled at the indoor trees and intricate paintings on the woodwork all around them. "This is quite a beautiful spot."

"I do enjoy it," Foster said as he pushed his menu to the side. "I don't need to look at this thing. I have it all memorized. And it doesn't matter anyway, because I always get the same thing. I highly recommend the Carne Asada."

"Done. One of my all-time favorites."

"Perfect. We're off to a good start," Foster said. He folded his weathered hands on the table and leaned in. "I think it's time I told you what I have on my mind."

"I'm all ears."

"Hardly," he said with a sly smile. "Journalistic integrity."

"Excuse me?"

"This country is off the rails when it comes to the news. Facts aren't important anymore. Opinion is seeping into every report, every story, every feature. Our top *news* anchors can't help but to pepper their reporting with their own thoughts on every issue. Our major newspapers are in trouble. Print is dying. No one wants to pay for news, so they consume crap. They end up with poorly researched innuendo and speculation and, worst of all, sensationalism. Click bait! What is considered breaking news these days troubles me dearly. Celebrity is considered the highest form of life—no offense to your other clients. But we, as a nation, bow down to it. I want to help change that culture. Forge a new path. A return to facts and a return to journalistic integrity. We shouldn't know who Anderson Cooper voted for in the last election. Peter Jennings shouldn't have a public opinion on income taxes."

"Oh goodness," Skyler said. "Peter Jennings died years ago."

"Yes, yes. It's just an example. But see? The evening news broadcasts aren't important anymore; I don't even know who anchors those programs."

She laughed out loud. "That's not true. You probably pay some of them."

"Okay, to be fair, you and *I* know who the anchors are." He gestured wildly with his arms at the other diners in the restaurant. "But I bet the average American could not even name one. But that's not the point. The point is the journalistic landscape has changed for the worse. And I want to fix it."

Skyler considered for a moment what the world's foremost media titan was saying. "Sir, you control a very sizable share of media outlets here in the United States and around the world."

"I do. And I don't."

"What do you mean?"

"I try very hard not to trip down the path that others have navigated quite recklessly. Without naming names, I think you can probably think of a few major news conglomerates that clearly have a corporate-governed political agenda. There are organizations that worship on both sides of the political spectrum and I don't think they are doing Americans any favors. I've made it very clear to my newsrooms around the world that we are to be 100% nonpartisan in our reporting of the news— and to only deal in facts—and I am generally very happy with the outcomes. The local affiliate stations, the papers, and the European satellite service, for the most part, comply with that way of thinking. But there are slip ups. And, more importantly, there are a lot more people working in journalism today who do not work for one of my companies, so I can't tell them what to do. But I can help mold the minds of the future with conferences, articles, videos, endowments, scholarships, perhaps even our own journalism school. And hopefully we can lead by example and set a few zillion current news people on the correct path."

Her mind was reeling. "That's a lot," Skyler said. "Who's spearheading the project?"

"I am, for now," he said confidently. "I quietly gave up running the day-to-day operation of the company a decade and a half ago, although I'm still chairman of the board. So, I have time on my hands. I'm meeting with potential executives and industry professionals to eventually operate the foundation because I'm just too old and too fidgety to be tied to a desk chair." He sighed deeply. "But it's been hard to convince these people who I've been courting to leave their current positions. I might have to pay ridiculous amounts of money to get them to agree to come work on the project."

"I imagine that you *have* ridiculous amounts of money at your disposal."

"I do. And I can't take it with me and I don't have heirs to speak of. Not any worthy ones, rather." He paused and smiled at the waitress when their meals were delivered. When she was out of earshot, he continued. "I outlived three wives. Collectively, we had seven children. Four of them have passed on, too. Two of them are housewives—actually, they're both grandmothers now; can you believe that? My children are *grandmothers!*—but they have no interest in my businesses or me, for that matter. We've all been estranged since the late-1970's."

"I'm sorry to know that," Skyler said, wondering why he was being so forthcoming about his personal life, although she suspected none of this was secret information given that several articles and tell-all books had been written about the man over the years. "That leaves one more, sir."

"Sasha."

"Sasha Martin. The current C.E.O. of Martin Media Worldwide. He's positioned to inherit everything?" Skyler asked.

"Hell no. He makes a tidy salary and he has tons of stock, but he'll never gain full control and he knows that. He always has."

She wasn't sure if she should keep asking questions.

"For several reasons, I've let him keep his job, but he's disappointed me many times. When I pass away, the company will be sold. Broken up into pieces, I presume. The vast majority of the assets will go to charity."

"You don't want Martin Media to outlive you?"

"I think the money can be used to help more people by breaking it up, my dear. My 71-year-old son has more than enough money to live out a very happy retirement. Most of the employees will still have jobs under new ownership. And the cancer centers and schools and libraries and museums and adoption organizations that I help to fund will flourish beyond their wildest dreams."

"It's all very admirable, Mr. Martin."

"Foster!"

"Foster. I'm so sorry. But for now, it's all about the future of journalism?"

"That's right. And I am going to throw truckloads of money at this. And I want you to help me spend it."

Skyler brightened. "I'm happy to help and I'm *very* good at spending money that isn't my own. Responsibly, of course. But more importantly, I'm very honored that you think so highly of my work that you'd trust me to help with such a worthy cause."

"I did my homework after Carissa Lamb recommended you. You have an amazing track record."

"Well, Mr. Martin, I would be honored to be a part of the team. It's a very worthwhile venture and something that I could certainly sink my teeth into. I bet Carissa and even Brenda Braxton—the celebrity chef and my best friend—will be enthusiastic donors to the effort. I know a few other people with deep pockets, for that matter. I just might be a de facto fundraiser for the…oh my goodness, I never asked. What is it going to be called?"

Foster's face crinkled up. "I don't have a name picked out yet." He fished a small green notebook out of his breast pocket and flipped through some tattered pages. I have a very long list of possible names. Maybe you can help me decide."

"Again, I'd be honored."

"If we are going to work together on this project, there would be a few stipulations."

"Alright."

"You are required to call me Foster. Never Mr. Martin."

"That's an easy one. Done."

"Plus, you'll need to drop all of your current clients and move to Las Vegas."

Skyler's mouth quite literally dropped open.

CHAPTER FOURTEEN

One of Brenda's recurring nightmares involved trying on new clothes. She absolutely dreaded the process and the humiliation she felt in and out of store dressing rooms, which is why in recent years, she employed a personal shopper to comb through every store in New York City to bring her scores of things to test in the privacy of her own home. She was not just overweight, like an alarmingly growing population of Americans, she was a tad shy of obese, and she required just the right type of outfits to compliment—or attempt to disguise—her ample figure.

She didn't have the typical, perfectly shaped television personality body, but for some reason the public liked her, the food she prepared, and her line of products, so it was working to her advantage. But Brenda knew that she was entirely too large and she was determined to do something about it…in the new year.

She promised herself the same thing every year right around Christmas time.

And then she went on to gain 10 to 20 pounds over the holidays and never would get around to changing the dangerous pattern. The need for new clothes was a constant one.

A vicious cycle.

And because she was in Santa Fe instead of Manhattan, without the use of her trusty plus-size stylist, she was standing in the back of an upscale New Mexican boutique while a sales clerk pinned the bottom of a pair of green slacks.

"I absolutely love that color on you," Georgia said from a velvet divan somewhere behind Brenda. She sipped champagne from a delicate flute.

"It's not *too* green?"

"No. It's *ever*green. It's classic. And perfect for this time of year."

The clerk got to her feet and looked at Brenda through the mirror in front of them. "With an oversized man's white oxford, with the collar popped, maybe?"

"You've read my mind," Brenda said with a smile.

"Not really," the clerk chuckled. "I watch you on T.V. I know your style."

"You're hired! Can you move to New York?"

Georgia finished her wine and set the glass down on a small side table. She got to her feet and grabbed a pile of sweaters. "Okay, I'm ready to try these on."

The clerk escorted Georgia to the last dressing room on the left then took Brenda back out to the showroom floor to look at a coral necklace that the chef had her eye on for Skyler. A young redheaded woman, who had been trying on a dozen different outfits in the back, left without buying anything, and then there were just two women looking through the racks in the store. Anna stood near the sales desk as she surveyed the room and her husband stood outside next to the idling car, which was parked illegally in front of the shop. He had his eyes on everyone walking up and down the crowded sidewalk.

A few moments after she was entered the dressing room, Massimo Modena clamped his large rough hand over Georgia's mouth and pulled one of her arms behind her back. She struggled, the two of them trampling the sweaters she dropped, but he was much bigger and stronger and his grip continued to tighten. He leaned backward allowing one eye to peek through the small gap in the curtain. There was a rack of clothes blocking the view of the store; the perfect cover.

He pulled her out of the dressing room and through a swinging door that read, 'Staff Only.' She'd struggled fiercely for a few moments but then seemed to lose her will to fight back. Georgia didn't resist as Massimo twisted and pushed her toward the back of the store. He popped the handle on the back door, propping it open behind him. In seconds, they were outside in the biting cold, standing in the alley between the store and a windowless brick wall. Parked next to a Dumpster, was a small compact car with its trunk open.

Five minutes later, Massimo pulled the car onto US-285 and headed north. His former client...his former girlfriend...the celebrated coloratura soprano...was riding in the trunk.

It took a full eight minutes before Anna sensed something was wrong. She worked her way to the end of the back hallway and stopped in front of Georgia's dressing room.

"Miss Reece? How's it going in there?"

Silence.

Anna ripped open the curtain to find a pile of sweaters, Georgia's blouse and coat, her purse, and an iPhone on the bench. She flew through the swinging door and scanned the storage room then peered into a darkened half bathroom. The retired police detective pressed the small button on her earpiece. "John. Georgia is not in the store."

As John bolted through the front door, Anna opened the back door and looked up and down the alley. Nothing. Her husband was on her back in seconds.

"What the fuck?" he screamed.

"She was in the dressing room. Trying on sweaters."

"And now?"

"She's not."

"Anna, for God's sake," he said. "How did we let this happen?"

She braced herself against the brick wall. "I don't know. We checked this door. It was dead bolted from the inside. It needed a key and the key was not in the lock."

"Did anyone even know we were coming here today?" John asked, not expecting an answer. "I'm going to have a look further up and down the alley. Go back inside and, I don't know, go see who else is in the store right now. Go!"

Anna hurried back into the boutique and found Brenda and the sales woman looking at necklaces on a large black velvet placemat. She sidled up next to the chef. "I don't want to alarm you, ma'am."

"What is it?" Brenda said in full voice.

"Keep your voice down, if you will. Miss Reece appears to be missing."

"How on Earth is that possible? She didn't come this way. This store is tiny; we would have noticed. She's in the back trying on all those sweaters we picked out."

"She is not back there, ma'am. She must have gone out the

back door. It's unlocked."

"She left on her own?"

"We have not determined that yet." Anna turned to the sales woman. "Do you have security cameras in the shop?"

"I'm afraid not," the woman said, her hands trembling. "We've never had the need."

Brenda put down the jewelry she was examining and pulled out her cell phone. "I can try calling her."

"Her phone is in the dressing room along with..." Anna struggled to speak. "Along with her blouse, coat, and purse."

"Well then she certainly didn't leave by herself now did she?" Brenda exploded. "Anna! How could you two let this happen?"

"I'm devastated, Miss Braxton. This has never happened to John and me before. We've never..."

Her husband suddenly appeared. He was holstering his weapon as he approached the three ladies. "I found nothing. There don't appear to be any cameras in the alley. How about in here?"

"No," the sales women, Anna, and Brenda all said in unison.

"Fuck!" John screamed. He startled the only other person in the store at the time, an elderly, frail looking woman who was sifting through silk scarves in a sales bin. "What the fuck?!" John said again under his breath.

"What do we do now, detectives?" Brenda asked with a decidedly sarcastic tone.

"I guess we call the police," John said softly. "Damn it to hell."

"Because that's worked so wonderfully up until now." Brenda started for the back of the store. "I'm going to get out of these God damned green pants. *Jesus Christ on a cracker.*"

* * *

Skyler nearly choked on a piece of steak in her mouth. "Excuse me? Move to Las Vegas?"

"Well, that's where I plan to base the foundation. It's where my house is—the only one I kept when I started downsizing my once-ostentatious lifestyle; it's up in the hills in Henderson—and I have a very good relationship with the University of Nevada there. U.N.L.V. could be a good place to launch the initial course work."

"But, Foster," Skyler said after she took a moment to force down the meat with a long sip of water, "I'm an east coast girl. I live in Washington, D.C. My staff all lives there. And I have a house in Wabanaki, Maine, where I spend the summer months. Plus, I have clients that I have become quite fond of. You wouldn't want me to abandon them without proper notice and, quite frankly, I don't want to stop working for any of them. They were all hand-picked and have become like family to me. It's not like you're asking me to leave a big firm where I'm just one of thousands. This is my own business. It's my own baby. I'm the *one.*"

The old man smiled and leaned back in his chair. "And I don't want you to do that either. I guess that was just a little test."

Skyler exhaled. "It was a *mean* test, if I'm being honest, Foster," Skyler said.

"I didn't intend to be mean. And I always want you to be honest, for goodness sake. Even an old codger like me realizes that this is the 21st century. Technology and ever-present screens have taken over. A person can work from anywhere he or she pleases. You can be in Washington or Wabanaki or even Waikiki, for all I care. We can get together for face-to-face meetings when it's necessary and the rest of the time we can meet virtually. Believe it or not—I actually know how to Skype. So? How's all that sound?"

Skyler sighed pleasantly. "I like is all very much, thank you."

"And, by the way, I'm absolutely gaga over the state of Maine. Perhaps I'll have to come up there next summer and we can do some work over lobster rolls and a Portland Pale Ale."

"That would be lovely. You'd love Wabanaki. People come to visit and then don't ever want to leave."

"I used to own a home on Cobbosseecontee Lake, just west of Augusta. Do you know it? Most call it Cobbossee, for short."

"Do I know it?" Skyler said with a laugh. "My aunt and uncle had the cutest little camp along Pond Road on the east side of the lake. I remember swimming in that ice-cold water and listening to the loons when I was a little girl. A magical place, indeed."

"Indeed. That was during my water skiing phase. I'd spend Memorial Day to Labor Day there in the 1960's. I'd water ski for hours on end. It drove the executives of my company crazy. Back then, it wasn't as easy to get ahold of people. No email and no cell phones, of course. And I didn't even have a landline at the lake. I ran my business through the United States Postal Service and frequent trips to a pay phone at a diner in Manchester. Those were the days."

"Unless you take a trip to Timbuktu or the Galápagos Islands, I don't think that kind of sweet escape exists these days."

"So very true." Foster raised his hand and indicated to the waitress that he was ready for the check. "This has been lovely, my dear, but I have trails to hike and Christmas cards to address."

"You don't do that yourself."

"I absolutely do. I've whittled down my list to just a few dozen people who I actually care enough about to hope that they have a Merry Christmas. No more empty sentimentality for this old man. At one point, perhaps as early as a dozen years ago, my corporate card list was in the tens of thousands. That's just a ridiculous waste of money."

Skyler felt the hairs on her arms stand up—she'd completely forgotten to arrange for anything holiday-ish for her clients. She made a mental note to call her assistant Enzo just as soon as she got back to her car.

Skyler and Foster parted ways in the lobby. They'd made plans to reconnect after New Year's, and Skyler was excited about the opportunity to work on such a worthy and important cause. While celebrity projects were lucrative and full of rewards—like promoting Carissa's clothing line and getting network television product placement deals for Noah's craft vodka—this was the kind of work that she could get newly energized about.

Back in her car, she called her office and pleaded with Enzo to come up with holiday gifts for her clients.

"Christmas is six days away, Skyler," her annoyed employee said flatly. "You're just thinking about this now?"

"The question should be me asking you, *why didn't you think about this three months ago?*"

"I did," he said softly. "But I guess it got pushed to the bottom of the pile when we started getting so darned busy."

"Alright, this is my mistake; let's stop with the blame game. Enzo, darling, can we pull off a Christmas miracle?"

"With enough money, we can do anything, *darling.*"

"Great." Skyler navigated out of the downtown area and pointed the car up into the hills. She marveled at the crystal-clear sky and majestic snowcapped mountains ahead of her. "Do we know where everyone is?"

"For the most part, yes," Enzo said. Skyler could hear him furiously pounding away on his keyboard. "I have the master calendar pulled up. It shows where everyone is supposed to be, at least. Carissa is spending Christmas in Las Vegas. Noah is at his step-mother's house in Tampa. Gretchen and Blake are…"

"Okay, too many details," Skyler said, cutting him off. "Find a few quality options—but make sure they're unique—and get back to me by close of business."

"Skyler, it's four o'clock here in D.C."

"Great! You have a whole hour."

* * *

At the Franklin-Lowery construction site, Carter was stony and quiet most of the afternoon which was very much not a part of his character. He usually confronted problems straightaway and was ready and willing to talk them out, especially with his twin brother. But this was different. A woman, surprisingly, had never come between the two of them before.

As he examined the final city-approved electrical diagrams in a space that was soon to become the meeting rooms at the rear of the hotel's second floor, he sensed that he was no longer alone. He turned around to find Sullivan standing with his cell phone up to his ear. He was listening intently and was holding up an index finger. After a few moments, Sullivan said 'goodbye,' and lowered the phone.

"What is it?" Carter asked.

"Darby."

"For Christ's sake. What now? Is he in jail?"

"Nope," Sullivan said as he walked over to the drafting table. "He's still clean, sober, and on the straight and narrow—or so he keeps telling me every chance he gets. He wants to spend Christmas with us."

Carter let that sink in for a moment. "What happened to that low-life girlfriend who he can't stomach being away from for seven minutes? I thought he was going to Cleveland to spend the holidays with her family."

"They broke up. He caught her with a coffee barista in Darby's bed. He told me the whole story in quite graphic detail. Apparently, the kid is 17 years old and still had on his Starbucks hat while he was going down…"

"Sully! I don't need to know any of this."

"I'm just setting the scene."

"Spare me!"

Carter continued, "Darby wants to be with us—which may be a first. He also wants to get out of the city so that he can lick his wounds. At least that's the way I read it. And he wants us to buy him an airplane ticket."

"What happened to his allowance? You insisted on giving him $5,000 a month. How does he blow through that so quickly?"

"I give him the money as long as he stays in school, Carter. You know that," Sullivan said. "And he's done that. He's maintaining a B-average, too. This is *monumental* coming from the biggest screw up in New York. He's turning his life around. It's a good thing."

"I'm skeptical, man, that's all I'm saying. We've been down this road before. Ever since Mom and Dad passed, he's been nothing but a damned headache. He doesn't appreciate that money and he's really never worked a day in his life."

"Well, he's working hard on school and he's proving himself. *Now,* at least. Let's give him that."

"I don't really want to give him anything." Carter shook his head in defeat. "When is he coming here?"

"I'll call Cynthia and have her book him for Saturday the 23rd. Newark to Santa Fe, through Denver, I guess. United seems like the best option to get here from there. And he'll get in in time for dinner."

"I'm surprised he didn't ask you to send him a jet."

Sullivan sat down on a folding chair and popped the top off a cup of steaming coffee. "Oh, he *did.* He wasn't happy about the idea of flying commercial at the holidays. But he'll survive."

"Screw him. Seriously. Tell Cynthia to put him in coach. A friggin' middle seat in the last row. Between the two fattest jerks she can find. Super fat jerks who haven't showered in days. No! Super fat jerks each with a friggin' screaming baby on their lap."

Sullivan laughed despite himself. "Jesus, Carter. Now I'm going to have that image in my head all day."

"I'm sorry," Carter said. "He just gets me all worked up, that one." He paused a moment, then continued. "Can we talk about Georgia?"

"The country, the state, or the opera singer?"

"Let's start with the opera singer, wiseass."

Sullivan took a sip of coffee, burning his tongue. "Fuck!"

"Funny. That's what I want to talk about," Carter laughed. "You slept with her last night."

"I guess I did, so?"

"You *guess* you did? You either *did* or you didn't."

"Why do you care, man? Are you into her?"

"I had sex with her Sunday morning, Sully."

"What?! No way. I had sex with her Saturday night after Skyler and Brenda left the house."

Carter shook his head and took a seat next to his brother. "Damn, dude. She's playing both of us. She's *fucking* both of us. Isn't that fucked up?" He paused for a moment. "It's fucked up, right?"

"Is it possible that she doesn't know *who* she's sleeping with?"

"No. *Right?* Come on. No. That's not possible."

"It's possible. We've encountered hundreds of people who can't tell which one of us is which, Carter. We have close relatives who still get confused. Even Darby mixes us up all the time."

"Crap. Maybe we do need time apart from each other."

Sullivan had thought about that, too, but he wasn't going to admit it. "I don't think we need to go that far. But I guess one or both of us should have a conversation with her about it."

"And what exactly are we going to say during this conversation? *Pick a Lowery brother, 'cause you can't have us both?*" Carter asked.

"*Could* she have us both?"

Carter suddenly stood up and took a step backward. His boot slipped on a pile of sawdust and he nearly toppled over. "What are you suggesting? That we share the opera singer?"

"We've shared girls before."

"One night stands when we were drunk out of our minds in high school and college. This isn't something sane, sober people do, man. Twins don't *share* a girlfriend. We're well known business men. She's an internationally known entertainer. What the hell does that do to our collective reputations when it gets out? No way. It's just too insane."

Sullivan waited for his brother to calm down. "Is it?"

"I'm heading back to the house. I'm exhausted and you've lost your mind." Carter grabbed his plans and headed toward the pre-function area, then started down the grand staircase that lead to the unfinished lobby. Sullivan was on his heels.

"Think about this," Sullivan said, placing a hand on Carter's shoulder when they reached the bottom of the stairs. "If we share a girlfriend, we each only have to spend 50% of the time with her. Half the money buying gifts and expensive dinners. Half the nights having someone hog the covers. *Half.* We've always shared everything."

Carter made a tight fist, pivoted, and punched his brother square in the jaw, sending him flying backward, off his feet. His body landed inside a wheelbarrow full of commercial electrical wiring. Sullivan was in shock. It was the very first time one of the twins purposely hit the other in order to inflict pain.

Carter shook his throbbing hand, turned on his heels, and headed out the service door and climbed into his rental car. He cried uncontrollably as he drove slowly down the alley toward the main road.

CHAPTER FIFTEEN

Early Wednesday morning, Skyler tiptoed into Georgia's kitchen and fished around in the cabinets and drawers for coffee pods for the Keurig machine. She would have preferred an old-fashioned pot of extra dark brew, but there was only the Keurig and it was too early for a Starbucks run.

Not that she'd be able to get out of the house on her own anyway. If it wasn't buttoned up tighter than Fort Knox before, the house certainly was so after all that went down in Santa Fe the afternoon before.

She'd hardly slept. Brenda had insisted that they share a bed on account of Georgia's apparent abduction, and the celebrity chef was a serious cover hog. That, and the fact that one or both of the dogs were on the bed at any given time throughout the night. Skyler was happy that she didn't have any fulltime animals of her own; Leonard was the only living thing she was interested in sharing a (*king sized*) bed with (and she was secretly happy when he gifted his old dog to a friend in Wabanaki before he moved to Washington with her).

And as if he could read her mind, her phone buzzed. It was Leonard.

"Did I call too early? I still can't get the time difference thing straight in my head," he said.

"It's 6:15 here. I just got out of bed and I think I'm the only one up. I'm on the hunt for coffee."

"I didn't see your texts until I got up this morning," he said. "How do you keep getting wrapped up in messes like this, Sky?"

Skyler finally found a stash of coffee pods and busied herself preparing the machine. "I don't know, Leonard. If it wasn't for Brenda, I think I'd be on the next flight to Maine. But Georgia is important to her and she feels an obligation to see this through. Whatever *this* is."

"Are the Mallard Protection people feeling like super dumbasses right about now?"

"Let's just say that they're none too happy. They spent hours with the local police yesterday and I understand that their boss— some guy named Archibald—is on his way to take control of the investigation. Well, the private one, anyway. And I think the F.B.I. might be on the case, too. They were here at Georgia's house for the bomb, anyway."

"Bombs and stalkers and opera singer abductions. Merry Christmas. Jesus Christ, honey."

"I know. But a very good thing came out of this trip, Leonard."

"And what's that?"

"I have a new client. Foster Martin officially asked me to head up the P.R. effort for his new journalism integrity foundation. It's going to be huge."

"Wow. That does sound huge. He's the television guy."

"Yeah. I think he may have *invented* the television set," she said. "He's in his early-nineties." Skyler could hear Leonard clicking away on his computer keyboard.

"Martin Media, is that it?"

"Yeah. Did you just Google him?"

"I did. He doesn't look 90."

"He doesn't, no," Skyler said. "He could easily pass for someone in his mid- to late-60's. He stays very active and he's wicked smart, too. I met him on the hiking path at the Four Seasons. But he may have been stalking me, come to think of it; Carissa suggested that he seek me out."

"It's a small world," Leonard said. "And now we are acquainted with superstar pop singers, billionaire businessmen, and celebrity chefs. Little ol' us."

"Well, to be fair, we've always known the celebrity chef."

"Yeah, but Brenda hasn't always been a celebrity chef."

"That is true." Skyler took a sip of coffee and nodded at a stone-faced Anna as she entered the kitchen. "Listen, honey, I need to run. Can we talk later?"

"Of course. There are still five days until Christmas, Skyler. Just remember that you can always leave the dangerous insanity of ol' Santa Fe and come join me here in the much less dangerous insanity of Wabanaki. I'd love for us to be together. And I'm sure Brenda would be able to manage without you."

"I'll give it some serious thought. Love you." She pressed 'end' and set the phone down on the counter. "Good morning."

"I'm not sure how good of a morning it is, ma'am," Anna said. The retired detective started her own cup of coffee and sat down at the breakfast bar. "John isn't talking to me unless it's absolutely necessary. I think he blames me for this whole thing."

"From how it was described to me," Skyler said, "it probably couldn't have been avoided. Brenda said that you checked the store thoroughly. The back door was bolted from the inside, right? Unless John or you were physically in the dressing room with Georgia—on top of her every waking moment—you two couldn't have prevented this. You can't blame yourselves."

"Thank you for trying to make me feel better. But Mallard has a top-notch reputation for V.I.P. protection. And we have failed miserably. We've never lost a client before. Well, we had one shot once, but we didn't lose track of him. And now our boss is forced to leave his family vacation in Aspen to come down here to clean up *our* mess. It's a disgrace. We'll be out of jobs come January." The woman sighed pitifully.

"You could still find Georgia and bring her home safely, Anna. The press doesn't have the story yet, as far as I know. That should protect Mallard's reputation and your jobs. Yes?"

"Maybe. We have a few leads we're going to follow up on today."

"And they are?"

Anna grabbed her mug and stood up. "We'll share the details later, if we can. I need to go see if John is ready."

When Skyler returned to her suite, she noticed that Brenda and the dogs had vacated her bed; presumably returning to their own room, since the perimeter alarm system was still activated.

She jumped in the shower then got ready for the day, dressed in dark skinny jeans, well-worn knee-high boots, and her favorite cashmere sweater. It was mint green and had been a Christmas present from Brenda the year before. It was thin, but warm; she absolutely hated bulky clothing, especially when she was working. She preferred layers that she could easily peel off as necessary.

After jotting off a few electronic missives to the troops regarding various ongoing projects, she realized that she hadn't decided on the holiday gifts. "Enzo works his ass off," she said out loud to herself, "and I'm the one who drops the ball. *Again.*" She rang his cell.

"I assumed you were just messing with me," he said when he answered. "Making me jump through hoops to earn my end of the year bonus?"

DAMN IT, Skyler screamed to herself. She hadn't remembered the staff, either!

"Listen, bucko," she said calmly. "I am still your boss and I don't appreciate the pushback. Things got really bad here last night, to say the very least, and Christmas gifts were the last thing on anyone's mind."

"Okay. Sorry. Really. I am sorry," a repentant-sounding Enzo said. "Is everything okay now?"

"It is not. But that doesn't mean Christmas won't come or that I don't want to keep the clients happy. Listen, I got your suggestions, I approve of them all, and I give you carte blanche to figure out how to secure the items and deliver them before Sunday. And when you finish that task, you may leave for the holiday and not look back until January 8th."

There was silence on the other end of the phone.

"Are you still there?"

"Yes, Skyler," he said slowly. "Are you telling me that you aren't changing a single thing on the list? You're even leaving in the Tiffany necklace for Carissa and the saddle bag for…"

"Everything, Enzo. You did an amazing job and I am learning to trust the capable people on my team, albeit slowly, I admit. But just make sure to sign *my* name to the card and not your own."

"Of course. And thank you."

Skyler pulled out her notebook and searched for a pen in her purse. "Where will you be for the holidays? It seems your bonus is going to be a bit delayed and I might have to send it next week."

"Cash, Skyler. Cash. I have everything else I need."

She threw the pen across the room. "Cash it is. Under the table though. If I wire it to you, you'll have to pay a ridiculously unfair tax rate on it."

"No, no," Enzo said, backtracking. "Please send it like you do the rest of my salary. I don't want anyone to get into any trouble."

"Oh, Enzo. Will you marry me?"

"I will not. I could probably sue you for sexual harassment for you even asking," he teased. "Is there anything else, boss?"

"Nope. Thanks for getting all of this done. I can manage on my own until we all get back together after the break."

"Good," he said, "because I'll be off the grid. I'm going to try a real holiday with no internet, no cell phone, and no social media. None of it. I'll be ice fishing with my father."

"Oh. Lovely. Well, you're a better man than I am," Skyler said. "I don't think I could be that unconnected for even a few hours. Merry Christmas, buddy. And thank you for all of your hard work this year. You really did hit it out of the park. You saved my ass many, many times."

"Thank you, that means a lot. Merry Christmas, Skyler. If there is an emergency, you can call my parent's house. That's where I'll be. The number is in my personnel file."

"That won't be necessary. Travel safe...and don't fall through the ice." Skyler ended the call and dropped the phone onto the mattress. She looked up and found Brenda standing in the doorway. "How are you able to appear out of thin air?"

"I don't really," Brenda said. "You just aren't very observant when you're busy with something. A one-track mind, I guess. I even made an extra effort to walk heavy so that I wouldn't scare you as I came down the hall."

"I've got Christmas presents squared away for my clients," Skyler said.

"Seriously? I took care of that back in August. Way to be on top of things, Ms. Public Relations Maven." Brenda lowered herself onto the edge of the unmade bed. "I think I liked having daily maid service at the resort."

"And I liked not spending the Christmas holidays in a prison. Brenda, what are we going do about this mess?"

"We will help the authorities and the ex-detectives out there in the other room find the missing opera singer, I suppose. Georgia and I aren't as close as you and I are, of course, but she's become a good friend to me. I instantly felt a connection with that woman. And now that we're here and a part of all of this, I think we have to stick it out. Or at least, I need to stay."

"I'm not going anywhere," Skyler said, rising to her feet. "I just wish Leonard was here. I'd feel better."

"Of course, *you'd* feel better," Brenda said with a sly grin.

"Stop!"

"I just spoke to John in the front hall. He and a cop are going to pay a visit to that Diego fellow."

"The poor construction guy who almost got his head shot off the other day? Diego isn't involved in this."

"How can you say such a thing?" Brenda spit. "He's literally the only lead these people have. Besides the twins and a few people associated with the opera house, he's essentially the only other person who has had any contact with her since she got to Santa Fe. He's an established fan of hers and he had access to the house. He may have even been the guy in the woods when we were in the hot tub, Skyler. I'm beginning to think he isn't just some innocent, small town *construction guy.*"

Skyler kneeled down and started rubbing Mulder behind an ear. Scully was instantly jealous and began poking her head in. "You watch too many procedural dramas on television. It most certainly isn't as easy as all that. The F.B.I. talked to him after the bombing. He was cleared."

"Well, then I don't know."

"I do," Skyler said sharply. She stood straight up and brushed her dog hair-covered hands off onto her jeans. "It's Massimo."

Brenda shook her head. "He's in Italy."

"Is he, Brenda? How do we know that he's not still in Santa Fe? The only person who has ever told us that he was in Italy, was Georgia."

"Oh…my…goodness," Brenda said slowly.

"Right."

"Where do we start? Do we tell John? Or the police?"

Skyler pondered that question for a moment. "Since their track record is rather questionable up until now, perhaps we should just look into this ourselves."

"We're not Cagney & Lacey."

"That's funny, because just the other night I was thinking about that Halloween we dressed as them. Do you remember that?"

"Do you remember that time I told you how much I hate when people bring up shit that two people did in the past and then ask, *do you remember that?*"

Skyler's face crinkled up. "You are being a royal *bitch* today."

"Jesus Christ, Skyler!" Brenda erupted.

"What? I'm sorry."

"No, honey, it's not you." She struggled to pull her cell phone out of her pants pocket. "We never told the twins about Georgia's abduction. They are going to be beside themselves!"

"Absolutely. Well, I know what you should say. Tell them it *just* happened."

"Have you lost your mind?" Brenda pressed a few buttons and lifted the phone to her ear. "Now you shhhhush. I have to think fast."

"Cry, if you can," Skyler whispered. "That always helps."

"It doesn't matter anyway," Brenda said after a moment, dropping her phone onto the bed. "It went straight to voicemail. I think we need to make a quick trip to the hotel to see them in person."

"Can we get out of this house?"

"I'm sure we'll figure it out."

CHAPTER SIXTEEN

The Santa Fe Opera Theater and the wide, sprawling grounds on which is stood was admired around the world by opera-goers and revered by orchestras and performers. Positioned next to a cliff with views of the Jemez and Sangre de Cristo Mountains and surrounding valleys, the open-air structure had won prestigious design awards attracting not just the usual monied, cultured 'elite,' but regular folks, too. During the summer, three productions were typically done in reparatory, so that visitors could come to Santa Fe once and see all of the season's shows in a three day stretch. And many did just that.

The rest of the year, there were a small smattering of administrative and grounds people working on the 150-acre compound, but late in December, the 'opera ranch,' as it was commonly referred to, was a virtual ghost town.

Miss Georgia Kennedy Reece, celebrated soprano who sang for kings and presidents and opera lovers worldwide, was not scheduled to perform at the Santa Fe Opera for many months. But she was in a darkened orchestra hall rehearsal room nevertheless, sitting on the floor in the corner, wearing yesterday's slacks, knee high socks, and a bra. She was tired, cold, hungry, and terrified. She didn't know what had become of her shoes.

And she was afraid this was going to end badly.

Massimo was in constant motion, moving in and out of the rehearsal room, agitated, in the middle of a long, passionate argument with himself. Periodically he'd stop and look at her with an expression of surprise, as if he'd just noticed her for the first time. During those moments of recognition, he'd include her in the argument and declare, "*I made you. I gave you everything. You are selfish and mean and ungrateful woman. Why do you do this to me? Why have you torn down everything we have built together?*" And then he'd scream, '*figlio di troia!*' Georgia didn't understand: she wasn't anyone's *son* and Massimo had never met her mother, who had been the furthest thing from a *bitch* as one could get.

She had been with him for a full day now. He'd given her no food or water. Every once in a while, he'd leave off his ranting, charge into the bathroom, and emerge after a few moments with water drops around his mouth and chin. She hadn't seen him eat. They were both running on fumes. The windowless room and lack of a clock, her watch, or a phone made time disappear. She guessed that it was Wednesday afternoon, but she couldn't be certain.

Massimo reentered the room, seemingly calm, and lowered himself into a crossed leg seated position a few yards away from her. He held a small grey handgun in one hand and rested his chin on the other. His hair was matted with sweat, despite the chill in the unheated room.

"What do we do now?" he asked quietly. It sounded to Georgia as is Massimo genuinely wanted an answer.

"I think you should dispose of that gun and get in that little car of yours and drive yourself down to the Santa Fe Police Department and turn yourself in." She shook hair out of her face and examined his reaction. It was slow in showing itself.

"You know I'm not going to do that," he said. "They'd lock me away for a very long time."

"What do you want to do?"

"I don't know."

"There has to be a plan, Massimo," Georgia said. She was growing angrier as the seconds passed and it was beginning to get the better of her. "You were always good with plans. You made all the rules. You made all the decisions."

"It was *you* who decided to end our relationship. You!"

"Our sexual relationship? Is that what you are referring to? Sure, I did. It wasn't healthy for either of us. You are a married man, if I must remind you for the thousandth time. It was a dumb mistake on both of our parts. You originally agreed with me on that, did you not?" She didn't wait for an answer. "*You did.*"

"My marriage is one on paper only at this point," he said. He scratched his forehead with the barrel of the gun.

"Oh my God, Massimo," Georgia exploded. "Don't do that."

"Relax," he said, dismissively. "It's not loaded."

The admission ricocheted through her consciousness in an instant. She threw herself forward and knocked him backwards. The gun flew out of his hand and skidded across the carpeted floor. His head hit the thick wooden leg of a table. "What are you doing, you crazy woman?!" he screamed.

She was kneeling on him, trying to pin his hands down. She screamed out all of the terror and anger of the past day, the past week, right into his sweaty face. "Asshole! Fucking asshole! Asshole!"

Without much straining, he twisted his body and hurled the singer to the floor. When he stood up suddenly, he swayed left and right, and Georgia thought for a moment that he might pass out. "Jesus Christ," he whispered.

Georgia rolled her body and struggled to her feet. She started toward the closed door leading to the hallway when she felt his hands—large, deadly, rough—wrap around her throat from behind. Because he was holding onto her hair, too, he couldn't get a tight grip, and she managed to squirm away from him. She turned and kicked him as hard as she could in the groin, sending him back down to the floor, doubled over in pain.

She could hear him screaming out in Italian as she ripped open the door and ran down the hall, rounded a corner and took the stairs, two risers at a time, up to the ground level. She'd only been in the building briefly before this, but she had amazing retention—*how else does one memorize dozens of three-hour long operas in a foreign language and never forget a single word?*—and knew exactly where to go. As she rounded another corner she had the exterior door in sight. She paused to rip a window curtain from its rod and wrapped the fabric around her shoulders then rocketed into the bitter cold daylight.

"Help me!" she screamed out. "Someone! Please!"

Nothing. No one for miles. She didn't scream again. No one could hear her, and she didn't want Massimo to follow her voice.

She jogged along the path toward the main parking lot, hoping she'd come across a security patrol or *anyone* left on the property. But there wasn't a single vehicle to be seen. She didn't even know where Massimo's rental was, not that she had the keys. A sudden memory came to her of a desperate woman on some television show, hotwiring a car, but she bitterly dismissed it. Sure, it looked easy on T.V. and in the movies, but she wouldn't even know how to begin to do that.

"There's no car to steal," she told herself out loud. She was near delusional and her heart was racing inside her chest. She couldn't focus, her thoughts were all over the place. She wondered if anyone was looking for her. She decided she'd ask Mallard Protection for her money back. She thought about her mother, and Christmas, and the Lowery twins. She wondered which of the brothers would come to her rescue.

Sullivan.

No, Carter. Yes, Carter. It should be Carter.

Damn! What am I doing?

Either one. Both! Who cares?!

I don't have time for this.

Crouched down between a large tree and a thicket of bushes, she tried unsuccessfully to collect her thoughts and focus on…

She heard a sharp, loud crack and was immediately overcome with pain, but she couldn't identify where it was coming from or how it happened. And then she blacked out.

CHAPTER SEVENTEEN

Brenda dreaded telling her new business partners about Georgia's abduction. She was already distraught about not including them the day before. She nervously chewed the inside of her cheek on the walk from a parking spot on the street to the hotel two blocks away, Skyler leading the way.

When they got to the hotel they found it deathly quiet inside. The twins were side by side, leaning over a table, heads almost touching, looking at blueprints.

"Did you send the crew home for holiday break already?" Skyler asked. She took off her coat and placed it together with her purse on the cleanest part of the desk she could find.

"No," a clearly exasperated Sullivan said. "It's lunch. They take a full 90 minutes here. I have no idea where in hell they go."

Skyler looked at Sullivan's face for the first time and her eyes widened. "What happened to *your* face?"

Sullivan absently touched his sore black eye. "Just a little construction accident. I'm fine."

"It looks horrible, honey."

"He's fine," Carter said flatly.

"I'm fine," Sullivan said. "What's going on?"

Brenda cleared her throat and wrapped her arms around her body and hugged herself. "I have some bad news, boys. I'm going to just come out and say it. Georgia…she…Georgia has been kidnapped."

"We don't know that," Skyler quickly added. "She *is* missing though. She disappeared late yesterday afternoon."

"What?" Carter looked bewildered. "I don't think I heard you correctly. What are you talking about—*yesterday afternoon?* Why are we just hearing about this?!"

Sullivan grabbed the back of a folding chair to steady himself. "I knew this was going to happen. I knew she wasn't safe. How could we have left her alone?"

"She wasn't alone," Skyler said. "She had Brenda and two highly regarded, former New York City detectives watching out for her."

The twins turned their outraged faces to Brenda. "No. No. Do *not* blame me," she said. "I wasn't hired to keep her safe. She walked right out of the back door of a dress shop and those useless Mallard people just let it happen."

"She didn't just saunter out the back door, Brenda," Skyler said. She turned to Carter. "Georgia disappeared, leaving behind her coat, shirt, and purse. It was freezing outside. We have to believe that someone must have forced her out of that dressing room and into the alley. She wouldn't have left with just a bra on. And without her phone, for goodness sake."

"What are the police doing about this?" Sullivan asked.

"As far as we know, nothing. Not yet." Skyler brushed sawdust off the top of a cooler and sat down. "The F.B.I. is involved. I mean, they were notified. But they're not moving on it yet. No demands have been made, and it hasn't been 48 hours yet."

"We have to wait 48 hours before someone will take this

seriously?" Carter exploded. "First someone breaks into the poor woman's house and trashes the place, then someone sets off a bomb at the Christmas party, and someone stalks all of us from the woods near our house. I mean, honestly. Must I go on? There's a pattern here. That woman is in serious jeopardy."

"Skyler has a theory," Brenda said calmly.

"It's not a theory, really. But I have to wonder, did Massimo really leave the country? He hit her, for God's sake. He was terrorizing her with that bogus contract. Manipulating and using her to line his own pockets for decades, according to Georgia. Massimo was devastated and very, very angry when she fired him. She was his bread and butter. His only income, as far as we know. Maybe this is some sort of revenge."

The unfinished hotel lobby fell silent as it all sank in. The only sound they could hear was each other's breathing, until the front door slammed shut, startling them all.

"I am so sorry, folks," Matteo said. "The wind got ahold of it."

"Skyler, this is Matteo Ferrera, our contractor," Sullivan managed to say. "Matteo, Skyler Moore. She's a friend of Brenda's."

"How do you do?" Skyler said.

"I do very well, and yourself?"

"I am much better now, because I just thought of something." She turned to the twins, "You two have been to Milan to see Georgia perform, yes?"

"We have. About two years ago," Carter said. "So?"

"Did you not visit Massimo's home and meet his wife and children? Isn't that where Georgia stayed when she was performing there?"

Sullivan brightened. "That's right. And his wife's name was Ava. She spoke both Italian and fluent English. She studied art history and English at N.Y.U., as I recall. She founded and directs a very successful Milanese art gallery now. She took us on a private afterhours tour and..."

"Christ almighty, Sully! Focus on what Skyler's saying," Carter erupted.

"Call Ava right this minute," Skyler said. She looked at her watch. "It's midnight there. She'll still be up. Sophisticated Italians eat late and stay up late, no?"

"Yes," Brenda said. "Skyler, you are a very smart biscotto."

"Well, we'll see about that."

Matteo looked puzzled. "I am so confused."

After an exhaustive search, and with the help of the twin's assistant back in New York, Sullivan finally got his hands on a phone number. With the group crowded around him, he entered the digits into his cell.

"Pronto."

"Ava Modena, please," Sullivan said. He pressed the speaker button and held the phone in the middle of the tight circle.

"This is Ava. Who is this? Do you have any idea what time it is, sir?"

"Ava, this is Sullivan Lowery. We met a few years ago in Milan when my brother and I came over from America to see Georgia Reece perform at the opera house. I apologize for telephoning you so late."

"Sullivan, yes, of course I remember you. Who's dead?"

"Excuse me?"

"Someone must be dead or you wouldn't be calling me at

this hour. Where are you? New York?"

"No, I'm in Santa Fe, New Mexico."

"Massimo is dead, isn't he? *Dannazione*! Is this why you are telephoning me?"

Brenda gasped and Skyler hit her on the arm.

"I don't believe anyone is dead, Ava. I was calling to see if Massimo was in Milan with you."

There was silence on the other end.

"Ava?"

"Massimo is spending Christmas there in Santa Fe. Surely you must know this since you are friends with Georgia. He said it couldn't be helped. He said he wanted to be there for Georgia's surgery. Is that why you are there, too? I must tell you, the children are heartbroken not to have their father here for Christmas." More silence. "Sullivan? Is Georgia having vocal surgery this week in Santa Fe? Massimo said the best vocal surgeon in the world practices there."

Sullivan quickly scanned the faces around him. His brother slowly shook his head and closed his eyes.

"No, Ava. There is no surgery. And she is not sick, as far as I know. But Georgia *is* unaccounted for. She disappeared yesterday after several attempts were made on her life this week. We are very concerned."

"Jesus. Where is my husband?

"Soon to be *ex*-husband," Brenda mouthed.

"That's why I am calling you," Sullivan continued. "He told Georgia that he was flying home to Milan. He supposedly did that several days ago. He hasn't been seen in Santa Fe since Sunday."

More silence. Then, they heard a long sigh. "I don't want to sound unsympathetic, but I must get back to bed. I have a very early morning tomorrow. Massimo is not in Italy, Mr. Lowery. And as far as I am concerned, he can stay in Santa Fe for the rest of his revolting life." And she terminated the call on her end.

"Holy crap," Brenda said.

"What now?" Carter asked.

"Well, we find Massimo and I suspect we'll find Georgia," Skyler said. "The Mallard people are at Georgia's house. And John and Anna's boss is due to arrive this afternoon. Let's go tell them what we know."

"Perhaps they can convince the police to track Massimo's phone somehow. That'd be a good place to start, right?" Sullivan asked. "They can run a check on his passport, too."

"It's the only thing we've got so far. It's worth a try." Skyler grabbed her coat and the group headed to the door leaving Matteo standing alone in the unfinished hotel lobby, quite literally confused.

* * *

Mallard Protection's Challenger 604—recently purchased from an Oscar-winning client who traded up to a new Gulfstream—touched down at the Santa Fe Regional Airport and taxied to Advanced Aviation, the fixed-base operator that serviced private aircraft. After the engines were shut down, the cabin door was lowered, and handrails were locked into place by the co-pilot, Archibald Grey and three of his favorite, biggest bodyguards descended to the tarmac and piled into a dark blue Ford Expedition. The engine was idling and the interior was pleasantly heated.

Within minutes, they were traveling north-east on Route 599 towards Georgia Reece's house with Archie at the wheel, controlled and steady, weaving expertly around cars and trucks at perilous speeds. He'd never before set foot in the state of New Mexico, but he did not trust G.P.S. navigation systems—one had failed him once when he got misdirected while transferring a very high-level V.I.P. client, and he vowed never to reply on the technology again. Instead, he studied Santa Fe-area street maps on the 45-minute flight from Aspen, committing his intended route to memory. It helped to pass the time and it got his mind off the fact that he was furious to be missing valuable snow skiing time with his wife and children—the entire family was only together a precious few days now that the kids were done with school and his wife refused to give up her job as a United Airlines flight attendant, despite the fact that they had more money than they knew what to do with—not to mention the cost of operating the jet and paying holiday double-time pay.

When they approached Georgia's front gate, Archie lowered the driver's side window and pressed the 'call' button. He identified himself and within seconds the gate swung open. He drove through and then immediately stopped the car. In the rearview mirror, he watched as the gate swung closed again before continuing up the driveway to the large house—it was a habit he tried to instill in all of his employees and clients. "Never take anything for granted," he reminded the men in the car. "The time you don't wait, the gate won't close and someone will slip in behind you."

John Sparks was standing alone in the driveway near the front porch. His hands were clutched together and he nervously shifted his weight. "Welcome to Santa Fe, boss," he said sheepishly.

Archie got out of the S.U.V. and stared down the man he used to consider one of Mallard's finest employees. "What. The. Living. Hell?"

"I am *so sorry* to drag you down here. Anna and I are absolutely horrified with ourselves and we won't blame you if you decide to let us..."

"That's enough, John." He started walking toward the front door and the ex-policeman hurried to keep up. "What's new since we last spoke?" Two of the bodyguards instinctively followed; the third was already out in front, opening the door. "Guys, do your thing," Archie said to the bodyguards. They each took off in a different direction.

"What are they going to do?" John asked as he closed the front door and offered to take his boss' coat.

"They're going to assess this house and report back to me. Is there anyone else in the home who should be warned that I'm here to take over?"

"Just me at the moment," Anna said as she entered the room from the kitchen. "Hello, Mr. Grey."

"Anna."

"Miss Reece has two houseguests, as well as one of the guest's two large dogs. They're out back. The dogs, not the ladies. The ladies are downtown, but they should be back shortly."

"Remind me who these guests are."

"Brenda Braxton of New York City. She's a well-known chef and restaurant owner. And Skyler Moore. She does public relations based out of Washington, D.C. They were here in Santa Fe for the holidays, were invited guests at Miss Reece's Christmas party this past weekend, and they have become very friendly with Miss Reece this past week."

Archie took a seat on the living room sofa. "Who else has been in Georgia's world since she moved to town?"

John cleared his throat and took a seat opposite his boss. "The hotel developers Carter and Sullivan Lowery. They are twin brothers and they are roughly the same age as Miss Reece. They are here in Santa Fe building a new property down near the Plaza. Franklin-Lowery is the name of the hotel."

"I know it well, John," Archie said. "There's one across the street from our offices in New York. Go on."

"By all accounts, the twins are very close friends with Miss Reece. I assume they became acquainted back in the city. And then there's Miss Reece's agent, an Italian citizen named Massimo Modena who..."

"Who we believe is still here in Santa Fe!" Brenda said as she bounded into the living room.

Archibald got to his feet and greeted Brenda, who was followed into the house by Skyler, Carter, and Sullivan.

"Miss Braxton," Archie said, "Why should we be concerned that Miss Reece's agent might still be in Santa Fe?"

Skyler stepped forward. "Because Massimo physically attacked Georgia last weekend. She filed a police report. She fired him as her agent. And as far as we were all aware at the time, he left the United States and flew home to Milan, Italy."

"When did he supposedly leave Santa Fe?" Archie asked.

"Saturday. But his wife says that he did not return to Italy," Sullivan said. He then told Archibald, John, and Anna all about the phone call with Ana.

"Suspect number one, fellas," Carter said. "We just have to find him and we'll find Georgia."

Archie made some scratchings in a small notebook. He turned to Anna, "Call Berta back in New York and get her to check all the possible ways this Massimo fellow could fly commercial from Santa Fe—or Albuquerque, for that matter— to Milan or nearby international airports in Italy on December 16th. My guess is that he couldn't have possibly arrived there until December 17th, at the earliest, given the time difference. Have her check all the passenger manifests. If anyone can find out if he flew to Italy, she can."

Anna nodded and left the room.

Archie turned back to the twins. "Does Massimo have the means to fly private?"

Carter and Sullivan exchanged looks. "I don't think so," Carter said. Sullivan agreed. "Georgia is comfortable, but not private jet comfortable. And Massimo took a cut. She was his only client."

"Too *large* of a cut," Brenda added. "He was ripping her off."

"Explain," Archie said.

Carter let out air. "Georgia told me that Massimo was taking 40%. He was robbing her blind. She was very unhappy about it."

"Yet she stayed with him for twenty years," Sullivan said. "Why?"

"Besides the guests and service people who were here for the party last Friday," Archie said, "Is there anyone else who has been in this house in the last week? Who fixed the damage from the bomb blast?"

"Diego Ferrera," Skyler said. "He's a very sweet local fellow. He was brought in after the original break-in to fix that plate glass window over there and then he came back to fix the wall on Monday. He was referred by the responding officer. Diego is the police officer's brother-in-law."

"And Diego is the brother of Matteo, the contractor who is overseeing the construction of our new hotel," Sullivan added.

Archie's eyebrows rose.

"Welcome to Santa Fe," Brenda said. "It's a very small town."

"Apparently."

CHAPTER EIGHTEEN

She was awake for a few moments before she was able to open her eyes—they just weren't cooperating. The throbbing in her head was constant and overpowering, and the rest of her body wasn't faring much better. Her legs felt like jelly, her torso sore. And her stomach was magnificently empty. She was aware that she was in some sort of enclosed space. She heard birds singing in the distance, but it was muffled. She seemed to be lying on some sort of upholstered surface. Her fingers traced the edge and then her right arm dropped down and she felt tight, thin carpet. And a coin.

When she finally willed her eyelids to open, she was staring up at the fabric covered roof of a car. She was alone in the back seat. There was a dim light outside. *Early morning or late evening*, she decided. She had no idea which. She'd lost all track of time, date, and place.

After a few long minutes of listening to her own labored breath, she sat up and slowly swung her legs to the floor. Blood rushed to, or out of, her head—she wasn't sure which—and she nearly blacked out again, but she was determined to stay conscious. The car was sitting to the right side of a single lane dirt road with thick groves of trees on both sides. She checked the ignition; no keys. There was a large McDonald's cup in the center console. Dehydrated, she took a sip from the straw without checking to see what was inside. It was relatively cold and virtually flavorless—day old, unsweetened iced tea, she surmised. She finished the beverage then searched the rest of the car, desperately trying to ignore the pain that seared through her body. All she found was a rental agreement from Avis. She opened it and saw that the car had been leased to Massimo a week earlier.

Had he run out of gas? Was he taking a leak in the woods? Would he be returning any moment? Did he get cold feet and abandon her? Georgia Reece was stunned and wounded but alive, and thankful for another chance to escape.

She scanned the perimeter and saw no sign of life, save a large black bird pecking at a small dead animal a few yards in front of the car. Wrapping the opera house window curtain around her, she opened the back door of the sedan and climbed out onto the dirt road. Startled, the black bird flew away and she was utterly alone. Shoeless, shirtless, lost, and utterly alone. But she was determined to save herself and see Massimo pay for what he had done.

It took a few long minutes, but she finally decided to go back the way the car had apparently come from, instead of going forward. She didn't know why, but it seemed the right thing to do. She began to walk, alternating between scanning her surroundings and looking down at the road just ahead of her numb, bare feet, in order to avoid stepping on rocks and twigs and other obstacles. Her mind wandered between the growing fear that Massimo would pop out of the woods, or appear around the next bend in the road at any moment, to her pain, her hunger, the cold winter wind that was picking up, her mother's ashes, her cozy new Santa Fe fireplace, her vintage Christmas ornaments back in New York City (where she wished she'd stayed), the lyrics to her favorite Italian opera, Sully's penis...or was it Carter's?

Are they different?

She walked for nearly an hour, she estimated, and it was now clear that the sun was setting instead of rising, somewhere behind the thick clouds that had rolled in. In another half hour, she'd be walking in the pitch-black December night. And that made her start thinking about coyotes and the inevitable newspaper headlines:

```
Internationally Acclaimed Opera Diva Found
Dead, Eaten by Coyotes in New Mexican Desert

A Pack of Wild New Mexican Coyotes Devour the
Once Breathtakingly Beautiful Face of Opera
Singer Georgia Reece

Renowned Soprano Georgia Reece's Throat Mangled
and Her Shirt and Shoes Stolen by Rabid Coyotes
Near Santa Fe, N.M.; Entertainment World
Mourns; Flags to be Flown at Half Staff,
President Orders
```

Georgia Reece may have been rightfully delirious, but she was wrong about two things; she wouldn't be eaten by coyotes that night...and she wasn't in New Mexico.

* * *

A command center had been set up in Georgia's dining room. Fitted with a laptop, tablet, cell phone, and the most high-tech headset money could buy, Archibald Grey worked every possibility as fast as he could. He had two of his men canvasing the downtown retail area in a fruitless search for surveillance video that may have captured Georgia's abductor and the getaway vehicle, if there was one. But most Santa Fe businesses didn't feel the need for the extra expense of security cameras; companies in larger cities and towns were apt to spend money on those.

Despite coming up empty-handed at every turn, Archie's team reported back regularly.

The third Mallard employee was at the police station filing the official missing persons report in order to get the much-needed, now official—since it had been two days since she had gone missing—attention from the authorities. Up until now, the police claimed their hands were tied despite the Christmas party bombing and Georgia's ongoing harassment. Archie saw it as a rinky-dink, small town law enforcement cluster-fuck, and it made him frustrated beyond belief.

And still blaming themselves, John and Anna were trying to track down and speak to every single person, save for the Governor, who had been inside Georgia's home since she purchased the house in early-December. This, too, was an arduous task, as many folks had left the state for the holidays.

Christmas Eve was a mere three days away, a fact that wasn't lost on any of the Mallard team members; each wished they could locate Georgia and hightail it home. That prospect was unlikely though, and Archie, for one, feared this job could be the straw that finally broke his precarious marriage apart. His wife was furious about his absence and was texting her displeasure nearly nonstop; the distraction messing with the security man's typical laser-focused concentration on the pressing matter at hand.

"Can I get you anything?" Brenda asked Archie. "Coffee? Something else? Have you eaten anything today?"

Archie considered the celebrity chef's offer for a moment— he almost opened his mouth to order a glass of whiskey, but instead said, "You are too kind, Ms. Braxton. I'm fine, though, really. You shouldn't trouble yourself with us."

"Alright," she said, "but the kitchen is very well stocked. Please help yourself."

Brenda padded off to her suite, took a few moments to pet Mulder and Scully, then sat down on the loveseat with her cell phone. She found the contact information for Leonard Little and initiated a video call. It was nearly 10 o'clock on the east coast, but she suspected he'd still be awake.

"Wow," he said when he picked up. "I don't think you've ever FaceTimed me before. Is everything okay?"

"My goodness, that beard! I've never seen you with facial hair. What brought this on?"

"Laziness. And it keeps my face warm. It's friggin' cold here, Brenda. One of the coldest on record, they're saying on the news. Global warming, my ass." He lit a cigarette.

"A beard *and* you're smoking again. Skyler would not be happy with either."

Leonard exhaled a cloud of smoke and leaned in close to the camera. "What she doesn't know won't kill her. Keep your mouth shut, woman."

"Listen," Brenda said, "I'm calling because I have an idea. My Christmas present to Skyler."

"Shit, I haven't sent her anything yet. What do you have planned? Not that I could match it."

"Shave off that muddled mess of hair, ditch the nasty cigarettes, and pack your bags. I want to wrap you up and deliver you to your girlfriend as a holiday surprise. Game?"

His eyes widened and his mouth slipped open. "Brenda. I've flown three times in my entire life. The flight up here, all by myself...that one almost killed me. I'm not sure I'm up for it again. Or ever, for that matter."

"You are the biggest baby I know, Lenny," Brenda said. "And it's not like I'm going to subject you to a commercial flight, or anything. I'm sending a private jet. Can you be at Advanced Aviation at nine o'clock tomorrow morning? At the Portland Jetport?"

He took a long drag on the cigarette and then stubbed it out. As he exhaled, he said, "I guess Wabanaki can deal without their temporary sheriff for a few days. Porter Maddox should be able to keep things in check. And I guess if I have to fly, a private jet would soften the blow a bit."

"Well, if you crash in a Gulfstream or a commercial 757, I still think you die either way."

"What is wrong with you?! I thought you were trying to convince me to come."

"While you're packing your suitcase, make sure to locate your balls, okay? You are a police officer, Leonard Little. Jesus Christ."

"Alright," he said like a defensive little boy talking back to his mother, "Just shut up about planes crashing. I'll come, I'll come."

"Perfect. Skyler is going to be thrilled. And, Leonard, I think we'd both feel better having you around. This place is on high alert. And there's still no sign of Georgia."

"I really don't know why you haven't cut and run. Let the authorities deal with it."

"That's the point," Brenda said. "They *aren't* dealing with it. They aren't equipped for kidnappings around these parts."

"Sounds familiar."

"Right? Plus, with the Mallard Protection folks here, maybe you can learn a thing or two. Skyler told me that you're interested in that field of work."

"I'd like that, maybe. Maybe not. I Googled that Archibald fellow after I talked to Skyler. He does a lot of work in and out of New York City. But he's not the best of the best, you know. He's had more than a few negative stories written about his outfit. Has a pending lawsuit or two. And he just comes across as an arrogant bully—on paper anyway."

"Geez. I didn't know all of that, no. And to tell you the truth, he and his crew are coming up empty while trying to locate Georgia. So maybe you don't want to emulate all of that."

"This is all very scary."

Brenda stood up and walked over to the window. "Okay. So, you'll come here? Good. I'm very happy. Bring your gun, okay?"

Leonard lit another cigarette. "Can I fly with a gun?"

"When you're flying private? Sure. Just alert the pilots. They'll probably have to lock it away for the flight though. Be ready for that. You're a police officer with a conceal-carry permit. You should be fine."

"Why do you know more about this shit than I do?"

"I've been around the block more than a few times and I haven't spent my entire life in Wabanaki, Maine. I'll see you tomorrow, honey. And for God's sake, go buy some Nicorette gum before you get on that plane."

"Yeah, yeah. How will I find you guys after I land?" Leonard asked.

Brenda smiled. "We'll find you, Lenny. Fly safe." And with that, she disengaged the video call before he could scold her for using the much-hated nickname again. It tickled her to tease him.

In her own suite, Skyler was wrapping a present she intended to overnight to Leonard the following day. She was seriously conflicted about focusing on Christmas revelry and tradition while Georgia was still missing, but at the same time, was secretly miffed that she was embroiled in the drama during one of her favorite holidays. *Again.*

She was still incredibly wounded from losing one of her lifelong best friends over the Independence Day holiday six months earlier. There were many times Skyler would actually pick up the phone to call or text Tanner Millhouse, only to suddenly remember that he was very dead. And it was Tanner who took Leonard's father with him, too, so she shared that loss with her boyfriend on a daily basis. They didn't talk about it often, but she knew that Leonard was still brokenhearted over the death of his father, the former sheriff of Wabanaki. Theirs was a complicated father-son relationship, she understood, crowded with the pains of a nasty divorce, various family members' deaths, and general parental disappointment, but love seemed to seep through the many cracks just enough to hold them together. It hadn't helped that Leonard's father was also his boss for so many years. It was strained, but there was love there.

Skyler's cell phone vibrated and the screen came to life, indicating that Foster Martin was calling from his personal number. She cleared her throat and stood up before answering the call.

"Foster! How are you this evening?"

"I am well, Miss Skyler Moore," he said. "I apologize for disturbing you at this late hour, but I wanted to let you know that I am leaving Santa Fe tomorrow, a few days earlier than I had originally planned."

"Oh, okay," she said. "I thought it was a tradition of yours to be here for Christmas."

"That was the plan, yes, but my plans change frequently. A very good friend of mine is having a big Christmas Eve party at her house in Maui. She's an honest to goodness Hawaiian Princess. Did you know that the island has its own royal lineage?"

"I guess I did not know that, no sir," Skyler said.

"Well it does, and she is quite the entertainer. The Princess has insisted that I come and since I am all by myself, I'm going to go, gosh darnit."

"Good for you. It will be wonderful to be around friends for Christmas."

"Will you come with me? I am sure she'd be more than happy to host you, too. She has the most amazing house right on the ocean and there are at least a dozen guest rooms. It's beautiful there this time of year, I'll tell you that. Not nearly as chilly as New Mexico."

Skyler laughed politely. "That's very kind of you, Foster. But I think I better stay here with my friends. And we're down one at the moment. Georgia Reece has gone missing."

"The opera singer? Missing?"

"Yes sir," Skyler said, immediately sorry that she'd brought it up. She gave him the short version of the complicated story.

"For heaven's sake," he said when she was done. "Well then, it sounds like this is where you should be right now. But I wonder if you'd agree to come meet me at my airplane tomorrow morning before I take off? I have some foundation documents that I want to give to you before I go—I believe I told you that I'm not a fan of sending sensitive things by email and fax and such. I just need a few moments of your time."

It was like the ultimate Christmas present and he didn't even know he was offering it up on a silver platter. Getting the chance to climb aboard Foster's jet—purportedly one of the most expensive custom-built private planes on the planet—would be the self-proclaimed plane nut's dream come true. She agreed without a second's thought. "Absolutely. What time should I be there?"

"I'm taking off from S.A.F. at Noon on the dot. Shall we meet at half past eleven? The bird is tied down at Advanced Aviation. I suspect you won't be able to miss her."

"I have no doubt about that," Skyler said. "I'll see you tomorrow at 11:30, Foster. Good night."

She finished up her present wrapping, filled out a sappy-sweet card to Leonard, then set out to find Brenda. Skyler had wine on the brain and she intended to suggest that they get a large amount inside themselves just as soon as humanly possible.

CHAPTER NINETEEN

After nearly getting shot at Georgia's house, Diego Ferrera was laying low and staying off the grid for a few days, but agreed to show up at the Franklin-Lowery construction site to assist his brother with an electrical problem. It was late, and the entire crew was gone for the day, but Matteo and Diego soldiered on; Matteo was determined to stay on schedule to avoid the wrath of Carter Lowery. The construction foreman wasn't fond of bringing his brother in on his projects given their powerful sibling rivalry, but Matteo was desperate. The main electrical panel wasn't operating at capacity—every time the central heating system switched on, the entire building went dark—and Diego had an uncanny knack for fixing such things.

They worked in silence until they heard a loud banging sound coming from the ground floor directly above them. Matteo left his brother to work while he investigated. With a large flashlight in hand, he made his way up the service stairs, through the lobby, and then cautiously approached the large floor-to-ceiling glass doors that led to the street. Two imposing white men stood on the other side.

"Can I help you?" Matteo shouted through the glass.

"We're looking for Diego Ferrera," Archibald Grey said. "Is that you?"

"Who wants to know?"

"Can you open the door so that I don't have to scream?"

It was late and he obviously wasn't thinking clearly—Matteo unlocked the door and let the men inside.

"Are you Diego Ferrera?" Archie asked again, skipping the pleasantries.

"I am not," Matteo said. "Who are you, sir?"

Archie sighed and fished into his blazer pocket for a business card. He handed it over. "Archibald Grey with Mallard Protection. I was hired by Georgia Reece."

Matteo took the card and examined it with the use of his flashlight. At that very moment, the electricity was restored and the construction lights flickered on above them. "Good job, gentlemen," Matteo said, as he pocketed the card. "I was told by Ms. Reece's houseguests that you lost her and that she still hasn't been located."

"What did you say?!" A shocked Diego stood in the doorway between the lobby and the service stairs.

"Are you Diego Ferrera?" Archie asked.

"I am," he said as he joined the group. "What is this about Georgia Reece? She's missing?" The handyman looked confused.

Archibald Grey's expression said he didn't believe Diego for a second. "Come on. Save yourself and everyone else a lot of trouble. Just between us, right here and now. What do you know about Georgia Reece's whereabouts?"

"Excuse me, sir," Matteo interjected. "What exactly are you implying? That my brother is somehow involved? That's ludicrous. He's done nothing but come to the aid of that woman since she showed up in this town."

"She's missing?" Diego repeated. "I don't understand. What does that mean, *missing*? Where was she last seen?"

The bodyguard who had accompanied Archie into the hotel had run out of patience. He strode forward and grabbed Diego by the collar, nearly lifting him off the ground and then slammed his body into a column. Matteo gasped, dropped his flashlight, and jumped onto the bodyguard's back to free his brother. Archie joined the scuffle, hitting Matteo hard on the ribs, sending the contractor to the ground. Archie pulled his handgun out of its holster and held it on Matteo.

"Terrance," Archie said, "Ease up on Mr. Ferrera, please."

The brute let go of Diego and backed away as the handyman collapsed onto the floor next to his brother. Both men looked up into the barrel of Archie's pistol.

"Something isn't adding up," Archie said calmly, "and I intend to get to the bottom of it. We've been doing some checking into your background, Diego. You have a thing for opera singers. An obsession maybe? We've seen your...what shall we call it, Terrance? A shrine? A sick-puppy, opera singer shrine? What is all that shit, Diego? What's your fascination with Georgia Reece?"

Diego didn't say anything. He closed his eyes for a moment and slowly let out his air.

Matteo sat up slowly. "Have you been inside Diego's house without his permission? That's certainly trespassing, gentlemen. You aren't police officers. Did you have a warrant? You aren't even from around here."

"Shut the fuck up, amigo," Terrance said. "No one's talking to you."

"I like opera," Diego said meekly. "It's not a crime. I haven't done anything wrong."

"Where is Georgia Reece, Diego?" Archie asked.

The front doors slammed open and two Santa Fe policeman entered the lobby each with a drawn weapon leading the way. "S.F.P.D.! Drop the gun!"

Carter and Sullivan Lowery stood on the sidewalk directly behind the officers. When it appeared that the situation was under control, they slowly walked in.

Terrance put his hands up, Archie carefully lowered his pistol to the floor, then turned around as he raised his hands above his head. "Officers," he said with a smile, "I think there's been some sort of mistake. We were just having a friendly, *private* conversation."

"Hardly," Carter said as he squeezed by the officers. "I think it goes without saying that we're pressing charges."

The officers patted down and handcuffed Archibald and Terrance after taking a handgun from the bodyguard's waist. Then they called for backup to transport the men to the city jail. The Lowery brothers helped the Ferrera brothers to their feet and the four men moved to the rear of the lobby, away from the intruders.

"How the heck did you know what was going on here?" Matteo asked Carter.

Carter pulled his iPhone from his pocket. "Security cameras."

"He's been fixated on that phone all day since the cameras went online this morning," Sullivan said. "And we were just around the corner at Café Pasqual's. Luckily, the cops were sitting in front of the Chuck Jones gallery on Water Street."

Carter turned to the Ferreras, "Basically, we were watching

you guys on our phones. I know; we're total creeps."

"Well thank God for the creeps," Matteo said. "And good thing the cameras have battery backup and infrared, because we've been in the dark most of the evening."

"I don't know anything about Miss Reece," Diego finally said under his breath. "I would never hurt anyone. Ever."

"We believe you, buddy," Sullivan said. "And trust me, Mr. Grey and his big bad bear of a henchman over there are going to have a lot of explaining to do. I guess that shit works back in New York, but it's not going to fly around here. And certainly not in our hotel."

Both sets of brothers stuck around to give their statements to the arresting officers and then were allowed to go. As Carter locked up the hotel, Sullivan, Matteo, and Diego watched from the sidewalk as the Mallard Protection men were loaded into the back of a squad car and driven away.

"We never did get to eat and I'm starving," Carter said as he rejoined the group. "Why don't you two come with us and we'll make it a foursome?"

And they did just that—after Sullivan called Skyler to update her on the unfortunate situation. He suggested that she might they to come up with a way to dismiss the rest of the Mallard crew post haste and Skyler readily agreed to start putting a plan into motion.

* * *

Skyler disengaged the call and picked up her glass of wine. "You simply *will not* believe what just happened at *your* new hotel." She gave Brenda the run down of what she'd just learned from Sullivan.

"Alright," the chef said as she topped off both of their glasses with what was left of a very fine cabernet sauvignon, a reserve from 2012 that Brenda found in a wine shop downtown. She'd never before tasted, or even considered, a New Mexican wine—every state in the union has at least a handful of wine making operations—but the cab, as well as the other selections from the Black Mesa Winery, were exciting her to no end. She made note of the wine on her phone and planned to feature some of the award-winning wines on all of her restaurants' lists. "I guess we know what we need to do." She took a large sip, savored the dry wine and its hints of black current and cherry for a moment, then swallowed. "We need to finish this delicious wine, then send that crew packing. This stuff'll give us the courage we need. And I hardly feel guilty. What have they done, but make a complete mess of this entire, ridiculous situation? I think Georgia should leave a strongly worded Yelp review when she gets back."

Skyler rolled her eyes. "Yelp review. You're insane."

"Well, people need to know, Skyler," Brenda spit. "Several of my friends back in the city use Mallard. Trust me, this is going to get out fast and then Archibald Grey's goose is really going to be cooked." She swirled her wine around in the glass as she reflected on that for a moment. "I hate goose. I've cooked *one*. Total. They're gross. Never again. Of course, the stupid birds deserve to be someone's dinner, because they are such nasty, unfriendly creatures, but I just don't like the taste or consistency. And now you know."

Skyler sighed and shook her head. "If we ask these people to leave, then we're right back to where we started—alone in a big scary house with an unreliable security system and no clue as to where Georgia is or who's still lurking around out there." She pointed toward the window and the pitch-black backyard.

"Forget that. Let's go stay with Carter and Sullivan. They're hoteliers; they'll love a few guests. And we won't be *here* being sitting ducks."

"Or gooses," Skyler said.

* * *

Georgia stumbled down the dirt road for what seemed like hours, but it was probably no longer than 30 minutes before she came across a dusty mailbox at the end of a well-worn driveway. With a new-found burst of energy, she navigated the tire rutted drive and came across a small bungalow. There were no vehicles on the property, but she banged on the front door.

Nothing.

The sunlight was all but gone and she couldn't imagine another minute alone in the dark, so when she discovered that the door was indeed locked, she searched the porch for a hidden key.

Nothing.

The windows were all locked, too. A nearby howl—*certainly a hungry coyote*—forced her to grab a small decorative gnome from a flower bed and shatter one of the panes of glass in the door. She reached in and unbolted the door and let herself inside.

From the looks of the well-appointed, cozy space— essentially a large studio complete with living, dining, cooking, and sleeping areas along with a tiny bathroom off to the side— it was a vacation or second residence. She couldn't readily find a landline telephone, but she did come across a thin plastic binder on the counter, written in both English and Spanish, welcoming guests to the vacation rental home. The interior pages included instructions on how to access the internet and how to operate the satellite television and security system. The text indicated that the four-digit code would have been forwarded to the guest prior to arrival.

"Security system," she said out loud. She hadn't noticed it when she entered, nor was there any beeping or loud siren. But to the right of the entry door she discovered the keypad. It was blinking red. She decided that was a good thing—she'd be saved.

Georgia found a bottle of water in the refrigerator and finished it in several fast gulps. She then searched one of the closets for something to wear; she intended to freshen up before the police arrived. She found a sweatshirt with a cardinal embroidered on the front, along with a pair of red bedroom slippers, among several items stored in a plastic bin on the top shelf, most likely the homeowners' private stash, she decided.

As she was taking a bird bath in front of the bathroom sink, it suddenly occurred to her that the address of the rental house was on the front cover of the binder. Georgia sprinted into the main room and flipped the cover over.

Welcome to Flagstaff!

"I'm in Arizona?!"

CHAPTER TWENTY

Skyler was giddy as she crossed the tarmac and approached the gleaming Boeing Business Jet. The customized 737 had been delivered to her new owner the summer before and was unpainted, save the familiar Martin Media double-M logo affixed to each side of the tail. The intense winter sun reflected off the silver fuselage, nearly blinding Skyler as she ascended the airstairs to the forward passenger door. She was met by a young, uniformed first officer who shook her hand and welcomed her aboard. After she removed her sunglasses and coat, the pilot closed a thin sliding door used to keep out the elements while parked on the ground.

"Mr. Martin is on a conference call in the rear of the aircraft," the pilot said. "He's asked that you wait for him in the main salon. It's just beyond the crew area and the galley, through that doorway."

"Thank you," Skyler said. She marveled at the rich beige and jet-black interior. The light-colored carpet seemed like an unwise choice to her, but it made the cabin seem especially spacious. She stepped into the main salon, a space that spanned the width of the jet. Forward, a well-stocked bar was surrounded by six stools that were anchored to the floor. On either side of that, underneath the windows, were small tables with three club chairs situated around each. Further back, there was an enormous U-shaped leather couch with a low wood coffee table in the middle, with an intricate chess set on top and a silver vase filled with picture-perfect white roses. Ultra-thin television monitors and drink holders dotted the space so that each passenger could have entertainment, news, and cocktails at their fingertips at all times. In the rear of the salon, there was a large dining table with seating for eight people, a divan along the right side, and two doors on the back wall. She assumed one was a lavatory and that the other led to the space Foster was currently occupying.

This was absolutely Skyler's mecca. She sat down on the couch and took a deep breath. The rich leather and carpet gave the cabin a new-car smell. But there was something else happening in the air. A scent was being pumped into the cabin, much like high-end hotels and casinos use fragrances to intensify a guest's experience. She couldn't quite identify it, but it had notes of cotton and sandalwood. Very clean and crisp and utterly relaxing.

A tall thin Asian woman in a tailored black pantsuit appeared with a small tray. She smiled politely and placed a silver bowl of mixed nuts and a glass of champagne on the coffee table in front of Skyler. "Welcome aboard, Miss Moore. My name is Susan," she said. "Mr. Martin will be out momentarily. Can I get you anything else while you wait?"

"I think I'm already in heaven, Susan," Skyler said. "I couldn't possibly want anything else, except maybe to fly with you guys to Maui."

"I'm sure Mr. Martin would be more than happy to have the company on the flight. He did mention that it might be a possibility—are you coming with us?"

"I am not, unfortunately. Perhaps next time."

The woman smiled politely and bowed ever so slightly. "I'll leave you."

Skyler pulled out her smartphone and opened the camera. She took a few clandestine shots of the interior and then texted a selfie—with a good portion of the lush cabin behind her—to Leonard. She captioned it:

We need one of these! #lifegoals #737

Just as the photo was delivered, one of the doors opened behind her and she jumped to her feet.

"Hi, Skyler," Foster said as he entered the cabin and sat down on the couch. "Sit, sit. Relax."

"This airplane is absolutely gorgeous, Foster. I've never seen anything quite like it."

"There *is* nothing quite like it. But it is my last extravagant creation, I imagine," he said as he looked lovingly around the salon. "At one point, Martin Media had a fleet of seven airplanes, can you believe that? Most of the executives fly commercial or with fractional jet cards now; it's just a lot more economical to fly first class or to rent a plane than it is to buy one and have the headache of employing pilots, cabin crew, and mechanics, and to rent hanger space and all of that boloney. But, Skyler, I just could not resist this Seven-Three. This is the Max-10 version; the longest one they make, at nearly 144 feet. It's the most fuel efficient, environmentally friendly, single aisle Boeing has ever produced; not that I have an aisle," he chuckled. "It has superior range, too. But, alas, I am boring you."

Skyler almost choked on her champagne. "You most certainly are *not* boring me, Foster. I am somewhat of an airplane aficionado; ask anyone. Please don't spare me the details. How far can you go?"

"About 3,300 nautical miles. I can get to Hawaii, for sure. I can fly from Las Vegas to my favorite resort in San Juan, Puerto Rico, or all the way up to Maine. I can't quite get to London without a stopover, or any other European city from Las Vegas, for that matter, but I've been to all those places more than enough. Too many times, really. I pretty much stay within the good ol' United States nowadays. I had a lot of fun working with the designers to come up with this interior." He gestured around the cabin like a spokesmodel on a vintage television game show. "It took nearly nine months to complete after Boeing delivered the plane to us, but it was worth the wait. Plus, I had my old G-6 to get me places in the meantime."

"It's gorgeous. There are just no other words for it."

"Thank you. So, are you flying with me today inside the new toy that my son didn't think I needed to waste $130 million on?"

"Oh, Foster," Skyler said as she grabbed ahold of his left arm. "I would absolutely *love* to, really I would. And it was very kind of you to invite me. But I've got my friends here for the holidays. Maybe next time?"

"Of course," he said, trying hard to mask his disappointment. "As I explained, I do have friends in Maui, so I won't be alone. And Susan—did you meet her? My stewardess?—she's a formidable opponent on the chess board."

"Well, then I don't feel so bad." It just sunk in what he had said a minute earlier. "$130 million dollars?"

"Outlandish, isn't it," he said. "And that didn't really include all the retrofitting we did. But what do they always say?—*you can't take it with you*. And I still have several hundreds of millions of dollars that I can use to help educate the people. With your help, of course."

Foster stood up and walked over to a credenza next to the divan. He picked up a large white envelope and handed it to Skyler. "Here are the documents I told you about. I didn't email them because I don't completely trust the world wide webs. I've been hacked more times than I'd like to remember. And I don't want word about the foundation getting out until we are ready for the world to know about it. Are you willing to do this C.I.A.-style so that we can keep a wrap on things?"

"I am. Absolutely," Skyler said, accepting the package and immediately hugging it to her chest. "And I will guard this with my life. I look forward to digging in. It will be refreshing to work with actual paper, for a change."

"I still buy all my books in hardback. I hate those newfangled electronic tablet things. It can't be good for peoples' eyesight."

"I do a little of each, I have to admit," Skyler said. "But there is nothing like a real, honest to goodness book and turning actual paper pages to see what happens next. And you can't put hundreds of e-books on your bookshelves either, now can you? I love looking at all of my old books, even if I don't have time to read them all. There is always a stack of books on my bedside table waiting to be read. Unfortunately, most of them are covered with dust. I'm only good for about 20 minutes before I fall asleep."

The old man chuckled. "It's the same exact story at my house. But I have maybe 10 minutes before I'm out cold. And my stack of books is very tall...but dusted daily, of course." He was quiet for several long seconds. "Will you be able to have a Merry Christmas, Skyler? Given all the..." Foster's voice trailed off. "All the unpleasantness you've experienced here in Santa Fe?"

Skyler crinkled her brow. "Gosh, I hope so. It's my favorite time of the year. But just being with my best friend is more than I could ask for and I'm confident that Georgia will be found soon. I mean, she's got to turn up sooner or later. Maybe we'll have a Christmas miracle."

"Well, I certainly hope so, my dear." He stood up, which was a clear indication that their meeting was concluded. "Thank you for coming, and we will be in contact soon into the new year."

"I look forward to it," Skyler said. She reached out to shake his hand, but he went in for a hug. She obliged, and he hung on just a tad too long—she was certain that she caught him smelling her neck. She pulled away ever so gently and gave him a big smile. "Merry Christmas, Foster."

"Merry Christmas to you," he said as he led her to the front door. Susan handed Skyler her coat then the flight attendant opened the sliding door and Skyler deplaned.

She ducked into the private jet terminal and found a comfortable seat next to the floor-to-ceiling window overlooking the tarmac. She had no intention of leaving the airfield until that beautiful sleek bird was airborne and out of sight.

* * *

Alon Leibovitz waited for his client to be escorted into the small interrogation room. He hadn't minded the late call from Archibald Grey the night before, pleading for him to fly to Santa Fe just as soon as was humanly possible, because he knew the payday would be worth the inconvenience of having to completely rearrange his packed schedule. This wasn't the first time he'd rushed to Mallard Protection's rescue and the steady legal work was largely how Alon and his wife were able to afford their palatial weekend house in the Hamptons, as well as their Park Avenue apartment.

"Thanks for coming, buddy," Archie said when they were left alone. The security man was dressed in yesterday's clothes, unshaven, and quite haggard looking. "Did you fly private? Is this going to cost me an arm and a leg?"

"Oh, yes sir, it is," Alon said. "An arm and a leg. Maybe two of each. But I think it's all going to have a happy ending. For both you and the goon."

"The goon doesn't actually like when we refer to him as a goon, I've come to find out."

"*Terrance*, then. My apologies. I've worked my magic and managed to get both of you off, scot-free. No charges have been, or will be, filed, they tell me. The Lowery brothers aren't pressing charges for trespassing and the Ferrera brothers aren't interested in taking this further. But, the local law has something to convey to you."

"Jesus Christ, Alon," Archie said. "Not fucking community service, please. I don't have time to be spending a hundred hours in this God forsaken town."

"No. Actually, you won't be spending *any* time in Santa Fe. Ever again."

"Oh." It wasn't the first time he'd heard this decree. "What's this now? Three states?"

"Yes, Archie," the lawyer said calmly, "Mississippi, Washington state, and now New Mexico. You are banned from all three."

"Fuck. Well, I can live without New Mexico, I guess. I just need to make sure never to take any business from Tom Ford or Julia Roberts."

"Do they live here?"

"Among many other celebrities."

"You need to be more careful," Alon said. "So, Terrance and you are being let go within the hour. Without your guns—they get to keep those. Sorry. You are to make your way to the jet and get the hell out of here just as soon as you can. The rest of the Mallard team needs to hightail it home, too. Nobody passes 'go,' Archibald Grey. And don't look back. If you ask me, you got off very easy this time. But it's Christmas and these people simply don't want to be bothered with you."

"Thank you," Archie said. "I owe you big time."

"Yes, you do, Mister. And you will be billed accordingly." The attorney got up and started placing papers into his briefcase. "Merry Christmas. My love to your wife and kids."

"Merry Christmas, Alon. Or, should I be saying, Happy Chanukah?"

"Chanukah was weeks ago. And we're doing Christmas this year, actually. The wife is having all her far-flung gentile relatives to the apartment. We even have a decorated tree for the first time ever. A live one."

"How festive."

"Enjoy Aspen. I'll see you back in the city. Don't pull a gun on anyone up there on the slopes." And Alon left the room without waiting for a reaction from his number one client.

Archie was taken back to the holding cell he had been sharing with his employee. "We're sprung," he said. "But, I hope you didn't get too attached to New Mexico."

"Why's that?" Terrance asked.

"Because you're never coming back."

* * *

Without an assistant within 2,000 miles, Brenda wrapped all of her presents by herself...and then she was bored out of her mind. And when she was bored out of her mind, she tested recipes. And ate.

She didn't actually *need* to test the crab cake recipe; it really wasn't hers originally and absolutely wasn't meant to be messed with. Like honest to goodness, authentic Maine lobster rolls—a *true* one, with nothing but succulent steamed meat and just enough mayonnaise to bind it together, mounded into a split-top long roll (she was partial to brioche hot dog buns)—Brenda was a traditionalist at heart and didn't feel the need to mess with a good thing. So many chefs had the tendency to add unnecessary filler. A real crab cake doesn't have minced red or jalapeño peppers, chopped parsley, or any number of add-ins. A real crab cake is *mostly crab, damn it.*

She took 15 saltine crackers and placed them in a gallon-sized plastic baggie and crushed them to smithereens with a rolling pin. In a large bowl, she combined a pound of picked over lump crab meat with a half cup of mayonnaise, a beaten egg, a tablespoon of Worcestershire sauce, and a few healthy sprinkles of Old Bay seasoning. While it sat in the refrigerator to meld together for an hour or so, she popped open a bottle of cold pinot grigio and pulled out her iPad. She opened a file titled, 'Beach House Cookbook-working title,' and added some notes to the bulleted list. The book was due to the publisher the following September and she'd only just started sketching out the outline. She wanted to evoke classic New England Americana with her seventh volume—simple, straightforward dishes geared toward big family get-togethers by the sea. The photography would have to be on point and she planned to pull together a huge team in order to shoot the entire book over a long weekend in Maine the following summer; she hoped to use Skyler's cottage as the backdrop. She'd need a cast, too, and started jotting down names of possible 'family' members since she had very few real ones to speak of; rather, no family members that she actually spoke to nor could stand to be in the same room with.

Brenda pulled out a cast iron skillet and heated a quarter cup of canola oil over moderately high heat. She rolled the crab mixture into two dozen, inch round balls, pressed them down a bit to form a disk, then began frying them in batches, two to three minutes per side (she rarely timed anything, unless she was baking; she just knew when things needed to be flipped and when they were perfectly done) until they were golden brown. Seventeen of them sat on a paper towel-lined plate, because she ate seven directly from the skillet.

Save for the dogs, there was no one in the house to eat her appetizers, so she popped four more into her face, then placed the rest in a small plastic container and put them in the refrigerator. She knew that they were just as good cold. She woke up the iPad and made a note that the recipe could also make eight entrée size cakes and that lemon wedges should certainly accompany the treats. French dressing, tartar sauce, or any number of accompaniments would also be suitable. She envisioned three of the smaller bites sitting on an appetizer plate with a heaping spoonful of her fresh corn kernel, bacon, and onion salad. She was partial to a poached egg and a simple hollandaise on an entrée sized cake for a great brunch, with a watermelon and feta side salad.

Despite all the crab she consumed, Brenda still felt hungry as her mind wandered through all the culinary possibilities.

The wall phone is the kitchen rang, startling her. She believed it was the first time she even noticed the antiquated thing.

"Pronto?" (She'd been waiting to use that as a telephone greeting since hearing Ava use it the day before.)

"This is Sergeant William Kern with the Arizona State Police. Is there a Mr. John Sparks there?"

"John Sparks? No, sir," Brenda said. "He and his entire crew should be leaving the state as we speak. May I ask what this is regarding?"

"Who am I speaking to, ma'am? Are you related to Georgia Reece?"

"I am not. My name is Brenda Braxton and I'm a house guest of Ms. Reece. Do you have information about her whereabouts, Sergeant?"

"I do."

"And?"

There was a pause, then, "Brenda Braxton the cook on television?"

Cook? "I'm a chef, sir. What do you know about Georgia?"

"She is currently at the Twin Oaks Hospital in Flagstaff,

Arizona, being treated for exhaustion, dehydration, and a concussion. But she is expected to make a full recovery. She apparently asked for Mr. Sparks to come fetch her."

"How did she get to Flagstaff?"

"I'm not sure I can divulge that information to you, ma'am," the police officer said. "But please know that she is safe and quite eager to get home. I've spoken to the police department in Santa Fe; they are aware of the situation and they've called off the search."

"Called it off? But Massimo Medina is still out there, officer! Unless you nabbed him. Did you nab him? Was Georgia with Massimo when you found her?"

"I couldn't say."

"You *couldn't* say?! Or you *won't* say? Seriously, we've been quite terrorized by that man for the past week. I think you better say something, sir."

"I'll refer you to the Santa Fe Police Department, Ms. Braxton. In the meantime, can you help make arrangements to get Ms. Reece back to New Mexico?"

"I will do that, yes," Brenda said. She was frustrated, but relieved. "Is there a phone in her room? Can I call her?"

"She sedated. She won't be able to have visitors or receive calls until tomorrow, but the doctors do believe they will be able to release her on Sunday. They asked me to pass that along."

"Sunday is Christmas Eve."

"Yes, Ms. Braxton."

"Okay. Thank you for calling, officer. We'll do our part."

"By the way, I'd keep this hush-hush until Mr. Modena is located," the officer said. "I'm telling you that off the record, of course."

"Of course. Thank you." And she hung up. "Well, shit," she said out loud to no one.

Incredibly frustrated by the fact that she was all alone with no one to tell the news to, Brenda picked up her cell phone again and dialed Archibald Grey's number.

"Why, it's Brenda Braxton," he said when he picked up. "We're at S.A.F. about to taxi down the runway. What can I do for you?"

"I thought you'd like to know that Georgia has been found alive and fairly well."

"That's very good news, indeed," he said. "I guess I needed that happy ending. I'm very thankful that you bothered to call me."

"No thanks to you and your duck people, Mr. Grey," Brenda spit. "Listen, I'm not a fan of Mallard's tactics or the professionalism we witnessed here. I know several people that use your services, you know?"

"I do," he said calmly, remembering who he was talking to. "And I am quite embarrassed. We're going to be making some significant operational changes and we'll be back stronger than ever in the new year. I promise you and all my clients that."

"I like to give people second chances, Mr. Grey, so I'll hold my tongue for now."

"How noble of you, Miss Braxton. But don't fret over this one moment longer, because the cat is already out of the bag. The gossip patrol have the story about my indiscretion and they ran it in the *New York Post* this morning."

"Oh good," Brenda said flatly. "That makes me feel much better. And *indiscretion* is certainly an interesting word for threatening innocent, good people with guns, but what do I know? Have a good flight, Mr. Grey." And she disengaged the call. *What an asshole*, she thought.

She grabbed the dogs' leashes and her purse and headed out to the car with Mulder and Scully following close behind. She was excited to be able to tell the twins the news in person. She wondered which Lowery brother would be more relieved.

CHAPTER TWENTY-ONE

Skyler secured permission from the F.B.O.'s customer service rep to step back outside the terminal building when Foster's beautiful plane started taxiing away from the terminal. She pulled her coat tight around her neck against the biting December wind, then found a spot on the patio with a good view of runway 2/20, the longest of the three. She suspected they'd need every inch of the pavement to get off the ground at the relatively small, high-desert airport.

An outdoor speaker on the patio was tied into the tower feed. She listened as a controller instructed Foster's pilots to hold for an arriving jet. "Citation 2-9-8-1 Charlie, cleared to land." She watched as a small private jet touched down, then the much larger Boeing moved into position. As soon as the Citation slowed and pulled off the runway, Foster's engines spun up and the gleaming 737 started rolling down the runway. It lifted off about three quarters of the way down the asphalt and began a rather impressive steep climb. It soon banked to the right and headed west.

When the plane was almost completely out of view, Skyler started back toward her car. As she passed a ramp attendant in the lobby, Skyler overheard him say, "Mr. Leonard Little. Got it," into his handheld radio.

Her heart skipped a beat. "Excuse me," she said, reaching out to grab the man's upper arm. "Did you say *Leonard Little?*"

"Um, I'm not sure I can confirm that, ma'am," the young man said, clearly caught off guard. "Are you here to collect someone?"

"Yes, of course. Mr. Little. Is he due in soon?"

"He just landed. The Citation is pulling up now." He pointed outside. "You can pull your car out to the plane. The gate code is 1-9-7-0." And he walked away.

She was left a little shell shocked. Clearly her boyfriend wasn't getting off that private jet in Santa Fe, New Mexico—he was thousands of miles away in Wabanaki, busy running the police department as a favor to the injured sheriff. But Skyler was intrigued, and she was now in procession of the airport's gate code, so she jumped into her car and drove up to the side of the jet just as the airstairs were being lowered to the tarmac. Feeling like a total idiot—*but at least I'll have a story to tell,* she told herself—she got out and opened her trunk then stood at attention waiting for someone—*Another Leonard Little? What were the odds?!*—to descend the stairs.

And then Leonard Little, *her* Leonard Little, the acting sheriff of the Wabanaki Police Department, poked his head out of the plane and looked around. That's when Skyler screamed.

"Stop it," Leonard said, clearly flustered. "Why are you screaming?"

She leapt into his arms when he got to the bottom of the stairs. "What are you doing here!?"

"It's Christmas."

She pushed him away from her to arm's length. "Yes, and you said you had to work. Is this Brenda's doing? It must have been Brenda."

"Do you think I have enough money to charter an airplane?" Leonard asked. "And would I even have thought such a thing was possible?"

"Well, certainly you *knew* such a thing was possible," Skyler said. She hugged him close to her body again. "I am so very happy. This is the best Christmas present you could ever give me."

"I didn't give myself to you," he said, "Brenda did. I brought you something else."

"What?!"

"I think you're going to have to wait until Monday for that."

"Oh crap," she said. "I overnighted your gift to Maine."

"Thank you. But all I need is you."

"I'm melting; that was the absolutely perfect thing to say." She took a moment to examine his clean-shaven face and she noted that he didn't smell at all like cigarettes. "So, welcome to Santa Fe," she said as she led him to the car. "It's beautiful, wide-open, extremely dry, and bitter cold right now."

"I'm used to the cold," he said. "So, why are you here at the airport anyway? I thought I was supposed to be a big fat surprise."

"You are a big fat surprise! But I was meeting with Foster on his *big fat* plane before he left for Hawaii. He just took off seconds after you landed. This is completely a coincidence."

"Or was it very well orchestrated so you'd be here when I landed?"

"Was it? Then Foster would have had to be in on it."

"Actually, I really have no clue. We'll have to ask Brenda."

One of the pilots brought Leonard's well-worn luggage and

briefcase to the car and placed them in the trunk. "Merry Christmas, Mr. Little. I hope you enjoyed the flight."

"I did not," Leonard said flatly, "but it had nothing to do with your fine piloting or the quality of that magnificent airplane. I'm just not a fan of flying. I'm afraid I white-knuckled it most of the way across the country."

"You made it in one piece," Skyler said. "That's the important part." She smiled at the pilot. "Thank you, sir."

They climbed into the car and Skyler drove back through the gate, navigated around the parking lot, and they were out of the airport in under a minute. She looked over and smiled at the man in the seat next to her. "I really, really missed you."

"Me too," he said. "My hand was starting to get tired."

"My goodness, you are so gross." But she smiled despite herself. "You won't need your hand here."

"Good."

"And I need to go straight home and shave my legs."

"Alright."

"I had no idea I'd need shaved legs here!"

"Okay."

"I'm serious."

"Great."

"Great." She pulled onto the highway. "Did you bring your gun?"

"I did."

"Good."

"Am I going to need it?"

"I hope not," Skyler said. She wasn't necessarily comfortable with the idea of her boyfriend brandishing a weapon—and the nations' obsession with guns in general was a sore subject for her—but she had to admit, given the current state of affairs, that she was happy he was packing heat. "But you never know."

* * *

Brenda was almost running as she entered the lobby of the hotel with Mulder's leash in her right hand and Scully's in her left. The dogs weren't used to the brisk pace, so they were jumping around in a frenzy wondering what the heck was happening.

"What the hell?" Sullivan yelled as he was nearly knocked off his feet when the threesome collided with him as he rounded the corner from the back hallway.

"I'm sorry, I'm sorry," Brenda said as she reined in the animals. She was out of breath.

"Calm down, woman. What's going on?"

"I heard from the police. They found Georgia and she is very much alive."

A huge smile covered Sullivan's face. "Well, that's the best news I've heard in a very long time. Where is she? Let's go."

"Hold your horses," Brenda said. "She's in Flagstaff."

"Arizona?"

"Yes. At the hospital. But don't freak out, they tell me that she's going to make a full recovery. She has a concussion and is severely dehydrated—and I don't know what else—but she's going to be fine and we're supposed to go collect her on Christmas Eve."

"How did she get to Flagstaff?"

"Massimo. I don't know one single detail beyond what I've already told you."

"Where is Massimo, Brenda?"

"What did I just say?" she exploded. "I don't know anything else. And the police won't tell us anything. Except that they don't have Massimo in custody."

"So, he's still out there somewhere."

"It would appear so."

"Who's out there somewhere?" Carter had appeared behind them and he was busy greeting the uncharacteristically alert dogs. "You know there are nails everywhere around here, Bren. Better watch the dogs' feet."

"Georgia is alive and in a Flagstaff hospital," Sullivan said. He filled his brother in on the few remaining details.

"We'll go get her on Sunday," Carter said. "If we go early enough, we can be back in time for a normal, quiet Christmas Eve at home. Although, we're going to be armed to the teeth."

Brenda sat down on a folding chair and the dogs curled up around her feet. "Would that crazy Italian really come back for more? I mean, what on Earth could his end-game be? He abducted her, drove to Flagstaff, and then somehow managed to hit her on the head and then lose track of her? He must be on the run. And if he's smart, he's going in the other direction. There is no way he is coming back to Santa Fe."

The twins considered that for a few moments. They had no words.

It suddenly dawned on Brenda and she glanced at her watch. "Shit. Leonard would have landed by now. I was supposed to go get him."

"Leonard?" Carter asked.

"Leonard Little is Skyler's boyfriend and I flew him in as a surprise Christmas present." She sighed loudly. "I was even going to get a bow."

"He's the cop? From Maine?" Sullivan asked.

"Yes. We all went to high school together. He's very down-Maine. Until last summer, I don't think he'd ever left the state. But he's a very nice guy and Skyler seems smitten with him. They're like night and day. So different. But it works for them, I guess. I mean, so far."

Carter was busy rolling up a set of electrical plans. "Do you think he brought his gun?"

"I told him to," Brenda said. "It's funny—his father never let him carry one, but that all changed last summer."

"I don't know what you are talking about. I just hope he has a gun," Carter said.

"His father wouldn't let him carry one?" Sullivan asked. "What does that mean?"

Brenda shook her head slowly and stroked Scully's neck. "His father was the sheriff of Wabanaki, where we grew up. He was sheriff for decades. It's a long story, guys, but it has a very sad ending. He died in July at the hands of another friend of ours. He'd lost his mind and took hostages and, well, it was all very messy."

The twins said nothing.

"I'm working very hard to forget last summer. And Leonard and Skyler are doing an exceptional job at pretending that they don't remember that horrible day. So, I really wouldn't bring it up when you meet him."

Sullivan couldn't help but laughing out loud. "Seriously? Did you just say that? Who do you think we are, complete idiots? *Hi, Leonard, I hear your father was gunned down by one of your friends last summer. Merry Christmas, though.*"

Carter chuckled. "We won't say anything. Of course."

"I might," Sullivan said. "Now that it's in my head. Oh shit. What if I say something about it?"

"Get a grip, Sully," Carter said. He turned his attention to Brenda. "Maybe we need to lock this place up and go home until Tuesday or Wednesday. I mean, honestly, will anything get done until after the holidays anyway? For that matter, maybe we should all just go back to New York and pick this up after New Year's."

"I really do like that idea given everything that's happened," Sullivan said, "except that we need to wait for Georgia to get released and then there's that other very annoying, very troubling, selfish person."

"I'm afraid to ask, but I will: Who is that?" Brenda asked.

"Darby Lowery."

"Crap!" Carter yelled. "I totally forgot he was coming."

"We can't decamp to New York when he's specifically coming here to spend Christmas with us."

"Darby Lowery?" Brenda asked.

"Our crazy brother," the twins said in unison, in the same exact pitch.

Brenda pointed at Carter but was looking at Sullivan. "You owe him a Coke."

* * *

Carter and Sullivan's brother descended the commuter jet's stairs and bristled when the cold wind filled his nostrils. He stuck his hands into the pockets of his hoodie and picked up his pace. He entered the tiny baggage room at the Santa Fe airport and scanned the small crowd for a familiar face. He couldn't find one.

He walked the length of the terminal and peered outside. Nothing.

"Merry Christmas, to me," he said. He fished out his cell phone and called Sullivan, the lesser of the two evils.

Sullivan skipped the formalities. "I am so sorry, buddy. Almost there."

"It's okay, Sully. Should I call an Uber?"

"No, no. I'm five minutes away," Sullivan said. "Sit tight."

"Alright. By the way, do you know that there isn't even a bar here? This is one small ass airport. Are you sure this is a good place for one of your hotels? Seriously. How do all the people get here?"

"Welcome to Santa Fe, Darby. It's small, but nice. Listen, we'll get you a drink, don't worry. I'll be there in a few. I'm in a dark green Jeep."

"See ya, dude."

"Goodbye, *dude.*"

CHAPTER TWENTY-TWO

When they found Georgia's house empty, Skyler and Leonard took very little time shedding their clothes and jumping into the large shower in Skyler's suite. Within moments of soaping each other, he was inside of her, lifting her body off the tile floor. She'd almost forgotten how strong he was and how full he made her feel, like no one before him. She purred into his ear and playfully bit at his neck, and soon, he grunted, then pulsed deep inside. He was done. She had just gotten started.

"Sorry," he said after they'd dried off and were lounging naked on her unmade bed. "You know I can last longer than that, right?"

"I do."

"And when it's not weeks between sessions. With a few drinks. And if I don't move much."

"I get it. I'm fine."

"Are you?"

"I could go again," she said with a sly smile.

"I need a minute. Or 30. I need 30-minutes."

She laughed. "It's cool." She stroked the hair on his leg. "I'm just really happy that you're here with me. This is the Christmas miracle I needed. The fact that you got on that airplane all by yourself, without having to hold someone's hand, well, that's something right there."

"It's not the half of it," Leonard said. When he noticed her staring at it, he pulled the sheet over his still-recovering penis and took her hand in his. "Kristin begged me not to come. She's not ready to let Porter run the show and she's totally not herself yet. She hardly gets around."

"Is she getting out of the house yet?"

"She has two broken legs, babe." Leonard rubbed one of his own legs in a kind of weird act of sympathy. "So, no. It takes three to six months for leg bones to heal completely. She'll be able to do some desk work soon, but she won't be in a car or in the field until well into next year. It's rough for everyone. And you know her; she's very antsy. She keeps saying that she'd rather kill herself than to watch another minute of daytime television or look at Facebook ever again. She's been living online."

"So, you're going back." Skyler hoped this wouldn't be the case. She wanted him back in D.C. with her.

"I think I have to," Leonard said solemnly. "At least until I go to Nevada for training."

"Nevada?"

"That's where that tactical school is. If I want to start my own protection agency, I'm going to need that kind of training. It's just outside of Las Vegas, which is cool, because I've never been there."

"You've never been anywhere," she said. "Do you really see yourself in the field, being a bodyguard for a Paris Hilton-type? Is that what you want to do?"

He shook his head. "It is not what I want to do, no. Who is Paris Hilton?"

"Are you being serious right now? The Hilton Hotel heiress?

Reality television star. Singer. Deejay. International pop culture icon. She has like 100 million followers on social media. What planet do you live on?"

"Not that planet," he said. "But if you think I should reach out to her, I will. But, seriously, I want to *run* the show. Hire the employees. Be the boss. I like being the boss, but I'm sure as hell not going to freeze my ass off while being the boss in Wabanaki for the rest of my life. Not even until Kristin is back behind the wheel. They're just going to have to learn how to deal without Leonard Little. I'm going to have people like Ferris Hilton to protect."

"*Paris*! Jesus."

"And you can do my agency's P.R., yeah? You'd do that for me."

She considered that for a second. "*Sure*," was the correct answer, for now. She wasn't completely confident that he could get such a business off the ground and that, of course, made her feel guilty. But *sure* was the right answer.

"And maybe we can get Brenda to talk me up to industry folks she knows. People in power, in broadcasting and stuff like that. And then perhaps Carissa Lamb, too. I mean, you work for her now and she must have tons and tons of celebrity friends who need all kinds of different levels of protection, I suspect."

"I guess that's got be true."

"And she likes me," he said with a wry smile.

That made Skyler cringe. "I think she likes you a little *too* much, yes." She noticed the sheet was tenting. "Are you kidding me right now? Why is *this* happening?!" She pointed at his crotch. "It hasn't been half an hour! Leonard Little, did this happen because you were thinking about Carissa Lamb and how she has a little crush on you? Honestly!"

He shrugged his shoulders.

"Honestly, Leonard. Gross."

He rolled over nevertheless, lowered his full weight on top of her, and stuck his tongue into her mouth. And then he was inside her again. And this time, he lasted well over 15-minutes, leaving her most perfectly satisfied.

* * *

After another shower, Skyler and Leonard dressed in jeans and sweaters and emerged from their suite to find Brenda, Carter, and the dogs in the living room. Introductions were made between the two men and then Brenda gave Leonard a long bear hug.

"I am so happy you are here," she squealed. She quickly turned to Skyler, "You ready for this? Georgia has been found and she's alive and well."

Carter, who was busy uncorking an expensive bottle of merlot, said, "*Well* isn't quite right. But she's alive." He encouraged everyone to take seats on the sofas while he filled four glasses.

"This is great news! Details, please," Skyler demanded. And she got them—at least she got what Brenda was told. "That is just amazing. I am so relieved. How do you think they ended up in Flagstaff and where the heck were they going? California? Mexico?"

"Flagstaff isn't really the right direction from here to get to Mexico if I remember my geography correctly," Brenda said. "But then again, Massimo is a deranged Italian lunatic who I suspect has never driven across the American southwest, so, gosh, who the hell knows."

"Crazy," Skyler said. "I'm just happy she's going to be okay. Who's going to get her?"

"My brother and I will go tomorrow. Haven't decided if we're flying or driving yet. I can't imagine it's easy to charter a plane on Christmas Eve at the last friggin' minute."

"You guys and your private jets," Leonard said. "Wouldn't a commercial flight work? It's got to be a lot cheaper."

"Bite your tongue with that blasphemy," Brenda said. "And anyway, you can't expect an opera singer of her caliber, who's just getting out of the hospital after having been abducted and knocked upside the head and left for dead in the God-forsaken Arizona wilderness, to fly coach on Southwest Airlines on Christmas Eve! It's unheard of."

"Southwest doesn't fly to Flagstaff," Skyler said matter-of-factly. "And all they have is coach."

"Well, how would I know any of that?" Brenda asked with an eye roll. "Why aren't you a travel agent, Skyler?"

"They don't make enough money."

"Mine does," the chef said. "He's boutique, high-end all the way. He drives a Bentley—it's second hand, but still—and he has a second home out on Fire Island. I don't know how he does it in this day and age of the internet, but he makes a mint and a half."

"I have got to warn you all," Carter said as he finally sunk down onto the sofa next to Brenda with his glass of wine. "A gentle warning. Our kid brother will be in town any minute now. And Darby is a first-class pain in our asses. A major fuck up, really. Well, until recently. Sullivan thinks the kid has pulled himself together and grown up a lot, but I seriously have my doubts about that. Just wanted to put that out there. He's a lot to handle. And he's cocky."

"Is he staying here?" Skyler asked.

Brenda shook her head. "No. I think we decided that no one is staying *here*. Pack up your crap, people. We're decamping to the twin's house."

Skyler sighed. "It's been a game of musical houses since we got here," she said to Leonard. She turned her attention back to Brenda. "Why another move?"

"Because Massimo is still on the loose, that useless excuse for a protective team has flown the coop, and the security system here in the house is seriously screwed up beyond repair. Or at least it's not going to be repaired before Christmas. We have no choice but to skedaddle."

Carter took a big swig of his wine. "But there's icing on this here cake, my friends."

"Which is?" Leonard asked.

Carter stood up and yanked up his sweater, revealing a hand gun strapped to his torso. "I'm armed."

Leonard smiled and stood up, too, revealing his own police-issued sidearm. "Me too. Twice." He pulled gently on his pant leg and the group could see a smaller gun—a purse-sized, semi-automatic .22 handgun that once belonged to his late grandmother—strapped just above the cop's ankle.

"Great," Skyler said, "the boys are comparing dick sizes." She looked over at her best friend and slowly shook her head back and forth. "It's going to be the O.K. Corral up in this bitch."

"Not *this* bitch," Brenda corrected. "The bitch on the *other* side of town." She pointed toward the north side of the house. "And I think it's high time we got packed up and get a move on. This place has lost its charm."

* * *

After Carter left to make sure the guest suites at the twin's house were up to snuff, Leonard got on his hands and knees, plugged in an extension cord, and then sat alone in the living room staring at Georgia's elaborate Christmas tree. He hadn't been there long enough to unpack, so he waited patiently while the girls shoved mounds of clothing, shoes, and beauty products into their many bags.

He was mesmerized by the twinkling lights and it took him back to a simpler time when his grandmother would go all out decorating her grand old house as if she were competing in some kind of neighborhood contest. All of her possessions were in storage now, but it warmed his heart knowing that all of her carefully curated things were somewhere he could get at them, if he needed to. Leonard wondered if Skyler would appreciate enough vintage ornaments to cover a half dozen live trees; his grandmother always insisted on fresh cut Maine Balsam Firs, he remembered clearly, each lovingly selected at Farr's Tree Farm in Scarborough. It was a family tradition that disappeared when she passed away, mostly because of laziness and partly because Leonard's father absolutely detested how the pine needles would linger in the bed of his truck for months after he hauled away the very dead, dried-up trees for his mother. She'd always stop watering them after New Year's, but hated to see them come down, so she'd wait as long as possible to pack up the forty or so boxes again. She amusingly claimed it was sacrilegious to leave them up until Valentine's Day, so that never happened. But she got damn near close a few times.

Lost in thought, he didn't hear when Skyler entered the room. "I wish we could take it with us."

"The tree?" Leonard asked. "I think that would be too much work."

"Georgia had a local design student pull it together. We could track her down somehow, I suppose."

Leonard stood up and turned toward his girlfriend. "A student? In the house?"

"How else would she do it if she wasn't *in* the house?"

"How did Georgia find this girl?"

"I don't recall, actually," Skyler said, looking confused. "Why do you care?"

"Was she vetted?"

"Oh my goodness, Leonard. I see where you're going with this. I don't know if the police talked to her, no. I'm not sure she was ever mentioned to the authorities or to the Mallard people, to tell you the truth. I guess everyone just forgot about her. If anyone thought about the Christmas tree—and I doubt anyone did, for goodness sake—then they probably assumed that Georgia did the decorating herself."

Leonard cocked his head. "You told me that when Brenda was with Georgia at the dress shop, that Grey's people checked the whole store and that the back door was locked before they allowed Brenda and Georgia into the shop. Isn't that correct?"

"Yes. That's what Brenda said."

"And there were two other people shopping in the store while they were there?"

Brenda heard part of the conversation as she struggled into the living room with her luggage. "Yes, Leonard," she puffed. "An ancient bitty and some young woman with glasses."

"Maybe a young *design student?*"

"Wouldn't Georgia have recognized her and spoken to her if it was the same girl?" Skyler turned to Brenda. "Did Georgia talk to the girl in the shop?"

"Not that I remember, no. I mean, no way. That place was tiny. I would have noticed and Georgia would have certainly introduced us. Right?"

"Maybe she was wearing a disguise of some sort. A wig? Maybe she didn't normally wear glasses?" Leonard asked rhetorically.

"I know you're a hunky cop," Skyler cooed, "but when did you become a clever detective?" She smiled widely.

"It's not rocket science." He went over to the tree and unplugged the lights. "She had access to the house like no one else has since Georgia bought the place. We need to know more about this chick and see if there's some kind of connection between her and Maraschino."

"*Massimo,*" Skyler and Brenda corrected in unison.

"Shit, we sound like the twins," Brenda laughed. "Okay, Leonard, will you please start hauling this stuff out to the cars? I'm hungry and I want to get settled over there and get cooking. I've got Christmas cookies to bake."

CHAPTER TWENTY-THREE

He'd been licking his wounds and laying low. There was nothing on the television news about it—he'd been watching regularly—but instinct told him Georgia had been found and was in the hands of the authorities...or maybe even back in her Santa Fe house already. And if that was indeed the case, the F.B.I. and the Arizona State Police would certainly be out in force looking for the accidental kidnapper.

He hadn't set out to abduct her, but she wouldn't listen to reason and none of his threats had worked. After decades spent laser focused on her career—*my entire adult life has been devoted to her!*—he was thrown away like garbage.

He *made* her.

She didn't care.

Massimo spent a lot of time cursing himself for his careless actions of the previous day. Thinking it was a good way to avoid the police, he decided to leave the highway a few towns east of Flagstaff and was navigating deserted country roads when the rental car ran out of gas. And since Georgia was still unconscious, he left her in the backseat when he went searching for another vehicle—at that point, he thought that stealing was a matter of survival—or for a place where they could hide out for the night. When that quest turned up nothing, he returned to an empty car. No Georgia and no iced tea. After walking in the desert for hours, he'd been imagining how satisfying the leftover McDonald's tea would be. He was dehydrated and exhausted. He hadn't slept for more than a few minutes at a time in several days.

But off he went again—what choice did he have?—searching for hours for the opera singer until it got too dark to navigate in the countryside. It was pitch black outside and when he stepped in a large hole, twisting his ankle so that he fell onto the ground, cursing in Italian, he'd had more than enough. He managed to limp to a main road and successfully hitched a ride to town with an old man in a vintage pickup truck, who probably should have known better about picking up strange Italian men in the dead of night.

Massimo checked into a cheap, 1950's-looking motor court across the street from a boarded-up Olive Garden restaurant. The seedy motel was the kind of place where one could lay a few twenties on the counter with absolutely no questions asked. No guestbook to sign. No identification checked. Of course, there were no frills either. A squeaky bed, paper-thin sheets, and rough grey towels that were probably crisp white a few decades earlier. He looked around on the nightstand and bureau for the television remote but couldn't find one. After few more moments he understood he wouldn't need a remote: the T.V. was huge, with a convex screen, and knobs and dials on the side. It took several seconds for Massimo to realize he had to pull one of the knobs out with his fingers to turn it on. He sat at the end of the bed. A bald man was telling the ugliest little girl Massimo had ever seen—*Dio mio! Scimmia!*—that the girl's performance had moved him to tears. *Not as much as having to sit across a table from her would,* Massimo thought. Then he remembered how he'd been moved to tears when he first saw Georgia perform, and his tears of gratitude when she agreed to have sex with him, and his tears of disbelief when she simply said, *Sure, certainly* to him when he asked for a 40% cut of her earnings.

Angrily, he reached and turned the channel dial. Static, then more static, then onto Fox News—he recognized the logo on the bottom of the screen—where one man was saying, "That's the problem with dressing rooms when you got all these athletes showering together—when one gets the flu, they all get it."

Just like that, Massimo thought to himself that Georgia and her friends probably thought he was as stupid and pathetic as this man speaking, and his anger came back.

He turned the dial again through seven or eight blizzards of static and then he landed at the only other channel the set picked up. And there was Georgia's new friend—that cow, *Brindle* or *Grendel*—no, *Brenda*, that's it—smiling and talking about her olive oils—and what did this *bovine cagna* know about olive oil? His great grandmother Nonna Cinghiale—Gramma Wild Boar, because of the long wiry hairs on her chin and cheeks—*now, she pressed genuine olive oil.* He turned the television off and lay back on the bed.

He was in pain, faint from hunger, dizzy from thirst, and now bored out of his mind.

But he had gone too far to turn back. He knew that he had to get back to Santa Fe to finish the job, whatever that job was. He was determined not to let her win, even if it cost him his freedom. He just wasn't exactly sure what he was going to do next. He successfully abducted her once, but he knew that the new friends she surrounded herself with would be extra diligent.

She'd never be left alone.

But what do I have to lose? he asked himself. He knew that he'd probably never make it back to Italy, nor would he see his family again, unless they deported him (a fact that he hoped would not come to pass, as he suspected American prisons were worlds more tolerable than Italian ones).

Is that my fate? What have I done? What have I become?

He had $92—boring American bills with pictures of long-dead politicians on them—left in his wallet. He couldn't use his credit cards for fear of being tracked. His cell phone was out of juice and he had no charging cords. And he had no clothes besides what he was wearing; his luggage was in the rental car somewhere out in the country. And it probably wasn't there anymore anyway. He decided that the car was most definitely sitting in an impound yard. It was evidence now. One of the scenes of his crime.

He pulled the knob and the television came back to life.

He watched as a plump blonde woman with a perma-smile plastered to her fat face demonstrated the wonders of some Tupperware-looking plastic food storage containers that were purportedly going to change the course of homemaker history for the better. Massimo watched in awe as the saleswoman went on and on about the stupid rainbow-colored boxes as if they were heaven-sent. He considered for a moment pulling out his credit card to make a purchase, but then he remembered his situation.

Massimo grabbed the Bible from the nightstand and threw it as hard as he could at the ancient television set then got off the bed. He stripped down and hobbled into the bathroom and into the mildew-stained shower stall. He wasn't going to waste any more time watching the Home Shopping Network in a Godforsaken, no-star Flagstaff, Arizona motel room. He had to figure out how to get back to New Mexico, ruin Georgia for good, and get his hands on a very large stash of cash.

Because that was who he'd become, and it made him quite sad, but more determined than ever.

* * *

Both Carter and Sullivan were equally flabbergasted by the buttoned-up appearance and sickeningly sweet demeanor of their younger brother. Darby was holding court on the living room sofa, between Skyler and Brenda, enchanting both ladies with his good looks and witty tales. He was sitting up straight up, his hair was perfectly coiffed, and he was smiling.

The twins stood several yards away in the kitchen unloading Brenda's paper grocery bags.

"I haven't seen that kid smile in a decade," Carter said. "What is he on?"

Sullivan shook his head slowly. "He says, nothing. The entire car ride from the airport, he talked about having turned it all around. No drugs, no binge drinking, no blacking out, no gambling. He claims that *on our parents' graves*—his words, not mine, especially since they were cremated—that he's cleaned up his act."

"And you're buying what he's selling?"

"Carter," Sullivan said, "look at him. Darby is a new man. Watch the way he is with the girls. They're eating it up. And I suspect that you can't fool people like Brenda and Skyler. They know how to see through peoples' bullshit. And it's not like we didn't warn them ahead of time."

"He wants something. Plain and simple."

"Maybe. But maybe he deserves something now."

"Maybe." Carter stuffed a carton of milk into the already crowded refrigerator. "Just make sure you always know where your wallet is. You tend to leave that thing in random places all over the damned house. If he gets his hands on it, you'll be cash poor and light of a few credit cards."

"You always think the worst of everyone."

"Not *everyone*, Sully," his brother exploded. "Darby's track record fucking sucks, excuse my language. But we shall see. It's Christmas. I'm willing to give him another chance. Jesus would want it that way."

Leonard walked into the kitchen and leaned up against the counter. "What are you guys talking about?"

"Nothing important," Carter said. "Say, how are you enjoying Santa Fe, so far?"

The cop shrugged his shoulders. "All I've seen is the airport, Georgia's house, and your house. And a lot of trees and mountains. What I can tell you is that I am dry as all get out."

"Yeah, the high desert will do that to you," Sullivan said. "It took us a few weeks to get used to it when we first got here. It's cocktail hour now, but I suggest having a glass of water with each drink you put away. You'll thank me tomorrow."

"Will do," Leonard said. "But I think I'll start with a beer."

"Coming right up." Carter fished a holiday pale ale from the under-counter beer fridge and handed it to Leonard.

"Thanks. So, I was thinking, I'd like to go with whoever is going to pick up Georgia on Sunday. Since you don't know what you might encounter, it would be good to have someone with a little bit of law enforcement experience along for the ride."

"I think that's a great idea," Sullivan said. "Carter just arranged for a King Air to take us. We're going at first light Christmas Eve morning. We should be back here at the house in time for a late lunch."

Leonard crinkled his brow. "You're going in an airplane?"

"It's a 400-mile drive from here, man," Carter said. "Even at 75 miles an hour, the roundtrip would take the whole damned day. We can get there in just over an hour in the King Air. It's a twin turboprop. You'll like it. Pressurized cabin, eight seats, has a lavatory on board, and she has a ceiling of 35,000 feet."

"Is that good?"

"For a prop? I think so," Carter said. "Ask your girlfriend about it. She's the plane nut."

"And I am *not*," Leonard said sheepishly. "But I still think I should go. It'll be good practice."

Sullivan looked confused. "Practice?"

"I'm toying with the idea of establishing a celebrity protection service. I know a few famous folks now and I'm just not cut out to be a small-town cop, that's for sure. I think it'll be fun."

"*Fun* is not the first thing I think of when I think of protecting celebrities," Skyler said when she appeared in the kitchen. She hugged Leonard from behind and kissed him delicately on an ear. "Honey, it's a lot of standing around and waiting. It's not at all glamourous."

"More glamourous than assigning deputies to go kick teenagers off of lobster boats in the middle of the night."

"What are teenagers doing on lobster boats in the middle of the night?" Carter asked.

"Drinking and screwing, usually," Leonard said. "What else are they supposed to do in Wabanaki, Maine in the dead of winter?"

"That doesn't sound very comfortable," Sullivan said.

"It's not," Skyler said.

Leonard turned to his girlfriend. "How do *you* know that?"

"I was a teenager in Wabanaki, Maine, remember?"

"Mmm," he said. "I guess I do."

Brenda marched into the kitchen and broke up the party. "I need all of you to move it to the living room. I've got to start cooking if we want to eat tonight."

And the celebrity chef didn't disappoint. After a few hours, the whole crew settled around the large round dining table and enjoyed a gourmet meal that would have cost several hundred dollars per head in one of her restaurants. They were first presented with her new signature Lobster Alla Chitarra, an appetizer portion of butter-poached lobster claw over thin pasta noodles with charred eggplant, zucchini, and parmesan—if it were to be served as an entrée, Brenda warned, "…it would kill you with richness." She followed that with an espresso cup filled with chilled pea soup paired with a toasted garlic bread crostini on the saucer. Next, the roasted veal tenderloin with truffle whipped mashed potatoes and cauliflower left everyone raving. And, as a sweet finale, Brenda produced chocolate-hazelnut mousse piped into champagne flutes. She dropped a spoonful of homemade whipped cream and a single red raspberry on top of each.

The chef sat down for the first time and savored the dessert.

"You did all of this on your own without a sous chef or any

assistance at all," Carter said. "So, why do we have to hire so many people for the hotel restaurant?"

"Please," Brenda said with a mouthful of mousse. "As much as I adore Santa Fe, darling, I am not going to be head chef of that kitchen. I'll get it started, I'll create the menus, and then I'll move on. Do you think Gordon Ramsey cooks every dish in every one of his hundreds of restaurants?"

"He was kidding," Sullivan said with a smile. "I am astounded by it all, Brenda. It's just so very impressive. And if we put your restaurants in all of our hotels nationwide, I am going to have one fat ass."

The chef wrinkled her brow and Sullivan felt bad for insulting her.

Brenda recovered quickly. She put down her spoon and raised a glass. "Since I am finally sitting on my fat ass and have a chance to breathe..." She turned to Leonard and whispered, "...by the way, you're cleaning that kitchen..." She glanced at the rest of the table, "...I want to propose a toast. To Georgia being found safe and sound; to a happy, *uneventful* Christmas; and, to a happy, prosperous new year for each and every one of us."

They all clinked glasses. Even Darby, who seemed to be watching his alcohol intake very carefully. "Hear, hear," he said. "And I want to propose a toast of my own." He pushed back his chair and got to his feet. "To my two big brothers. Thank you for believing in the brand new me. I won't let you down. *Again.* You're all the family I have in the world and I treasure you both. Merry Christmas."

"Merry Christmas," the assembled said in unison.

"I hope you mean that, buddy boy," Carter said after he took a sip. He looked at the younger Lowrey and noticed, for the slightest of a second, that familiar devilish look he knew so well. The one of contempt and foolhardiness and greed and laziness. It was there and then it was gone. Darby forced a smile and raised his glass again.

"I will not let you down, Sully."

Sullivan closed his eyes. Skyler stopped breathing for a few seconds; she'd just met them but even *she* knew which Lowery twin was which.

Carter cocked his head. "My name is Carter. But I'm letting it slide this time, baby brother, because, admittedly, we haven't spent much quality time together lately. I hope that will change and you'll be able to tell your brothers apart tout de suite."

Darby was doing his best to mask his embarrassment, and a tinge of resentment, with a forced smile. It was all there, right below the surface though. Carter saw it. "Time will tell," Darby said quietly.

"Well," Skyler said, "I think we should all pitch in and clear this table and clean the kitchen and I bet we'll have it done in 10 minutes." She turned to Brenda. "I think it was a great idea for you to suggest that Leonard take on kitchen duty, but trust me, you do not want that man washing a single dish or glass. I have seen firsthand his handiwork and it is not pretty."

"I am not inept," Leonard said.

"Honey. The last time you cleaned up after dinner, I had to re-wash nearly every single thing in the cabinets." She turned to the others. "He emptied an entire dishwasher full of stuff, but it was all dirty. I hadn't run it yet."

Leonard stood up causing his chair to topple over and hit the stone floor, making quite a racket. "I didn't risk life and limb to fly across the country to spend Christmas with you just so you could embarrass me in front of all of these people." He turned to Sullivan. "I'm sorry about the chair. I'll pay for it if it's broken."

"Honey," Skyler said carefully. "I was just kidding. Nobody cares about…"

"But *that* actually happened."

"Yeah. And I'm sorry."

"Whatever." And he stormed out of the room.

"Geez," Darby said. "He sounds like the old me."

"Drink your wine and shut up," Carter said.

"I think I better go talk to him." Skyler topped off her wine glass and followed Leonard outside onto the covered patio.

It was lightly snowing, and for the first time since they'd all arrived in town, there wasn't a bit of wind. It was cold, but still and silent. Leonard took a pack of cigarettes out of one pocket and fished a lighter from another.

"Before you say anything," he said, "I am going to have this one cig and that's it for today. I have been very good and I think having one a day, while I try to quit for good, is me doing pretty damned good."

"I think so, too," Skyler said softly. She sidled up close to his body for warmth and before he could put the pack away, she snatched it out of his hand and took a cigarette out of the box. She put it to her lips and waited for it to be lit. "Come on."

"No. What? What are you doing?"

"You can have one, I can have one. After a big fat meal like that, I bet it's going to be so good."

"You don't smoke."

"I have. And I can. I can if I want to. There was a three-month period in college when I smoked every day with some girlfriends I was trying to impress. I gave it up for a boy and never looked back, but I think it's like riding a bike, right?"

"I guess so," he said, producing a flame and igniting the end of her cigarette. Then he lit his own and took a long drag. "Oh, that's good."

Skyler took a baby drag and didn't inhale at first. She worked her way up to pulling the smoke into her lungs. Then she exploded in a fit of couching and nearly threw up her dinner all over the patio. She handed the cigarette back to Leonard and then finally managed, "I think maybe I won't be smoking ever again."

"Good idea." He put an arm around her back and pulled her close. "I don't want a girlfriend who smokes, anyway. I love you, you know? I'm sorry if I acted like a child in there. Do you think they all hate me now?"

"Are you kidding me? No one *hates* you. And Carter and Sullivan are as eccentric and crazy as the rest of us. And from what I hear about Darby, well, he's got some demons, too."

"I don't have demons."

"I didn't say you did."

"You said, *too*."

"Well, we all have demons. In any event, it's fine. And I'm sorry that I told tales out of school. I didn't mean to embarrass you. I just thought it was an amusing story. It was funny, Leonard."

"Alright," he said, stubbing out his cigarette. He then started smoking hers. "I'll forgive you."

"Good. And I will let you have your way with me tonight if you promise to brush your teeth three times before bed."

"I have to say, that is a very strange requirement," a voice said from behind them. Skyler and Leonard spun around to find Darby standing on the patio holding a glass of wine and an unlit cigar. "I'm sorry if I'm butting in. I thought you heard me come out."

"Jesus, Darby," Skyler said, "we were just fooling around."

"Apparently there won't be any fooling around unless the cop brushes his teeth three times." Darby grinned like a crazed Batman villain, then lit his cigar with a long neck fireplace lighter he found on the mantel inside the house. "I'm kidding, of course."

"Of course," Leonard said dryly. "If you'll excuse us, I think we're going to go inside and help clean up that kitchen."

"I hear you're not very good at that, but go for it, man."

Skyler gave the young man a weak smile as they passed him to enter the house. When the door was shut behind them, she turned to Leonard. "That one is starting to show his true colors."

"Yeah. I didn't like the kid the minute I met him."

CHAPTER TWENTY-FOUR

On Saturday morning, after a late-night hour of aerobic love making and a well-earned good night's sleep, Skyler stole into the kitchen wearing one of the rental houses' plush bathrobes. The twins liked to keep the place at a lower temperature than she was used to in the wintertime, so she also had on the thick socks that she'd pulled on after the post-coitus shower. The house was dead quiet except for the instantly recognizable tapping of a laptop keyboard. She discovered young Darby sitting on one of the Great Room sofas with a Mac on his lap. He suffered from severe bedhead, he was wearing eye glasses that she hadn't seen him wear before, and he had nothing on his body save for a baggy pair of well-worn red plaid boxer shorts.

"Good morning," she said. "Did you start the coffee by any chance?"

He continued to type, ignoring her.

"That's okay. I'll do it."

"Sorry," Darby finally said. He abruptly closed the laptop and placed it on the coffee table in front of him. "I'm drinking tea. I'm off coffee for the time being. But there's one of those pod contraptions by the bar. There seems to be a whole assortment of different things to choose from over there."

"Thank you." Skyler made her way to the bar. "How'd you

sleep?"

Darby got up and walked toward her, one hand flattening his hair and the other finding its way into the front of his shorts. "Apparently, I'm the lowest dude on the totem pole. My brothers each have a room, Brenda has one, and Leonard and you have the fourth. I'm in the stupid loft upstairs. It has a pullout soda bed with a shitty mattress and the room has no door. I felt very vulnerable up there and I'm pretty sure I slept on an exposed spring all night."

"My goodness, Darby. I'm so sorry. Maybe the twins'll move people around to make it fairer tonight."

"Maybe a house full of millionaires could afford better accommodations. I mean, my brothers are supposed to be experts at hospitality, for God's sake."

Skyler shrugged her shoulders and tried not to look at the kid's midsection. She made the mistake of glancing in that direction and it looked like he was either extremely hung or inappropriately excited to see her. "Can I make you some more tea?"

"Naw," he said, "I'm all teaed out. I've been up since half past five. I'm working on a novel and I'm at my best first thing in the morning, before all the chaos of the world gets going."

"That's pretty exciting. Is this your first book?"

"Third, actually. I self-published the first two, mostly because they were total pieces of crap that no publisher wanted to buy, but I'm feeling much better about this new one. It's more mainstream, too."

"Commercial or literary?"

"Commercial," Darby said as he slumped into a dining room chair and spread his legs wide. "It's a thriller with lots of chases, guns, murders and…some hot sex."

Skyler took a sip of her coffee. "Good. Sex sells."

"You've represented some authors. Can you help me?"

"After it's published, maybe. I don't really have literary agent or publishing contacts. I do P.R. after the fact for a few clients. But most of them were already famous when they came out with a book. It's easier that way."

"No shit," he said through a heavy sigh.

He was absently fondling himself and it was unnerving Skyler. "I'm going to take this coffee back to my room and get ready for the day. I still have a bunch of things to do to get ready for Christmas."

"Are we doing all of that?" he asked with disgust. "I hate Christmas."

"I thought you came to Santa Fe to be with your brothers for the holidays. How can you hate Christmas?"

"It wasn't always that way. I used to love it when my parents were still with us. Man, our mother used to go all out. She won decorating contests. The newspaper would take photos of our house and they even published one of her Christmas cookie recipes one year. I'm telling you, it would take her a full half hour to wrap one present because she was so meticulous. The woman had several themed trees. She really got into the spirit, which was funny, because she wasn't really all that religious or anything."

"Sounds a little bit like me," Skyler said. "So, what happened? Couldn't you carry that tradition on in her absence?"

"Me?" Darby asked. "No. It's just not the same. It's just us three boys now and Carter and Sully don't really give a crap. My present from them last year was that laptop and it wasn't even wrapped. Christmas is something for other people now. Families with kids and stuff. And stores. The stores love it."

"What did you give your brothers last year?" she asked as she narrowed her eyes.

"Nothing. They're worth millions."

"It's not about the value, is it? It's the sentiment. The thought behind it. Surely you learned that from your mother."

Darby was growing agitated. "You're acting like her right now. I don't need another mother, lady."

"I'm not nearly old enough to be your mother," Skyler said as she padded off to the back hall. "I'd kill myself first," she added, under her breath.

"Dude, you need to put some clothes on." Sullivan had appeared in the kitchen, already dressed for the day in jeans and a cable knit sweater. "Do you realize that your dick is hanging out of your boxers? Come on! Skyler or Brenda could come out here at any moment."

"Like they haven't seen massive dicks before." Darby shoved his penis back into place and got himself off the couch. "What bathroom am I supposed to use? The one out here is just a half."

"Go take a shower in mine. There are tons of fresh towels on the shelf in there."

"Cool."

"What happened to that *nice* kid I picked up yesterday? The one who supposedly turned it all around? The one who charmed the pants off the ladies last night?"

Darby walked past his brother toward the bedrooms. "That nice kid checked out when he found out he had to sleep on a sofa bed when he could have checked in to the Four Seasons."

"You're a spoiled brat," Sullivan called out after him.

"I think there are too many people in the showers all at once," Carter said when he joined his brother in the kitchen. "I just suffered through a nearly ice-cold shower. It was not fun."

"Sorry," Sullivan said. "I guess we should have orchestrated this better, but it sounds like Skyler, Brenda, and Darby are all in their bathrooms right now. I keep forgetting that we don't have hotel-sized hot water heaters in this place."

"Where is *Darby's* bathroom?"

"He's using mine."

"Is he still acting like he's miraculously turned into a good guy?"

"He is not," Sullivan said with a sigh. "He's foul and grumpy today. Back to normal."

"Fantastic." Carter got busy pulling out frying pans and mixing bowls. "By the way, I'm determined to make a hearty breakfast that will impress that celebrity chef staying under our roof. She outdid herself last night and I want to pay her back." He beat eggs, prepared slabs of bacon for the oven, and even mixed up a batch of honey butter for the sourdough toast. He sliced tomatoes and popped open a huge can of baked beans, too, intending to give his meal a British flair—that was one of the standouts he remembered from a trip to London a few years earlier.

While he cooked, the rest of the houseguests found their way to the kitchen and they lined up for coffee. Everyone crowded around the island, except for Darby, who found his way from Sullivan's shower into Sullivan's bed. He was fast asleep.

"What's on the agenda for today?" Leonard asked the group.

"I'm going to walk the dogs before I go food shopping,"

Brenda said as she tore into the bacon and scrambled eggs set in front of her. "I'm going to try to get everything we need for meals through Christmas Day. But, I do wonder if we might go out for one dinner—would that be okay with everyone?"

"Of course," Carter said. "No one expects you to cook for all of us, Brenda. That's not automatically your job just because…well…because it's your job."

"Good," she said. "Because I was thinking we might have our Christmas Eve dinner down at The Compound restaurant. I called them. They have room for all of us and the menu looks absolutely marvelous. With Georgia, it'd be seven. Do we think she'd be up for going out to eat almost immediately after getting home tomorrow? On second thought, maybe that's a bad idea."

Skyler swallowed then said, "I'm all for it. I think breaking from tradition and going out to eat for a holiday meal is kind of fun. And Carter is right; you shouldn't feel like you have to do all the shopping and cooking. I mean, I can help."

"Oh lord," Brenda laughed. "That's the last thing we want."

"What? I'm a decent cook."

"Not really," Leonard said. "She can manage spaghetti and calling out for pizza. That's about it."

"I will admit that I am good at calling for take-out. I singlehandedly keep several Dupont Circle restaurants in business, trust me."

"And the restaurant owners are very grateful," Brenda said. "Trust *me*."

"Who the hell is that!" Leonard shoved back in his chair and rounded the table as he sprinted toward the floor-to-ceiling windows that looked out over the hot tub on the patio outside. "Someone was just outside. Right there!" He squatted down and extracted the small .22 from under his pant leg; his larger, police-issued gun was holstered and hanging on the back of his suite's bathroom door. "I'm going out."

"Be careful, Leonard!" Skyler was right behind him. She ripped his jacket off a peg near the front door and threw it at him. "It's cold out there." The jacket fell to the floor as Leonard opened the door. "It's not *Maine* cold, Sky. Come on."

Carter sprinted to his room to grab his own weapon. "I'll be right there!"

"They're going to shoot each other, aren't they?" Brenda asked.

"God, I hope not," Sullivan said as the two hurried to the bank of windows. "I can't finish the hotel on my own. Who do you think he saw? Was it Massimo? No. It couldn't be."

"I have no idea." The chef stood up on her tip toes and craned her neck. "Right there! Behind the wood pile." She turned to Skyler who was standing at the open front door. "Skyler, tell him to head toward the wood pile."

Skyler stuck four fingers in her mouth and whistled with all of her might, then pointed wildly when Leonard looked back at the front door. She was shoved into the door jam when Carter barreled out of the house, his weapon drawn. "Jesus Christ!" She righted herself and massaged her right shoulder.

"Are you okay, honey?" Brenda was behind her and placed a hand on her back.

"I'm fine. That one should get a job as a linebacker for the Redskins."

"I'm calling the police," Sullivan said. He pulled out his phone. "I don't see them anymore, do you? Where did they go? I should call the police, yes?"

"I'm going out there, too," Skyler said as she headed down the front steps to the gravel walkway, but she was stopped at the bottom when someone grabbed her left arm and ripped her back around.

"You most certainly are not!" Brenda bellowed. "Do you want your boyfriend or that trigger-happy Lowery brother to shoot *you*? Get back in the house. Leonard is a police officer. He's got this."

Skyler reluctantly obeyed. "I can help. I need to do something, Brenda."

"Uh, huh. Inside!"

Sullivan slammed his cell phone down on the front hall table after the girls were back inside and the door was closed and locked. "I didn't get through. The reception up here royally sucks. It's better at night. It's worthless during the daytime. I have no idea why that might be."

"Is there a landline?" Brenda asked.

"Is it 1987?"

A quarter mile from the house, Leonard was down on one knee trying desperately to control his breathing. He'd lost track of the subject in a thick grove of trees somewhere in front of him. He didn't hear running anymore. He listened for any sound of human movement, but all he could hear were light footsteps behind him.

Carter was inches away. "Anything?" he whispered.

"No." Leonard looked to their right. There was a steep embankment sloping away from them. "Go that way and make a large arc back to the left. And *don't* shoot me as I come toward you. I'm pretty sure he's wearing black. I'm wearing *red*.

Remember that."

"Roger that." Carter took off.

Leonard waited a few beats before moving. It wasn't police training that prepared him for this moment—it was instinct. The Maine Police Academy never sent trainees out into the cold winter woods to track down potential stalkers. This was more like hunting deer with his father, but there'd be no venison on the table after this was over.

He pushed forward, careful to move branches without making too much noise. He held the gun down at his side; he was determined not to kill Carter—or anyone for that matter. He knew the mounds of red tape would ruin Christmas.

A flash to his left. Something moved quickly. He changed direction and picked up his pace. He was sweating as if it were a mid-summer afternoon instead of a brisk New Mexican morning in December. He had trouble catching his breath, too. He knew he had to quit smoking once and for all or he'd never catch anyone in the woods.

A tree branch slapped him across the face as he started running toward the figure. It was moving faster.

And then he ran straight into Carter and they fell to the ground on top of one another. In the same instance, Carter's gun fired. The sound echoed through the trees and seemed to last several long seconds.

"What the fuck, dude?"

"Oh my God, I'm so sorry," Carter said. "I didn't mean to pull the trigger." He carefully placed the handgun on the ground and got to his feet. He put out a hand to help Leonard up. "Oh shit, oh shit."

"What is wrong with you?" And then Leonard felt it. His

upper arm was searing with pain.

"Leonard, man. Oh my God, man. I shot you."

The cop felt lightheaded. "No fucking kidding."

"Was that a gun shot?" Skyler had been standing on the front porch. "I hope they didn't kill anyone. I'm going out there."

Brenda grabbed her friend by the arm for the eighth time that morning. "Do I need to tie you to a bed or something? What is wrong with you?"

"What is wrong with our life that gun shots are the new normal?"

"It's not our new normal," Brenda said, escorting Skyler back into the house. "But if there are people hell bent on screwing with us, well, then I'm glad Leonard and Carter have guns."

"Carter has never fired that gun, has no license, and has absolutely no training," Sullivan said. "It was our father's pistol and it was locked in a box for decades. I didn't even know we had ammunition for it."

"Why did he bring it to Santa Fe?" Skyler asked.

"He was certain this was the wild west and that everyone would be carrying guns out here. And this is a very different world than New York City, I'll give him that. Can you imagine him grabbing a gun and chasing a pickpocket down Madison Avenue in broad daylight?"

"This is insanity," Skyler said. "Sullivan, try calling the police again."

The front door opened and a stone faced, shirtless Carter entered first, followed by Leonard. Carter's shirt was tied around Leonard's upper left arm. It was soaked with blood.

"Massimo shot you?" Brenda asked.

Skyler rushed to her boyfriend and grabbed each cheek in her palms. "Oh my God, what happened?!"

"I'm fine. We need to get the bleeding stopped. I'm just grazed, so don't get all excited. An inch lower though and it would have gone straight through my damned arm bone." He shot a look at Carter. "I want your gun, by the way."

"You shot Leonard?!" Sullivan screamed.

"It was an accident," Carter said. He slumped down into a chair. "And she got away."

"She?" Skyler asked.

Leonard stood in front of the hall mirror and examined his wound—it wasn't very deep and not as ugly as he'd imagined it would be. It had pretty much stopped bleeding. "It was a woman, yes. Or at least she looked like one. She was much too short and thin to be someone named Massimo."

"He's right. It was *not* Massimo," Carter said.

Brenda went to Leonard's side and examined his upper arm. "We need to get you to the hospital."

"No, we don't," he said, pulling away from her. "I'm going to go take another shower and then we'll get this bandaged up. I saw a first aid kit under the sink in our bathroom."

"Honey, we have to have a doctor check you out," Skyler said.

Leonard turned to face his girlfriend. "And then what happens? We would be barraged with a thousand questions. The police would get involved—hospitals legally have to report gun shot wounds. I know a little bit about this kind of thing. It will take many hours, Carter will have to surrender his *unregistered* and *unlicensed* gun, and, well, it'll just be a royal pain in all of our asses the day before Christmas Eve. I'm fine. We'll all be better off if we just keep this to ourselves."

"Will we?" Sullivan asked. "Carter *should* lose that damned gun once and for all. And the police have got to be told that there's yet another person terrorizing us. Am I right?"

"We were hardly terrorized," Leonard said. "But we do need to up our game."

"What does that even mean?" Brenda asked. "Perhaps we should pick up Georgia and then get the hell out of Santa Fe. That's what we should *all* do. Why would we stay here and be on edge twenty-four-seven? We could fly over to Las Vegas and have Christmas at the Golden Cactus. Anything is better than this. The authorities are already looking for Massimo. We just have to tell them that we had a new intruder on the property today, so that they'll be officially looking for her, too. And then we can cut and run."

"Sully and I can't leave Santa Fe, Brenda. Not now," Carter said. "We have a hotel to finish. We've got millions of dollars on the line. You all can certainly leave if you want to, but I'm afraid we've got to stay. We've got crews returning to the site the day after Christmas. We have to be here."

"What the hell is going on? Can't a guy get some sleep around here?" A completely nude Darby stood in the doorway between the kitchen and the back hall, scratching his ass.

"Merry Christmas to us," Skyler said.

"Indeed," Brenda said with a big smile on her face. "Merry Christmas."

CHAPTER TWENTY-FIVE

After he purchased a ticket with the last of his cash, Massimo carried his pharmacy shopping bag of toiletries, underwear, and socks to the Albuquerque-bound Greyhound bus and found an empty seat in the second to last row. He'd never before rode on a bus and he was unnerved by being so close to so many people, together with all their many bags of giftwrapped packages. He assumed that they were collectively on their way to relatives' and friends' homes for the holidays. He wished he was anywhere but the Flagstaff, Arizona bus station two days before Christmas, his first holiday away from his family.

The trip was bumpy, but uneventful. They stopped every two hundred miles for bathroom and cigarette breaks and arrived in downtown Albuquerque at half past three in the afternoon.

He knew it was risky, but he located another pharmacy and purchased a cold tuna fish sandwich, a bag of potato chips, and a banana. He used his debit card and asked for $100 cash back, the maximum the store allowed.

After devouring the late-lunch on a chilly park bench, he went back to the Greyhound station and inquired about buses to Santa Fe. Not one seat was available. The clerk suggested the commuter train and he stood in line for over a half hour just to discover that they were oversold, too.

An elderly Native American man approached Massimo in the waiting area. "Hey, mac, can you spare a few bucks for a veteran?"

Massimo was annoyed, but not altogether uncaring of his fellow man. "For what?"

"I'm trying to get home to see my grandkids for Christmas."

"Where is home?"

"Roswell."

"And Roswell is where?"

"About 200 miles from here. I've got $30 but I need…"

"200 miles in which direction? I'm not from around here."

"Well, I could tell that from your accent," the man said with a hearty laugh. "Roswell is south. It's south-east, actually, as the crow flies."

Massimo didn't think about it for very long. "I don't know about this crow you speak of, but I think this might be your lucky day, signore," he said. He knew the purchase would be beneficial…for both of them.

Massimo used one of his credit cards to buy a one-way bus ticket for the very grateful old man, then he set out to find a himself a good Samaritan who might offer him a ride in the opposite direction.

* * *

Back in Flagstaff, an incredibly antsy opera singer was going out of her mind. She repeatedly asked the hospital staff to release her early, but her doctors were determined to keep her under observation for another 24 hours. Besides a slightly sore scalp and a few abrasions here and there, she felt like her normal self again—despite the diet of barely edible hospital 'food,' including a mushy Salisbury steak that she was absolutely certain wasn't actual meat—and her normal self wasn't used to laying around in bed all day doing nothing.

She did vocal exercises until the woman in the next room complained and a nurse came to ask her to stop. She tried to watch the wall-mounted television, but all she could find were trivia game shows, pathetic people confessing dreadful things in front of dreadful audiences, and overwrought anger and crying on soap opera melodramas. She'd always had a low opinion of these shows and the kind of people who watched them. And she'd already read three well-worn issues of *People Magazine* that were each a few months old. So, she did what was most natural to her, she asked around until she found someone who could recommend a hair and makeup person and she asked that they come just as soon as was humanly possible. She had no intention of letting the twins see her in her natural, unkempt state.

When the pretty young woman arrived late in the afternoon, Georgia found her bubbly and enthusiastic and hoped that she knew what she was doing. She guessed correctly that Flagstaff, Arizona beauticians didn't work on too many celebrities.

"I've seen you on television," the girl admitted. "One of those weekend morning news shows, I think."

"*C.B.S. Sunday Morning* did a profile on me last year, yes," Georgia beamed. "I didn't know anyone actually watched that."

"Oh, tons, I'm sure. I was fascinated by your story. I even watched one of your operas on P.B.S. on-demand that very day. I didn't understand a word, of course, but there were captions at the bottom of the screen, so, you know, I could read along. You had such passion and poise and, wow, you really belted it out, huh?"

"Thank you," Georgia said. "Do you remember which opera it was?"

"I want to say, *Butterfly?*"

"*Madam Butterfly*. It's one of my favorites. I believe that particular production was filmed in high definition at the Palais Garnier. In Paris, of course."

"Of course."

"I'm glad you enjoyed it."

"I did, very much," the young woman said. She set a large plastic case on the bedside table and wheeled it into place. "So, are we doing a stage look or something more every-day?"

Georgia let out an emphatic belly laugh. "I don't think I want to fly home for Christmas wearing eight pounds of pancake makeup and three sets of false eyelashes, no. I want to look presentable, yet stylish."

"Hair, too?"

"Hair, too."

"How much time do we have?"

"About 18 hours. I get released in the morning."

The girl's face fell. "Oh, Miss Reece, if I do you up now, I'm not sure what it's going to look like come tomorrow morning."

"That's the beauty of having so much time," Georgia said. "I thought we could do it once now, as a rehearsal of sorts, and then you could come back again in the morning and get me ready for my departure."

"I guess I can do that," she said. "But it's going to cost a bit more."

Georgia produced the FedEx envelope that her bank's wealth manager had overnighted to her at the hospital from New

York City—she called him an 'absolute lamb' for seeing to it so quickly on the Friday before the holiday weekend. She pulled out a small stack of $100 bills and a brand new American Express Platinum card. "Cash or charge?"

CHAPTER TWENTY-SIX

Darby was loosely wrapped in a terrycloth bathrobe and was sitting on the end of Sullivan's unmade bed. His long hair was sticking up and out in every direction because after he took a shower, he got right into the bed with wet hair and it dried that way. Carter thought he looked like that famous police mugshot of the actor Nick Nolte from the early 2000's—he was just missing the wild Hawaiian floral shirt. *And Nolte's talent.*

"What the fuck is wrong with your brain?" Carter asked. "Excuse my French, man, but you can't just parade around the house buck naked, even if it were just the three of us here. Seriously. No one thinks this is funny. You're just...just...you have no class, man. No class."

Darby was unfazed. "I don't think the word *fuck* is French, actually."

Carter shook his head in defeat.

"What's up, buddy?" Sullivan was more optimistic. "What can we do to help you? Is it drugs again?"

"I am *not* on drugs. I haven't even smoked weed since I've been here. I don't even have any with me. The worst thing I've had since I've been in this Godforsaken place is a few glasses of wine and a cigar or two. I'm clean as a whistle."

"So, what's with the attitude? And nudity?"

"I'm free with my body, Sully," Darby said. "I don't need to be ashamed of my nakedness. My maleness. My essence."

Carter exploded. "Your essence is a big pile of stinking bullshit, is what it is! *Essence, my ass.*"

"At least I didn't shoot anyone with Daddy's gun today."

Carter lunged forward and grabbed Darby around the throat. They both went flying backward and toppling off the bed onto the floor as Sullivan jumped on the pile and feverishly tried to extract the eldest Lowery from the youngest before someone was choked to death. "Stop it, guys. Please. Stop!"

Darby was fighting back, pulling on Carter's hair and trying desperately to position his knee in order to deliver a...

"Mother fucker!" Carter screamed, then he couldn't catch his breath. Darby's knee was indeed delivered, squarely, and quite forcefully, to Carter's balls. The oldest brother rolled onto his back, tears escaping from his closed eyes.

"Why'd you do that?" Sullivan asked as he pulled Darby to his feet. "Hasn't he been through enough today?"

"Has he? He doesn't give a shit about me. He never has."

"Have you given him a reason? You've been nothing but a pain in everyone's ass since day one. Even Mom and Dad thought that."

"Sully! Dude. That hurts."

"Oh, *you* are hurt?" Carter asked. He managed to prop himself up against the dresser. "I think I need to go to the hospital."

"Walk it off," Darby said. He turned back to Sullivan. "I'm sorry if I have been less than pleasant on this trip. I really am committed to becoming a better person. That wasn't a lie. Getting screwed over by my girlfriend has taught me a few things about life."

Carter massaged his crotch and tried desperately to control his rage. "I don't want to fight with you. But if you won't start acting like a normal, civilized person, you're going to have to leave this house. This is no way to spend Christmas."

"You don't have to leave," Sullivan corrected. "We want to know what's going on with you."

"I'm good," Darby said quietly. "I'll *be* good. I promise."

Carter exhaled deeply and managed to get to his feet. "Super duper."

"But there is one thing I really could use some help with." Darby swallowed hard and tried displaying a small crooked smile before he continued. "I sorta, kinda owe a guy named Amancio Granada $750,000 by New Year's Eve."

The twins were speechless.

"Say something, guys."

"That's a lot of money," Sullivan managed.

Carter shook his head slowly. "We don't have that kind of cash lying around, dude. Everything Sully and I have in the world is tied up in new hotel projects right now. We reinvest every damned dime in order to grow the company." He took a deep breath, but it wasn't helping. He started to get angrier. "Are you *serious* right now? Who is this Granada person? A drug dealer? There is no way that you could have possibly racked up…"

Sullivan threw a hand up in Carter's face and then sat down on the edge of the bed next to Darby. "Amancio Granada, the Broadway producer? Is that who you are talking about? Why on Earth would you owe him money?"

Darby was staring at the wall.

"Darby. Three quarters of a million dollars, for *what?*"

"I kind of told him that Franklin-Lowery was interested in branching out into the entertainment business and that we wanted to invest in his new musical. It all happened so fast. I was on the spot." He got up and fished his wallet out of his crumpled jeans on the floor. He dug out a business card and passed it to Sullivan.

Darby Lowery
Business Development
Franklin-Lowery LLC

175 5th Avenue
New York, New York 10010
212-555-0229 /
DarbyLowery@franklinlowery.com

"Where did you get this?" He handed the card to Carter. "You don't work at Franklin-Lowery. You never have." Carter crushed the card in his fist. "You can't commit us to investments if you don't work for the company. This is just about the most insane thing you've ever done, buddy, and you've done some seriously screwed up stuff in your short lifetime. I'll make this very simple for you: You need to get yourself out of that deal."

"Contracts were signed."

Carter started out of the bedroom, but then stopped short and turned around. "You signed a contract by misrepresenting *yourself*. You! Sully and I have nothing to do with this. The company has nothing to do with this."

"Actually, that's not quite true," Sullivan said calmly. "Darby technically owns a third of our shares of Franklin-Lowery."

It took a few long seconds for him to realize what his brother had just confessed, then Carter slumped against the doorjamb. "Mother. Fucker." He waited a few beats and then said, "Damn it, Sully."

"I own what?!" Darby yelled. It was starting to sink in. He jumped off the bed and crouched down like a football player waiting for the quarterback to call the play. "I own a third of Dad's company and you never told me?" He stood straight up and put a hand on his forehead. "I don't understand. I was faking that I worked at the company and I could have been doing it for real? Why would you guys keep this from me? How do I own a *third* of the company? How did this happen? A third? Really?"

"It's a very complicated story," Carter said. "But the lawyers were in agreement with us and we all decided to keep it from you for your own damned good. When Dad died, you were in rehab for the second time. But maybe you don't remember that."

Sullivan approached his younger brother and placed a hand on his back. "We were going to tell you. Eventually. We were waiting for you to grow up."

"Well, damn. I'm rich."

Carter shook his head. "You aren't that rich."

"How much am I worth? Like, on paper."

"Somewhere in the neighborhood of 30. But most of it is tied up in the hotels, obviously. You can't get at it. But you get dividends."

"Thirty?" Darby asked, literally scratching his head. "Thirty, what?"

"Million," Sullivan said matter-of-factly.

Darby let out a bloodcurdling scream that the tourists in downtown Santa Fe most likely heard.

* * *

"What the hell is going on back there?" Leonard asked Skyler when she joined him in the Great Room.

"A family squabble of some sort, I imagine. I couldn't hear much. These walls are too damned thick."

"It's basically a log cabin. Not great for eavesdropping."

"I wasn't eavesdropping," Skyler said. She sat down on the couch and put a hand in Leonard's lap. "Okay, I *was* trying to listen. It's all so juicy."

"I couldn't care less. I want to go help get this Georgia person and then I want us to hightail it out of here. Brenda's onboard, too. She just went to her room to see if she could make a Skype call since the phone service sucks so much."

"Who is she calling?"

"A charter service. We're going to Vegas to finish out this trip."

"Christmas in Las Vegas does not sound right to me." She gestured around the cavernous room complete with roaring fire in the stone fireplace and the commanding view of the trees and mountains outside. "*This* is Christmas."

Leonard took Skyler's hand in his own and gently squeezed. "Let me get this straight. Now you'd rather stay here, in a cabin, miles from town, with people we hardly know, and multiple madmen on the loose? And risk your boyfriend being shot again in the woods? *That's* Christmas to you? I thought you were ready to leave."

Skyler's face wrinkled up. "It sounds crazy, I know. But Georgia is a very good friend of the twins. The twins are Brenda's business partners. And Brenda is my best friend in the world. So, this seems like the place we should be. For now. If we had family we wanted to be with somewhere, I'd probably feel differently. But since I am not at all eager to go watch my nieces and nephews tear open gifts at 5:30 in the morning, and because a smoky Vegas casino is just *not* the place I really enjoy at all…then this is it."

"But your best friend in the world is in there getting a plane to take us out of New Mexico. If she's comfortable leaving the insanity behind, I think we should be, too."

"I'm conflicted."

"I'm not."

"So, you're just going to go get Georgia and then run? Not see this through? Where's the Christmas spirit in that? I really do feel like we should help, Leonard. It's what we do. And let's not forget that the local police have not done a damned thing. The security team Georgia hired was a complete nightmare. Even the F.B.I. seems uninterested. We are her best bet, and you know it. Plus, you saw what Carter did."

"Saw?" Leonard exclaimed. "I *felt* what that idiot did. And it still smarts."

"We really should go to the hospital."

"You need to drop it. I'm fine. And I've already explained why that isn't going to happen."

They sat in silence for a few moments, staring at the fire.

"Carter isn't an idiot," Skyler finally said.

"Maybe he's not, I don't know. But I do know that he has no business handling a firearm."

The next few hours were spent hemming and hawing about leaving New Mexico. Skyler wanted to stay, Leonard was ready to leave, and Brenda had become indifferent, especially when it became clear that she wasn't going to be able to charter a plane because of the holidays. She contacted every outfit she could think of and absolutely nothing was available. There were options on American and United, but getting to Las Vegas from Santa Fe meant changing planes in Denver or Dallas, and it didn't matter anyway, because she refused to fly commercial with two large dogs in tow. She'd rather walk the 630 miles than put Mulder and Scully in cages and ship them in the belly of a freezing, dark airplane.

So, it was decided that they'd hunker down and make the best of it in the Lowery's beautiful rented house. Brenda hatched a plan to stock the kitchen. Skyler volunteered to find a Christmas tree and decorations. And the twins—when they weren't fielding 7,000 questions about the family business from their ecstatic new partner—decided that it would be best to let Georgia take the lead on which Lowery brother (Darby not included) she wanted to share a bed with upon her return. Vying for the same woman was a situation Carter and Sullivan had never been in before, but one thing was made crystal clear that afternoon: They would *not* be sharing her. Carter was still sore that Sullivan would even suggest such a 'perverted arrangement,' as he called it.

When Brenda, Skyler, and Darby left to run errands, Leonard helped the twins move furniture around the Great Room to make room for the tree. When they were happy with the new arrangement, they popped open three beers and sat in front of the fire.

"I confirmed the King Air," Carter said. "We're taking off from S.A.F. tomorrow morning at 8:30. The pilot is getting double time for flying on Christmas Eve, so it wasn't all that cheap. But, I don't see that we had much of a choice since we ruled out driving."

"I'll be ready," Leonard said. "I'm not excited about it, but I'll soldier through. I'm bringing my gun, by the way, in case you need to alert the pilot." He turned to Carter. "And you are *not* bringing your gun, buddy boy."

"Holy shit," Carter said. "My gun." He placed his beer on the coffee table and got to his feet. "Holy shit!"

"Where is the gun?"

"I never picked it up after I shot you," Carter said. "Unless you picked it up. Tell me that you picked up the gun."

Leonard shook his head. "I did not. I was too concerned about bleeding to death in the woods."

"Then it's out there lying in the brush."

"I think someone needs to go out there and get that damned gun," Sullivan said. "And you guys better be more careful this time. And please don't forget that there's a crazy woman on the loose out there and maybe even a lunatic Italian man. Not to mention all the bears and coyotes."

"Thanks, Sullivan," Leonard said. "That makes me feel much better."

Carter and Leonard bundled up for a late-afternoon trek back into the woods, then left a weaponless Sullivan with the dogs to guard the house.

After nearly two hours of attempting to retrace their steps, they finally came upon the spot where they thought the gun went off. When Leonard found and removed the slug from the side of a tree, they were certain.

They feverishly searched the ground until just after sunset, but the unregistered weapon was nowhere to be found. They stood in the nearly dark woods, both breathing heavy.

"Now what?" a distraught Carter asked.

"You better start praying," Leonard said. "How many bullets were left in it?"

"Five."

"Pray *real* hard."

* * *

When everyone returned to the house, the six of them worked as a team redecorating the Christmas tree that Skyler and Darby commandeered from Georgia's house. Everyone was able to table their various anxieties for the evening—including Darby, who was still riding high on the news that he was actually a very well-off young man—and they enjoyed pizza and beer around the Great Room fireplace, then all retired at a reasonable hour. It went without saying that they knew the next few days would be eventful ones.

CHAPTER TWENTY-SEVEN

On Christmas Eve morning, Brenda woke up with a start, worrying about Froment du Léon cows.

During her time as an apprentice at Joël Corentin's L'Atelier Delphine in Paris, she learned about the plight of the French breed of dairy cattle from the restaurant's chef, who was quite obsessed with the topic. If you would listen, he would talk about the cows ad nauseam and, besides cooking, the chef had made saving the cows his life's passion.

In the early twentieth century, there were thousands of the brown and white horned bovines, and they were, and still are, revered for their yellow, high fat content milk that is used to create the most decadent butter. By the middle of the century, the population was dwindling fast, and by the late-1970's, their numbers were reduced to a mere 50 head.

A breed society was established and ever so slowly, their numbers began to grow again. In the early twenty-first century, there were a few hundred, and it continues to grow, albeit too slowly for many who care about such endangered things. Like Brenda's old teacher.

Brenda knew every last detail about the effort to save the majestic cows who lived in France's north-west coastal region, because of her teacher's new book, "Sauvez les Bovins: Froment du Léon." It went into great detail about the effort to preserve the breed and included some pretty amazing recipes, too. It was written in French, *naturellement*, and the exercise of forcing herself to read the fat tome was not only educating her about the cows and their milk, but she was brushing up on her rusty French at the same time.

It was all going to her head and staying there. Especially when she took the book to bed late at night and then dreamt of fatty butter until morning.

She swung her legs over the side of the bed and found her bathrobe amongst a giant mess of clothes and other belongings on the floor. *I'm as big as a Froment du Léon and as messy as a porc*, she thought, which caused her to laugh out loud. She was still chuckling when she entered the kitchen as Leonard and the twins were preparing to head out the front door.

Skyler raised up on to her toes in order to reach Leonard's lips for a kiss. "Don't forget to ask Georgia the name of the design student."

"I won't," Leonard said as he zipped up his jacket. He bellowed over his shoulder as he held open the front door for the twins, "Good morning, Brenda. See you soon. I hope."

And they were gone.

Brenda looked at a now sullen Skyler who had sat down at the table. "I'm sorry I slept so late. I was dreaming about endangered cows."

"That's nice."

"What's wrong with you?" Brenda asked as she fiddled with the coffee maker.

"Look outside."

Brenda hadn't put in her contact lenses yet. She pulled

her glasses off the top of her head and glanced out the picture window. It was snowing and there was a light dusting on the limbs of the trees and on the rocks. "Snow. So?"

"Leonard and the boys are about to get on a tiny prop plane and take off in *this*? I love airplanes, but I do not love airplanes mixed with snow and ice. It's not a good combination."

"What are they predicting?"

"Scattered snow showers off and on all day," Skyler said. "Maybe heavier tonight. Maybe not. The television weather people are useless and they mostly talk about Albuquerque anyway. They don't know what's going to happen here in Santa Fe any more than the dogs do."

Mulder and Scully looked up from their nap causing Skyler and Brenda to chuckle.

"The boys will be fine," Brenda said as she lowered herself into a chair at the table. "The charter pilot won't take off if he thinks it's in any way unsafe. What about the weather in Flagstaff?"

"Clear."

"Good." Brenda took a long sip of the dark roast and gently placed her mug on the table. "I have a few trinkets for Leonard and the twins I can put under that tree. But I don't have anything for Darby or Georgia."

"Presents? Oh, goodness. I have next to nothing. I shipped Leonard's stuff to Maine, remember? I have something for you, of course. That's it. Should we go shopping? Do you think they'll care?"

"Georgia is getting back to reality after quite a dreadful ordeal. The woman was kidnapped, knocked unconscious, escaped, and spent the last few days in the hospital all alone. We should try to give her some semblance of a normal Christmas."

Skyler pointed at the tree. "Hey, I did that, didn't I?"

"That was very nice of you, yes," Brenda said. "And thank you for packing some clothes and essentials from her house, too. She'll appreciate all of it, I'm sure."

"I hope I picked out stuff she'll actually want to wear. My goodness, I completely forgot to mention this last night..." Skyler picked up her iPad and pulled up a photo of a front porch. There was a large, smartly wrapped Christmas present sitting to the left of the front door. She showed it to Brenda. "This is sitting on Georgia's front porch. It doesn't have a card or a tag and I didn't have the guts to touch it."

"Rightly so," Brenda said. "It could have exploded in your face. We should alert the authorities."

"I think so, too," Skyler said. "I put that F.B.I. agent's information into my contacts file. I'll text him right now. I'm sure he'll be thrilled to hear from me on Christmas Eve."

> This is Skyler Moore. I was a guest at the Reece party. Sending photo of a mysterious gift left on her front porch. We decided not to touch it.

Good call. I will send someone to have a look. Have tried calling Ms. Braxton but got voicemail — We have a ping on Modena's credit card. He's apparently on his way to Roswell. Local police investigating.

> Thank you for the update. Cell service is not good here. Text is best.

Roger. Merry Christmas.

> Merry Christmas. And
> don't call me Roger.

☺

Skyler laughed out loud. "At least he has a sense of humor."

"What did he say?"

Skyler handed over her phone. "Read it. My coffee is kicking in. I'll be right back."

Relieved that one of the main suspects was probably not lurking around outside, the friends busied themselves with a bit of housework, then retired to their respective suites to take showers and get dressed for the day. They decided that if the snow let up a bit, they'd brave the winding country roads and head into town for a few last-minute gifts, including something special for the opera singer. And Brenda wanted to pick up some more wine. There could never be too much wine, she always said.

* * *

The storm clouds had pretty much cleared out over the Santa Fe Regional Airport when the boys pulled up in front of Advanced Aviation. They checked in at the front desk and were directed to take seats in the lounge. Minutes later, a young man of about 23 or 24 years old, dressed in tan slacks, a brown leather bomber jacket, and aviator sunglasses approached.

"You must be the Lowerys? And Mr. Little?" the young man asked as he took off his glasses and extended a hand to Carter. "I'm Cody Thalhimer, your pilot."

"Nice to meet you, Cody," Carter said as he got to his feet. "I have to say, you don't look old enough to drive, let alone fly."

"Carter, really," Sullivan scolded. "Cody, hello, I'm Sullivan Lowery. This rude person is my brother Carter, and this is Leonard Little. He's the acting chief of police of Wabanaki, Maine, and he has a police-issued weapon that he'd like to bring on the plane." He studied the kid's face for a few moments. "How old *are* you?"

"I get this a lot, gentleman," he said pleasantly. "I have over 3,000 hours, I've been type-rated on the King Air 350i for most of that time, and I first soloed when I was 15; I started early. And the company has no problem with the service weapon coming aboard, but it will have to be locked in a box we have located in the exterior baggage compartment. That's the deal, I'm afraid."

"It's an easy deal," Leonard said as he showed his badge to the pilot.

"Let's go." Cody lead the way out onto the tarmac and not more than a few yards to the waiting plane. It was a beautiful, white and teal painted, twin turbo prop and it looked like it had just come off a showroom floor. The passenger entrance was on the left side of the fuselage. Stairs were attached to the back of the door, which was hinged at the bottom and folded down to the ground. After the gun was locked away in the compartment, Leonard, Carter, and Sullivan climbed inside and selected their seats. Leonard sat facing forward. The twins took rear-facing seats across from Leonard. Cody closed the rear door then squeezed past the passengers and entered the open cockpit.

"Only one pilot?" Leonard asked.

"This thing is easily managed by one person. No worries," Carter said.

"You are white as a ghost," Sullivan said. "You gonna be okay?"

The cop nodded. "I'll be fine. I just need to concentrate." He glanced out the window as the props whirled to life. "I don't know how you guys can ride backwards. That'd certainly make me sick."

"Are you going to be sick?" Carter asked. "You could have stayed at home, you know. I'm certain that we're capable of getting Georgia out of that hospital and back onto this plane without incident."

"I'm sure you could, too," Leonard said. He was gripping his armrests as the plane began taxiing toward the runway. Then his cell phone vibrated. He fished it out of his pocket and read the text from Skyler. "Ah. I guess I really could have stayed behind."

"Why's that?" Sullivan asked.

"Apparently your friend Massimo has been tracked to Roswell, New Mexico. The police are moving in. That's over 200 miles from here, right?"

Carter beamed. "Now *that's* the best Christmas present I could have possibly received."

The plane was cleared for takeoff and the engines spooled up to full power. Leonard wanted to close his eyes, but he also didn't want to look like a total dolt in front of the twins, so he looked out the window, forced a small smile, and prayed to the little baby Jesus as the King Air lifted off the runway and began a steep climb into the New Mexican sky. He was all but certain that they were going to slam into the mountain side, but Cody banked the plane to the left and reached their cruising altitude of 21,000 feet in no time. And a quick 50-minutes later, they started their descent into Flagstaff's Pulliam Airport.

And a relieved Leonard survived another flight. He was a little weak in the knees as he climbed out of the aircraft and immediately lit a cigarette while he waited for his firearm to be freed from the baggage compartment.

*　*　*

Massimo stuffed his plastic drugstore bag behind a planter on Emma Wade's front porch then rang the bell. After a few moments, the door cracked open and she peeked out.

"What are *you* doing here?" Emma asked as she opened the door slowly to allow him to enter her apartment.

When the door was closed again, he locked it then walked into the kitchen. "Do you have any liquor? I need a drink."

"I don't drink alcohol, Massimo. You know that. I have milk and water. Maybe a diet soda or two."

He rummaged around in her refrigerator. "Not even a beer."

"No," she said, growing agitated. "I thought you were taking Georgia and leaving town. I thought I was done with this. Why are you here?"

Massimo slammed the refrigerator door, causing several telephone books that were stacked on top to tumble to the floor. "You could say that it did not go as planned. None of it. She escaped."

"I've been watching the news," Emma said. "There's nothing. Absolutely nothing. They've kept it all very quiet. Where is Georgia now?"

"I'm not entirely sure," he said. "But I suspect that she's on her way back here to Santa Fe."

"You aren't going to kill her."

"That was never my intention, no. I explained this to you. I thought you understood me. But I can't let her get away with this. I made that woman what she is today and she has completely and 100 percent rejected me. Threw me away like garbage. *Spazzatura*!"

"I'm so sorry. But I am not surprised."

He went to the living room and flopped down on the girl's thread bare couch. "Has anyone approached you? The authorities?"

"No. No one."

"The American F.B.I. is not very thorough, are they?" he said. "Although, to be fair, I don't believe *you* were ever on their radar, *mio caro*. Georgia never named you after the bombing as someone who'd been in the house. You slipped her mind completely. That was convenient. For both of us."

Emma sat on the ottoman opposite him. "I did everything you asked me to do."

"I know that," Massimo said quietly. "But it was not enough. I should have planned this better."

"What is your end game, Massimo?"

"I do not know."

"Well, I can tell you this, you really should have killed her. She's going to talk. She's going to implicate me."

"Why would she do that?" he spit. "She doesn't know you did anything to her. But on the other hand, if she were dead it would make you the infamous decorator to the recently departed celebrity opera singer? It could help your interior design career, no? Is that why you want her dead?"

"Did I say I wanted her dead? I don't think I ever said that."

Massimo exploded. "You just said, 45 seconds ago, that I

should have killed her."

"That's different from saying that *I* want her dead. I don't want her dead. Not that."

"You are confusing me, young lady. I'm too tired for this." He closed his eyes. "I'm not going to kill her, Emma. It's just not in me. I may have done some screwed up things in the last few weeks, but I'm not a murderer. I'm just extremely mad about all of this. At *her*! Mad and frustrated and disappointed. And now I'm fucked."

"But you came back to Santa Fe nonetheless. And everyone must be out looking for you. What do you intend to do?"

He thought about that for a few long moments. "I'm going to take her most prized procession. I'm going to take away her voice."

"How?"

"I have no idea."

She put her hands on her hips. "You can't stay here."

"You have no choice about that," he said straightening up. "I'm going to stay here until I come up with a plan."

"I have roommates. How will I explain you being here?"

He opened his eyes. "Where are they now? I see no one."

Her face crinkled up. "They're home for the holidays. School is out until January 6th."

"Perfect. Then I'll stay awhile." He closed his eyes again.

"I really wish you wouldn't."

"One anonymous phone call and you'd have a slew of cops on your front porch. You helped me with a kidnapping, my dear. You broke in and trashed her house. You planted the bomb at a party attended by the New Mexican governor, for God's sake. You're as guilty as I am. Maybe more so. They already know that

I'm involved, obviously, but no one else on Earth, besides me, knows that you had anything to do with any of this. *Yet.*"

"Yet?"

"Mmm hmm. Yet."

"It's Christmas Eve and you are in my house threatening me because you need a place to hide out."

He opened his eyes. "That's exactly what's happening, yes, Emma. *Buon Natale.* Don't ever say I didn't get you anything."

A few very uncomfortable hours later, Emma quietly left a napping Massimo in the living room and locked herself in her bedroom. She got on her hands and knees in front of her over-stuffed closet and gently pulled out a banker's box from behind a mound of shoes and boots. Inside, scores of high school snapshots, her junior and senior yearbooks, greeting cards sent to her from her father and grandmothers, and a shiny handgun.

After she heard the gunshot in the woods the day before and watched until the two men retreated to their house, she doubled back and literally stepped on the weapon near the base of a tree. And, now more than ever, she was most thankful that she'd kept it.

She thought, for a moment, that she'd use it on Massimo, but he was the least of her problems.

CHAPTER TWENTY-EIGHT

Georgia was looking photo-session perfect, but still dressed in a thin cotton hospital gown when the boys arrived at Room 312 to collect her. Before anyone uttered a word, she bolted up right in her chair and extended her arms.

"Tell me, please, that you brought me some of my actual clothes that I can put on," she said excitedly.

Sullivan smiled and handed her a duffle bag. She grasped it to her chest and he leaned in to kiss her lightly on a cheek. "We brought you your very own clothes and your cell phone. I charged it up. And I'm glad to see you in one piece, by the way."

"I'm glad to be in one piece," she said. "And I can't wait to get out of this hell hole. Tell me that we are not driving. Tell me that we are flying first class. *Please*. It's Christmas. It's the absolute least you could have done."

"Even better," Carter said as he stepped forward and hugged Georgia. "We're flying private."

"That is the best thing I have heard in a very long time," she cooed.

"Georgia Reece, this is Sheriff Leonard Little," Sullivan said. "He's here to see that we all get back to Santa Fe unscathed." He lowered his voice to a whisper. "He's packing heat."

Georgia rose out of her chair and shook hands with the

handsome police man towering above her. "I'm pleased to meet you, Leonard Little. Skyler has told me nothing but wonderful things about you. She's a very lucky girl."

"Well, that was nice of her and very nice of *you*, too," Leonard said. "Skyler lies, but I love her. And I'm thrilled that I was able to get away from Maine to be in Santa Fe for Christmas."

"Which is where I want to get to A.S.A.P, gentleman." She walked to the hospital room's private bathroom and closed the door. From inside she yelled, "Give me five minutes."

Exactly an hour later, Cody fired up the King Air again and the foursome were ferried back to New Mexico without incident. When they landed at S.A.F., thick white clouds were starting to spill into the valley.

"Looks like you're in for a very white Christmas," the pilot said as he handed Leonard his gun from the locked compartment. "I'm going to hightail it out of here and get back to my family in Phoenix before it starts coming down again."

And before the Lowerys, Leonard, and Georgia had even driven off the airport property, Cody was back in the air.

On the long car ride back to Carter and Sullivan's house in the hills east of town, Georgia and Leonard sat in the backseat and she gripped his hand for a few seconds. "Thanks for being here. It makes me feel so much safer."

"It's my pleasure."

"I really mean it. If I were a sane person, I'd get on an airplane and fly right back to New York, but I like it out here in the high desert very, very much. Despite the insanity of the last week or so, I'm so happy to be in Santa Fe. New York City will *always* be my home, but it can also drain the life right out of a person. Especially at the holidays."

Leonard smiled awkwardly. The opera singer seemed to be trying desperately to believe what she was saying. "I was there in New York City this past summer for the first time in my life. It's a very different world from the one I grew up in down Maine. I think Santa Fe is probably more my speed if I had to pick."

"Well, yes, the city is not for everyone. I'm curious, how did you and Skyler meet?"

"Grade school, actually," Leonard said. "We both grew up in Wabanaki. It's a very small town where everyone pretty much knows everyone else, whether you like it or not. But it wasn't until this past July that we took the friendship to...well...to a new place. It was kind of unexpected on both our parts. I'd just lost my wife."

"I'm so sorry to hear that," Georgia said, squeezing his hand again. "I had a husband die not too long ago. We're too young for such things, aren't we?"

"We are."

"How'd she go?"

Leonard swallowed hard. "It's a long, complicated story. The short version is that she was murdered in a seafood restaurant's bathroom."

"My goodness. I'm so sorry." There were a few minutes of awkward silence, then, "We should change the subject. Talk about happy things. It's Christmas Eve. And I'm back."

"And it's starting to snow," Sullivan said from the front passenger seat. "Oh, shit, Georgia!"

"Why are you screaming?" a startled Georgia asked as she hit

Sullivan on the shoulder. "What is it?"

"I forgot to tell you: Massimo has been tracked to Roswell, New Mexico. He's a good 200 miles away. We can all relax a little bit tonight."

Georgia turned to look at Leonard. She managed a weak smile. "I'm not relaxing until he's in custody. Tell me they'll get him, Leonard."

"I'm not from anywhere near here, Georgia, but I have the utmost confidence in local police departments. Massimo appears to be using his credit cards. It shouldn't be too hard to track him down, bring him in, and lock him up. I think you can relax a little bit."

"I hope so," she whispered.

"By the way," Leonard said, "what was the name of the design student you hired to help at the house?"

"Emma Wade. Why on Earth would you want to know that?"

"What was that?" Sullivan said from the front seat. He turned around. "What did you say?"

"Emma," Georgia said. "He's asking about the girl who Massimo found to..."

"Massimo found her?" Leonard asked.

"Oh my goodness." It started to sink in. The singer put a hand on Sullivan's shoulder. "I never mentioned Emma to the police, Sully. To the Mallard people. To anyone. What is wrong with me? Was she working with Massimo? She was quiet, but sweet." She turned to Leonard. "No. I just can't see it. Not Emma."

"Do you know where she lives? Is she still in town?"

"I don't know the answer to either of those questions. I don't even know what school she goes to. What is wrong with me? I never even asked."

Leonard patted the distraught singer's hand. "We'll get this figured out."

There was a large popping sound and the car started rapidly losing speed and was pulling to the right.

"That was the back-right tire, I think," Carter said from behind the wheel. He slowed the vehicle and pulled off the road into the dirt. "A complete blow out. *This* should be fun."

* * *

Skyler was holed up in her room wrapping the last of her Christmas presents when her phone made the 'V.I.P chime' for the second time in the last ten minutes, indicating that she had another text from a close friend or a top client. The first time it was Leonard, letting her know that they'd been delayed, and now it was Carissa Lamb, her second most important account since she took on Foster Martin.

```
Merry Christmas, my darling. About
to go on stage. Wishing we were all
together. New Year's, maybe? My love
to Lenny and all.
```

She knew Carissa had shows scheduled for New Year's Eve at the Golden Cactus and wasn't quite sure she wanted to spend the last night of the year in Las Vegas for what was arguably one of the busiest tourist seasons there, so Skyler politely tabled the discussion.

> Merry Christmas, Carissa. I'll
> talk to the troops about NYE.
> It's snowing here! Miss you.

Thank you for the necklace! It
is absolutely stunning. You have
impeccable taste. I sent you
nothing. I suck. I'm sorry.

"*Enzo* has impeccable taste," Skyler said out loud as she tapped away on her screen.

> Thank you...and no worries. You
> write me fat checks! LOL Let's
> chat in a few days. Love you.

Enjoy the snow, darling.
Ho ho ho. XOXO

Brenda and the dogs filed into the suite and the chef flopped down on the bed. The dogs started playing with shreds of wrapping paper that had piled up on the floor next to the folding table Skyler was using as her wrapping center.

"Are you done yet? I want to start drinking," Brenda said with a huff.

"Why does my wrapping of presents stop you from drinking?"

Brenda consulted her watch. "It's only half past two. I should wait. When do the boys return with the abductee? It seems like they should have been back by now."

"Any minute," Skyler said as she shooed the animals away from her mess. "They landed some time ago, but they got a flat tire on the way back. They couldn't get the nuts off, so they had to wait for a tow truck to come save them."

"I hate when guys can't get their nuts off."

Skyler snorted with laughter. "Now *that's* funny."

"I try."

"We have an invitation to go to Las Vegas for New Year's Eve, by the way."

"Carissa, I assume?"

"Uh huh. She has two shows that night, but still wants us there, and she's planning a party on The Strip for the countdown to midnight and for the fireworks shows. It wouldn't be my first choice of destinations, but if we went, and we were with her, I'm sure we'd be comfortably insulated from the unwashed masses."

"That's so elitist of you," Brenda said. "But I get it. And I agree. Wholeheartedly, actually."

"Could we even get rooms at this point?"

"Probably not. The suite I usually stay in would have been booked months ago for Christmas and New Year's Eve. I can usually get something when I want or need to be there, but I've never even tried to go on a holiday before. I can call and reserve us the private wine room at *Brenda's Kitchen* though. I was just talking to the Las Vegas restaurant manager yesterday; it's still available."

"I don't want to sleep in a wine room," Skyler joked. "Are we sure we want to go to Vegas?"

"Yes. It'll be fun. Once we get Georgia settled and I do a few more things at the new restaurant downtown, I should be able to get out of dodge for a while. I think I am all Santa Fe'd out for the time being."

"Agreed. Me too," Skyler said. "This has been one hell of a drama filled year. We deserve to celebrate in style."

Brenda propped her head up with her right arm. "If we can't get decent rooms at the Golden Cactus, we could probably talk our way into staying at the Carissa Lamb estate. I've never even seen it. She lives alone, and it has like a gazillion bedrooms, a ballroom, an amazing Strip view, and pools."

"Pools? With an 's' on the end?"

"Indoor and outdoor."

Skyler smiled. "Sounds lovely. Let's talk to Leonard and see how he feels. Maybe he can fit it in before heading back to Wabs."

"Hey! That can be my Christmas present to you. I'll fly us to Vegas."

"My Christmas present from *you* was that you flew Leonard to Santa Fe to surprise me, Brenda. You've spent enough on private jets."

"Bite your tongue. It's just money, and I still have lots of cash left in my transportation budget for the year. We're good, honey. And besides, I don't have children to leave my fortune to, and because of Q.V.C., it keeps growing. Like me."

"Stop," Skyler said as she playfully hit her friend. "Alright. I'll let you fly us there. Anything beats commercial."

"Don't I know. Cool. New Year's in Las Vegas. If I can find us a plane, that is. That seems to be my new full-time job. Why do my assistants insist on taking the holidays off, damn it?"

"If you can get a plane and let's not forget that this is all dependent on getting Leonard on board. Move over," Skyler said as she joined her friend on the bed. "It's very quiet in this house, by the way. Where's Darby? Is he still on top of the world?"

"He's annoyingly giddy, but at least he's acting like a semi-normal person now and not acting like a total shit all the time. Last time I saw him he was sitting near the fire making a list of all the stuff he was going to buy."

"He's going to blow through all the money like a lottery winner and then he'll have nothing."

Brenda shook her head. "I suspect the twins won't let that happen. Did you hear what they did with his profits all of these years? They funneled them into a money market account. They've kept half in cash and invested the rest. That kid is worth millions. And he'll still get annual hotel profits for years to come. But here's what I would be worried about if I were Carter and Sullivan…" She lowered her voice to a loud whisper, "If I were Darby, I'd sue the pants off of them. They kept the fact that he owned a third of the family company from him and invested his money without him even knowing it existed. If that kid has any brains at all, he should be livid. I'd be scared he'd walk away with the entire company if he won in court. And he'd have a good case."

"But they did it for his own good," Skyler said. "He's been a drug user since high school. In and out of rehab. They were *protecting* his money."

"The courts might not see it that way. Their father wanted him to have a third."

"He *had* it. He just didn't know it."

Brenda shrugged her shoulders. "Just calling it like I see it. In any event, he might be too stupid to even think of such a thing. He's too excited with his new inflated bank accounts. And, now he's a Broadway producer. That's what Sullivan told me.

He's investing in some new show."

"What's the show?"

Brenda's eyes widened. "A musical about the holocaust. Sounds like a real good time to me."

"Yikes. Well, that should keep him busy," Skyler said as she went back to her wrapping. "Everyone needs a project. And my project right now is to get these gifts under the tree before everyone gets back." She held up a small gold box topped with a white bow. "This is for Georgia. The bracelet."

"From both of us."

"From both of us."

Brenda struggled a bit but managed to get her feet back on the floor and stood up. "Come on, Mulder and Scully. Momma is going to go look at the wine bottles." She started out of the suite.

"Look at them?"

"I might have to open one or two to test them. To make sure they're not poisonous." And she was gone, with her babies in tow.

CHAPTER TWENTY-NINE

It snowed heavily for the rest of Christmas Eve afternoon and well into the evening. And because Santa Fe wasn't used to more than a dusting at a time, the entire city and surrounding areas came to a virtual stand-still. With very few plows and sand trucks available to treat the roads, most people were stuck at home or in their hotels, and many of the independent restaurants were forced to close. Brenda's dinner reservation downtown was cancelled, but the twin's rental house kitchen was more than fully stocked, so with her third glass of wine in hand, she began prepping dinner with Sullivan serving as her sous chef for the evening.

After Leonard left a message for the lead officer at the Santa Fe Police Department about Emma Wade, he joined Skyler, Carter, Darby, and the newly sprung Georgia in the Great Room. They could all see the wintery mix outside but appreciated the warmth of the roaring fire inside the house. Everyone had a glass of wine or a cocktail in hand—Carter saw to that in his role as self-appointed bartender—and the conversation drifted from the wintery weather, to sports, to future Franklin-Lowery hotel locations, to New York City real estate prices, then ending up on Broadway. That's when Darby became quite animated.

"I think I really could make a go of this," he said. "Now that

I have the means. I bet I could get some innovative, ground-breaking material off the ground. I think *Shoah: The Musical* is a good start, too."

"And here I thought you had no interests besides screwing up your body with illegal substances," Carter said, then displayed a wicked smile. "I kid, of course."

"You're an asshole, Carter."

"I'm sorry, dude. Seriously, I am very proud of you. And maybe it's good that all of this business stuff finally saw the light of light of day. I guess we couldn't have kept you in the dark forever."

Darby placed his drink down on the coffee table. "Dad would be spinning in his grave if he knew what you two did to me. But, I've decided to be the bigger man, so I'm not going to be pissed about it. I'm going to move forward and do good things with my new-found riches despite my greedy, inconsiderate, most definitely unethical brothers."

Carter rolled his eyes.

"Good for you, Darby," Skyler said. "I haven't been to a Broadway show in several years. I'll look forward to coming to town to see what you cook up. It's very exciting. Just don't revive *Cats* again, whatever you do. For the life of me, I just don't understand what people love about that horrid musical."

Darby laughed. "Maybe we can do *Dogs*."

"Hear, hear," Brenda said.

"I've never been to a Broadway show, or any stage show for that matter," Leonard said. "Not sure I could sit through anything longer than an hour. I don't have much of an attention span."

"Then whatever you do, Leonard," Georgia laughed, "do *not*

go to the opera."

"Are they long?"

"You could say that. There are a few that are over four hours, like Philip Glass' *Einstein on the Beach*, but most are in the two and a half to three-hour range. I guess that really isn't much different than Broadway shows, come to think of it."

"I'm primarily interested in one act plays," Darby said, "because I can't sit in one place for very long, either. Get in, enjoy it, and get out. Most shows' second acts suck anyway."

"Speaking of second acts," Skyler said, turning her attention to Georgia, "have you given any thought to new representation for the new year?"

"Oh goodness. I don't know. I'm sure that I can ask around and see who other people are using. I've never been a free agent before. Massimo was with me from day one. It's all kind of foreign to me."

"Well, the best part about that is that you won't be royally screwed anymore," Carter said. "You'll go with someone reputable and start paying the customary percentage instead of the insane amount of *half*. You're going to be much better off…in more ways than one."

Georgia raised her glass of wine into the air. "I'll drink to that."

And as the group sipped their drinks, the music suddenly stopped playing mid-Christmas carol and the room plunged into darkness. The house was nearly pitch dark, save for the light coming from the fireplace.

"And there goes the electricity," Brenda said from the kitchen. "Good thing this place has a gas stove and oven."

"And gas heat," Sullivan said as he joined the others in the

Great Room. "We won't freeze to death out here in no man's land. I'm actually surprised that this house doesn't have a generator. I'm going to look around for some matches and candles."

"I have a lighter," Leonard said.

Skyler tsked at her boyfriend then walked over to the window. "It must have been caused by snow and ice building up on the wires. It's really coming down now. And it looks heavy and wet."

"I need light over here," Brenda said. "I can't see a thing and I'm at a critical stage with almost everything."

Sullivan returned with a flashlight from his briefcase and two candles he'd found in the bathrooms. "Here ya go, Chef. You're the most important person to us right now. You stand between us and certain starvation."

"I feel so special," Brenda said before taking a long sip of her wine.

"What's on the menu?" Leonard asked when he approached the kitchen island to light the candles.

"We'll start with a simple salad with grapefruit, red and golden beets, and goat cheese—it's one of my favorites. Then, a New York strip roast with a Burgundy and mushroom sauce paired with barley risotto and butternut squash, balsamic green beans with pearl onions, and homemade snowflakes rolls with a sweet and spicy honey butter I whipped up. Then, afterwards, a sweet potato crème brûlée. I've never made it before, but I am very excited to give it a whirl. I don't have a blow torch, but I can broil it."

"Too bad you're going through all this work with no television cameras here."

"I cook like this because I love it, *Lenny*. I don't do it just for the cameras. Plus, it's Christmas, damn it. This is what I do."

"I didn't mean to belittle you. I love you and I love your food and I will eat it and shut up. I'm truly grateful, because if I were back in Wabanaki, I'd most likely be eating my Christmas dinner alone at the Popeye's out near the 95 exit."

"Thank you, I guess," she said. "Now go find some more light for this joint or no one will be able to see what they're eating."

After a spirited conversation over Brenda's over-the-top Christmas Eve dinner by candlelight, the seven delightfully stuffed, snowed-in revelers moved to the Great Room, leaving the dirty pots, pans, and dishes for the light of day. Carter poured snifters of 1985 Delord Armagnac and Darby helped pass them out. When everyone was around the fire, a large crashing sound came from the roof.

"What the hell was that?" Brenda asked.

Skyler was the first to her feet. "I'd guess Santa Claus and the reindeer, but we don't have any kids here." She grabbed Sullivan's flashlight and started toward the back stairs. "I'll go have a look." Leonard didn't like the sound of that—he'd seen enough slasher flicks to know exactly what a statement like that meant in a dark, creepy house. He was right on her heels as she disappeared into the darkness at the back of the house.

"That girl needs a leash," Leonard said.

"It was probably just snow falling off the roof," Georgia said.

"I don't think snow makes such a loud thud," Brenda said. "We should probably all be in bed under the covers. It's most definitely Santa."

"Or Massimo," Carter said softly.

Sullivan nearly choked on his after-dinner drink. "Seriously? Why would you bring up his name? He's not even in Santa Fe."

"Why? Because the police told us that he wasn't? What do they know? They couldn't even locate him in Roswell today."

"What are you talking about?" Georgia asked as she straightened up in her seat. "You said he was 200 miles away and that they were moving in on his position."

"Skyler's been in contact with the lead guy on the case, apparently," Carter said. "He said that Massimo's credit card was used to buy a bus ticket to Roswell. But he didn't get off the bus at the other end. He's not there."

"And you're just telling me this *now?*"

Carter moved over and placed an arm around the singer's back and pulled her in tight. "You can't see outside right now, Georgia, but it's a virtual blizzard. He's not out there. No one is out there. Even the coyotes and bears have taken cover."

"That's not making me feel better."

"Not even in my arms?"

"Sully, please," Georgia said.

Carter recoiled, and from across the room Sullivan said, "I'm over here, babe."

Darby laughed.

"Jesus Christ," Brenda said under her breath.

"My goodness. I'm sorry." She looked into Carter's face then grabbed each of his cheeks with her cold hands. "I know who's who, Carter. I've just had too much to drink and I'm tired. And it's dark in here. It's been quite a day."

In the loft upstairs, Skyler and Leonard approached the exterior glass door that led to a small second floor balcony. Skyler directed the flashlight at the snow piled up on the wood planks. There were fresh footprints just on the other side of the glass. She gasped, and Leonard reached around her and checked the doorknob. It was unlocked.

Skyler knelt down and felt the carpeting. "It's wet."

"Holy shit," he said. "Get downstairs and make sure all the doors are locked. I'm going to go get my gun."

"Please don't shoot anyone inside this house, Leonard!" Skyler yelled as they hurried down the stairs in the dark. They fell over each other and landed in a heap at the bottom. "Are you okay?"

Leonard scrambled to his feet. "Yup. You?"

"I'm fine."

Brenda and Darby appeared in the back hall with flashlights. "What is going on?" Brenda asked as she helped her friend to her feet.

"Someone was out on that balcony off of the loft space. We saw footprints."

"Is that all?" Darby said with a sigh. "That was me. I was puffing on my cigar a bit after we finished dinner."

"Jesus," Skyler said.

"Not Jesus," Darby said. "I didn't see Santa out there either. Or the Abominable Snowman. Just a butt load of snow and a lot of darkness."

"I think it's about time we all retreat to our suites and call this Christmas Eve over," Brenda said. "Seriously. Everything is going to be a lot more pleasant when that damned sun comes up."

Leonard came out of his suite, gun drawn. "Why aren't you checking the doors?"

Skyler put a hand on Leonard's arm. "Lower the weapon, Officer. It was Darby on the balcony. He was just out there twenty minutes ago smoking his cigar."

"Oh. Good." Leonard turned to return to his room. "It must have been ice falling off the roof. I'm getting into bed. I'm beat. Go check the doors anyway." And he was gone.

Skyler smiled at Brenda. "I think you're right. Time to hit the hay."

"Is that all you'll be hitting?" Darby asked.

"Gross," Skyler and Brenda said in unison.

"I knew the real Darby would return," Skyler said. "Goodnight everyone. Go check the doors, kid." And Skyler disappeared into her suite and shut the door.

After a short discussion on revised sleeping arrangements, Darby reluctantly returned to the loft—noting that he planned to buy the house and burn it down one day—and the twins agreed to bunk together in order to give the diva her privacy.

"I'm just going to pass out, if that's okay with you both," she said sweetly.

"Of course. You've been through a lot," Sullivan said. "I'll go move my stuff into Carter's room."

Carter shrugged his shoulders. "Sully and I haven't shared a bed, or even slept in the same room, in a couple decades. I guess a Christmas Eve slumber party won't kill us. You know, we used to sleep together every Christmas Eve when we were kids because we were so excited and…"

Georgia placed a cool hand on Carter's cheek as she pushed

by him on her way to the back hall. "That's nice, honey. I'm fading fast. Goodnight." And she was gone.

"Rude," Carter said under his breath. He went to the bar and fumbled around with the bottle of Armagnac. He poured a few ounces into a juice glass and then padded off to his room after blowing out the remaining candles.

Within a few minutes, the house was dark and quiet. It was just after 10 o'clock and the snow was tapering off outside. The clouds began to clear and a three-fourths moon shone brightly on the blanket of white below.

CHAPTER THIRTY

Skyler was the first out of bed at about half past six on Christmas morning. The house was freezing cold and she really didn't want to leave Leonard (the human heating pad that he was), but she had work to do. The stockings weren't going to get hung by themselves.

It was silly, and she didn't know if the gesture would be appreciated by the Lowerys and Georgia, but she knew Brenda would get a kick out of her remembering their tradition—Brenda cooked and Skyler played Santa. It's how it'd been for as long as either one of them could remember. And they liked it that way, whether there were men in the picture or not.

The stockings were handmade needlepoint creations, each one different, adorned with various snowmen, Santa Clauses, Christmas trees, wreaths, angels, and the like. Since she hadn't had time to get them monogrammed, she made a list of who was to receive which stocking design and filled them accordingly. It was just small trinkets and candies and mementoes of Santa Fe, but it would do the trick. Or, at least she hoped so. There was even one for herself, filled by herself, so she'd have something to open, too. Brenda never remembered to do it and she knew it would have never in a million years dawned on Leonard. She didn't care though, it was her task and it was important to her.

"Merry Christmas," Darby said from behind her. "He is risen."

"That's what you say on *Easter*, not Christmas, silly. Today is his birthday."

"Actually, Biblical scholars think Jesus was born in the summer. December 25th is a bogus date."

"Nevertheless," Skyler said, raising one of the stuffed socks into the air. "Santa brought stockings for all of us."

"How'd he get through all that damned white stuff out there?"

"He flies, silly."

"Ahh yes. I forgot." Darby made his way to the coffee bar. Skyler was thankful that he had clothes on. "Can I pour you a cup? Black, right?"

"Yes, thank you. That would be most appreciated. How'd you sleep?"

"I was more awake than asleep most of the night. All I can think about is money."

"That keeps a lot of people up at night," Skyler said. "But usually because of a *lack* of it."

"The poor peasants."

Skyler stood at the window and noticed that the snow was melting fast. She suspected that as soon as the sun was fully up over the mountains, that the rest of it would be done away with fairly quickly. It was then that it dawned on her, the electricity was back on.

Darby handed her a mug. "Here you are."

"Thank you," she said. "We have power."

"That's how the coffee got made, ma'am. According to the clock on the kitchen stove, it's been on for just over three hours now."

Skyler felt something warm hit her face just as she heard the plate glass window to her left shatter. A small powerful burst of wind whisked by her right ear. It all happened at the same time, in a fraction of second. For Skyler, time seemed to come to a screeching halt for that split second, just like in the movies— slow motion for the ultimate dramatic effect. Skyler wasn't fully aware of what was happening while it happened. And she felt like she couldn't breathe; there was no air around her face. Yet she dropped her coffee mug and instinctively put both arms out in order to grab Darby's body as it slumped forward toward her. As she cradled the young man in her arms, the combined weight—along with something slick and thick on the floor below them—sent them down. It was then that Skyler realized that Darby was bleeding heavily from the base of his neck.

Skyler lay on the floor with the unconscious man on top of her and listened to voices coming from the direction of the kitchen.

"Are you okay?" Leonard screamed. "Skyler!"

She couldn't speak.

Her boyfriend rolled Darby over and grabbed her around the waist and brought her effortlessly to her feet. He held her close and asked again: "Are you okay? You're covered in blood."

"I think so. I wasn't hit."

"We need to move." He picked her up and carried her like a ragdoll out of the Great Room and into the back hall of the house. Brenda was right on their heels.

"Is he dead?" Brenda asked Leonard.

"I don't know. I'll go back and see." He placed Skyler on their bed and turned to Brenda. "Look her over. I'm getting my gun." He struggled with his suitcase. "I need my damned shoes. Mother fucker!"

Carter and Sullivan appeared in the doorway in matching boxer shorts and socks to see Skyler absolutely covered in blood.

"What happened?" Carter demanded.

"Oh, my goodness, Skyler!" Georgia was in the room now, too, dressed in a long nightgown. A black eye mask was pushed up onto her forehead.

Leonard finished pulling on his boots from a seated position on the floor then sprung upright like a gymnast. "I want everyone to stay in this room and to stay down low. Now! Away from the windows." He bolted out of the room as he racked his firearm.

"Someone please tell us what happened," Sullivan pleaded. "Skyler, where are you bleeding from?"

"I'm not bleeding," Skyler managed to say.

Brenda, who was on her knees on the floor in front of Skyler looked up at the twins and Georgia. "Get down here, now!" she screamed. "Didn't you hear what he said?"

They all got down on the floor.

"Come on!" Brenda screamed at Skyler.

Skyler let herself slide off the bed on to the floor. She looked at the twins. "Someone shot Darby in the Great Room."

The brothers immediately sprung to their feet and were gone.

"I hope it's not too late," Skyler said.

"On Christmas morning," Georgia cried. "Where was he shot?"

"In the living room," Skyler said, her voice shaking.

"We know *where* in the house," Brenda said. "Where on his body?"

"His neck. He was losing a lot of blood. But Leonard made us move. Someone had a gun pointed at the house. That big front window is gone. Completely shattered."

Brenda snatched Skyler's cell phone from the bedside table. "I'm calling 9-1-1."

"Good luck with that," Skyler said. She wiped blood off her forehead and smeared it onto the sheets. "Oh my goodness."

"Honey, go into the bathroom," Georgia said. "There are no windows in there. Get cleaned up."

Brenda dropped the phone into her lap. "I can't get through. I'm getting nothing. Nothing!"

Skyler started crawling toward the bathroom. "Come with me. We'll text them from the bathroom."

Leonard was outside on the front porch listening carefully for any human sounds. The snow and ice was melting fast and all he could hear was dripping water from the roof together with the sound of his heart racing. He descended the slushy stairs slowly, holding the gun straight out in front of him. When he got to the ground, he started toward the right and was soon standing in front of the broken window.

It took just a fraction of a second for him to realize: the broken glass was on the *outside* of the house.

Carter and Sullivan were on their knees on each side of Darby's limp body. He was still breathing and the blood flow was slowing from the wound at the base of his neck. Carter grabbed one of Skyler's Christmas stockings, dumped the contents onto the floor, and pressed it against the entry point. Sullivan had his hand on the back of Darby's neck and felt blood flowing through his fingers.

"It went all the way through," Sullivan said. "We need to stop the bleeding in the back." As he pressed his fingers as hard as he could onto the exit wound, he looked up when Leonard rushed back through the front door.

"The shot came from *inside* the house!" Leonard said.

"Okay, okay. We need to move him," Carter said. He started to get to his feet but slipped in the thick pool of blood and fell backwards into the Christmas tree, sending it toppling over. Sullivan let go of Darby's neck and helped Carter to his feet.

"Let's pick him up and get him to our room. There's a first aid kit in the bathroom under the sink."

Nothing else mattered. They worked together, each taking an arm and a leg. They moved as quickly as they could through the kitchen and down the back hall to the room they had been sleeping in. They tossed Darby onto the bed and Carter scrambled into the bathroom to get the kit while Sullivan locked the door to the hall. He then grabbed his phone and sent a texted to 9-1-1:

> 1417 encantado place
> ambulance police gunman hurry

As soon as he was done, he put both hands firmly around his younger brother's neck again.

"God damn it, Carter," he screamed. "Hurry up."

Leonard ran into his bedroom suite and found the girls gone. He saw that the bathroom door was closed so he rushed to it and tried the handle. It was locked from inside. "Skyler?" He banged on the wood. "Open the door, honey. It's me."

No response.

He threw all of his weight into the door and it easily popped open. He fell against the interior wall and then lost his balance on the loose area rug that covered the tile, falling to the floor. There was no one besides him in the bathroom.

He heard a commotion coming from the end of the hall, so with his weapon drawn, he made his way as quietly as he could toward the laundry room. He rounded the corner and saw Skyler, Brenda, and Georgia backed up against the washing machine and dryer, all looking in the same direction. Leonard didn't have much time to decide what to do; rushing into small rooms with his gun drawn didn't work out for him in the past. He didn't want to accidently get one of the girls killed.

He tried desperately to control his breathing. He wanted to go outside to get a look through the laundry room window, but there was little time. A woman started yelling and it didn't seem to be Skyler, Brenda, or Georgia's voice.

Then Brenda cried out, "No, please!"

"Emma, why are you doing this?" Georgia pleaded.

Leonard sprung forward and pointed the gun toward where he thought the woman had to be standing. Startled, she whipped her body around to face him and she pulled the trigger on the gun she was holding. Her bullet missed him but he shot back at the same instant, hitting her in the right shoulder. She dropped her gun.

Skyler scrambled to the ground and retrieved the weapon, then pointed it at the wounded woman slumped against the wall and slowly collapsing toward the floor. Her eyes were closed tightly and she clutched at her shoulder with both hands. She started to cry.

"Back out of the room," Leonard directed his friends. "Skyler, give me the gun." She handed it over and now he had one in each hand pointed at the woman. "Call 9-1-1."

"We texted," Brenda said. "They're on their way. They confirmed."

Leonard examined the pistol in his left hand and immediately knew that he'd seen it before. That was twice that Carter's weapon had discharged in his direction that week.

A shrill beeping sound started coming from somewhere behind them. Georgia and Brenda ran to investigate.

The Christmas tree had fallen into the gas fireplace when Carter toppled it and it was entirely engulfed in flames along with the drapes, the wrapped presents, and the couch. The house was filling fast with a thick black smoke.

Brenda ran to the front door and ripped it open. She could hear sirens in the near distance. She turned back to Georgia. "Let's get everyone out of the house. They're on their way. I can hear them coming."

"Where are the dogs?" Georgia asked.

She was already pale, but the very last of the blood ran out of Brenda's face. She had no idea where her babies were. "Oh my goodness. I don't know!"

CHAPTER THIRTY-ONE

Leonard was wrapped in a Santa Fe Fire Department blanket and standing in the fast-melting slush next to an ambulance. He told the commanding police officer on the scene everything he knew about the events of the past few hours. Inside the vehicle, paramedics worked on Darby and they successfully controlled the bleeding from his gunshot wound. They were about to head to the hospital and explained that only one of the twins would be allowed to ride along. Sullivan quickly volunteered, and Carter reluctantly got out and closed the back doors. When the ambulance had driven out of sight, he joined Leonard and the officer.

"Where's the gunman?" Carter asked.

"In the other ambulance," the officer said as he pointed up the driveway. "It's not life-threatening. An officer is in there with the paramedics."

"Who is he?"

"He is a *she*," Leonard said.

The officer continued to take notes. "And the gun that she had, tell me again where it came from."

"It's mine. I lost it in the woods just over there," Carter said, pointing toward the evergreens to the north.

"When was this?"

"Two days ago. On the evening of the 23rd," Leonard said. "We were chasing an intruder on the property. She got away."

"You're assuming it was Emma Wade?"

"We think so, yes, in hindsight. Especially since she showed up with the gun. We didn't know it was her at the time."

"And how exactly do you lose a handgun in the woods, sir?"

Carter and Leonard exchanged looks.

"Gentleman," the officer continued, "I'm trying to help you."

"Mr. Lowery's weapon accidently discharged after we lost the subject—we had been pursuing her when we saw someone lurking around the house from inside. Carter dropped the gun in the snow after it fired and, well, we forgot about it. When we remembered it and went back to the spot to retrieve it, the gun was gone."

"I assume you have a permit for this weapon, Mr. Lowery?"

Carter said nothing.

"Mr. Lowery?"

"He does not," Leonard said. "It's vintage. It was his father's weapon and he brought it here to Santa Fe from his home in New York City, on a private aircraft."

The officer exhaled and shook his head. He continued to make notes. "Wonderful. I could arrest you, sir."

"I'm sorry," Carter said meekly. "I meant no harm."

"We're keeping the gun," the police officer said. "Go be with your brother, but please don't leave town. We still have some major shit to figure out. Merry Christmas to us all."

Brenda couldn't stop hugging her dogs. Mulder and Scully had been hiding under the bed in her suite when she found them, and quickly escorted them out the back door of the house. Her knees were soaking wet from kneeling down in the snow and mud.

"We're leaving this place immediately," she said to Skyler.

"If not sooner."

"Is the fire out?"

"I think so," Skyler said. She handed the dogs' leashes to her friend. "They let me back in to get stuff, so I guess it's under control. The real damage is to the front of the house. The suites are fine."

"Let's pack up our stuff and head to the airport," Brenda said. "We still have time to save this monumentally cruel Christmas."

"And what about Georgia? What about the hotel project?"

"Let's bring Georgia with us. I am certain that the last place she wants to be is here in Santa Fe with Massimo still on the loose. And that hotel and the new restaurant are the least of my worries right now. The twins can figure it out. I've had just about all I can take for one year."

"I hear ya," Skyler said.

While Brenda went to pack, Skyler found Leonard in the front yard.

"Brenda wants us to high tail it to Las Vegas. She suggested we take Georgia with us."

"I think that's a very good idea," Leonard said as he rubbed his hands together to warm himself. "How long is the drive?"

Skyler crinkled her face. "Drive? Honey, no."

"I've told the local authorities everything I know. They want to talk to Georgia next."

Georgia appeared with coats. "I found these inside," she said. "Put them on."

"Who is this Emma person?" Skyler asked as the lead police officer joined them.

"Her name is Emma Wade. Or so she said. She is a local interior design student who helped me put the house together. She did the Christmas tree, too. She did a lot for me and she had unfettered access to my house, now that I think about it. And she's the one person I forgot to tell the F.B.I. about after the bombing. She totally slipped my mind."

"Why would she terrorize you like this?" Leonard asked. "What could possibly be her motive?"

Skyler placed a hand lightly on Georgia's back. "Could she be some kind of deranged opera fan?"

Leonard had to suppress a chuckle.

"That crossed my mind," Georgia said. "But I really don't know. She was odd, but rather sweet...up until today."

"What exactly did she say to you this morning?" the officer asked.

Georgia squinted her eyes. "She was rambling. Screaming about a car." She turned to Skyler. "Didn't she mention a car? I don't even *have* a car since I don't drive anymore."

"She started screaming about a car *accident*," Skyler said. "But that's when Leonard shot her. Could she have been talking about the accident you had last December in New York? No. That can't be it."

"Oh my God," Georgia said, her eyes widening. "I can't imagine how she'd know about that or why she'd even care. It must be something else."

"What accident did you have last year?" the officer asked.

Georgia reluctantly retold the story about how she fell asleep at the wheel and a man died because of her negligence. When she was done, she lowered her head and closed her eyes. "It crushes me every time I think about it."

The stone-faced officer was taking notes. "What was the man's name?"

"Michael Dawes. D.A.W.E.S. It was mid-December, last year, on Long Island, New York."

"Alright, that's enough for now," he said.

"Officer," Leonard said, "Brenda, Skyler, Georgia, and I are planning to leave Santa Fe this afternoon. For Ms. Reece's safety…"

"…and our sanity," Brenda interrupted.

The officer shook his head. "A little recap, people. An allegedly mentally unstable young woman broke into this house on Christmas morning with a stolen gun and threatened the ladies. She shot Darby Lowery and shot at Sheriff Little. Sheriff Little shot her. The entire house almost burned to the ground and we still don't know why any of this happened. And you want to leave town?"

"Yes sir," Leonard said. "You know that Ms. Reece was abducted last week and found in Arizona. Her kidnapper is still on the loose. Perhaps Emma Wade knows something about that, perhaps not. But we're not sticking around to find out. I don't hink you have grounds to hold us. You have all of our cell numbers; you can reach out to us any time you wish."

Skyler was proudly beaming. Brenda couldn't mask a grin.

"Fine," the officer said after a few long seconds. "Where are you going?"

"We'll tell you when we get there."

CHAPTER THIRTY-TWO

In a partially draped recovery area of Santa Fe General Hospital's emergency room, Darby Lowery had his eyes closed, but he wasn't asleep. His brother Sullivan sat next to him scrolling through his social media feed on his smart phone.

"This is both the crappiest and the best Christmas ever," Darby said quietly.

"I wouldn't put anything that's happened today in the *best* column. What are you talking about? Are these the drugs talking?"

"They didn't give me any drugs, Sully," Darby said. "I turned everything down. I can't risk it. I've been addicted to enough crap to know I'd fall right back down that rabbit hole. I was talking about the business."

"Oh."

"You guys really shouldn't have kept it from me."

"We know that now."

"But I understand why you did."

"Thank goodness."

"Were you afraid I was going to sue my own brothers?"

"It happens," Sullivan said softly. "And maybe. Alright, yes, we were afraid you might possibly do just that."

"Well, I'm not going to. Onward and upward. But I want to

be involved, Sully."

"Okay."

"I want a say so, Sullivan."

"I said, okay, *Darby*!"

"I mean it."

"I believe you. I hear you," Sullivan said, growing frustrated. "I. Hear. You. Darby."

Darby opened his eyes and slightly turned his head to look at his brother. "Thank you."

"You're welcome. When can we leave this place? I hate hospitals."

Darby closed his eyes again. "No one likes hospitals. And I don't know yet. The bullet didn't hit anything major, they say. I'm going to recover quickly. I can feel it. They said if it was a fraction of an inch higher or to the left, I could have been killed instantly."

"Jesus Christ."

"I'm not sure if he had anything to do with it, but today is his birthday. I guess someone up there must be looking out for me."

"That's something, I guess."

"You aren't happy about my Christmas morning miracle?"

"Carter and I would be a lot better off financially if you hadn't made it," Sullivan joked.

Darby didn't react. He kept his eyes closed. "You're a shit. You shouldn't talk that way on such a holy day."

Carter appeared from behind a curtain. "How is our patient doing?"

"I'm fine," Darby said. "You guys sound exactly the same, ya know that? It's still so weird to me."

Carter and Sullivan exchanged eye rolls.

"He must be drugged," Carter said as he took a seat next to his twin.

"He's not. He's just delirious from the pain in his neck."

"A pain in our collective necks, I'm sure," Carter said. "When can we leave here? I called and booked us a two-bedroom suite at the Four Seasons. All of our stuff from the house is in the back of my car." He paused for a few long seconds and then said, "I don't think we're going to be getting the security deposit back on that house."

"I want my own suite," Darby said, eyes still closed. "And a cheeseburger."

* * *

Georgia was busily packing suitcases in her massive master bedroom closet while Skyler, Brenda, and Leonard sipped coffee in the kitchen. Mulder and Scully were curled up within a band of sun that was heating the tiled floor.

They'd all returned to Georgia's house one final time because the opera star insisted that she needed a whole new wardrobe for the Las Vegas New Year's Eve trip. Leonard agreed on the pitstop, but only after he searched every square inch of the mansion while the girls and dogs waiting in the locked car.

"I called in some pretty big favors to get this jet for us today," Brenda said. "It's Christmas, you know. I basically had to agree to cater the owner's damned birthday party next summer. In Myrtle Beach, of all places."

"We are well aware of your sacrifices for us," Skyler said. "And we thank you from the bottom of our hearts. And I will go with you to Myrtle Beach to help. I promise. If I'm not too busy."

"I don't thank you from the bottom of *my* heart," Leonard said, "but I guess I'm getting a little better at stomaching the idea of flying."

"You are very strange," the chef said. "And I'm afraid that you are going to be just a *tad* more inconvenienced today, Lenny. We need to make one more stop before we go to the airport. If I'm leaving Santa Fe for a while, I need to shore up a few details regarding the restaurant project. The boys are going to meet us at the hotel site. They're leaving the hospital now."

"How's Darby?" Skyler asked.

"He's going to recover and could be out of the hospital fairly quickly," Brenda said. "He's a very lucky young man."

Leonard got up to refill his coffee cup. "I'd say so. Isn't modern medicine amazing? Released from the hospital within a dozen hours of being shot in the neck."

"The bullet apparently missed all the important stuff," Brenda said as she cringed. "Imagine."

"We don't have to," Skyler said. "We saw it with our own eyes. I believe I've seen enough people shot this year, thank you very much." She looked at her hands. They were still slightly blood stained.

Brenda hoisted her coffee mug. "I'll toast to that."

"Why are we drinking coffee?" Skyler asked. "We should be drinking champagne."

Brenda smiled. "On the plane, dear. On the plane."

* * *

A few miles away, Massimo sat on the floor of Emma's living room with a pair of headphones on. While he was mildly concerned about his hostess's whereabouts—she'd been gone all night—he was consumed with plotting out his next move. At the same time, he was obsessed with listening to the live audio feed. After hours and hours of nothing but the hum of a refrigerator and the heating system fans, he finally heard voices and his heart began to race.

The small microphone was positioned out of sight above and behind the lip of the molding of the highest of Georgia's kitchen cabinets. It was broadcasting via her wi-fi signal to a relay device that he'd plugged in to the back of her high-speed internet modem, the very modem that he installed for her when she moved in. Massimo knew that Georgia would never touch the box, for she had absolutely no understanding of, or interest in, such things. And because of the modifications, he could tune in to the audio feed from virtually anywhere in the world with a password. He marveled at how easy the components were to obtain online and how simple it was to set up. He did curse himself for not installing a similar system in his Italian home when he suspected his wife was having an affair, but quickly brushed that aside. He had more pressing matters: the people in Georgia's kitchen were talking about leaving Santa Fe. But first, they were all headed to the hotel.

The deserted, under-construction hotel.

CHAPTER THIRTY-THREE

After Darby was taken away for a few final tests to determine whether he was well enough to be released, the twins escaped from the hospital and made their way downtown to the hotel. Being that it was Christmas Day afternoon, traffic was nonexistent, and they made the trek across town in record time. The snow and ice had almost completely melted away due to the intense desert sunshine and the temperature had soared to a very comfortable 55°. Carter found a parking spot directly in front of the main entrance and the brothers made their way inside.

"It's colder in here than it is outside," Sullivan said as he zipped up his jacket.

"I'll get one of those space heaters," Carter said as he disappeared into the office behind the front desk. "I'm just happy that we have reliable power now."

Sullivan ran his hand over the newly installed reception desk. It was impossibly smooth from being polished and sanded dozens of time. He was thrilled with the woodworkers' finished product and it was absolutely the perfect complement to their vision for the lobby. He looked up at the antler chandeliers hanging above his head and made a mental note that they needed a good dusting before the light bulbs were installed. Sullivan turned around and leaned back against the desk marveling at what they'd created. The space was nearly complete and he expected they'd open the hotel on-time, if not early. *Early would be tremendous*, he thought to himself, *because we can work out all the kinks before the official public launch.*

"We have never opened early," Carter said as he reappeared. It was as if he was reading his brother's mind, which was actually not uncommon. "Looks like we might have a *first* on our hands."

"We've had a whole slew of firsts on our hands this month," Sullivan said. "I think I'd be quite content with a whole lotta normal, every-day kind of stuff on our hands." He looked at his own hands and noticed that they were still bloodstained despite three good scrubbings. He held his palms out for his brother's inspection. "Look."

"I know. Mine, too." He had to fight a sudden urge to tear up again. "This is not how I expected to spend today."

"No one could have expected any of this."

There were a few moments of silence as they each inspected various items in the lobby. Then Sullivan walked over to his brother's side. "We might not see Georgia for some time after today."

"And?"

"And we haven't really determined where these relationships are going."

Carter's eyes narrowed. "Do you and I get to decide that? Or does she?"

"Well she doesn't call all the shots. I mean, what do you want?"

"I'm indifferent, Sully. I like her a lot, but I'm also pretty damned busy, she's got a lot of baggage, and I seriously doubt she is going to come right back to Santa Fe after Las Vegas anyway. We're never in New York long enough to have girlfriends and once she's back to work, she's going to be on the road all over the world. What kind of future could we have?"

"That seems defeatist."

"And if she was your girlfriend, would it be any different? After Santa Fe is up and running, we're off to Palm Springs. There are no opera companies in Palm Springs that I know about."

Sullivan sighed.

"You know I'm right."

"I liked having sex with her."

"Gross."

"Really?"

"No," Carter said. "So did I. But can we table this discussion for the time being, please? She's leaving on a jet plane today."

"Alright." Sullivan shuffled away and busied himself with inspecting a bank of light switches on the north side of the lobby until the front doors opened and Skyler, Brenda, and Georgia entered the hotel.

"Leonard is parking the car," Skyler said as she peeked Sullivan on the cheek. "How's Darby?"

"He's being released this evening."

Skyler shucked her heavy coat. "It's simply unbelievable. Shot in the neck in the morning and home in his own bed that same night. Incredible."

"I guess so," Sullivan said absently, trying to erase the image in his head of the blood gushing from his younger brother's neck. "When are you taking off?"

"Presently," Brenda interjected. "We're getting the hell out of Dodge."

"Well, Brenda Braxton," Carter said as he approached, "you have a new restaurant here in Dodge that needs your attention."

"I am well aware of that fact, Mr. Lowery," Brenda said, "and I fully intend to keep my commitments to Franklin-Lowery. But given the circumstances, I'm making an executive decision to skip town for a little while. But rest assured, I'm replacing myself with reinforcements."

"What exactly does that mean?" Sullivan asked.

"My number two will be here in three days." That's when Leonard walked in. His eyes widened.

"What the heck are you talking about?" he asked. "Why are you talking about your number twos?"

Brenda shot a look of disgust at the cop. "You will forever be a revolting 13-year-old boy, Lenny. For goodness sake, grow up. I was talking about my second in command." She turned back to the twins. "His name is Ernie Sommers. He's an absolute wunderkind and he knows more about my restaurant empire than I do. He's been on-site for all of the build-outs, he cooks almost as good as I do, and he's gorgeous and gay."

"I don't know that *gorgeous* and *gay* is going to help you, guys," Skyler said, "but Ernie is marvelous. You'll love him."

"He arrives on Thursday," Brenda said. "I convinced him to give up his New Year's skiing trip to Park City, so he's not happy with me, but that won't affect his performance here."

The twins exchanged nods. "Cool," they said in unison.

"So cute," Georgia said with a sweet smile. "I'm going to miss you boys. Please don't be mad at me for abandoning you. I'll be back. I promise."

Sullivan shrugged his shoulders. "We're not mad at you, honey. You've been stalked and bombed and kidnapped and nearly shot. Like we said earlier, if it wasn't for all of this…" he gestured with his arms "…we'd be on the first flight out of New Mexico, too."

"Don't forget ransacked. She was ransacked, too," Skyler said.

"*Ransacked*, stalked, bombed, kidnapped, and nearly shot," Sullivan said again.

Georgia leaned in and whispered into Carter's ear. "And *screwed*."

Completely caught off guard, Carter choked and pulled away from the group.

"What did she say?" Sullivan asked. He turned to the opera singer. "What did you say?"

Georgia just shook her head and walked off to admire the front desk.

Sullivan looked to Skyler. "What did she say?"

"Why are you asking me? I don't know."

"Whatever it was, she probably doesn't even know which of you she said it to," Brenda said with a hearty laugh. "Listen, let me get to work so that we can get to the airport. We have a very expensive bird waiting for us." Brenda started toward the restaurant, a notebook in hand.

"Bird?" Sullivan asked Skyler.

"An Embraer Phenom 300E. It's a Brazilian beauty."

"I didn't understand anything you just said."

"Seriously? Come on. It's an airplane," Skyler said. "This one seats six passengers and has a ceiling of 45,000 feet. I'm just sad that we're only going a short distance to Las Vegas. We'll be up and down before we know it."

"Ahh," Sullivan said. "I don't usually notice what kind of

airplane I'm flying in. I just get onboard and plug in my earbuds and try to zone out."

"Not me," Skyler said. "I drink in every aspect of the plane I'm flying in. I love every second of it. Delta once let me sit in the co-pilot's seat at cruising altitude—of course that was way, way before 9-11. Next, I want to be up there for a take-off. That's my favorite part."

"Why don't you have your pilot's license? Given your affinity for airplanes, I'd think you'd want to fly a plane yourself."

"It's a huge investment of time and hell of a lot of money," Skyler said. "I've certainly thought about it. I did take a few lessons in college in a small Cessna. But I never really wanted a career in aviation, so I tabled the idea. Brenda and I have had friends who have owned their own planes. It's a very expensive hobby. These days, I'm just happy riding along."

"Anything is better than commercial."

"You can say that again." Skyler looked up at the wood beams above her head. "This room is gorgeous. You guys are going to have a hit on your hands. I see a *Condé Nast Traveler* award in your near future."

"From your mouth to the magazine gods' ears," Sullivan said. "Come with me. I want to show you the gym. The equipment was delivered yesterday. All brand new, state-of-the-art stuff."

Leonard and Carter were walking from room to room on the third floor, inspecting bathroom audio speaker installations. Brenda was making notes in the restaurant's kitchen. Sullivan and Skyler were walking side-by-side on treadmills equipped with satellite-television screens. And Georgia was sitting on the reception desk, tapping away on her smartphone, alone in the lobby. She was quite oblivious to the man standing five feet away from her.

He cleared his throat.

Startled, she looked up.

"Massimo," she said calmly. "I'm going to scream."

"You will not, *mio caro*," he said. He was dressed in jeans and a pullover sweatshirt and had on a black baseball cap with the logo of the opera house in Milan embroidered on the front. She'd given it to him years earlier. He pulled his hands out of the kangaroo pocket of his sweatshirt and aimed the small handgun at her. "I have a gun."

"I see that."

"Why did you leave the car?"

"In Arizona? Massimo, seriously? Why on Earth would I just sit there and wait for my crazy captor to return from wherever it is that you went? Honestly."

"I was not your captor," he said, clearly hurt. "I am your best friend. I was rescuing you."

"You're my best what? My *friend!?* Are you mad? You hit me hard over the head. I had to be hospitalized. Friends don't do such things. And who exactly were you rescuing me from?"

"That deranged girl. Emma."

"Emma. Are you serious right now, Massimo?!" She said his name rather loudly in hopes that someone else in the hotel would hear her. *Where were they?*

"Keep your voice down, Georgia."

"We've come to find out that Emma Wade helped you get me out of that boutique. How were you saving me from *her?*"

"Never you mind that. We're leaving this place." He gestured with the gun. "Get down from there and let's go."

"I will not be going anywhere with you ever again," she said defiantly. "I used to trust you. Heaven knows why. You screwed me, Massimo. You stole from me. You lied to me. You used me. And you made that poor girl do all those horrible things to me. How did you convince her to do such horrific things…"

"I made you!" he exploded. He realized he was being too loud and tried to control himself. "I made you who you are today, Georgia. Without me, you'd be doing summer stock at some little community theater in New Hampshire."

That made her laugh. "You don't even know where New Hampshire is."

"I know *all* the United States," he said. "I took American history in school."

"Good for you," she said. She realized that she still had her phone in her hand and she tried to navigate to the messaging app without directly looking at the screen. "If I went with you, where would we go? Back to Arizona? To *New Hampshire*? And no matter where we went, how do you think it would end? You've gone entirely too far for us to even go back to normal."

"There is no normal anymore." He suddenly looked exhausted. "I realize that much."

"They'll be looking for us."

"They won't find us."

She thought she'd pulled up the app. She glanced quickly at the screen and saw that it was Skyler that she'd last texted. She moved her thumb to the 'H' key. "I'm not leaving with you right now, darling." She was calmer than she thought she should be. "You should go on without me, Massimo."

"We don't have much time to quarrel over this, Georgia.

Let's go. Get down from there."

She managed to type an 'E.'

"I mean it. I have a gun."

"I see the gun, Massimo," she said as she typed an 'L.' "Where did you get that? You've never used a gun in your life. Did you bring it from Italy? Is that an Italian gun? Are there such things as Italian guns?"

"What are you talking about?" he spit. "Why do you care where the gun came from?" It's then that he noticed the phone in her hand. He lurched forward just as Georgia hit the 'send' key.

He swatted the phone out of her hand and it flew across the room and bounced off the tile floor and shattered. Georgia let out a little scream as she propelled herself backward, falling off the reception desk. She landed with a thud on the dusty floor. Stunned but newly energized, she scrambled into a seated position and looked desperately for a weapon of some sort.

Massimo ran to the end of the desk and rounded the corner. The gun leading the way, he darted toward the singer just as she sprang to her feet and launched a bucket of construction debris toward him. Dust, wood chips, a few broken lightbulbs, and a hand full of large screws filled the air, momentarily disorienting the Italian.

Georgia ran for her life. She had no idea where she was going.

CHAPTER THIRTY-FOUR

The cell phone in Skyler's back pocket vibrated. She kept walking on the treadmill as she pulled it out and glanced at the screen.

"It's from Georgia," she said. "It says 'Hel'. What does that mean?"

Sullivan snatched the phone from Skyler's hand. "Help? Could it be the beginning of 'help'?"

"Oh my God," Skyler said.

They both stopped their machines and took off running toward the grand staircase that led up to the lobby. Skyler managed to speed dial Leonard along the way.

"What is it? Where are you?" Leonard asked when he picked up.

"Get to the lobby, NOW!" she screamed into the phone and then put it back in her pocket without hanging up.

Leonard darted into the bathroom of the guest room. "We need to go back downstairs right now." He took off running without waiting for a response.

"What's happening?" Carter was right on the cop's heels.

Leonard unholstered his handgun as he ran toward the service stairs. "Is this the way?" he yelled over his shoulder.

"Yeah," Carter said. "Two flights down to the lobby. The doors aren't marked yet. It's dark. Be careful."

Georgia had her head turned as she ran full speed ahead, and she connected hard with Brenda, sending them both tumbling to the floor. Brenda let out a scream as her notebook went flying through the air.

"My God, Georgia," the chef managed. "What's going on?"

Georgia scrambled to her feet and extended a hand to help Brenda up. "Massimo is here. Let's move."

"We can handle him," Brenda said confidently as she brushed off her pants and started in the direction of the lobby.

Georgia reached out and grabbed a fist full of Brenda's sweater. "Stop. He has a gun."

Skyler and Sullivan scanned the lobby. Nothing. They listened. All was quiet. Then they heard pounding on the stairs behind them and turned just as Leonard and Carter came into view.

"What is it?" Leonard asked his girlfriend.

"We don't know," Skyler said, "but I have a feeling it isn't good."

"Where is Georgia?" Carter asked.

"We don't know anything," Sullivan said. "Georgia! Georgia!"

Carter knelt down to pick up the shattered smartphone. "This must be hers."

"Emma is in custody," Leonard said, "so this must be Massimo."

"You think he's here?"

"Let's find out. And let's stay together." Leonard led the way toward the restaurant. "Where is Brenda?"

"I believe she's back here somewhere," Skyler said as she checked her phone. "She's not responding to my texts."

"Call her," Leonard demanded.

Brenda and Georgia retreated deeper into the kitchen. It was a maze of hallways and spaces with separate areas for cooking, food prep, dry storage, dishwashing, an office, a wine cellar, and a walk-in deep freeze. In the very back there was a double service door leading to the loading dock. It was chained and secured with a large padlock.

"Why?" Georgia asked.

"The door installers forgot to put in the locking mechanism, so we had no way of securing the building until they can come back. Hence the chains." Brenda put a hand on her forehead and tried to remember if there was another way out.

"This seems like a safety violation," Georgia whispered.

"Indeed," the chef said. "But the place isn't open yet and the next city inspection isn't until..." She cut herself off. "Why are we talking about this? Who cares? Let's move. There's a door in the back of the wine cellar that leads to the dining room. I think."

"Great."

They held hands and started looking for the wine cellar.

"Do you have a phone?" Brenda whispered.

"Massimo made me drop it."

"Damn it," she said. "I don't know where mine is. I must have set it down somewhere while I was working."

Leonard could hear Brenda's cell phone ringing and he

hurried toward the sound with Carter and Sullivan close behind.

Skyler was in the rear, looking at her screen. She tripped over a rolled electrical conduit and fell face-first into a door jam. A trickle of blood started to flow down her right cheek and she could taste it as it made its way into the corner of her mouth. "Oh my gosh," she said out loud. Her head ached. She looked up and didn't see the boys anywhere.

Massimo was crouching behind a stack of boxes when he saw Leonard and the twins enter the dry storage room. The door opened out into the hallway. He sprang forward, slammed the door shut, and locked it. He heard someone moving to his left, so he moved quickly down the hall toward the wine cellar.

"What the fuck?" Sullivan yelled.

"Find a light switch," Leonard demanded as he fished his phone out of his pocket. He fumbled with it for a moment then managed to turn the flashlight on. He pointed it toward Carter.

"There are no lightbulbs in the overhead fixtures yet," Carter said with a shrug.

"Of course not."

"Skyler was right behind us. What is her number?" Sullivan asked as he produced his own phone. "Damn it. Never mind."

"What is it?" Leonard asked.

"There's no service in here. The walls are stone. And they're like 18 inches thick."

"Well then, we're going to have to blast our way out," Leonard said.

The twins looked at each other. "Did he really just say that?" they asked together.

"I did. Stand back."

In the dimly lit, empty wine cellar, Brenda was about to open the door to the dining room when she heard someone approaching from behind. Georgia and she turned to find Massimo had entered the room and closed the door behind him. He was aiming the small gun at them.

"Don't open that door and don't make a sound," the Italian said. "This is over."

"Massimo, darling," Georgia said as sweetly as she could muster, "We can figure out some kind of compromise here. Let's you and me try to negotiate some sort of settlement. Okay? Put down the gun and let's go somewhere and talk. Just the two of us. Brenda has nothing to do with this. Let's let her go on her way."

"I'm not leaving you," Brenda said. She started to reach for the doorknob and Massimo fired off a shot. The bullet pierced the door a few inches above Brenda's head. Both women screamed and Massimo seemed just as startled as they were; he hadn't meant to discharge the weapon.

"I'm sorry," he said. Then he recovered. "But be quiet and do not move or I won't miss next time."

"Were you trying to kill one of us?" Georgia asked in a loud throaty stage whisper. "What good will that do any of us? If you hurt me, there's no money anymore. Seriously, Massimo, this must stop right this instant."

"This won't end well," Massimo said. "For any of us. There is no escape. For any of us, sadly."

"I am not going to die in this wine cellar in Santa Fe, New Mexico, Massimo," Brenda said defiantly. "I had my fortune read several years ago, on a whim, really. Anyway, the oracle told me that I am going to die an old lady and that I will die in my sleep in my own bed. So, unless we're going to be staying in here for a very, very long time…"

"Shut up, lady!" Massimo screamed. "Georgia, come to me. Walk toward me."

Georgia didn't move.

"We're all going to die in this room," Massimo said with a sigh. "Your stupid fortune teller was wrong. It happens sometimes."

Leonard wasn't answering his phone. Brenda's phone was going directly to voicemail. And Skyler had no idea where the boys went. She wiped a glob of blood off her cheek and rubbed her hand on her pants. That's when she heard a gunshot followed by screams. Then, quickly, another muffled gunshot. She heard what sounded like one of the twins cry out. She had no idea what direction it all came from. These rooms were like caverns and everything echoed.

Skyler picked up a two-by-four and walked carefully into the dining room. She heard a commotion behind a door to her left. As she approached it, she saw the bullet hole. She stopped and tried to hear over the thumping of her own heart in her chest. Then she heard a gun cock.

Instinctively, Skyler opened the door and held the piece of wood high above her head.

Brenda, who had been leaning against the door on the other side, flopped backward onto the dining room floor.

Massimo fired his gun. Georgia screamed again and hit the floor hard. Skyler threw the two-by-four with all of her might at the Italian and it made direct contact with his head just as he squeezed off another shot.

Massimo dropped the weapon and fell backwards out into the kitchen. Georgia scrambled forward and retrieved the gun at Massimo's feet just as Leonard knelt down and held his own gun to the man's temple.

"Don't even think about moving, buddy boy," Leonard said.

Massimo closed his eyes and exhaled deeply. "*Scopami*," he whispered.

"Fuck you, is right," Georgia said when she was on her feet. "Fuck. You. Massimo."

After Skyler helped Brenda to her feet she turned back to her boyfriend who was busy tying Massimo's hands behind his back. "Should I call the police?"

"I think so, yes," Leonard said with a laugh.

Carter and Sullivan appeared behind Leonard. Carter was holding Sullivan upright. "And an ambulance," Carter said. "Sully is going to go join Darby in the hospital."

Sullivan looked at Skyler. "Your cop boyfriend shot me in the thigh."

"I did no such thing," Leonard said. "It ricocheted when I was shot out the doorknob. And I said I was sorry."

Sullivan shook his head. "Okay, cool. He apologized. Everything is fine now."

CHAPTER THIRTY-FIVE

The same Santa Fe Police officer who had been on the scene at the twin's house that Christmas morning responded to the hotel and he was none too happy when he encountered another bleeding Lowery brother and a man tied up with string.

He was a little less gruff—and secretly a little gleeful—when he realized he was about to arrest a suspect that the F.B.I. hadn't yet tracked down.

After Sullivan and Carter left in an ambulance and Massimo was carted away in handcuffs, Leonard and the women answered the authorities' questions.

"We've attempted to interrogate Emma Wade at the hospital," the lead officer said, "but that hasn't gone well. She's not talking, and she's requested an attorney. It's slow going, as you can imagine, since it's Christmas Day. We haven't been able to assign representation for her yet. We have no idea what her motivation was to break into the house with Mr. Lowery's weapon."

Something sparked in Skyler's brain and she stepped back from the group and pulled her smartphone out of a pocket. She did a quick Google search for 'Emma Wade' and 'Georgia Reece' and came up with a *New York Times* article from the previous December.

"Miss Moore," the officer said to her as she was slowly walking away from the group while she read the online story. "We're not done here. And you really should be treated by the paramedics."

She lowered the phone and put a hand to her forehead. "I'm quite alright, Officer."

"Are you refusing care, ma'am?"

"Skyler, let the doctors have a look at you," Leonard said. "You went down hard."

"In a minute," she said. She scanned more of the story, then sidled up next to Georgia. "Take a look at this." She handed her phone to the diva.

Georgia read quickly, saying, "Oh my God," more than a few times. She then looked up at the officer. "Emma Wade is the step-daughter of the man who died in the car accident that I was involved in last year."

"You didn't know that until this moment, Ms. Reece?" he asked.

"Of course not," Georgia nearly screamed. "I had *no idea.* Massimo is the one who reached out to the design school to find the young woman to come work on my house." Her mind was reeling. "Oh my goodness." She exhaled slowly. She was trembling. "This all...this all makes a weird sort of sense, now."

"It was a team effort to take you down," Brenda said. "To scare the living shit out of you. Oh, honey. I am so sorry."

"It looks that Brenda might be right," Skyler said, wrapping an arm around the opera singer. "I am so very sorry, Georgia."

"Well, I brought this on myself," Georgia said in a defeated tone. She walked backward toward the reception desk for support.

It took a few more hours of questioning and paperwork before they were cleared to leave the hotel. When they were finally released, Leonard locked the front door of the hotel with the keys Carter had given him and then drove the women back to Georgia's house, where she intended to stay.

"I have a lot of decompressing and processing to do," the singer said, "and I want to do it alone."

*   *   *

At a quarter to six, Leonard, Brenda, and Skyler climbed aboard the small Embraer jet and each took a seat. As the pilot stowed their luggage, Skyler peered out at the darkened ramp. She watched as a group a passengers who were lined up in the cold waiting to board a small commercial jet a few dozen yards away. She thought it was probably a Bombardier CRJ900, but she couldn't be certain without looking up the tail number. She was about to do just that when Brenda let out a little laugh. "What is it?"

"Carter," the chef said. "He just texted me. Sullivan's surgery is complete. He's going to have to spend the night. They're keeping Darby a little while longer, too, so they put them in the same room together. Carter says that he's certain that when he goes back tomorrow morning he'll find out that they've killed each other."

"I'm sure they'll all be just fine," Skyler said. "And Georgia? Have you heard anything else from her?"

"Not yet, but she must be relieved. And she's finally safe, the poor thing. I bet she's happy to be back in her own bed tonight.

I wonder just how alone Carter's going to let her be though."

They set their sights on Las Vegas, Carissa Lamb, and much deserved New Year's Eve revelry as the plane's engines roared to life and they started speeding down the runway.

Leonard gripped his armrests and closed his eyes.

Skyler and Brenda looked at Leonard then smiled at each other as they each took a long drink from their champagne flutes.

"Onward and upward," Brenda said.

"Absolutely."

"Oh, and Merry Christmas," Brenda added as she raised her glass into the air.

"We'll see. We still have a few hours left." Skyler looked out the window at the twinkling lights of Santa Fe as they climbed over the mountains and headed west.

THE END

Skyler Moore and friends will return
for another adventure…in Las Vegas, Nevada.

AUTHOR'S NOTE

Many thanks must go to Jonathan Dixon for his invaluable guidance and to Holly Canada Barlow for her thoughtful suggestions—you both set me straight again and again. Thanks also to my sounding boards—my whip-smart sister Laura Wallis and her uber-talented husband (my brother from another mother) Jay Cooper. And last but not least, thank you to Dale Blades, for being the best friend, co-host, and partner-in-crime a guy could have.

I've got to thank my parents Richard and Dale Wallis, too, because without them, there would be no me.

I also greatly appreciate my friends Kristin (this book is dedicated to her because she's my best girlfriend on Earth), her cool cat of a husband Rob; my new in-laws Sherry, Dale, Tracy, Joyce, et. al.; my best cruise buddies Michael, Jim, Marci, and Ally; my German angel Jacqueline; my hero Carlos; plus, Henry, Annie, Catherine, Matthew, Jeri, Marge, Elaine, Joanna, Monica, Melissia, Tracy, Taylor, Brent, Shelene, Carolyn, Susan, Chris, and the many others who continue to support me and enrich my life in so many ways. Thank you all.

A big fat thanks must go to my entire **Advance Team** who are kind enough to read early versions of my books and provide the feedback every writer needs to improve. I couldn't do what

I do without you all. Go team!

Thanks too, to the good old United States, because I am forever grateful for this great land of ours. She inspires my work every day. From the rocky coast and picturesque lakes of Maine where I spent childhood summers, to the arid deserts and striking mountains surrounding my homes in New Mexico and Nevada, to the majestic wildlife and stunning scenery in Alaska, to the oceans and seas where I am most at home, well, I am in total awe. I will continue to travel throughout the U.S.—and encourage you to get your butt to every state, too—for the pure pleasure of it and to spark my imagination for new fictional adventures to come. (Up next for Skyler—Nevada this fall, Alaska early next year, then California, Virginia, we'll go back to Maine, and beyond. I love them all!)

And, last but not least, I thank you, dear reader. You've helped make my lifelong dream come true by ~~buying~~ reading this book. Because without you, Skyler Moore would be just a bunch of words strung together deep inside my laptop.

— Scott

ABOUT SCOTT

R. Scott Wallis is endlessly inspired by his surroundings and adventures. And he thrives on new chapters and creating unique projects to keep himself out of trouble.

Scott started his working life as an advance person and assistant to a sitting United States Vice President. Later, he served as the creative director for a leading Washington think tank. That led to working directly for one of the richest men on Earth, conceiving and executing exclusive events for his billionaire friends.

Tired of working for the man, Scott ventured out on his own, becoming a celebrity interviewer and pop-culture podcaster in the top 2% of iTunes, while also dabbling in both the worlds of clothing manufacturing (creating his own baby clothes brand that was sold in over 300 stores nationwide) and retail sales, with his own well-received men's clothing store.

Always willing to lend a hand or donate what he can, he's an enthusiastic philanthropist, championing causes such as childhood bullying, suicide prevention, and animal adoption and welfare.

A wide-eyed world traveler, Scott has been to four continents, mostly by sea. While he loves exploring Europe and the Caribbean islands, it's the vast United States that he likes best.

He's been to Alaska four times, Hawaii twice, and can't wait to explore the eight states he hasn't been to yet.

Technically a Connecticut Yankee, Scott grew up in historic Williamsburg, Virginia, and lived for 25 years in the Washington, D.C. area, before recently discovering that the American West is where he is most at home. He lives in Las Vegas, Nevada, with his husband and their two rescue dogs.

Learn more at www.rscottwallis.com

Scott in Santa Fe, New Mexico, 2017

Made in the USA
Middletown, DE
30 May 2019